Variables

James Allan

Grosvenor House
Publishing Limited

This book is published by
Grosvenor House Publishing Ltd
Link House
140 The Broadway, Tolworth, Surrey, KT6 7HT.
www.grosvenorhousepublishing.co.uk

This book is a work of fiction. Any resemblance to
people or events, past or present, is purely coincidental.

A CIP record for this book
is available from the British Library

ISBN 978-1-80381-882-5
eBook ISBN 978-1-80381-883-2

A worm in a peach may know the inside of his peach with a precise and "scientific" knowledge, but it requires another worm, perhaps no better or more knowing, to tell the first worm that his peach hangs on a tree.

W. Beran Wolfe

As soon as questions of will or decision or reason or choice of action arise, human science is at a loss.

Noam Chomsky

The manager of a nightclub was told that loud music resulted in hearing loss, and that club members should be warned. Learning that the finding was based on albino rats, he replied, 'If an albino rat should arrive at my club, I'll warn it of the danger.'

Ratology

1

Neil Denton stared into the void above his bed and ruminated on the problem. Usually, when waking at some early hour beset by a problem, he would mull it over until an answer revealed itself, get up, and write it down, convinced the solution would erase forever if he went back to sleep. But this problem, the cause of his sleeplessness and other symptoms, offered no solution, required no written record, would not erase.

The problem was, he was unsure if he believed in psychology anymore.

His heart jumped as if attached to Milgram's shock machine, only this time the truth evoked the shock. My name is Neil. I am... What, exactly? If psychology was a religion, he would be an atheist. No, not an atheist; an atheist is certain of his disbelief, whereas he lacked all certainty. An agnostic, then? He wondered for a moment if an agnostic psychologist could successfully research and teach psychology, reminded of the agnostic vicar he read about who claimed he could still function as a vicar; no certainty of an afterlife or revelation, or God, even. What was left? The vicar could go through the motions, he supposed: pastoral work, read sermons, offer prayers. 'I don't know if it's any use but let us pray.' Should he go through the motions of research? Pretend to believe? Or simply ignore the problem?

But the problem was manifold, and everywhere. For every theory there was a counter-theory, for every interpretation of results a counter-interpretation. And every study came complete with a set of methodological criticisms: the sample size, the research design, the interpretation. Above all, the interpretation. Even the experiment, exemplar of science, was usually short on relevance, and if relevant, such as Milgram's much vaunted obedience experiments, it left you with another problem: how to interpret the results. What did they mean? And were they applicable to life beyond the laboratory? It was easy for Matlock to say control all variables but one, but how does one know how many variables there are, the unknown, unseen unidentified variable licking its chops waiting to polish off your experiment? Of course, there were non-experimental methods such as the 'softer' participant observation, stepping out of the laboratory, mingling with and observing subjects. But this too had weaknesses. No, he was caught between two stalls: hard results, variables controlled, replete with columns of statistics (said to be objective but of little relevance to real life); and soft results, such as small group participation, low in statistics, subjective, but engaging with the external world. Quantity or quality? Whatever the approach, both had limitations, collapsing like papyrus clutched from a tomb.

Then there was psychology itself, the discipline, indefinable, plethora of schools, methods, and subject areas from social psychology to physiology, a catchall subject that inexplicably held together. What did it all mean? What relevance was psychology? He supposed it was knowledge or truth knowing why we don't know, knowing what little was knowable, being better at explaining what was wrong with a theory or study than what was right. But the result was uncertainty, inertia and mental constipation. He couldn't decide anything anymore. Whatever happened to facts? And the problem now extended into his teaching, colleagues telling him he had become notorious for demolishing findings, criticising studies, being negative, and unsettling students. 'Came here to learn some facts, increase knowledge, but I seem to know less now than when I started', a common refrain. Bloody students! If students thought a degree answered all the questions, gave them 'the knowledge', then wasn't that their fault? A degree surely showed the problems; showed why we don't know.

Matlock recently warned him not to be too critical or negative. 'It's the hallmark of science to be skeptical and open-minded, but not to the point of nihilism, that postmodern malaise'. Neil's colleagues argued similarly. 'You've got to try. We know the problems, the weaknesses, but if we listened to you, we'd all be out of a job'. That worried him. His research was at a standstill, while they battled on doing pointless or inconclusive research. He sighed. Whatever research one did, however meticulous, the enemy – those so-called peers – were at the gate, axes firmly in hand, or scalpels poised, waiting.

First, they would kill the study with a single blow, then dissect the corpse: the design, sample size and composition, ecological validity, experimental realism, demand characteristics; each X-rayed and held up one by one. And the murderous ritual came complete with its own clinical jargon, cold and cerebral. God, it was so depressing. And he was part of it. Worse even, a notorious serial killer of others' research. Then there was that other problem, the problem of the problem itself. Was it the problem, or his attitude to the problem, a principle now enshrined in cognitive behaviour therapy, the most fashionable of therapies? Did it all boil down to attitudes? Was *he* the problem? Neil pulled the sheet over his face to block the light feeling its way across the room, hoping for another hour of sleep. Did anyone outside the cloistered world of psychology take psychology seriously? He pulled together negative experiences, ridicule and rejection by outsiders who often confused psychology with therapy: 'Better be careful what I say', or responded with hostile dismissal: 'You psychologists think you know everything', to which he recently replied, 'Correction, we psychologists know nothing, and if you were to study psychology you would end knowing less than you think you know, or know why you know so little'.

Maybe he should emulate the osteopath recently met at a party. Slightly drunk, he had told the osteopath that research, using a control, showed that osteopathy made no difference; cure was all in the mind. 'You know, I have a vague memory of being told that while training,' said the osteopath, and grinning broadly switched to another subject. He was still practising a year later. Mindful of Festinger's rule that the dissonant must change contrary information by rationalising or change behaviour, the osteopath appeared to do neither, his dissonance, had he any, overcome by not caring – Orwell's doublethink.

Now wide awake, he wondered if he was depressed. Surely these were classic symptoms? Momentarily this caught his interest, a new, exciting but worrying thought. He sat up and switched on the angle poise. Lifting down a substantial tome, *Diagnosis and Statistical Manual of Mental Disorders* (or DSM for short), he turned to the symptoms of depression under DSM-1V-TR and read through the list. Yes, he had some of the symptoms, which gave him a strange satisfaction, but simultaneously found himself questioning the criteria. Who ordered the classification? Who decided what a symptom was? And classifications weren't fixed but changeable over time, reflecting social attitudes. Until 1973 homosexuality was included but removed following protests from gay activist groups. He was finding fault again. He must dwell on the positives, follow the advice of Selena de Vaux and her favourite quote from Beck: 'We behave the way we think'. In other words, most problems are no more than disordered thoughts and feelings. Negative thoughts beget negative actions (or inactions in his case). But was it that simple?

Pretending for a moment to accept the criteria, he read that to qualify as depressed, symptoms such as depressed mood had to last two weeks or more plus four additional symptoms, such as loss of appetite, difficulty concentrating, suicidal thoughts, loss of energy, sleep disturbance and/or feeling worthless. But what if he had only two or three symptoms? What if they lasted only seven or eight days at a stretch? What did that make him? 50 per cent depressed? Whatever the percentage, depressed or not, he still felt research was pointless. But did research seem pointless because he was depressed, or was he depressed because it seemed pointless?

The first glimmer of sunrise squeezed through a chink in the curtain. He wouldn't sleep now. He threw the book aside and got up. He felt fuzzy, unable to focus. He needed some pills to help him sleep. If only he could get a good night's sleep. He would see the doctor that morning.

2

Even before Neil sat down, the doctor was asking what was wrong, making notes without looking up. He explained his sleep problem and suspected mild depression. He would like some pills.

'Getting to sleep or waking early?' she asked tersely.

'Waking early.'

'Then pills won't help you.'

She made a note. Checking his blood pressure, she asked the usual questions about smoking, weight loss or gain, duration of his sleeplessness, other symptoms. She looked up and asked, 'Are you in a relationship?'

'Sort of. I think so. It's complicated.'

'Ah, that's not a medical problem. You need therapy for that.' She glanced towards the door. But I can't help you myself.'

'I didn't come for –'

'You appreciate we are very busy. If I gave therapy to all my patients, I'd never get done. As for your depression, it's not severe enough for antidepressants.' She shrugged wearily. 'Do you want a certificate?'

'No. I'm going to work.'

'Good. Concentrate on the positives.' She made another note.

He sighed. Another CBT convert.

Outside he lit a cigarette, inhaled deeply and wondered why he was smoking again. Remembering the psychologist Bem who maintained we discern our motives from our actions, and not the other way round, he decided he was probably smoking because he was depressed, but consoled himself with the knowledge he was only smoking lightly, a mere four a day, and didn't inhale deeply, so his depression must be correspondingly mild. But the problem with the explanation was that he hadn't smoked for years; starting again on his first date with Selena. Imitation perhaps? Only partly. She smoked heavily and inhaled deeply.

Driving away from the surgery, he drew on his cigarette and cursed doctors. Of course he didn't want antidepressants or therapy. He had deliberately said, 'bit depressed,' minimising his symptoms. Had he wanted to be diagnosed clinically depressed he would have used the full DSM or ICD panoply, the same used by doctors, called the shirker's bible by some tabloid. That was a bit harsh, but anyone faking mental illness would be advised to get a copy, and it amused him to imagine it circulating neighbourhoods notorious for benefit fraud.

'Useless, useless manufacturers of miracles,' he shouted out loud. To illustrate the problem of sorting out correlations from causes, Neil would tell students the story of a doctor who wrongly told someone he had only a month to live. The person went to a faith healer, and a year later was still alive. 'A miracle,' he told everyone, 'The power of prayer.' Apocryphal no doubt, but the sort of story you want to believe.

Doctors reminded him of therapists, who reminded him of Selena, the very private, very aloof and very non-tactile Selena de Vaux. Touching, he now realised, was a problem for Selina. Her general aloofness was the main reason for taking an inordinate amount of time asking her out, going no further than various hints, telling her finally that a new restaurant had opened nearby.

'Why don't we go some evening?' she said. 'Preferably a Tuesday.'

He had quickly arranged this and told her the date, noting her surprised but pleased expression. The evening went well enough. At one point she casually revealed a very distant husband living in Paris, met periodically at her behest. He had heard she was married (one of two rumours circulating about her).

'You sound as if you wouldn't care if you never saw him again.'

She laughed, all the time fixing his eye. 'Probably. He writes shape and sound poetry and is famous in avant-garde circles. He once swallowed a microphone to record bodily sounds such as the faint rustle of nasal and other hair.' She was amused at Neil's expression. 'I'm not putting you off your food?'

He had talked more than she had, mostly autobiography, she encouraging and attentive. At one point she looked troubled and said, 'It's unfair.'

He looked uncertain. 'Unfair?'

'I now know so much more about you than you know about me. That's what comes from doing therapy.'

He smiled. 'Feel free to talk about yourself, Selina. Darkest, deepest, and all that.'

She looked away, falling silent. Then smiling at him, her eyes piercing, she said, 'Later, perhaps. I need to drink more before I can talk freely.'

The restaurant was busy, every table full despite being midweek, and he noticed her searching the room, perhaps fearing a familiar face, insisting before entering he look inside for university staff. He thought this strange but saw it as another aspect of her aloofness. She filled her glass, (her third, and still only thirty minutes into the meal) and, taking a drink, placed the glass close to his, her arm remaining outstretched. He thought about touching her hand and felt his pulse race, not from passion so much as fear of offending her, felt a numbing inertia; the hand, as one psychologist put it, an intimate zone requiring invitation, not trespass. Was there a hint of invitation in that careful placing of the glass, the outstretched arm, the proximate hand? He realised he was a long way from asking her back to his flat, a lengthy incremental haul of weeks, even months.

He became aware it was raining heavily. The windows of the restaurant streaked, a taxi unlikely, and a quick dash to the university soaked through the evening's dismal conclusion. They had left their cars at the campus car park, the restaurant a short walk from the university. As predicted, there were no taxis available. Selena suggested they share her umbrella and walk to the university from where they could have a last cigarette and sober up before driving. He thought about taking her hand, but it was beyond reach, firmly gripping the umbrella. She was just not very tactile, perhaps not tactile at all, not a tactile type, never seeing her touched or touching, not even touching or being touched by other women, or Kelvin, a colleague and close 'friend'. Neil often saw her with Kelvin, or 'Kel' as he was known to the secretaries and other doting females, parading his tandoori tan bought weekly at some tannery. Perhaps Selena had Scottish ancestry, recalling a study of body language which claimed Scots were the least tactile and most distant, Arabs the opposite.

Much of the building was in darkness, the work of the vigilant caretaker, the only light a distant orange glow from the car park. The steps down to the general staffroom were steep and very dark. She became anxious, frantically drawing her hand along the wall. Her voice rising, she said, 'Where's the bloody light switch?'

She moved ahead, out of reach, descending swiftly. In the staffroom, all lights blazing, she relaxed slowly, but sat on the opposite side of Neil's desk as they smoked a final cigarette.

Sometime later she indicated she was ready to go home, thanked him for the evening and started for the steps, where she turned and said very softly, 'That was nice.'

'Yes. We must do it again some time,' he said.

'Yes, definitely.'

As she switched off the lights, he reached out and touched her sleeve, which was dimly outlined by the distant glow of the car park lights. 'Selina, do you realise I've known you a year and have never touched you?' He touched her hand and she stiffened, immobilised.

She released her hand and said a little coolly, 'Right, I think you have touched me enough. Can I go now?'

Feeling very foolish and imposing, even obtrusive, he said, 'Yes, you can go now.'

He headed home feeling wretched, telling himself he should have apologised, and asking himself over and over why he had used the strange lines: 'I've never touched you,' and, 'You can go now.' Ordinarily he would just touch, a tentative precursor, but Selina, he reminded himself by way of an excuse, was not ordinary, was a very private person. And definitely not tactile. Maybe he was nervous? Selena made him nervous. Bem again. 'You can go now' because he was nervous; he knew he was nervous...

As Neil ruminated on his problems, he reached the roundabout and the exit for the university. Was he going in or not? He circled round, indicator blinking continuously, and approaching the exit a fourth time noticed a police car parked on a slope, four eyes peering at him intently. Controlling a powerful urge to accelerate away, he took the exit calmly and headed for work. Entering the car park, he remembered he was supposed to arrange a meeting with Professor Matlock. *Urgent*, his note read. *See my secretary*. That was more than a week ago.

3

Professor Matlock, head of social psychology, harboured no doubts or crisis of faith as he peered down at the small group of freshers, seating carefully arranged, he proximate, all-seeing and seen. He had carefully choreographed the situation, surrounding the students with the trappings of research. They were to choose a module to supplement their main subject and he aimed to persuade them to take psychology. There would be five groups in total and the inductions would take up most of the day. He could have combined them in the hall and given one lecture but considered the hall 'situationally inappropriate'. The laboratory was the only context: clinical, white walls, impressive apparatus, he in a white lab coat, but not too white, not off-the-shelf crisp white, but long hours in the laboratory white, worn and faded. The coat was integral to the performance, along with his title and the lectern borrowed from the lecture theatre. Situationism was the hallmark of social psychology, but Matlock went further, believing one's persona varied from situation to situation, his own and the students now shaped by the props of the immediate context, he both the shaper and shaped. The scientist created the laboratory, and the laboratory created the scientist, a transmogrification requiring no Jekyll drug or philosopher's stone, just the immediate, all-powerful situation.

Stepping back to a huge three-panel, wall-mounted roller board, he wrote in capitals: *The situation*. Turning, he said, 'Most people understand we are shaped by two forces in life, commonly known as nurture and nature, our upbringing and our genes, or the interaction of the two. But there is a third variable, commonplace, pervasive and easily overlooked: the immediate situation.' Returning to the lectern, voice rising, he said, 'Situations are all around us, are external to us, often beyond awareness, invidiously shaping us. Take architecture.'

He paused momentarily and slowly looked round the laboratory, the students following his gaze to the high-vaulted ceiling. 'Architecture,' he repeated. 'Wasn't it Churchill who said, "We shape our buildings; thereafter they shape us". A soaring cathedral points towards God. We are awed, and worship. The illuminated circus tent and supporting music excites. We are prepared to have fun. The solid facade of a bank assures us. We deposit our money. A prestigious university epitomises knowledge. We study.' He peered over his glasses, and added, 'We hope.'

The laughter resounded round the laboratory, and as it subsided, he said with levity, 'And within that prestigious university a laboratory, and within that laboratory a professor issuing commands. We obey.' He paused, the word *obey* a cue for the predictable question.

'Obey?' asked a voice from the back row.

'Yes, obey. Some of you will be familiar with obedience studies at A-level, or with parodies on television. You will recall ordinary people obeying the command to apply what they took to be electric shocks, to what they believed to be genuine learners. In the baseline experiment there are two subjects: one a teacher, the other, a learner. One subject is genuine, the other an accomplice. The procedure is rigged so that the accomplice is always the learner. Most obey to the very end and apply the highest shock levels for wrong answers, even when the learner protests, pleads to be released, bangs on the wall and finally falls silent.

'At the time, some dismissed Milgram's now classic study. They said it was American, only what you would expect of Americans. The English, they said, are different. The criticism of Americans gave me an idea. Some years ago, I replicated the entire study in England, here at this university. I got similar results. English obedience was slightly lower, but only slightly. Regardless of personality, education, sex, class or nationality, most obeyed and administered what they thought to be dangerous electric shocks to people they didn't know and bore no animosity. Obeyed the situation, you understand. These were not bad people, but ordinary people in a bad situation.'

He stepped back to the board and wrote: *Situations equal behaviour*, and connected it to the word *situation*.

'Milgram was probably the first to study obedience experimentally, and there have been numerous replications and variations across cultures and across time. All show similar levels of obedience, and all show obedience has not declined since Milgram did his pioneering study in the early sixties.'

He piled on more studies, showing the power of the situation over the individual, how a powerful situation overrides disposition, personality and attitudes.

'We like to believe we are not controlled by others. We like to believe we are free and independent. You see, you can't rely on what people say. That's why we need experiments. If you remember one thing today, remember this: who we are is less important than where we are.'

Stepping back to the blackboard he wrote, again in capitals: *Experimentation.*

'What words come to mind?' He lifted his arm. 'Give me some key words.'

'Control.'

'Control of variables.'

'Testability.'

'Good. Excellent. Control and testability are key words. Separating cause and effect. And how difficult that is, and how easy to confuse correlations with causes, coincidence as cause *and* effect. But there is something else; something missing. Control, testability and...'

After some hesitation a student said, 'Replication?'

'Excellent. To be a true experiment it must be open to replication.'

Matlock wrote the three words on the board.

He decided on a short break to let them wander the laboratory to peer in at the various soundproof cubicles running the length of one side, and be awed by the impressive equipment, particularly his shock machine. They broke into small groups and roamed the laboratory. Helmets resembling hair curlers caused a few giggles. Matlock mingled, explained apparatus. He noticed a group standing near his shock machine taken out of storage, cleaned and polished for the occasion. He felt deep satisfaction at the interest being shown. As he approached, part of the group fell silent, averted eye contact and moved away. One he recognised, arms folded throughout his lecture, recalled his failure to laugh at his jokes.

*

Seated at the front, arms folded, the student looked from side to side and said, 'We have a question. 'Didn't Orne say volunteer subjects in experiments want to help the experimenter succeed, work out the result the experimenter wants and act accordingly? Not obedience after all, just a wish to please. "Demand characteristics", isn't that the term?'

Matlock nodded.

'Doesn't that invalidate experimentation on humans?'

Taking control of the knowledge, Matlock stepped forward, leaned over the lectern and said, 'Professor Martin Orne, to give him his full title, professor of psychiatry and psychology at the University of Pennsylvania. Ingenious as Orne's arguments are, he is wrong about the obedience experiments.'

The student smiled skeptically.

'Now you're thinking, he would say that, wouldn't he?' He paused for laughter. 'How could he possibly know the subjects of his experiments were not pretending?'

His voice now brisk, he said, 'How did I know? Two kinds of evidence. For a start, subjects visibly suffered during my obedience experiments. For Orne to be correct, we have to believe subjects feigned stuttering, sweating, trembling and hysterical laughter, all to please the experimenter.' He shook his head. 'Still not conclusive, you're thinking? God, you're a skeptical lot. And rightly so. What was needed was a test, so I asked three independent observers to debrief a random sample of subjects and load the question in favour of Orne's hypothesis. "C'mon, you surely saw through it? You must have worked out what the experiment was about?" Over ninety per cent said they were convinced the experiment was genuine. A few had doubts. Just a few.'

Once he would have cited Sheridan and King's replication using puppies and real electric shocks, where most of the male and all the female subjects obeyed to the end despite the puppies visibly squealing and jumping around; obeyed to the end despite showing obvious conflict and distress, some crying. A decisive repudiation of Orne. But animal welfare was now a moot point. He wanted to win over the students to psychology, not alienate them, and momentarily consoled himself knowing other disciplines had similar problems, the liberal malaise everywhere. Even literature. A colleague told him he had stopped teaching George Orwell's *Shooting an Elephant* due to protests. Orwell, a colonial officer in pre-war Burma, is forced to shoot a rogue elephant which has caused mayhem, including a death. Orwell doesn't want to shoot the elephant but feels pressured by the situation, namely the huge crowd of local Burmese looking on expectantly. Orwell pumps bullet after bullet, but the animal just lies there making a dreadful noise. For years the students sympathised with Orwell's dilemma, some even showing amusement at the elephant's stubborn refusal to die. Then slowly concern shifted from Orwell to the elephant, first a lone voice, then a chorus, then a crescendo: 'He didn't have to kill the elephant. He had a choice'.

'Right, that's Orne dealt with. Now the Freudians.' Matlock's tone was happier; Freud easier to refute than Orne. 'Some Freudians told me the subjects didn't so much obey as enjoy, the experiment an opportunity to release sadistic desires found in all of us, the experiment legitimating those desires. Hysterical laughter and stuttering, they said, are well-known expressions of joy. Not the situation after all, but disposition, something they brought to the experiment.'

He beamed at the audience. 'I was prepared for them. That's why I included all those variations, testing one variable after another to separate cause and effect. How do you explain, I asked, when given a choice over shock levels, most subjects gave lower shocks? How do you explain Experiment 28, where the experimenter gave orders by phone and most cheated by giving lower shocks, and lied about the shock levels given?' He turned to face the students. 'You see the importance of manipulating different variables? Only the experimental set-up separates variables, making it a true science.' He paused momentarily. 'Freud has a place, I suppose.' He stared vacantly at a point the far end of the laboratory, as if visibly struggling to find Freud's place, evoking smiles and a small ripple of laughter.

'Contrary to Hollywood depictions, psychoanalysis is a small and declining part of the whole, and therapy itself has moved on. Most therapists today are not Freudians. Of course, you still find Freud knocking around English departments worming his way into literary texts, eating the heart out of authorial intention, but as one contemporary critic said of Freud's *Interpretation of Dreams,* "In this book anything can mean anything". Then there's Freud's sample, a theory built upon a few hundred middle-class Viennese neurotics in the 19th century. And from that small sample selection of an even smaller sample of successes for publication, which he gave sensational names such as the Wolf Man and the Rat Man. As much showman as therapist. We now know all his case studies are suspect. Take the Wolf Man. Sixty years later, when interviewed, he claimed he was never cured of his obsessional neurosis, and dismissed Freud's explanation that his condition and wolf dream arose from observing his parents making love when he was an infant as "terribly farfetched".' He paused and leaned over the podium for emphasis. 'No, only experimental psychology is a true science. Hard evidence, prediction and replication. Causes carefully separated from correlations. Less exotic than Freud, perhaps, but...

'You may have come across press articles ridiculing experimental psychology. No relevance to the outside world, or if relevant, proving the obvious.' He shook his head. 'Not obedience research pioneered by Milgram and replicated by me. Research not for the moment, not for a decade, but for all time, relevant to one of life's enduring problems: obedience to authority. This resulting in the worse example of obedience in human history: the holocaust.'

The hall went quiet, expressions serious.

'Obedient Germans slaughtering innocent Jews. This led to the "Germans are different" hypothesis, popular after the war. Milgram initially intended studying the Germans, but his wholly unexpected obedience findings in America caused him to drop the idea.'

The student with folded arms raised a hand. 'I take it you are familiar with Goldhagen's historical work, *Hitler's Willing Executioners*. According to Goldhagen, Germans willingly killed Jews; were willing executioners. Goldhagen cites an occasion where a group of Germans were given a free choice, to kill or not to kill, and almost all of them volunteered to kill Jews. Not obedience but willing killers. Explain that.'

'A good question,' Matlock said, stalling.

Only recently published, Matlock hadn't read or heard of the book. He rarely read psychology these days, less still history. *How was this bastard so well-informed?*

Still stalling, he said, 'History isn't an experimental science, of course. Historians don't agree on the causes of the Second World War or the Holocaust. You can't replicate history, take out variables such as Hitler or Chamberlain or the Versailles Treaty. You can't control or replicate it in a laboratory. That's why we need experimental psychology, such as obedience research.'

The student was about to protest, but Matlock had moved to firmer ground. 'Of course, as you all know, not all research is truly scientific. Control has lessened. Studies are increasingly comparative or observational, the so-called qualitative approach.' He paused and leaned forward. 'But infinitely more accurate than psychoanalysis.'

When the laughter subsided, the student persisted. 'So, you're saying Goldhagen was wrong?'

'I'm saying history can't control variables, unlike psychology.'

'Wasn't it cruel to deceive and stress the subjects in your obedience experiments? Make them suffer. Was it ethical? What do you say to those who argue that the experimenter's obedience to science and inflicting pain on subjects resembles the Nazis obedience to the Fuhrer? Science *their* Fuhrer.'

There was a gasp from the audience.

Matlock recognised the student as one of a type, a leader, more shaper of a situation than shaped, a non-obedient championing another attitude shift: subjects' rights in experiments, their human rights; no longer subjects even, persons, individuals with names. Animal experiments in psychology were out. Well, almost. Even if you got permission there would be protests, even sabotage. But times changing or not, this student was gaining control, the rest enjoying his challenges, and had to be stopped. Nodding towards the student he said, 'You ask, was it ethical? A good question. Debriefing showed that the majority thought participation worthwhile or gave a neutral response. This is the same for Milgram's original research, and all other replications.'

'But not every subject?'

Matlock avoided the question, saying other students had questions and time was running out, pointing to a student at the back whose arm was raised.

*

Matlock was offered a professorship because he came with a long string of publications (boosting the department's meagre offering at a stroke and solving the publications crisis), and a substantial research grant to replicate Milgram's American study.

At the time, psychology in general was suffering from a relevance crisis and Matlock's obedience replication solved the problem for City Centre University, gaining a brief respite from relentless media ridicule. Combining interest, rigour and surprise, depth and popular appeal, obedience was a media sensation belying the belief that Brits are different from Americans and psychology has no relevance. At the time of his arrival, much psychological research at CCU was trivial and empty, and if rigorous, laboriously demonstrated the obvious, such as the television research led by Odlum. After two years the study concluded that, contrary to earlier research claiming we are totally shaped and conditioned by television, we are selective when watching television, and different audiences interpret programmes in different ways. Unlike rats or pigeons, we have minds, can choose, think and reflect.

Local radio, adopting an ironic tone, set out the great discovery as a conversation. 'We don't have to watch a programme. We can, and do, switch the television on and off and choose between channels. You know, the TV control.'

'Really. Who would have thought of that?'

'What a clever lot these psychologists are.'

Locked into an internal debate with the behaviourists at a rival university, Odlum and his team were oblivious to the outside world, that ultimate funding agency, the taxpayer. Thereafter, the local press, radio and television took unusual interest in psychology research at CCU, now a symbol of all that was wrong with the discipline.

There followed the queuing study, ongoing when Matlock arrived. He thought this might offer something, some insight, a situational study after all. But after a year studying queues, all they came up with was trivia couched in the most pretentious jargon, perhaps hoping it would compensate for the findings. Queue jumping became situationally inappropriate queuing behaviour response, those at the front of a queue, and more likely to obtain tickets, situationally advantaged queue members. Then there was situationally appropriate queue place maintenance (those queuing kept each other's places while they bought food or went to the toilet). At first Matlock thought the study might be more self-indulgent than mindless, a ruse to attend football matches and concerts, until he found none had entered stadia or concert halls.

But no ridicule affixed his obedience research. Even local media managed qualified praise.

A spin-off was the Replication Team. From replicating Milgram, the department embarked on a series of replications led by Odlum, and the department was now seen as a centre of replication, attracting grants from major funding agencies.

4

Neil found a note in his tray from Rachel Probender: *Come to my room to discuss Frankenstein. Urgent.*

He began telling Rachel about his insomnia and visiting the doctor that morning.

'Never mind that, I need some help. Think Frankenstein. That's why you're here, remember. We can come to your problem later.'

Neil wasn't exactly certain what Rachel's research entailed, certainly the Gothic novel, something about childhood influences on characters ranging from the Brontës to Mary Shelley. She was searching for an angle, a focus. Annoyed by her abruptness, Neil said provocatively, 'Frankenstein? You mean the monster with a bolt through his head?'

She sighed. 'No, you idiot. Victor Frankenstein's the scientist, the monster is his creation.' Her tone conciliatory, she added, 'You're not alone making that mistake. Mary Gaskell confused Victor Frankenstein with his creation. And definitely no bolt. Get that out of your head.'

They laughed together at her unintended pun.

'Read the novel. Forget the films, especially Boris Karloff. Forget everything you've learned about the monster. People have wrong ideas about the monster. The monster does some bad things but isn't all bad. He starts out with good intentions.'

'Bad things?'

She waved her hand dismissively. 'Oh, takes revenge on Victor Frankenstein for rejecting him. First, he kills Victor's best friend, moves on to Victor's family, kills his little brother, and then strangles his wife on their wedding night.'

'But not all bad?'

'Not his fault. The monster isn't born evil. That's the whole point. Given a chance he would have been different. You see, Mary Shelley believed we are products of our circumstances, not some nasty inheritance, at least in the 1818 edition. Very Enlightenment. Rousseau? Noble savage?'

Neil looked blank. 'Rousseau?'

'Too difficult to explain. Another time. The monster desperately wants to be loved. He's initially kind to a poor family, hides from them but helps in various ways. But once he reveals himself, they flee in horror and the villagers banish him.'

'Even so, going on a killing spree, targeting the innocent...'

She shrugged. 'Still not his fault. You see, the monster is intelligent, articulate and sensitive, not a grunting Neanderthal. He only becomes cruel when rejected and, ironically, on learning that people are cruel and deceitful. You see, he comes into the world an innocent, a tabular rasa, and learns about evil from human society. Mary Shelley is making a point about human nature. We are corrupted by society.' She sighed wearily and stood up. 'Let's have some coffee. I need to explain the novel before you read it. That'll take some time as it's you.'

Neil smiled. It never occurred to Rachel to ask if he had the time to spare. But he knew his role; knew he must be Rachel's sounding board.

'Don't smile. I know that smile. Anyway, Frankenstein's about science and relevant to your research. The first science fiction novel and written by a woman.'

He settled in his chair as she made coffee.

'You see, Victor Frankenstein is the problem. He's the creator after all, but totally inept. He creates a man but forgets about his appearance. His creation is hideously ugly on the outside, has yellow skin which, Frankenstein tells us, "Scarcely covered the work of muscle and arteries beneath". OK, he has lustrous, flowing black hair and pearly-white teeth, but these, Frankenstein tells us, sets a horrific contrast to his "watery eyes that seemed almost of the same colour as the dun-white sockets in which they were set". Add to that a shrivelled complexion, straight black lips, giant limbs, eight feet tall, and your monster is complete. What chance for the poor thing? You see, Victor found the parts in various mortuaries.'

'Mortuary for giants? Weren't most people much shorter around that time?'

She sighed witheringly. 'That's not the point. Victor doesn't intend to create a monster. He does so by default. He tells us he has difficulty working with small body parts and searches around for large ones. That's a key point, man subservient to science. Frankenstein's out of symmetry, a one-sided scientist pursuing his career regardless of other considerations: the aesthetic, the moral and the social. He deliberately isolates himself, is freed from social constraint and driven by unrestrained ambition. At one point, Clerval, his friend, criticises him for being antisocial. You see, Clerval symbolises the social. Remember that phrase: *Unrestrained ambition*. It explains a lot. Frankenstein's a specialist. "In the extreme", said Bernard Shaw, "the specialist is an idiot".'

'You got that from the vice-chancellor. He uses it to justify integrating disciplines.'

She went on hurriedly. 'So what sort of idiot is Frankenstein? For a start, he shows no consideration for his creation and no moral responsibility. He can't even bear to look at him and flees. But he can't escape that easily, and the price is terrible suffering on himself and others. Had he considered the aesthetic and social dimensions, created a beautiful creature, or even a passable one, the disaster would never have happened. The creature, initially well-intentioned and good-natured, would have gained acceptance; his creator, success and fame. So I'm saying, if the creation of the monster had been teamwork – Frankenstein, Clerval and Elizabeth – we would have had a more rounded creature.'

'Elizabeth?'

'I'm coming to her.'

She handed Neil a coffee. 'Victor Frankenstein's central to the novel, though his creation usually steals the limelight, particularly in those fucked-up film versions. But remember, title and subtitle refer to Frankenstein, not the monster.'

'I still don't understand why the monster goes on a killing spree.'

'Spree is not the word I would choose. Hated, feared and rejected, he becomes consumed with self-loathing, rage and revenge.'

'Low self-esteem?'

Her laugh was ironic. 'That's putting it mildly. And a bit limp. I hope you can come up with some meatier theory than that.'

'Adler's inferiority complex, an ugly-neglected child. Rejected and hated, aggression is his way of gaining validity and significance.'

She nodded. 'Better. Fits what the monster says: "I will revenge my injuries; if I cannot inspire love, I will cause fear".'

Handing Neil a second coffee, she said, 'Now, let me clear up another myth, shaped by various film versions. You probably think Frankenstein is an anti-science novel.'

Neil smiled and nodded.

She shook her head. 'The novel's more about the misuse of science, man's arrogance, one-sidedness, fallibility. Proof of this – yes, I said proof. I saw your eyebrows lift slightly. You know, if I was limited to an experimental framework as espoused by your Professor Matlock and applied that framework to analysing literature, vainly trying to isolate variables, no criticism or biography would be possible. If only you could do a re-run of someone's life, take out a single variable, say, Mary's mother dying giving birth to her. Would Frankenstein have been written? Did Mary feel responsible for her mother's death? Did her father hold her responsible? Maybe he didn't reject her as some claim, but he certainly gave her scant attention. And she herself loses a child. Does she feel guilty? Remember, Frankenstein is an appalling parent, doesn't even give his creation a name. Even the worse parent gives a child a name.'

'Couldn't the monster give himself a name?'

'That's not the point. Now concentrate. Is Frankenstein a replay of her own life? Decidedly psychoanalytic, but you see the possibilities. I see connections, albeit loose, and in a way I do manipulate variables or hypothesise them. My question earlier, what would happen if Frankenstein had created a beautiful creature? Did Mary intend the reader to sympathise with the monster? Does the text and other sources support this? But first, you need to know how the novel is structured.'

Neil shifted in his seat.

Rachel shook her head. 'I see, low attention span. You're worse than some of my students.'

'I'm tired, that's all.'

'Oh yes, your insomnia.' She handed Neil a strong, black coffee.

'The story takes the form of a narrative inside a narrative, rather like a Chinese box or Matryoshka doll. It opens with Walton, a sea captain, writing to his sister about his voyage to the Arctic to discover a new passage through the icy waste. Like Frankenstein, Walton has scientific aspirations to benefit society and hopes to find the source of the magnetic pole. Walton tells his sister how he rescues Frankenstein from the icy waste. Frankenstein then relates his story to Walton, his pursuit of the monster following the deaths and final meeting with the monster. At that point, the monster becomes narrator and tells his side of the story to Frankenstein. Frankenstein dies and the story concludes. Each narration within a narration is in the first person.

'Now concentrate. This is important. Walton parallels Frankenstein. Walton's voyage is dangerous, for himself and the crew, but ambition, his thirst for new knowledge, overrides this initially.'

She looked at Neil. 'Listening? You see, that's the difference. Unlike Frankenstein, Walton is not completely isolated. No Ingolstadt retreat for Walton.'

'Ingolstadt?'

'I'm coming to that. He can't ignore his crew. They are increasingly close to mutiny, and he reluctantly turns back. He is controlled by his crew. The crew symbolises the community. Frankenstein, you remember, works in complete isolation, is unrestrained, so the flaw here is man, not science. You see how evidence works in lit crit? You see why Shelley has the Walton parallel? Science and polar exploration are neutral, man in isolation and excessive ambition the problem. The weakness is man, not science. You'll better understand this when you read the book.'

'What about Mary Shelley's intention?'

Rachel wore a pained expression. 'Authorial intention? Good question. And shows you're listening. The novel starts out as a horror story and becomes a deeper philosophical work, which is reinforced in her 1831 revision. She never quite sheds the horror aspect singled out by the popular film versions, such as the Gothic devices; the monster seemingly all-powerful and ubiquitous, threatening storms, perilous locations, pervading fear. There's no single meaning to a text, of course, no single truth. Writers don't always know what they are doing. They make unconscious assumptions; make mistakes. Contradict themselves, steer a different course part way through.

'Evidence, before you ask. The clue is in the triad, introduced by Mary in the 1831 revision to flag up the one-sidedness of Frankenstein by contrasting him with the others. That's a crucial piece of evidence regarding authorial intention. Clerval can be seen as part of a triad, each representing a segment of the organic whole. Against Frankenstein's cold and flawed rationality, Clerval is moral, altruistic and chivalrous, composes heroic songs, is a perfect friend, occupying himself, Frankenstein tells us "…with the moral relations of things". Visiting Frankenstein in Ingolstadt, Clerval lectures him on his failure to respond to his family's letters. Elizabeth represents the aesthetic. Frankenstein tells us: "While Elizabeth contemplated with a serious and satisfied spirit the magnificent appearances of things, I delighted in investigating the causes". Feminists are none too happy with the depiction of Elizabeth, but even today literature departments are female-dominated, science departments male-dominated. Does it matter? Feminists I know, ask why so few women do physics? But rarely ask, why do so few men do literature? Somehow, that's not seen as a problem.'

Neil nodded. 'They implicitly accept the superiority of science. Literature valued less.'

'What does psychology say about subject choice?'

'One theory is that women prefer literature because it's about relationships between people, whereas natural science is about relationships between inanimate objects, which are cold and impersonal. Psychology is somewhere in between, the students split fifty-fifty. Males dominate the staff side though, and most professors and top management are male. Same in sociology, that bastion of liberalism. Why? Some stress nurture, male prejudice, the glass ceiling, others nature. Can't separate the two, of course.'

'Interaction of the two?'

Neil shrugged. 'Probably. We just don't know.'

'Even if Mary Shelley had wanted to counter the stereotype, she couldn't have a female Frankenstein, no more than Dickens could have made Scrooge female and his office full of female clerks. Were there any female scientists in 1818? Whatever, Mary obviously sees Frankenstein's one-sided obsession the problem, male or female. As I keep repeating, Frankenstein is not an anti-science novel, just critical of unregulated science and unbounded ambition.' She pushed the book towards Neil. 'And finally, the title.'

Neil looked at the title. '*Frankenstein*?'

'And underneath?'

'*Or The Modern Prometheus.*'

'Exactly. The book is subtitled *The Modern Prometheus*. The theme of unbounded ambition is indicated by the subtitle. Why have a subtitle? Frankenstein is a modern Prometheus who usurps God's and society's power but has none of the roundness of a real god. You know the Prometheus myth?'

Neil shook his head.

'Don't you know anything?' She sighed witheringly again. 'The simple version for you. Prometheus rebels against God by giving mankind the gift of fire and is punished.'

'Punished?'

'Bound to a rock, has his liver eaten, regenerated daily and re-eaten by vultures. Frankenstein is the modern Prometheus because he usurps nature or God by creating life. Prometheus is punished by Jupiter for his presumption, Frankenstein is punished by his creation. Frankenstein is unbounded and presumes he alone can create life and usurp nature. Remember – and this is important – characters are not real people. Critics often go wrong here. We have the text, or what the author put into it; we have information about the author: letters, diaries, and so on. We can link these to a novel, perhaps work out what informed the novel. This is where you fit in. What I want is some theory or theories to fit the themes of the novel.'

Aware Rachel was silent, Neil looked across.

'You were drifting. You're even worse than my First years. OK, five-minute break. I'll make some more coffee. Black for you.'

*

Laying her watch on the table, Rachel was saying, 'Frankenstein has generated numerous interpretations. The Marxist O'Flinn, obsessed with revolution and capitalism, claims the monster symbolises the vengeful working class rejected by the bourgeoisie, a sort of rampaging mob. Then there are feminist and psychoanalytic interpretations. All appropriate parts of the text to support this or that ideology. Admittedly, there's no single, true interpretation of a text, the position held by Derrida and Barthes.

'Isn't that a bit obvious?'

'Of course it's fucking obvious. I'll hit you in a minute. You use some structuralist, post-structuralist, deconstructionist or postmodernist shit or die. You're not recognised unless you pay homage to some turgid, pretentious French bullshitter, preferably two. Old wine in new bottles; not even new bottles, just badly glued new labels. It's extraordinary. Some arsehole comes up with the vague term postmodernism, and millions of words are written debating what it means, when all the time it means what you want it to fucking mean –'

There was a knock at the door.

'It's open,' shouted Rachel.

A tutee tentatively put her head round the door. 'Rachel, can –'

'Go away, see me later.' The door closed and Rachel continued her rant against postmodernism.

Those who didn't know Rachel might easily cast her insensitive and abrasive, even a people-hater she used the word hate so often, but Neil now understood she would usually start by 'hating' those she didn't know, taking an instant dislike to Neil their first meeting and regularly putting him down, until one day he reacted strongly, telling her to fuck off. They didn't talk for some time. Finally making up, she said, 'There was I thinking you were arrogant, pompous, too self-assured, but now I know you're sensitive, insecure and rather modest.'

Soon realising abrasiveness was a condition of their friendship, he now merely smiled and waited for the onslaught to end. Her abruptness and rudeness towards the student were belied by the queue of students outside her room well into the evening seeking advice on finance, academic issues, even relationship problems. From freshers to PhDs, she patched up their personal lives, much to the consternation of Selena de Vaux, the department therapist and councillor.

Occasionally Neil asked himself why he tolerated her barbs and put-downs. The truth was, he didn't know exactly and would turn to Bem's self-perception theory: we judge our motives and infer our attitudes from our actions. 'I'm eating a lot today; I must be hungry... I'm applauding madly; therefore, I must be enjoying the concert' (especially if the ticket cost the earth). I put up with a lot from Rachel, therefore I must be... What, exactly? Weak? Dependent? Tolerant? He preferred tolerant. That put him in control, superior even, tolerant a positive word. Another clue, he told himself, was the balance of their relationship, gaining far more than he lost, insults easily dismissed as a game played along with. For this was another rule of friendship devised by Rachel, and she decided the rules, or as Goffman would say, defined the situation. Matlock told people he was a different person with different people, depending on the situation, and the standing joke, whenever you mentioned Matlock was: 'Which Matlock are you referring to?' Was he a different person with Rachel? Rachel, of course, was always Rachel, transcending situations. Recently invited by the vice-chancellor to a conference, Rachel, a vegetarian, had aired her usual concern about the food, saying it was mostly meat dishes and therefore discriminatory. One professor asked her what sort of food she would eat, and the VC called from an adjoining room, 'What does she eat? She eats department heads and vice-chancellors.'

Recently the VC had his room decorated, with reddish-pink wallpaper. Rachel was appalled.

'Looks like a brothel,' she exclaimed loudly so the secretaries could hear.

One, looking horrified, said, 'I'm not listening to this,' and started to move away.

That moment the VC emerged from his office, grinned broadly and said, 'No, no. You must understand, this is Rachel.'

Yes, he had the right personality for a friendship with Rachel, the right attitude, mostly adapting to her rules, though for his own protection he would implement a range of deflectors, defusers and avoiders cultivated long before knowing Rachel. 'Insults out the way, can we…' 'Now you've scrutinised my jacket, perhaps we…' Sometimes, when tired and his defences weak, he would negotiate. 'You can come round to my place on one condition, you don't criticise my colour-scheme or pictures.'

She would laugh loudly at this and say, 'OK, you win. This time.'

Well, that was as close as he could get to explaining why their friendship worked so well.

'As I was saying, postmodernism's only a word, a sound, a mouthful of air. Right, now listen carefully. Your question about authorial intention. I repeat, Mary Shelley re-wrote *Frankenstein* and added the triad. Why? Obviously to clarify her intention that Frankenstein was one-sided and lacked aesthetic and social dimensions. That was her intention. See what I mean by evidence? Surely an author has intention? Ask yourself, why create an ugly monster if she didn't want to show Frankenstein as one-sided? There must be some limit to interpretation, otherwise you could read the same text and turn it into whatever you want. No need to read all of Shakespeare's plays. Read *MacBeth* and interpret it as *Hamlet* or *Richard III*. The problem today is that Freudians and most postmodernist critics give scant attention to the author's intention. Incidentally, I'm meeting up with a sociologist next week, a Durkheimian, or something. Do you know anything about Durkheimians? Said to be the opposite of Marxists. Sounds promising. Now, about your insomnia…'

*

Neil had described his symptoms to Rachel – sleeplessness, fuzziness, apathy – and how he had tried going to bed early. 'Someone in biology went on about circadian rhythms, my body clock.'

'A gene slave.' Her tone was disapproving.

'Selena suspects a trauma.'

'Do you believe that?'

'I've racked my brain but can't recall a single traumatic experience, not even years back. She said it's there but dissociated.'

'You know how Selena reduces symptoms, something means something else, all buried in the distant past. It's axiomatic with her. My advice is, forget Selena and try the Rachel Probender Method. Your problem is you worry about it, get anxious about it. Fear it.'

He nodded.

'That's where you're going wrong.'

'The doctor –'

'Sh-ss. Listen, forget the fucking doctor, forget pills, forget the body clock, and forget Selena. As I was saying, don't fear it, fight it, and stay awake, that way the bastard insomnia can't control you. Don't try to sleep. Don't go to bed. Nothing pisses off insomnia more than that. Get plenty of exercise, go for long walks, and exhaust yourself. I could soon cure your little ailment. I'm off to Brontë Country this weekend, walk where the Brontës walked. You're welcome to join me. If you do, get some waterproofs and the right shoes. I'll cure your insomnia.'

Rachel told Neil not to sleep the night before going to Brontë Country. He thought he might sleep in her car on route, but she lectured him on the Gothic novel, and if he showed signs of drifting, she made him repeat points. 'You can sleep tonight. I want you fit tomorrow. We've got a long circuitous walk to Ponden Kirk, said to be inspiration for Penistone Crags in *Wuthering Heights*. I don't want you falling over the edge when you crawl through the hole.'

'Hole?'

She laughed. 'All will be revealed.'

*

Friday night he was barely awake, but she refused to let him go to bed early, making him talk, nudging him if he showed signs of drifting, which was often. He slept for ten hours. The next day he woke refreshed, fuzziness gone. But what had done the trick? Was it the Rachel Probender Method, or something else? Perhaps the change of scenery, being away from the university, sharing the problem with Rachel, or Rachel's presence.

'Of course, it might have gone away spontaneously. Or your presence, a well-documented psychological phenomenon called the Hawthorne Effect.'

'Hawthorne Effect?' she echoed flatly.

'The name given to an American study where productivity increased whatever changes the researchers made to the working environment: heating, lighting, whatever. The researchers eventually realised an uncontrolled variable was causing the rise in output: their own presence. The workers were responding to the attention and interest shown. Perhaps –'

He stopped, aware that Rachel's posture had stiffened.

'Neil, I'll hit you in a minute.'

'Only joking,' he lied. 'I really am grateful.'

'I hope so, after all my efforts. OK, I've cured your insomnia, that's one symptom out the way, but your procrastination is different. You have a touch of the Hamlets of late, that's all. It'll pass. You know the *Hamlet* story? Hamlet wants certain knowledge before he can act but sees endless problems and outcomes, the result inertia. He can't even commit suicide because of the uncertainty of what follows death. Hamlet Complex, we'll call it.'

'Hamlet Complex. I like it. Make a good research project. Methodology would present a problem, of course, and –'

'Ever on duty. Can't you think about something else?'

'By the way, what happened to Hamlet? Does he resolve –'

'Absolutely. Then he dies. The whole play is about death. "To be, or not to be", and all that. All the main characters die.'

The moors surrounding Haworth seemed little changed since *Wuthering Heights*, and Rachel was feeling close to the Brontës knowing that the sisters walked the same route so long ago. She explained that the novel needed the moors as a setting, the wild, rock-strewn terrain, Wuthering Heights storm-tossed and defended with aggressive thorns and large jutting stones, windows set deep into the walls (as much fortress as house), and how you couldn't imagine the raw passions taking place in a neat suburban two-up two-down next to a well-tended local authority municipal park. After Brontë Bridge and Waterfall, they headed for Ponden Kirk, a gritstone outcrop and megalithic portal of jagged rock protruding from the hill. They rested before the short but steep descent to the hole, clinging to vegetation. The hole, perilously close to the edge, went right through the rock and was sufficiently large enough to crawl through.

Rachel seemed hesitant. They sat on a rock and she explained the legend. 'It was once believed that if a maiden passed through the hole she would marry within a year. If she couldn't pass through, she would never marry. Bit phallic, if inverted. Doesn't say what happens if you don't try, or if you're a man.' She smiled. 'You go first. I'll take some pictures.'

Neil duly crawled through. Re-emerging, head peering out, Rachel took more pictures. 'Like a badger emerging from a burrow.'

He was a bit miffed when Rachel refused her turn. 'What was that stuff about walking where they walked?'

She laughed. 'As far as I know, no Brontë ever crawled through any holes.'

Next was Haworth village and the parsonage, now the Brontë Parsonage Museum. Rachel explained that the museum was more dedicated to Charlotte, partly because she outlived Emily but mostly because she was rated the better novelist for a long time, also her own estimation. 'Charlotte was a bit critical of *Wuthering Heights*, considering it immature and far too violent, claiming Emily had little knowledge of real people. Today, *Wuthering Heights* is classed as one of the great novels of the 19th century. Even Somerset Maugham grudgingly admitted such, but couldn't resist a barb or two, saying the novel was clumsily constructed because it was her first novel, a two-generation novel beyond her capabilities, implying the two generations are not properly connected.

'The novel is open to interpretation. Quintessentially writerly, no omniscient third person (unlike Lawrence), and avoids the limitations of chronology. Wonderful time shifts, all meticulously constructed to create suspense and mystery. The opening depicts inexplicable events only later unravelled.

She explores the destructive nature of passion and class snobbery, culminating in Heathcliff's cruelty and revenge. You see, Catherine marries Linton, who is part of the gentry, for status, and realises her error. If written today it would be postmodern because Nellie, the main narrator, is considered unreliable. But – and it's an important but – Nelly's comments on Catherine provide enough information for the reader to form their own conclusion. More than can be said for many of today's postmodernist offerings.

'Maugham, in his article, derides her style and selectively nit-picks. He ignores one of her most eloquent passages: "My love for Linton is like the foliage in the woods: time will change it, I'm well aware, as winter changes the trees. My love for Heathcliff resembles the eternal rocks beneath: a source of little visible delight, but necessary. Nelly, I am Heathcliff!" Any failing in style is more than compensated by that one passage. Heathcliff is equally passionate, driven to cruelty and terrible revenge, whereas the next generation is balanced and breaks from the past, symbolised by flowers replacing thorns at the Heights. But not too civilised or genteel, not the deadening, passionless, orderly, refined, civil and very dull world of Linton. So you see, the first part of the novel is about extremes, the second part about reconciliation and balance. Maugham missed that.'

Earlier, Neil had asked about the Brontës and men. Other than Charlotte, who married and became pregnant, were they all virgins?

'Who knows,' Rachel had replied. 'Just because there is no evidence is not proof they were. What is it you keep saying, absence of evidence is not evidence of absence? You forget your own quotes. They met men professionally, publishers and writers, travelled unchaperoned to London. Who knows? Maybe secret lovers. Putting aside propriety, the risk would have been great. Contraception was rudimentary. The scandal.'

5

'You can't go in yet.'

Neil could hear Matlock moving around his office, chairs banging against a table.

His secretary chuckled. 'He's preparing the room.'

'Doesn't he always?'

Matlock was sitting at the far end of his large rectangular table when Neil entered. There were three empty seats, one next to him, one to his left and one facing him. Neil headed for the one furthest from Matlock. Matlock scowled. 'Not that one. That one,' pointing to a chair to one side of the table. 'Some ongoing research. May as well use staff as subjects. You don't mind?'

Neil had heard about Matlock's mini study, an attempted reversal of earlier research into seating choice. Nodding his assent, he vaguely recalled the earlier study. If the meeting is confrontational, people sit face-on either end of the table. If co-operative, they sit side by side. If intent on discussion, they occupy a corner. The study found intention determined seating. But what if choice was denied? Would dictating where we sit shape our response, the situation shaping attitude? Neil thought this unlikely, more so in his case as he knew the aim of the research.

'How are things?'

Neil wanted to say, what kind of things exactly? My finances, my relationship with Selena, my health, my research, my insomnia? Operationalise your concepts, Professor Matlock. What things?

Neil shrugged. 'So-so.'

There was an awkward pause and Neil focused on rows of East Light lever arch files, the distinctive green fan motif, very old, warped and overloaded. Matlock's obedience data. He remembered Matlock saying they had been water damaged not long after compiling them, explaining the drained colour on some and ad hoc labels on others. Recalling this, he now detected an odour and suppressed an urge to sneeze. Next to these was a bookcase full of tomes of varying age, feathered with torn paper markers, showing they were read, but an absence of sticky notes indicated long ago. Neil was surprised to see a row of Goffman, and one of his favourite works: *The Presentation of Self in Everyday Life*; surprised because Goffman was a sociologist.

Matlock was not adept at starting or concluding meetings or small talk. His two openings 'Winning?' and, 'How are things?' said a lot. Staff dreaded walking a stretch of corridor with him, conversation and partings painful, particularly the latter. Neil blamed those long years of study and research, little time for socialising, a theory, he believed, that also explained doctors. Three straight As to get into medical school, years of slog thereafter, cerebral as the Mekon but no people skills. He knew he was generalising, based on a sample of four, the four he had known, and coloured by his recent encounter.

'Ah yes, I asked to see you, Neil.' He looked at his diary. 'Why have you taken so long?'

Neil gave an explanation.

'Let's get this clear. Are you here because you want to see me, or in response to my request to see you?'

'Both, really.'

Matlock sighed. 'Let's say you are seeing me in response to my request to see you.' Adopting a grave voice, he levelled his gaze and said, 'I'm very worried.'

'Worried?'

'Do you know why I am very worried?'

Neil remembered an incident at school, called up before the head at assembly. 'Do you know why I have called you up?' On that occasion he had confessed to all kinds of misdemeanours, much to the merriment of those assembled.

'Cuts?' said Neil, hoping to keep the issue general.

'Yes, I am worried about cuts. We should all be worried about cuts. But to be more specific, I'm worried about you. You're good with the students, Neil, and students are money, bums on seats. Good MA and PhD idea, and you were progressing so well. Now everything's stopped. As I said last time, you either do individual research or join an ongoing team.'

'I looked at the ongoing research as you suggested.'

'And?'

Neil shrugged.

'What about evolutionary psychology? New area, massive funding, openings likely.'

'Too speculative and reductive for me. Whatever problem comes up, be it gender differences, fear of spiders, depression, laughter, you name it, Shelrack always brings it back to evolution, the animal under the surface. Everything is in the past, nothing in the present. And situation-free.' Neil knew Matlock would like this last point. 'It's not that I don't believe in evolution, the evidence is compelling for animals and plants. But humans. Everything?'

'Not very scientific, I grant you, and as you say, devalues present situations. Just-so stories. Attracts funds, though. Funds,' he repeated. 'What else did you look into? Remind me.'

Neil went through the list of ongoing research, faulting them all.

'Even Wendy's suicide and gender study? You can't fault that for relevance. Comparative method, of course, but relevant. Male suicide over twice the rate of female suicide. No ambiguity there. Ready-made research topic.'

Prompting Neil he said, 'I'm a bit out of touch. What explanations have the team come up with?'

'Oh, the usual cross-referencing to other studies that show men are in a different situation to women.'

'Situation. Good.'

'Men are predominantly breadwinners; the current recession, cuts, unemployment, business failure. Hits men hard.'

'Sounds good.'

'Would be, if it were true. But it relies on official statistics.'

'I'm not with you.'

'Suicide isn't a fact, it's a definition. Coroners decide if a death is a suicide based on the limited evidence before them, and different coroners use different criteria. A whole load of people are involved in the final definition: the police, relatives. Relatives may cover up, destroy evidence like a suicide note. Coroners are crucial. How do we know if a death is a suicide? It might be an accident, a plea for help gone wrong. Murder even.'

'If someone's found with an axe buried in his head, it's murder.'

'Yes. But it's mostly not that clear-cut. That's the point I'm coming to.'

Matlock laughed. 'Cut and point, double pun. Sorry, couldn't resist. Please go on.'

Neil smiled politely and suppressed a sigh. 'Suicide statistics are no more than coroners' interpretations, not facts at all. Suicide statistics are socially constructed.'

Matlock's smile withered. 'Socially constructed.' He looked fixedly at Neil. 'You've been talking to the sociologists.'

'As part of my research.' Neil went on hurriedly. 'I've been reading up on phenomenology. As I said, coroners have the final say regarding suicide, their so-called facts hardly a scientific basis for research. If someone takes an overdose it could be recorded as accidental or labelled an open verdict. A hanging or shooting is almost invariably labelled a suicide, suicide note or not.'

'So what's the problem?'

'Men are more likely than women to use violent methods. Women are more likely to overdose. Pills are less reliable, but if successful, might be labelled a plea for help gone wrong, or just an accident. You're unlikely to hang yourself accidentally. Because of the unreliability of pills women are more likely to survive suicide attempts. These ways men appear more frequently in the official suicide statistics. If men took pills or more women turned to hanging, gender differences might disappear and there would be no problem to research. Why men and women tend to choose different methods of suicide is a better question. I think Wendy's team might be researching a non-existent problem, that's all.'

'Sociology, you say.' His tone indicated a negative. 'A discipline of comparisons and correlations unable to separate cause and effect. It's dangerous to sociologise psychology. A psychological fact should only be explained by another psychological fact. Don't you agree?'

'Integration,' said Neil, avoiding Matlock's conundrum. 'Isn't the VC keen on integration?' Neil knew this had sufficient emotional charge to distract Matlock. The new vice-chancellor regularly enthused about integration, his oft stated 'cross-fertilisation of ideas'. Disciplines acted in isolation, creating competition, hostility, paranoia, stereotyping, extreme specialisation and myopia. 'In the extreme, the specialist is an idiot,' he often said, quoting Bernard Shaw, until someone asked, 'So you're saying we are all idiots?' But he had a point. Psychology was almost completely isolated from sociology, history from both. Literature was currently embattled with sociology for offering a new MA in the sociology of literature which they did everything to undermine. Each subject belittled other subjects, the sociologists depicting history as a chronological list of facts, the historians characterising sociology as vague and over-generalised. At a recent and embittered meeting about cuts, everyone, including the VC, claimed psychology didn't even exist, an indefinable no-man's land sandwiched between sociology and biology. Neither one thing nor the other, said one professor, bits and pieces stolen from other disciplines. Matlock countered by saying that psychology was the interaction between biology and society, between nurture and nature, scientific and measurable, a hyphen which joins, a buckle which fastens, recalling his Walter Bagehot from A-level British Constitution. 'Hyphen which joins?' queried the VC. 'Where's the biology in social psychology? What precisely is the difference between micro sociology and social psychology? You both study small groups, extol the situation and interactions. OK, social psychology is more experimental, but how much current research in your department is truly experimental?'

Unfortunately for Matlock, the VC was a sociologist and, of late, a born-again phenomenologist, meaning he saw the boundaries between disciplines socially constructed, and therefore arbitrary. Matlock suspected an ulterior motive, phenomenology a rationale to end 'needless' duplication, merge disciplines, even departments.

Ignoring Neil's question about the VC, Matlock said dramatically, 'Post-traumatic stress disorder. Up-and-coming area. Big research grants up for grabs. All the rage. And so many areas: ambulance medics, firefighters, soldiers, jurors forced to go over all that gore in a murder case, all those graphic descriptions and pictures. Think of the litigation alone. You'll be sought after by lawyers across the land.'

Neil was silent, frantically manufacturing an excuse to avoid involvement.

'Slokem, over in biology,' Matlock continued, 'has worked out a brilliant way of traumatising rats and observing later behaviour.'

'Ratology.' Neil shook his head.

'I'm no rat man myself, as you know, but it backs up Kel and Dunk's study, and the rats integrate with biology. The VC approves.' He waggled a finger towards Neil. 'And it's experimental. Two groups of rats, one group traumatised. Did you know, some soldiers have recurring symptoms, months or even years later? Many have difficulty adjusting to civilian life, symptoms galore, including recurring nightmares.'

Neil was tempted to ask if the traumatised rats have recurring nightmares, and how Slokem knew, but said instead, 'An uncle of mine took to drinking when he left the army.'

'Exactly. Typical symptom.'

'Only he saw no combat or anything. Never killed anyone or saw a dead body. Did a spell in Germany then Cyprus. No conflict, just our presence there. Boring, he told me, but at least Cyprus is in the sun. Is boredom is traumatising?' Neil paused for Matlock to laugh, but he remained stony-faced, and Neil hurried on. 'He just couldn't adjust back to civilian life. Driven mad seeing his family every day. That's my mum's theory. He missed his comrades. He missed the discipline, the routines. No responsibility, plenty of company, clear hierarchy.' Neil glanced towards the row of Goffman. 'Bit Goffman, really. Bit total institution. He was institutionalised.'

'Maybe he left because of his drinking.'

'Definitely took to drinking after.'

Matlock wagged a finger again, this time from side to side. 'Statistic of one. Not very scientific. You know that.'

After a long silence, Matlock reached a summation. 'Look, Neil, I'm not surprised you find research confusing. That's what comes of moving away from the laboratory and straying too far. Sociology, for instance.'

Again, Neil glanced towards the bookcase and fixed his gaze on Goffman's *Asylums*. 'Isn't Goffman a sociologist?'

'Wrongly labelled. More social psychologist. Got in with the wrong lot, that's all.'

A contradiction of Festinger proportions, Matlock resolved the dissonance by claiming Goffman's people were context-dependent, defined and shaped by setting or situation. Goffman could safely be admitted to the club.

Matlock looked quizzically at Neil. 'Straying too far?'

'Part of my research into dogmatism. Remember? Need a sample of sociologists. Requires socialising with them.'

'Socialising, you say.' He shook his head. 'But do you retain your objectivity? Contamination is the downside of integration. The VC forgets that.' He sat back into his chair and swivelled round to face Neil. 'You know, this is not a good time for self-flagellatory criticism. Aren't we in enough difficulty? We need to stand together. Thatcher's gone, but Thatcherism lives on, first Major and now Blair, a crypto-Thatcherite. We need to publish. We need research. We need it now. You are very good at criticising research, Neil, perhaps you could produce some for a change? OK, your criticism of suicide shows you are thinking, shows you are not idle, but taken too far no research would get off the ground. Obviously, we're in the business of challenge, being open-minded. I took you on because of your critical mind, your inventive criticisms, but not to the point of paralysis, not so open-minded that your brain falls out and gets kicked around by our enemies. Go away and think about what I've said. Think positively. Think research.'

Now desperate to leave, Neil shuffled in his seat, but Matlock was saying, 'Don't misunderstand me, skepticism is good, but how do you persuade anyone to fund research if you believe it all pointless? These postmodernists are thinking their way out of a job.'

'I'm not a postmodernist –'

'If everything is relative and nothing better than anything else, why do we teach and do research? Strange how these esoteric theories emanate from France. Grand narratives, metanarratives, mini narratives, no French intellectual complete without a theory, however absurd, and all said before in less pretentious language, of course. Whatever some postmodernist relativists say, approximations of the truth are better than no truth, and the closest approximation is the experiment. That's where Lyotard is wrong. At least as far as I understand him. No apology for getting him wrong, that opaque jargon. His rejection of grand narratives, such as science, is itself a grand narrative, and therefore self-refuting, and he disappears up his own anal orifice.'

Keen to dissociate from postmodernism, Neil said, 'Extreme postmodernists claim all knowledge is equal and no truth is possible. My position is that we need to find better ways of getting to the truth.'

'Better ways? Better than the experiment?' He deliberated. 'Next meeting, perhaps.'

Matlock stared past Neil, seemingly fixed on a crack in the wall. Had the meeting ended? He waited for Matlock's signal. Matlock looked at the clock and said, 'Is that the time?' He rose from his seat and stumbled against a wastepaper bin as Neil headed for the door and depressed the handle.

'Just remembered,' Matlock said.

Neil released the handle and turned to see Matlock pushing a huge tome towards him. 'Goldhagen. *Hitler's Willing Executioners*. Claims the Germans were not obeying the situation and authority after all but were willing executioners of Jews. Complete refutation of obedience research. See what you can make of it. Find the flaw. I'm planning an article.'

6

'Breakthrough!' Rachel repeated, as she made two mugs of coffee. 'You remember that sociologist I was telling you about?'

Feigning innocence, Neil said, 'Henry Hollow?'

'Henry? Fuck off. That Marxist idiot. I hate him. No, the Durkheimian. Durkheimians are a rare breed apparently, and there's one here at the university. Incredible luck. And you've never met him. Doesn't say much for your sample.'

'How long has he been here?'

'Oh I don't know. How should I know? The point is, the Durkheim fits *Frankenstein* like a glove, the whole novel and historical context. Takes in Mary Shelly as well. Sit down. You must hear this.'

Thrusting a steaming mug at Neil, she said, 'Remember I said Frankenstein is egotistical and isolated, the monster a product of his one-dimensional approach? Remember the triad?'

Neil nodded.

'Remember O'Flinn, the Marxist? His monster the mob personified. Well, I've found his match in Durkheim. Forget the mob. Frankenstein is a product of what Durkheim calls anomie and egoism. Egotistical ambition unaffected by other considerations. Unregulated ambition. Remember that word: *unregulated*. A key Durkheimian concept.'

Neil was wondering how the Durkheimian, whatever that was, had escaped his sample.

'I outlined the novel to him, adding a bit on Marx, and without hesitation he said, "Forget Marx, read Durkheim".

Turns out he's an authority on Durkheim, a 19th century rival to Marx and the first official sociologist. "Read *Suicide* and *The Division of Labour*", he said, "all about the dangers of specialisation, unregulated ambition, social fragmentation, egoism and anomie".

'God, it was a labour, rambling, meandering Victorian epics. Durkheim needed a good editor. But worth it. Gave me a structure and context for my chapter on *Frankenstein*. And definitely not Marx, despite responding to the same problems, such as the enormous changes wrought by capitalism and industrialisation. I would have hugged him, only he's in his sixties, bald with a shiny dome. So away with dreary class conflict and social revolution; in with disintegration, de-regulation, excessive and unconstrained individualism and reduced moral regulation, summed up by Durkheim as anomie and egoism.'

'Does Durkheim's reject individualism?'

'*Unrestrained* individualism. Individualism is good, allows creativity and choice, but the price is high: increased pathology, suicide, family instability, crime, industrial conflict, loneliness, selfishness, dissatisfaction. And that's not all. At the other extreme is altruism, or too much regulation. Some cultures suppress the individual and force them to die for the group. He gives the example of old Eskimos in time of food scarcity encouraged to commit suicide. You see, the group's more important than the individual. Remember Walton, the captain who rescues Frankenstein? He is less isolated than Frankenstein and feels under pressure to give in to the crew because they are becoming mutinous.'

She picked up a huge tome, and for an anxious moment Neil thought she was about to hand it to him to read.

'Durkheim talks about the cult of the individual. Specialisation results in greater fragmentation of work and increased individualism. People are more isolated, more selfish and pursue individual goals. Listen to this: "Where man is God to mankind, the individual is readily inclined to consider the man in himself as a God". Could be a comment on Frankenstein, usurping God and society by taking on the role of creator. I felt lightheaded when I read it.'

Neil was about to speak but Rachel held up her hand. 'Just listen. I must get this clear.' She picked up some typed sheets, a draft of her article:

The 19th century was a period of increasing anomie or normlessness. Society was undergoing fundamental change. The church was being questioned and the world demystified; old truths about man questioned; science was on the ascent; revolutions occurring; new classes emerging; the economy becoming freer; insecurity abounding. The old order no longer certain, in panic.

She looked up and grinned at Neil. 'After all, there had been a revolution in France, aristocrats' heads lopped off. The English upper classes feared the same and meted out harsh punishment to machine breaker, such as hanging or transportation. Mary worried such harsh measures would antagonise the mob and feared for her own safety. Specialisation also brought in its wake a science unregulated by morality or aesthetics, a point taken up by Mary Shelley in *Frankenstein*, symbolised by Frankenstein and his monster.' She laughed. 'You could create a monster then, no ethics committee.' She continued reading:

Cantor points out that the Shelley circle was even more anomic and egoistic than the wider society. They were outsiders, acutely aware of their marginality, of being "wise but unhappy". While recognising there was an element of posing, suffering and self-torture seen as part of the creative process and self-parody all the rage, suicide and breakdown were common to their circle. They opposed traditional values and institutions, and the price was insecurity. Their anomie is evident in other ways. They were sexual radicals, or at least Percy Shelley was, pressuring Mary to have sex with his friend Hogg, styling it his free love experiment.

Rachel put aside her notes. 'Significantly, Mary removed all evidence of Hogg from her diary, the pages ripped out. Percy's constant screwing around couldn't have been easy for her to bear. OK, she paid lip-service to free love, but there is no solid evidence she practiced it. They were a rootless lot, living abroad periodically, living apart, ostracised by society. O'Flinn observes that the novel is studded with examples of the dangers of acting alone, and disaster only avoided by the intervention of others. Notice how close he comes to Durkheim. Frankenstein symbolises Mary's unregulated lifestyle.'

Neil asked, 'What about the monster? How does Durkheim fit?'

'Yes, the monster. I'm working on it. Not the mob personified, not some Marxist super Luddite, I'm working on the idea the monster relates to Mary's life, not incest or similar Freudian crap, but her general sense of isolation from wider society.'

'Incest?'

Rachel chuckled. 'Between Frankenstein and Elizabeth. It's a convoluted theory involving Mary's father. Hardly worth bothering with. Too reductionist; too Freudian. Feminists oozing psychoanalysis from every pore treat novelists and texts as case studies, disguised wish fulfillments, a royal road to the writer's hang-ups (or the researcher's). Psychoanalytic interpretations of Mary are all female stuff: fears about childbirth, guilt over killing her mother, father/daughter incest, marital problems.'

'Explain reductionist.'

'Devalue author and text; modern day alchemists magically changing a text into something else, the unconscious their philosopher's stone. I'm closer to the surface than that and need evidence. Freudians don't need evidence, other than Freud's version of evidence, his anything can mean anything. Saves effort and time, of course.'

'Matlock says the same about Freud.'

She grimaced. 'What I want from you, Neil dear, are some theories that fit the monster. Not Freud. Something new. You were a great help with *Breakfast at Tiffany's* and the Brontës.'

Neil often supplied Rachel with theories, once helping her with an article about Holly Golightly in *Breakfast at Tiffany's*.

'Not the early years and all that psychoanalytic tension-reduction crap. Something different,' she instructed.

'The future. Whither not whence,' said Neil.

'Whither not whence... Go on.'

Neil had explained it was a quote from Alfred Adler, Freud's hated rival and early phenomenologist.

'Freud was steeped in 19th century science, was mechanistic. All causes are in the past. Think of a snooker ball.'

'Snooker ball?'

'The cue strikes the ball and it moves. There is no goal because the ball has no will, goal or purpose. 'Adler emphasised the future, what we are moving towards. We may have faulty schema, wrong or mistaken attitudes, private logic such as his famous Yes-But attitude. The neurotic cannot say "No", must say "Yes", and solves the problem by offering excuses that absolve them from the task. "I could have succeeded, but my brother was favourite..." "I would work, but..." Always some excuse absolving them from the task. Not facts or causes as such, more interpretation of, or response to, facts or causes. It fits CBT, but uncredited. Someone may be handicapped by high expectations or are too self-critical. According to Adler we are not totally caused by events, we respond to them. "No experience causes success or failure. We do not suffer from the shock of our experience – the so-called trauma – but make of them what suits our purpose".'

'All said long ago, of course. "There is nothing either good or bad, but thinking makes it so". *Hamlet*.'

'Take snakes.'

Rachel smiled and repeated slowly, 'Snakes.'

'Adler gave the example of being frightened by a snake. Someone sees a snake and recoils in fear, and we say the snake caused them to recoil. Someone else shows no fear, but we don't say the snake caused their fearlessness, we say it's their attitude. Adler also explained behaviour more by looking to the future than the past, a sort of goal determinism.'

'A cause set in the future? I like it.'

'Adler recognised we are also shaped by past events, but once goals are set in motion we're pulled not pushed, drawn not driven. The past shapes the goal. CBT emphasises the present, but Adler put more emphasis on the future linked to the past. What are we moving towards? What do we gain, or hope to gain, from our actions? Holly's impermanence results from dissatisfaction with her present self. She is what she wants to become: a self, set in the future. The future explains her denial of the present.'

Rachel was impressed. 'Fits the unpacked boxes, the unnamed cat, and the symbolic fire escape and window she escapes through on one occasion. Open spaces feature a lot in *Breakfast*. Her name – Golightly – is airy, flighty, rootless. Yes, the future explaining the present. Brilliant. I'll treat you to dinner tonight.'

*

'Adler's fictional finalism,' Neil explained over dinner. 'We act as if we are going somewhere. There are concrete goals and vague guiding goals. "Guiding fictions" Adler called them. Holly's drawn, not driven.'

'The problem is, Holly doesn't know what she wants.'

'Adler's said goals can be vague. We act as if we are moving towards something, from a minus to a plus, and along the route we set up concrete goals. Holly vaguely aspires to material success, her minus to a plus. We can't live without goals, an idea Adler got from Vaihinger's As-If philosophy. We act as if there is a goal. You see, academic psychology explains people causally, past occurrences leading us to where we are now, dependent and independent variables, and all that. Adler linked present behaviour to the future and got around simple cause and effect explanations. It's fashionable to link present behaviour to some trauma, a linear causality. We also look back to the past for some explanation, some cause and search for a scapegoat, some long-forgotten trauma. But are these causes, fashionable explanations or excuses?'

'Back to Holly. You know Capote modelled Holly on Isherwood's Sally Bowles? In turn modelled on a real-life Jean Ross, a British actress and singer. Isherwood's autobiographical novel *Goodbye to Berlin* is the original, followed by stage and screen productions: *I Am a Camera*, *Breakfast at Tiffany's*, *Cabaret*. Capote's Holly is more removed from Sally, and Audrey Hepburn's Holly is rather more refined than Sally in the novella, and the film has a moralising ending. But all the derivative characters have Sally's sexual abandon, directness and rudeness in common, while remaining loveable.'

More recently Neil had helped her with an article on problems of identity in the Brontë novels. She had quoted Charlotte and Anne Brontë respectively: "A private governess has no existence", and "It seemed as if they gazed on vacancy".

'Any theory that fits?'

Neil had directed her to Goffman's *Behaviour in Public Places* and the example of the servant, a non-person.

'A Goffmanesque interpretation. Sounds promising. Goffmanesque. Like the term.'

As they separated, she smiled sweetly and said, 'Remember, theories that fit the monster. Something meaty. Durkheim's the competition.'

She called after him. 'Thinking of Yes-But, what's your excuse?'

Neil turned. 'Excuse?'

'I would like to do research, but...'

7

Occupying the only chair available, the rest carefully stacked in one corner, Neil faced Matlock. The crunch meeting. The word crunch brought to mind a mince pie, a particularly dry mince pie, crumbling at first bite and dropping from his mouth in front of Matlock onto an off-white carpet, his other hand shackled to a glass of dry sherry, obligatory fare at one of Matlock's obligatory Christmas sherry parties. He remembered Matlock's secretary rushing forward with a small dustpan and brush, the sudden silence as the gathering looked on. But this was not the moment for Proustian involuntary memories, particularly unhappy ones, evoked, no doubt, by the situation, namely Matlock's presence and a pervading sense of dread.

Matlock cleared his throat. 'I'm still very worried.' He paused, shifted in his chair. 'Something is holding you back. Your colleagues are commenting. They suspect something in your attitude, but I suspect something in your situation. Problems with your research, perhaps?'

'Not my situation, no. More the situation of psychology.'

'Interesting. Go on.'

Neil paused. 'As you know, I'm having doubts about research. It all seems so pointless.'

'Go on.'

'For every study there's a counter-study, for every theory a counter-theory, for every interpretation a counter-interpretation. Then there are methodological criticisms. Even the experiment, the gold standard of research, is flawed. No matter how meticulous, no matter how large the sample, no one agrees on the interpretation. Whatever you do, someone demolishes it. It's pointless. Then there's bias.'

'Bias? You're not suggesting staff in the department –'

'Absolutely not. Unconscious bias, at the most.'

Matlock's face darkened.

'No, not even unconscious bias,' he added hurriedly. He glanced at the row of works by Goffman and, settling on *The Presentation of Self in Everyday Life*, said, 'It's not enough to be sincere, we must appear sincere, or in this instance, not enough to be unbiased, we must show we are unbiased. Goffman?'

'You're on about blinds again. As I said before, all our research is partially blind.'

'But not double or treble blinds. I've been reading up on the albino rat study, Rosenthal and Fode?'

'Rosenthal and Fode. That's going back some. As I recall, psychology students were asked to test the maze running abilities of rats. One group were told their rats were fast learners drawn from a bright strain, the other that the rats were slow learners from a dull strain. The "bright" rats were judged faster learners than the "dull" rats, when all the rats were randomly drawn from the same population. They concluded that somehow the observers' expectations influenced the rats, expected the bright rats to do better. Expectancy effect, wasn't that what they called it?' Matlock leaned back and smiled, pleased at his recall of the study.

'That's only one interpretation, of course. I've thought up an additional interpretation.'

'Go on.'

'Let's say there was uncertainty about a given rat's performance. If thought to be a bright rat you give a favourable judgement, if dull…'

'The glass half full or half empty. Interesting interpretation, and interesting how you criticise research yet believe in the truth of this study, and a rat study. Tell me, was the study blind?'

Neil hesitated. 'No. Not as far as I know. It doesn't say so.'

'Meaning it wasn't. Then how do we know their research into research wasn't itself showing observer bias? After all, they used the same type of research design they were criticising. Maybe they saw what they expected to see, albeit unconsciously?' He leaned forward for emphasis. 'Maybe it has the same flaw as Rosenthal's *Pygmalion in the Classroom* study. You know, we tried replicating it some time back and failed. Other attempts at replication had the same problem. Some flaw in the original, I recall. Look it up.' He leaned back and beamed. 'No such problem with obedience, of course. Replicates every time.'

Neil felt his pulse accelerate as he said, 'Could be replicating design error.'

'Design error. Really? Enlighten me.'

'None of the studies used blinds. If there were single and double-blinds, say the experiment conducted by assistants unaware of the purpose of the experiment, and the findings analysed by assistants also unaware of the purpose that would test for observer bias. Even the Catholic Church uses blinds to investigate so-called miracles today. The Holy Shroud, identifying saints. Blinds –'

Matlock leaned forward, his swivel chair mimicking his move. 'Neil, I'm perfectly aware what blinds are. Do you have any idea what it would cost? The extra staff? And where does that leave our existing stock of research? Above all, obedience research? None of the seminal studies used double or treble blinds; Milgram, Asch, Zimbardo, almost all the research undertaken in the history of psychology and most of the studies undertaken by this department. Are we supposed to bin the lot? Start again? Is that what you're suggesting? We'd be a laughing stock. The media would love it. Isn't psychology sufficiently under attack? Do you want to give ammunition to our enemies?'

Neil was shaking his head vigorously. 'No. Of course not. But –'

'But?'

Neil saw the idea was preposterous, logically sound, but preposterous. 'As I said before, it's not about being unbiased, it's about *showing* one is unbiased.'

'Anyway, parts of my research were blind. If you recall, to test Orne's assertion that subjects see through experiments but play along to please the researcher, I employed three independent observers to ask a sample of my obedience subjects if they realised they were being hoaxed. We deliberately loaded the question.'

'Did the observers know the purpose of the experiment?'

'Of course they knew the purpose. OK, it wasn't properly blind. OK, OK. When I did my Milgram replication some of my data was analysed by two research assistants. Their results concurred with my own, suggesting no bias on my part. There, a blind study, if ever there was one.'

'Did they know –'

Matlock thumped the table. 'Blind!'

Neil was about to ask if the assistants knew the purpose of the research, making them only partially blind, if blind at all, especially working under a professor, an authority figure, probably knowing what result he was hoping for: to show that Brits are no different from Americans. How euphoric Matlock must have been when the results showed Brits almost equally obedient, how keen the assistants were to fuel his euphoria. Matlock showed obedience decreased if the experimenter left the room, increased when he was present. Didn't the same apply to his assistants? Was Matlock breathing over them as they did those calculations? Did they depend on Matlock for advancement? For their jobs even?

'Field studies,' Matlock was saying, 'complete refutation of Orne. Remember Hofling's field study? Nurses asked to administer a drug overdose on instruction from a bogus doctor by phone. Twenty-one out of twenty-two obeyed but were stopped at the point of administering the drug. No chance there of guessing the purpose because they were unaware they were part of an experiment. And a real situation. Fault that if you can.'

'Weren't the nurses alone in the ward when the bogus call came through?'

'I believe so.'

'Isn't there a counter-study by Rank and Jacobson which challenges the ecological validity?'

Neil suspected Matlock was unaware of the study stumbled across by chance, just one of the thousands of studies published each year, overlooked or forgotten and rarely cited in the textbooks.

'Remind me of the study.'

'They followed the same procedure as Hofling but changed two things: they substituted a familiar drug for the made-up unknown drug used by Hofling, and they allowed nurses time to confer with peers and senior staff about the excessive dosage prescribed. In this condition only two out of eighteen obeyed. In real life nurses are part of teams and have contact with peers. So Hofling's situation was contrived and unreal.'

Matlock was silent and Neil hurriedly added, 'It's similar to your obedience variation where the subject witnessed two confederates refusing to obey. In that situation most subjects also refused when it was their turn.'

Smiling, Matlock said, 'I bet there's a flaw here somewhere. There is a flaw, isn't there? Don't keep me in suspense.'

Neil hesitated. Feeling compelled to own up he said, 'A possible flaw is that the nurses were asked if they were willing to participate in an experiment. Ethics, and all that.'

Matlock roared with laughter. 'Orne would love this.'

'But they weren't told the purpose of the experiment, where it would take place or when, only that they would be part of an experiment sometime in the future. One became suspicious and was excluded. Debriefing showed the rest were unaware they were part of an experiment. When conferring with peers none raised the suspicion that it was a hoax.'

Matlock leaned back. 'Blinds?'

'Single only. The nurses. But no different from Hofling. Whatever the validity of Rank and Jacobson, their point about Hofling's situation being unreal and contrived stands.'

Leaning forward, Matlock spoke very slowly. 'Are you sure all this criticism is not rationalising? Self-handicapping?' He paused to polish his glasses, allowing Neil time to digest this point. 'Ask yourself, Neil, where does all this criticism leave us? Lots of people are attacking the sciences today: the media, the greens, postmodernists, animal rightists.'

Neil braced himself for the eulogy, the tiresome example of the fridge freezer.

'It's fashionable to decry science. Some say it is a belief like any other belief, no better or worse than theology or magic, a grand narrative, a story, relative cultures, and all that postmodernist crap. They say we have faith in science the way people in medieval Europe had faith in religion and God.' Matlock leaned forward, finger pointing. 'But science gets results. Yes, the church has its so-called miracles, people cured of illnesses, the piles of crutches at Lourdes. Strange how it is always crutches, or as one early commentator put it, "What, no wooden legs? "Does God hate amputees?" And why hasn't the Virgin Mary performed a useful miracle, such as a fridge freezer before they were invented? A thousand nuns praying for fifty years would not produce a single fridge freezer. Only science can do that.'

Neil was tempted to say, nor would a thousand psychologists researching for fifty years produce anything as tangible as a fridge freezer. Natural science got tangible results, produced useful objects. There was no argument about a fridge freezer, it worked. It cooled or froze food. It wasn't open to interpretation. Where was psychology's fridge freezer? He wondered a moment what kind of fridge freezer Matlock had at home and what he kept in it, the importance he attached to the object.

'I don't need to remind you that a lecturing post is coming up soon. Spooner's close to taking early retirement, probably a year from now. From the start I had you in mind. That surprises you, doesn't it? But be careful. Kelvin's doing great work. As you know, he's teamed up with Slokem over in biology researching post-traumatic stress disorder. They're looking at civilians, such as nurses and ambulance drivers, supervised by Odlum. Eight publications under his belt, two in prestigious journals, two peer-reviewed. He knows how to spin the research, break it down into components, halving or even quartering.' Matlock chuckled. 'One study alone generated four articles.' He briefly fixed his gaze on Neil. 'And conference papers galore. Impressive style, knows how to make the commonplace sound profound. Remember that phrase he used recently, multifaceted aetiology.'

'Mixture of causes,' translated Neil.

'Exactly. But doesn't multifaceted aetiology sound so much more.' He leaned forward. 'He's a whizz on the newfangled Internet. Sends emails.'

'I tried sending emails but gave up. Some arrived garbled and others disappeared into the system. Same with the replies. It took so long it was quicker to phone.'

'See Kel. As I said, whizz on the computer.' He sat back in his chair and smiled. 'OK, he gets up some people's noses, I know. Can be abrasive, insensitive, I'm told, though never with me. But he delivers. When it comes to promotion, Kel is the competition to watch. You're thirty, older than Kel, and a school teacher for a number of years. That goes in your favour.'

Apart from his tan, Kel boasted greater height, easily two inches taller than Neil. 'Taller men gain more promotion,' he once explained to Neil. 'Those in power are taller on average.'

Neil was skeptical, but Kel had pressed on, citing studies, such as Wilson's experiment. 'The same man was introduced to different groups but given a different status, such as professor or student. When asked later to estimate his height, those believing him to be of higher status judged him taller.'

Neil had remained silent, as Kel added, 'Why else do we say, under someone's thumb, and walking tall?'

Neil heard that Kel had recently approached Spooner and said bluntly, 'When exactly are you retiring?'

Spooner had told him, 'When I'm good and fucking ready.'

Kel, as usual, remained nonchalant, insulated by an evenly tanned thick skin, a skin for all seasons, boasting that a healthy appearance aided promotion.

'Does research back that up?' someone asked.

'Absolutely,' his reply.

Neil knew, if pressed, he would have come up with some study plucked from the hundreds laid to rest in journals, or just make one up.

'Thinking about Kel's thesis,' Matlock was saying, 'your dogmatism research –'

Neil sighed inwardly. Hadn't he explained this? 'Contaminated results, you remember. Debriefing showed that some had heard about the experiment, explaining why so many lacked dogmatism. It didn't ring true. So I eliminated them.'

'How many? Remind me.'

'Almost all. Campus rumour didn't help. It's not easy researching researchers. Suspicious lot. If only they were rats.' He paused for Matlock to laugh, but his jaw remained tight, lips closed and straight. 'They guess what you're up to. Then someone revealed the identities of the dogmatists and it sort of ended there. Especially when local radio got wind.

That's why I changed the research design from individual dogmatism to more general dogmatism in science.'

'Great pity,' said Matlock. 'Did you have to own up to the problem? Of course you did, of course. What am I saying? But you've come to a standstill. That's the problem. We need some way to get you moving again. That's why I asked you to look into ongoing studies, just to help out. Some of the studies are behind schedule.'

He adopted a fatherly, soothing tone. 'Getting back to your inertia, these things always boil down to situations. Something, something in your situation. You know what I think? What's really troubling you is not loss of confidence in psychology, but loss of confidence in yourself, a situational response. Did you find out who revealed the names of your subjects and circulated them? Thought that reporter friend of yours might know. Seed something or other. Andy Seed?'

'As I said, haven't seen him for some time. He's a newspaper reporter, remember, nothing to do with radio.'

Matlock chuckled. 'Odlum was furious.'

'I know. Quite a few staff were.'

Neal had gone to great lengths protecting the anonymity of his subjects, but someone had obtained their names and position on the scale and circulated them. The data was then leaked to local radio which ran an amusing discussion on dogmatism in science, highlighting a senior psychologist high on the dogmatism scale, contrary to the popular stereotype of academic objectivity and openness, more especially being noted for his liberal views. Everyone knew it was Odlum. Convinced he had kept the identities of his subjects secure, Neil was baffled. There followed a parade of irate lectures, some withdrawing co-operation, others challenging his methodology. Odlum accused him of carelessness. Where did he keep his computer password? Learning it was secure, Odlum homed in on copies. Where were his floppy disks kept? The relevant disk was kept in his briefcase, albeit unattended from time to time. There were limits to security, and no one warned or predicted this might happen. What possible motive was there? He had contacted Andy. Did he know the source? But Andy said his contact with local radio was limited.

There was a long pause and Neil ruminated on his ruined research, long even by Matlock's standards, and Neil knew Matlock wanted to say something, something disagreeable, had felt this all along, cued partly by the confrontational seating.

Matlock became animated, and in a rush said, 'Fancy being a fake schizophrenic?' He laughed at Neil's bemused expression. 'You like challenging labels. What I'm going to tell you is very hush-hush. No one must know. Especially the press. This reporter seems to have it in for us. Andy, Andy Seed, Seedling.'

'Seedbank.'

'Whatever. The Replication Team is currently researching schizophrenia and planning to replicate Rosenhan's hospital study. You know, fake patients. One of the great situational studies.'

Neil shook his head.

'Codenamed *Thud*. Should get us noticed in the press. Television, even. The journals will love it. But that's a long way off. Odlum's supervising the study, wants to see if it obtains here in the UK and still relevant, given all the changes since the sixties. Very hush-hush. That's why you don't know about it. No one outside the team knows about it. Don't want to alert the media yet. Above all, hospital staff mustn't be alerted. We're not doing an exposé as such, you understand, it's mostly about how patients are treated now that the large hospitals have been replaced with smaller units. Fancy being a fake schizophrenic?' He chuckled. 'It'll mean not washing for a week and claiming you hear a voice saying "thud".'

'Thud?'

Matlock chuckled. 'Yes. That's all the Rosenhan fakes had to do to gain access to mental hospitals. Well, "hollow" and "empty" as well. Half a mind to join myself. Sorry, couldn't resist that one. Odlum needs help with the archival side, digging out related studies, reviews. That's where you would come in.'

'But my research. The time.'

'But you're at a standstill. You need a change of situation. Yes, *situation*. This will kick-start you back into research mode. As you know, the VC is keen on integration, and your contacts with sociology suggest to me you are of similar mind. The VC wants us to get away from individual, isolated topics towards teamwork. Even wants to break down barriers between disciplines. Tried to tell me micro sociology and social psychology are the same thing. Hinted at integration, a merger. Of course, I pointed to experimentation and its absence in sociology.'

Matlock drew his hands together. 'Of course, the hospital study is far from scientific, mainly covert observation. Things are loosening up in psychology. Observational studies are on the increase. If anything defines psychology, it's the experiment, and we're in danger of losing our identity.'

'You don't think observation is of any use?'

'Some merit, I suppose. Observing the treatment of patients, fallibility of diagnostics. Once in a hospital setting, everything you do is evidence of mental illness. Psychiatrists diagnose the context not the person.' He paused and said thoughtfully, 'Or so Rosenhan claimed. You see, Rosenhan and his team couldn't manipulate the situation, only observe. Rosenhan could have been biased for all we know, seeing what he wanted to see. We only have his or his co-workers' word for what went on. Then there's the limit on what questions could be put to patients and staff without arousing suspicion. As you know, in my laboratory-based obedience research I was able to isolate numerous variables: the status of the professor, status of the organisation, presence of peers, and much more.' He sighed. 'For all its weaknesses, it's research. We must never forget that. There's a substantial grant and it should keep the VC off our backs.' He brightened. 'And it's situational. At least it should get much needed positive publicity when the results are out. Meanwhile, under wraps.' He fixed Neil's gaze. 'You've got to compromise, Neil. We've all got to compromise. You can be too committed to the truth. Perfection is the greatest imperfection. It stultifies.'

Matlock had all but demolished Rosenhan's research, fuelling Neil's growing opposition, but before he could refuse, Matlock said, 'I think you should join Odlum's team.'

'But –'

'Enough. The department requires that you join.'

'But –'

'It is absolutely essential that you join.'

'But –'

'You have no choice. Join.'

*

Feeling his usual discomfort in the presence of Odlum and eager to escape, Neil hurriedly said Matlock had given him the basics, such as pretending to hear the word "thud".

Odlum grimaced and said testily, 'Matlock's out of touch. Ask yourself, when did he last do research or read anything? He's a manager now, more fundraiser than researcher, if that. Lives off the fat of obedience. No, Rosenhan's just a starting point. Since Rosenhan criteria has tightened. Rosenhan's fakes breezed in, said they heard voices and were instantly labelled schizophrenics. Those days have gone. Read up on DSM-4 and ICD-10. Symptoms must persist for months, and

two or more symptoms are required.' He smiled thinly.
'Voices, of course, and I've added impaired hygiene for good
measure. No one must wash for a week.'

'Bet Kel's far from enthusiastic.'

'As it happens, he was the most enthusiastic.'

Kel not washing for a week? Neil shook his head. Fake
patient, fake tan, fake enthusiasm. Odlum was genuine, of
course, suffering for science, enjoying the suffering of others,
his one pleasure denying others pleasure. Ascetic and sadist
rolled into one. But not washing for a week... In that moment
he was glad to be on the archival side.

Odlum explained that the idea was to see if much
had changed since Rosenhan's early seventies study in the
wake of new drugs, outpatient treatment and the recent
DSM revision. Odlum paused, stared at Neil a long moment,
and said gravely, 'This is the most secret research ever
undertaken by the department. 'I sweated blood getting the
hospitals and other units to cooperate. Psychiatric units
are coming in for a bashing of late. Only the guarantee of
complete anonymity swung them. And my natural objectivity
and fairness.'

'They know you're coming?'

'The nurses and psychiatrists on the wards won't know,
only top management. Anyway, the upside is we'll get
feedback from the staff and access to their notes. Rosenhan
did the same. It's all agreed.'

Odlum became very serious. 'The press mustn't know
anything, at least, not until after publication. This time,
complete control. You know how they misrepresent everything,
distort and simplify. Especially that so-called journalist,
Seedhouse.' He looked sideways at Neil. 'Friend of yours,
I hear?'

Odlum's voice was rising in pitch, and Neil recalled his
mauling by local radio and press over his media study. Andy's
article was particularly biting.

'Seedbank, not Seedhouse. We graduated together, that's all.'

Odlum's silence was meaningful by its length.

They were under pressure to get the submission together and Neil was given a deadline to gather as much information as possible about Rosenhan.

'Reviews, letters, books – anything useful for the bibliography, advised Odlum, walking towards his room. 'I want you to give a presentation. And read up on schizophrenia, DSM-4 and ICD-10.'

'Is there a difference?' Neil shouted.

'Find out for yourself.'

'Thanks.'

Neil repeated to himself, 'I am doing research; therefore, I must be a researcher.'

*

Neil headed for the library to gather material on Rosenhan. He was feeling aggrieved. Of all the people to work under, how could he end up with Odlum, assistant professor and… somewhere far along the spectrum from normal to…

Neil remembered discussing Odlum with Rachel.

'Odlum came out high on my Belief Scale, highly dogmatic.'

'But he's a paragon of liberalism, a bible of political correctness. You should see him perform on the ethics committee. Even claims to be a feminist. Don't believe it, of course. There are few women on his team. He once corrected me for saying lesbian lecturers are more likely to get promotion because they are childless. "A dangerous viewpoint", he said, "ammunition for the homophobic misogynist extreme right". Suddenly I was cast a fascist. He didn't even say, be careful, Rachel, people will think you are prejudiced, or experience what you say as prejudice.

So I said to him, why do you think so few women get promoted? He banged on about lack of role models and his support for feminism. Then why are there so few women on your rat pack team? I said.'

'You said that to him?' Neil's tone was full of admiration.

'Yes, but he didn't reply. Can't be as simple as role models. Literature's female-dominated, yet most top journalists are men. Same with hairdressing. Why are most top hairdressers men? It's fucking obvious when you think about it. Not role models; not some glass ceiling crap. Children hold women back. It's common sense. Common to everyone but extreme feminists and Odlum.'

'You're missing the difference, Rachel. There's common sense and there's Odlum sense.'

Rachel laughed, and Neil added, 'Odlum may be a paragon of liberalism, but it's the way he holds his liberal beliefs that counts. This was Adorno's mistake. His Fascism Scale measured only right-wing intolerance, but anyone can be intolerant, even a liberal, according to Rokeach. Some people show higher intolerance than others. Some evolutionists are no better than creationists according to my research. Odlum holds his liberal views in a rigid, threatening way. You will be a liberal. You have no choice. All clear thinking, unselfish people are liberal. It is essential for the department that you are a liberal. He's the sort who would sack someone for failing the political correctness test, disguised as protecting minorities, of course.'

'Intolerant liberal, illiberal liberal, an oxymoron. Something in psychology after all,' Rachel said thoughtfully. 'Yet Odlum's very intelligent. As much as we hate him, that's got to be admitted. Wouldn't he see the contradiction?'

'I found no correlation between rigidity of beliefs and intelligence. The intelligent rationalise at a higher level, that's all.'

'The intelligent rationalise more intelligently. I like it.'

'Liberalism is changing. It's more dogmatic now, more authoritarian. We're moving into a new politically correct Victorianism. Odlum's the future.'

'God. What a thought. But why?'

'Why? Because they are now the majority. Today's liberal views, once condemned, are now mainstream. When you're a minority, on the defensive, you value freedom of expression. When the majority, you condemn those with opposite views.'

Making coffee, she was saying, 'You're right. Got to be so careful what you say today. No doubt you have a theory to cover it?'

'Fits Goffman, self-presentation. Appearing more important than being. Presentation changes over time. Makes you wonder how sincere our responses are. Bit like chameleons changing colour to fit context. Are our public responses genuine? Or are we just saying the right things in different situations at different points in time? There are things I said ten years ago I wouldn't say today, least not in public. There are more threats today.'

'Mostly low-cost, safe liberalism, of course. Don't-have-to-do-anything liberalism. Reminds me Mrs Jellyby. Her telescopic philanthropy?'

Neil shrugged. 'Jellyby?'

Her sigh was withering. 'Haven't you read anything? Jellyby is a character in *Bleak House* who supports distant charitable concerns in Africa, while at home she neglects her family. Dickens describes her philanthropy as telescopic. Some of today's liberals have distant concerns, the past, not the present. They re-live and redress past injustices, weighed down with pseudo guilt about our colonial past, and agonise about the slave trade. Not today's sex slaves, of course, girls trafficked into prostitution from Eastern Europe. Might have to do something. No, just cosy, safe, armchair, no cost liberalism.'

Rachel was sometimes accused of hypocrisy, her critics unaware of her work for Amnesty International and other causes, hours spent writing letters to prisoners and no hope of a reply.

'I hate Odlum,' she said suddenly. 'His trousers don't cover his bony ankles.'

'Same with his pyjamas.'

'Pyjamas?' She paused, nodded slowly. 'How do you know? Surely you –'

'Went on a residential with him, and he knocked on my door wearing pyjamas.'

'Suspicious.'

'Not really. Didn't make a pass, or anything. Not even his notorious plastic arm.'

*

Neil entered a long corridor of metal racks, the light switching on automatically, and looked despairingly at the rows of journals, thousands of studies sweated over, an endless torrent. Did anyone read them? Valhalla for research articles. He was in there somewhere, an article submitted and accepted, summarising the main part of his revised research: *Anomaly in Kuhn's The Structure of Scientific Revolutions.* He moved along the rack, found the journal and read a short passage from his article:

Contrary to the belief that scientists are objective, tolerant and open to criticism, Kuhn maintains that science is necessarily dogmatic and operates within overarching paradigms. Contrary evidence, what Kuhn calls anomalies, is dismissed as flawed research or put to one side to be dealt with later when the tools become available, but in reality, only addressed when they accumulate and threaten the prevailing paradigm, at which point a new paradigm emerges, called by Kuhn a scientific revolution. Kuhn was describing natural science, and my aim is to see if dogma also pervades the social sciences.

Replacing the journal, Neil reflected on Odlum's traits, starting with his lunchbox. Everything was separated into discrete packets, as if fearing the cheese might pollute the tomatoes or the cucumber offend both. A rumour circulated that one of his children had put a drawing on the toilet wall at home, contravening the same separation of categories, and Odlum had made her remove it. This indicated something, though he was uncertain what.

Odlum controlled departmental rooms with similar rigour, counting, numbering and organising chairs and other furniture, even specifying the type of chalk, and relentlessly campaigning against 'alien' chalk circulating the department. One day an anti-dust chalk clandestinely entered Odlum's controlled environment comprising a hard outer blue coating which left hands clean. Chalk was messy, the staff regularly covered in dust, and the 'alien' chalk successfully reduced dust. The problem was it also damaged the board, the hard outer coating leaving an impression. Odlum banned the chalk and confiscated any found, but sticks of it hung around, mainly in lecturers' pockets, bags and hiding places of increasing ingenuity.

Odlum was recently perplexed by the impression of a solitary letter N on the new blackboard in the recently refurbished lecture theatre, presumably done using the same 'alien' chalk. Unable to identify the culprit perplexed him further, as if the perpetrator inconsiderate leaving such a dearth of evidence. 'Why would anyone write the single letter N on the board? Why uppercase? Why to the side of the board, suggesting something should follow?'

He approached Neil. 'You used the room recently, Neil.' He paused, perhaps expecting a confession. 'Did you notice the N? I'm trying to narrow it down. Not accusing you of anything.'

'Bit like Holmesian deduction,' Neil quipped. 'Eliminate the variables one by one and the one remaining must be the cause.'

'It's no laughing matter, Neil. Do you know what boards cost?'

Odlum quickly ran out of variables, the elusive singular capital N beyond his control or imagination, such as Neil introducing himself to a new group of students.

'My name is Neil Denton but call me Neil.' He had begun writing his name on the board and stopped at the first letter. 'No need to write it down, it's on the handout.' Later, he wiped the board, leaving a ghostly N etched into the surface.

Odlum took to secretly observing lecturers, peering through windows or entering a room under some pretext, typically inspecting blinds. Finally spotting a lecturer poised to write on the blackboard with the non-designated blue coated medium, he had flung the door open, bounded across the room and snatched it from his hand saying, 'So it's you who vandalises the boards.'

'I wasn't aware of the ban and thought it was a joke or one of his breaching experiments, such as tossing chalk at the students,' the lecturer explained to Neil later. 'You know the stuff, breaching situational assumptions about behaviour and observing reactions. So I said, 'Thank you. Experiment over, can I have my chalk back?' "Experiment?" he hissed. "Are you mad?" He stormed out, leaving me chalk-less.'

Neil gained some satisfaction knowing Odlum resented supervising the Replication Team. Of course, everyone praised the idea in principle. Wasn't there a need for replication, a basic principle of science? An ad hoc team had been cobbled together comprising reluctant researchers drawn from various research areas. Rival departments soon dubbed it the Resurrection Team, and John Odlum found himself styled Resurrection John and made the subject of endless jokes about resuscitating corpses, research robbing or snatching. Which was curious because replication was supposed to safeguard science against error or fraud, a tenet enshrined in every manual and textbook, yet identical replications were rare as most funding agencies and prestigious journals favoured novel or groundbreaking studies, and the few replications undertaken usually differed in some way from the original to claim novelty and funding, such as Matlock's obedience study transposed from sixties America to nineties England, a different time and culture. And his shock machine was slightly modified, the *Danger, high voltage* sign altered to read, *High voltage*.

8

Neil was commenting on the improbable science and improbable coincidences in *Frankenstein*.

'Frankenstein is in the Orkney Islands and begins creating a female companion for the monster, but ends up destroying it, fearful the world will be populated by monsters. One wonders where he got the body parts in that remote place. That moment the monster appears, is enraged and swears revenge on Frankenstein's family and later murders Frankenstein's friend, Clerval, in Ireland, though there is no explanation what Clerval is doing there or how a very conspicuous eight-foot monster got there undetected. Unaware of Clerval's death, Frankenstein leaves Scotland by boat, goes adrift and lands in Ireland, the very place where Clerval has been murdered. He is then accused of the murder. And as for Mary Shelly's depiction of science...'

Her gaze steely, Rachel said, 'You're looking at it the wrong way. Despite your reservations about psychology, you're still steeped in narrow scientific method, probability and reality, just like your Professor Matlock. When told *Vertigo* was not true to life, Hitchcock said, "I make slices of cake, not slices of life... Films are like life with the boring bits cut out". I spoke to your Matlock recently. All he could talk about was control, the usual shock machine stuff and some hideous example of traumatising rats. What's the fucking point to that? I asked him and he said, "Well, you can't traumatise people". I bet he would if he could. Life just isn't that simple, I told him. Literature isn't that simple. Take Macbeth. He kills Duncan because he is ambitious and wants to be king, but ambition alone isn't enough to explain the murder. The witches' prophecy that he will become king influences him, gives authority, but only because he believes in witches and the power of witchcraft. More than anything there's his wife, encouraging, prompting, goading, orchestrating. Then there's opportunity: Duncan staying the night. And Duncan's naive trust. The real world isn't the simple interaction of two variables fighting it out in some fucking laboratory.'

'Is that what you said?'

'Well, I didn't say fucking. I asked him how he would analyse a work of literature experimentally. "You can't, that's the point", was his smug reply. "Literary analysis isn't a science, just elevated opinion. A waste of time and ripe for a cut". Arrogant shit. I asked him if he had set up an experiment to choose his wife. He didn't answer.'

Neil laughed.

'Have you met her? You and Matlock must understand, *Frankenstein*'s not famous for its scientific, sociological, psychological and historical accuracy. If that was the measure of literature, Shakespeare would be out. Forget psychology.'

'Even so…'

'Forget psychology. Forget everything you've learned. Above all, forget your Professor Matlock. Look at me. Now concentrate. Literature's not your subject. Literature isn't reality. Literature isn't your trite, boring dung heap reality picked over by psychologists. Literature escapes reality. Now, have you come up with any theories about the monster?'

'The monster. The monster,' Neil repeated, stalling. He shrugged. 'It's difficult to find a theory that fits. The psychology of monsters isn't that developed.'

Rachel tried to suppress a laugh. 'Oh c'mon, you're not going to blank on me. You're not going to do your *Hamlet* routine. Save that for Matlock. I want a theory, pristine, and now. What's the latest in psychology? What's all the rage?'

'CBT.'

'CBT? What the fuck's that?'

Neil leaned back, grateful he now had something to say, something Rachel knew nothing about. 'If you promise to stop shouting, I'll tell you.'

Rachel glared.

'Promise.'

She made a sign of submission, smiled sweetly, and Neil said, 'Cognitive behaviour therapy. It's everywhere. Originates from America. Not very scientific, according to Matlock, but he's mostly lukewarm because it's more about attitudes and not situations. "Attitudes don't spring from nowhere", he told me recently, "the situation's in there somewhere". He tolerates it because it brings in funds. As I said, all the rage. Even my doctor's a convert. Odlum likes it or pretends to.'

'Odlum? Wish you hadn't told me that. Makes me hate the theory even before I know what it is. Odlum hates women; rarely includes women on his team.'

'Wrong causality. Women hate Odlum. Avoid working with him. Female students hate to be alone with him.'

She nodded knowingly. 'His plastic arm. Heard about it from female researchers, his avuncular pose and comforting hug. If he put his arm around me, I'd break it. Women lack aggression. Why are so many women so fucking meek? Take Dunk. He has a reputation for staring at female students' bodies. The other day I was in the coffee bar with a student and Dunk sat opposite. His eyes roamed about my body then settled on my tits. Finally, I said, Duncan, will you stop staring at my tits. That's the way to deal with Duncan.'

Noticing Neil's dismayed expression, she said, 'What's wrong?'

Neil explained Dunk's condition. 'Face blindness. Can't recognise faces so concentrates on other things for clues: dress, voice, hair colour. Surprised you didn't know.'

'So what you're saying is, I'm just tits to Duncan. Is that what you're saying?'

'I'm saying that's his way of recognising you. It's the first clue, that's all. If you had unusually large feet or a missing arm…'

She smiled mischievously. 'Are you sure about his condition? He had no difficulty spotting Selena the other day in the library. Watched him glide over to her. No tits worth talking about.' As she said this, she was scrutinising Neil's face, and he quickly wore a poker expression. She laughed. 'Too late. You gave it away. You are interested in her, aren't you?'

Ignoring the question he said, 'Was she wearing socks?'

'Yes. Bobbysocks.'

'That explains it. She always wears ankle socks. He recognised her socks.'

'God, I feel bad. Why didn't you tell me? Poor Dunk. I've always thought him a bit strange, Asperger's, or something.'

'You should have spoken to him the moment he sat down. He would have recognised your voice.'

'How the fuck was I supposed to know that?' There was a pause. 'Right, if you're not going to tell me about Selena, back to CBT.'

Neil clasped his hands behind his head. 'It's all about how people construe the world, their self-concepts and attitudes. It's one's attitude or interpretation that counts. Adler long ago said the same. Some people carry around negative beliefs that are self-defeating or self-handicapping, such as expecting to be loved by everyone. In short, they create their own problems.' Rachel didn't respond so Neil hurried on. 'Cognitions determine emotional states, not the other way round. Some people are unhappy because they dwell on negatives and ignore positives. They have faulty cognitions. The therapist encourages them to look on the positive side. Called cognitive restructuring.'

'Cutting through the jargon,' said Rachel, 'isn't that a bit like saying count your blessings? Always look on the bright side?'

Neil now suspected it was hopeless but pressed on. 'Someone is troubled by a misshapen nose and wants it reshaped, but should they just change their attitude or wrong thought? This is Goffman's point in *Stigma*. Someone has a nose job but nothing changes. CBT is all about attitudes, expectations, evaluations, and positive and negative thoughts. One method is called thought stopping. An elastic band is worn round the wrist and snapped to interrupt the negative thought. After a time, the band is no longer needed.'

Rachel laughed. 'Cyrano de Bergerac has a long nose, fights duels and waxes lyrical about his nose to his opponents, and all the time it's just a wrong attitude. Imagine Cyrano going to a therapist and saying he wants his nose shortened. "Don't have that operation on your nose, Cyrano, it's not your nose but your attitude. An operation is expensive and unnecessary".'

Neil tried to interrupt but Rachel was in full flight.

'"Tie an elastic band round your nose and snap it every time you have an angry thought. Better still, take a picture of it, frame it and put it on your wall. Make Christmas cards of it and send them to friends and family. Be proud of your long nose".' She looked mockingly at Neil. 'If CBT had stopped all that ridiculous dueling we wouldn't have a story or those eloquent speeches.'

Neil ploughed on. 'The idea is that the patient harmlessly re-enacts the problem during therapy. It's a kind of catharsis. Selena was telling me about a patient –'

Rachel shrieked with laughter. 'Cyrano dueling with Selena. Harmless, you say?'

Neil sighed. 'Metaphorically speaking.'

'Anyway, it's all been said long ago. "…there is nothing either good or bad, but thinking makes it so". *Hamlet*.'

There was a long silence as Rachel made some coffee. 'Any other ideas?' she said over her shoulder.

'Maybe the monster makes unrealistic demands?'

'You mean, if he didn't want love and acceptance his problem would disappear? Anything else?'

'A negative attitude?'

'Wouldn't you have a negative attitude if you were rejected at birth, nameless, looked hideous and hated by everyone?'

'PTSD, then. Post-traumatic stress –'

'I know what the initials stand for, but how does it fit the monster?'

'The monster's reaction is delayed. After all, he isn't always vengeful. Being created and rejected must have been traumatic and confusing, later manifesting itself as anger and revenge.'

'You're forgetting, the monster tries to make contact, is sociable and wants to love and be loved and takes revenge because he is hated and rejected. It's a conscious decision. Hold on, this sounds like Selena. You haven't been discussing the monster with Selena, have you? He's not a fucking basket case for Bobbysox. If she got to the monster, he'd be on some anger management course.' Peering out the window, her back to Neil, she said, 'No. I still think Durkheim is the better bet. Facing Neil, she said, 'Sorry, it looks like the Durkheimian sociologist is leading here. Maybe you can conjure up a better theory for Victor Frankenstein?'

Beginning to feel competitive, Neil said, 'Situational psychology.'

She grimaced. 'Matlock goes on about the situation. The lot of you are Matlock situation clones. Oh, go on, then.'

'Frankenstein would not have created the monster in a different situation.'

'The problem is, Frankenstein deliberately creates a situation where he is free of constraint, a separate, solitary chamber. Frankenstein isolates himself in Ingolstadt, cut off from Geneva where he is surrounded by companions. That's not responding to a situation as *absenting* oneself from a situation. Is the absence of a situation a situation?'

'Walton, then. He –'

'Yes, it fits Walton. At first, like Frankenstein, Walton's disposition overrides all, then slowly he responds to the situation: the attitude of the crew. In the end he cannot ignore the crew and turns back. You're in with a chance. But forget the CBT crap.'

'Selena's critical of CBT. Doesn't get to the root, she told me.'

'Selina only sees the so-called fucking root.' She paused, smiled ironically. 'Hold on. Don't tell me: you really are interested in short socks. Ms Bobbysox. No, not Ms, Mrs. We mustn't forget she's married.'

Neil was silent.

'You are, aren't you?' She smiled enigmatically. 'We must discuss it. But not now.'

As he reached the door, Rachel said, 'How's the schizophrenia research going?

Neil grimaced. 'It's secret, remember. Can't discuss –'

'Bollocks. So secret you told me, beanbag you. Come back a moment. There's an amusing story about James Joyce and schizophrenia. I've been meaning to tell you about. You know his daughter was schizophrenic, and one symptom is incoherence.'

'Word salad.'

'Exactly. Joyce was living it up in Switzerland, gratis wealthy patron, and asked the eminent Carl Jung to treat her. Wondering if schizophrenia ran in the Joyce family, and ignorant of developments in literature, Jung obtained a copy of Joyce's incoherent *Finnegans Wake*, and concluded it did. In the extreme…'

*

'Aren't you a bit old for her? She can only be twenty at most.'

'Thirty, actually. How could she be twenty with a degree and PhD?'

Rachel pouted. 'Doesn't look thirty. It's those short socks she insists on wearing, that half-adult, half-child look. Forties bobbysoxers come to mind. Girls swooning over Frank Sinatra. No tits to talk about.'

Neil sighed and shifted in his chair. Rachel insisted on this ritual demolition whenever he showed interest in a female.

'The socks put patients at ease, are non-threatening.'

'Patients or clients?'

'I'm not sure.'

'Patient, I bet. Very medical. Controlling. Contradicts the non-threatening socks. She's a walking contradiction.'

Before Neil could respond, Rachel was asking, 'And she's married?'

'Sort of. She mentioned a husband of sorts. Alphonse.'

'Alphonse.' She pouted. 'Alphonse de Vaux.'

'Lives in Paris. Artist of sorts. Swallowed a microphone and recorded inner space, or something. Writes shape or shaped poetry. Famous in avant-garde circles.'

'Shape poetry? Say no more. Circle of two, three at the most. Wasn't it John Lennon who said avant-garde is French for bullshit? So she has got a husband. That's established at least, and French, explaining her surname. He's been a phantom up to now, rumoured to have turned up at last year's Christmas party, but stayed in the corridor in the shadow of a pillar.'

'Selena told me he hates English cuisine. Calls it a contradiction. Quite good, really. More than anything, he hates English Christmas dinner.'

'If it's turkey, I can understand. The person, thought to be him, jumped out from behind a pillar and asked a passer-by, "Is it over?" He was struck by his haunted expression, grey features and sunken eyes. Selena, of course, hates parties but drags herself along. Not exactly the sociable type.'

'She told me distance is part of her counselling role. Not enough to be impartial, she must *appear* impartial.'

'Interesting defence, but you expect that from a therapist. Anyway, I've asked around for you – discreetly, of course – but no one seems to know anything about her, other than the rumoured husband.' She looked mischievously at Neil. 'Most men think she's gay, the husband a cover.'

'Men often say that if a woman is distant. Do you think she's gay?'

'Thirty, you say. Lives alone?'

He hesitated before answering, and looking towards the window said, 'She lives with a female friend.' Then hurriedly, 'But if she's gay, why ask me out?'

After a long pause Rachel said, 'This friend, she isn't...' She laughed loudly, head on the table banging her fist, while Neil looked on dismayed.

'You think that is final proof?'

'Not necessarily.' She laughed again. 'There are no absolutes, no final proofs: your words. Didn't she tell you about gay friends coming over from America to visit? Why mention their sexual orientation? You wouldn't say heterosexual friends over from America.'

'Could be she's proud of her liberalism, her way of publicising it. She told me the other day she was showing a black friend around London. If the friend had been white, she wouldn't have mentioned colour. No, it's her liberalism.' Looking at Rachel, he said, 'Anyway, she's asked me out again.'

Rachel leaned back, hands clasped behind her head. 'My advice is go easy. Offer her friendship. Even if she is interested in a relationship, she'll take a long time. Months I would imagine the kind of person she is. Don't rush things. And don't touch, not until you are certain. God, it's like talking to a child. Fat lot of good your psychology degree. Aren't you supposed to know about – What do you call it?'

'Boundary understandings, intimate zones.'

Rachel chuckled. 'I repeat, don't enter her intimate zones unless invited.' She leaned forward and rubbed her chin. 'It may offend your male ego, but maybe, just maybe, she wants friendship. Some women do with some men. Would explain why she disliked being touched by you. Or maybe its repulsion, like Frankenstein fleeing when the monster reaches out to touch him.'

'Thanks, Rachel. Very comforting.'

'If it's not that, if she's naturally non-tactile, she won't be much fun in bed.'

Neil was silent, waiting for her to desist.

'And she's far too serious. Rarely smiles, the sort who says prune, not cheese, when photographed.' She smiled broadly, a deliberate display of perfectly straight white teeth, and speaking through these said, 'Maybe she has awful teeth?'

Neil was silent.

'Has she got awful teeth? She has, hasn't she?

Neil sighed, and said irritably, 'There's no problem with her teeth. I like her teeth. And she does smile, occasionally.'

Realising the absurdity of the question, they both laughed.

*

Neil watched as Selina neatly cut her underdone steak into small manageable pieces, a habit acquired living in America for a time.

She smiled across at him. 'It's delicious.'

He noticed again her slim body, covered as usual in a long, wide, pleated dress, formal but fashionable, shoes, black and simple, and the very short pink socks. Conflicting messages, he thought, mixture of innocence and sophistication. A presentation to tax Goffman. Her legs were apart at that moment, and the skirt, loose fitting, dipped in the middle, contouring her thighs, her crotch. Momentarily he thought about sex with her, but Rachel's 'Don't rush things... she'll take months I should imagine' came to mind.

His hopes had been rekindled when, a week after the disastrous first date, she rather shyly suggested a drink or meal, preferably distant from the university. 'We don't want prying eyes, do we?' The evening seemed successful, though not without confusing messages.

Moving the conversation on to her flat, he was about to ask about her flat mate when she cut him short.

'Don't.'

'Don't?'

'Don't say it. Don't ask.' She pushed back her chair, an awkward silence as both searched for a new topic, interrupting each other. Neil asked about her friends from America, leading to the issue of gays. Both expressed liberal leanings. Neil, keen to impress, told her about a residential he once organised on the very topic, inviting two gays to speak, one male and one female. On arrival, the female looked decidedly butch, a stereotype he'd hoped to play down, but later it was explained that the female gay couldn't make it and the butch lesbian transformed into a rather effeminate male. Thinking this amusing, he was disappointed when she merely smiled politely. She became very serious and talked about her flat mate; not flat mate exactly, a friend staying temporarily, who would occasionally wake in the early hours anxious and stressed by a recurring dream and climb into her bed for a cuddle. Her pause suggested to Neil she wanted him to comment.

Perhaps ease the way to saying she was gay? There again, she could be bisexual. Complicated but... Uncertain how to respond, the moment was lost and they had moved on. At least she had clarified the 'gay friends from America'. Not her friends after all, her temporary flat mate's. But if her flat mate's friends were gay... Out of this ambiguity he clung to the fact that Selena had initiated this second date, was keen to see him, and at most she could be bisexual.

They were at the Trip to Jerusalem, Nottingham's oldest inn. Relaxing outside, the evening warm, she giving some very positive signs such as looking at him intently from time to time, and showing, by her standards, a certain laxity, slouching, arms dangling or moving freely, but always out of reach, neither touching nor touched, ever the demure, sophisticated, reserved and reticent Selina de Vaux.

Smiling graciously, she was saying, 'People seem to feel threatened when in the presence of a therapist, as if I am reading their minds.' She smiled. 'Please don't feel threatened.'

The truth was, he felt no threat from therapy or therapists as such but harboured a niggling concern about what the students said about him to Selena, a concern engendered when first introduced, and her remark: 'So *you're* Neil Denton.'

But she had asked him out.

The evening drew on, the main meal and sweet over, she sipping a brandy and smiling across at him. Had he ever seen such a wonderful smile, eyes offering so much, yet rejecting as well as offering, her whole persona that mixture of conflicting messages: warm yet distant, sensual yet aloof, at times almost virginal? How he wanted her. But the evening was ending, the most he could hope for another date. Would it always be a restaurant or pub? Should he make some proposal now, define the situation as Goffman would say, but Rachel's advice came to mind: don't rush things, offer friendship. This seemed appropriate. He was uncertain about her feeling for men, and even if she was interested in him, she might, as Rachel so bluntly put it, only be interested in friendship. So he adopted a serious tone, said he understood the situation, how he liked her and thought her very attractive and would like to see her more, but was not committing her to anything and understood if all she wanted was friendship.

All through his little speech she had watched him fixedly, elbows on the table, and when he concluded she said enigmatically, 'I think we're both a little drunk.'

He felt slight alarm. What did it mean? Had he completely misinterpreted the situation again, offended her, another embarrassed farewell, awkwardness at work the next day? At least he hadn't taken her hand.

She stared at him intently for some moments, drew heavily on her cigarette several times, and looking down at the ashtray as she extinguished the remainder, said: 'This is our fantasy. No one must know. No commitment either side. Not yet anyway. Be normal during the day.' She paused. 'My flat mate's away this weekend, can you stay the night?'

She was obliged to repeat the invitation.

9

'All that was missing was guttering candles, clanking chains, perpendicular walls soaring to a black void, howling wind and grating doors on rusting hinges.'

Wendy Woodbine was relating Odlum's drug talk and preparations for the Rosenhan replication. Neil was pleased she was talking to him again. She had cooled following his criticism of her research into suicide and gender. Nothing was said, just distance, and curt replies from her and the team. He would be careful what he said to Matlock in future. The talk took place in a disused area of the old asylum building, part of the psychology block. City Centre University initially occupied a Victorian asylum closed in the eighties, vast, rambling and mainly one level. Rapid expansion followed and later arrivals, such as sociology, were advantaged with a glistening tower block while psychology languished in neo-Gothic gloom.

Worried some of the volunteers might weaken when in the presence of a psychiatrist and other hospital staff, take prescribed drugs and spoil the experiment, Odlum had played on the dangers of antipsychotic drugs, such as side effects and withdrawal symptoms. Given a box of placebos each, they were instructed to slip medication under the tongue and told to practice for ten minutes. This was easier than expected as the pills were not sugar-coated, adhered well and easily removed.

Wendy told Neil that most of the volunteers were stressed knowing they would have to deceive hospital staff. It seemed wrong. 'Easy to say act naturally once diagnosed.

Acting truly naturally would mean owning up, surely, not maintaining a pretence.'

Neil nodded his agreement.

Symptoms, Odlum explained on their return from placebo practice, had to be more extreme today to gain access to hospitals and other units, but short of paranoia and claims of self-harm.

'You don't want to appear dangerous to yourselves or to others. They might force drugs on you, force on you the ultimate drug, the drug you can't control, the drug you can't spit down the toilet: the slow-release depot injection.' He drew out the last word, expression deadpan.

'It was night-time,' Wendy explained, laughing. 'Walls covered in decades of yellow paint, now peeling to reveal garish red tiles; high ceilings in shadow, hanging lights with dark shades. One shade, caught in a draught, was swinging, casting a long curving shadow. The Gothic props weren't needed, of course, Odlum's creepy enough, prowling back and forth in front of the blackboard, casting a crooked shadow. I'm surprised he had any volunteers left after his over-the-top account. Two withdrew, one during the meeting, another later. This was after he gave them a choice. "Some of you", he said, "may be having second thoughts. I understand. Say so now if you don't wish to continue". Later he was less understanding. "Not committed to science", he told Kel. "Like psychology in the cosy abstract but not the messy reality. Fair-weather researchers". That's their careers over, I thought.'

'Anyway, the list of long-term horror side effects of prescribed drugs seemed endless: uncontrollable facial twitches and lip smacking, slower reaction times, drowsiness, stiffening muscles, memory problems, mild Parkinson's such as repetitive body movements, massive weight gain, nausea. And if that wasn't enough to put you off taking a drug, hormonal imbalances such as enlarged breasts and milk discharge in women and men. He did manage to identify some positive effects for patients such as disappearance of voices, but emphasised none work for very long, and even when they appear to work, the side effects are so awful you won't notice or care.

'The performance included a litany of medications none of us could spell: risperidone, clozapine, quetiapine, perphenazine, to name a few, all recited effortlessly in a mesmerising chant as we struggled to write them down, when all the time he had them written on the back of a large roller board, suddenly emerged from his trance, leaped towards the board and rotated it at speed to reveal the words. "Surely the drugs can't be that bad", I said to Odlum. "The whole of psychiatry can't be that wrong. What does the research say?"'

She smiled at Neil's approving nod. 'Of course, Odlum ignored my question. Odlum has a way of discouraging criticism. Later he saw me alone and asked me if I still wanted to participate. Talk about fixing your sample, the bastard. Made me feel bloody insecure. Kel put his foot in it. At one point he sounded off about psychiatry, liquid cosh or chemical strait jacket for drugs, psychiatrists on a par with witch doctors, no doubt thinking Odlum would approve. Odlum's tone oozed patronage. "I fully understand your feelings, Kel, but we need to be objective". Odlum objective! "We're not out to pillory psychiatry and psychiatric units. If the hospitals aren't as bad as the media says we must say so, of course". Totally contradicted his standard diatribe. Why does Odlum hate psychiatry so? Makes you think. It's more than research to Odlum. Too messianic. Bet he's had treatment. Suitable case. He wants control over psychiatry. Look at the way he keeps on about making fools of them.'

'You're right. Usually he's lukewarm about replications, resentful even.'

She sighed. 'Pity you weren't there, Neil. You would have challenged him. He needs deflating.' She reached over and fleetingly touched Neil's hand. 'Unlike poor me. But I've forgiven you.'

*

Nothing was left to chance. Odlum employed an acting coach from an agency, appropriately called Faking It, to train his 'volunteers' to give convincing performances. The fee took a quarter of the grant, but if it stopped them falling at the first hurdle...

Everyone was sworn to secrecy, friends and relations to be told only at the last moment. Volunteers only knew their own hospital or unit and their own pseudonym. On no account was the media to be contacted, a point repeated at every meeting. Meetings were held at night in the same unused area of the former Victorian asylum. 'Away from enemies, particularly the sociologists,' Odlum explained.

The research was about three related issues: diagnostics, patients' choice and the ongoing power of the situation. Each volunteer would adopt a pseudonym and give their own life-history minus real profession. Once diagnosed, they would drop symptoms and behave normally. Odlum again emphasised the importance of only pretending to take drugs, how drugs would impair observation and the perilous side effects.

Now a member of the team, Neil attended the talks, and tonight's was on the medical model of schizophrenia. Odlum's delivery was lighter than usual, even getting some laughs. 'Someone hears voices, goes to a psychiatrist and says, "What's wrong with me?"

"You have schizophrenia", the psychiatrist says.

The patient asks, "What is schizophrenia?"

The psychiatrist replies, "In your case, hearing voices".

'This is not the same as waking covered in spots and going to a doctor. If he says, you have chickenpox this denotes an underlying cause. If asked what chickenpox is, no doctor would say, spots. Similarly, if I go to a doctor and say I'm feeling listless, urinate a lot, feel unusually hungry and thirsty and my vision is blurred, the doctor might suspect type 1 diabetes and suggest a blood test to determine insulin level. The doctor would explain how insulin deficit affects the body, low insulin causing high blood sugar levels, and so on.'

Odlum paused and smiled triumphantly. 'There is no test of schizophrenias available to the psychiatrist. They have antipsychotic drugs, though all the evidence suggests they do not reverse or cure the symptoms, merely mask them, rather in the way alcohol can mask unhappiness or pain. I repeat, the label schizophrenia is a re-description. It doesn't denote an underlying cause, though this is often assumed. Diagnosis and symptoms are the same. Another problem is that schizophrenia includes a wide range of symptoms: hearing voices, paranoia, word salad, various deficits such as insomnia and inappropriate emotion. Any one of these could have a different cause but unlike physical disorders, which have blood tests or X-rays, there are no further tests for schizophrenia. Therefore, psychiatry is pseudo-medicine. So don't feel bad about deceiving them.

Pausing, he stepped forward. 'Critics of Rosenhan predicted that diagnostics would improve as criteria were refined. Almost a quarter of a century has passed since Rosenhan's study, DSM has been revised twice, but no underlying cause has been found.'

Odlum expounded on schizophrenia, how one isn't schizophrenic but has schizophrenia. Someone with schizophrenia is more than the label, is a father, son, brother or daughter.

The disability coordinator, a volunteer for the research and strongly attached to labels, particularly dyslexia, interjected. 'Does that mean your Professor Matlock shouldn't be called professor? By the same logic he is more than his academic status. Should we say he has professorship, recognising he is a father, son, brother, and so on?'

Irritation evident in his voice, Odlum said tersely, 'Schizophrenia is a negative and dangerous label, professor is not. Schizophrenics are lumped together by the media. A schizophrenic kills someone and the rest are labelled potential killers. "Why are they let out?" shriek the tabloids.

Most of those labelled schizophrenic are not paranoid killers. Most are not even paranoid. Two people labelled schizophrenic can have totally different symptoms. We should just describe problems and abolish labels. One person hears voices, another talks incoherently, yet another –'

'All labels?' interrupted the disability coordinator.

'All.'

'Surely not dyslexia. Having dyslexia is not the same as having schizophrenia.'

The disability coordinator was noted for her zeal supporting students with dyslexia, and each autumn launched what Dunk dubbed Dyslexic Season and the Great Dyslexic Hunt. She was also researching dyslexia. Many believed she and her team over-supported the students, gave undue help with coursework. She had fallen out with the educational psychologist because his criteria for dyslexia was too restricted. He maintained that many of her 'dyslexics' were not dyslexic at all, and no different from many other students who never presented for the label, and literacy was generally lower at CCU because many courses did not require a pass in GCSE English. She replaced him with one deemed 'objective'. She was cool towards Neil ever since he challenged her over a particularly difficult student, un-co-operative, sneering, and eventually complaining about Neil, prompting her to see him. 'You must understand,' she said, 'he's dyslexic.' She related his 'story', how he was bullied at school, criticised at home, and not to blame.

'But that implies some people are to blame. Why are some excused and not others? Give an example of a blameworthy student.'

She turned and faced Odlum squarely. 'It's been a hard struggle getting dyslexia recognised. Labels help us clarify; give recognition. Labels give comfort. How many children were once wrongly thought stupid or lazy? All those I support like the label dyslexic because it proves they are not stupid. Often, they say to me, 'At school, they thought I was stupid. I was bullied. I'm not stupid, I'm dyslexic.'

Dunk mumbled something from the back.

'What did you say?'

Odlum cuts in hurriedly before Dunk could elaborate. 'We're not saying dyslexia isn't a real condition. Of course not.'

Dunk persisted: 'If someone has a reading problem, we offer help. The problem exists. What we don't need is to waste time deciding if they are dyslexic or not, have dyslexia or not or worry about what dyslexia is. Why do we dream up label after label? Labels can be an impediment. In the case of dyslexia, a crutch even. An excuse for inaction.'

'A crutch,' she said slowly, repeating the words to herself.

'If someone can't draw, we say they can't draw, we don't devise some pseudo-medical term. It's obvious they can't draw. If someone can't compose music, we say they can't compose music. If someone has difficulty writing, why can't we say they have difficulty writing, and give them support? We don't need the label dyslexic. It's an umbrella term, anyway. Do all so-called dyslexics have the same reading and writing problems? In the end you identify their individual needs to give individual help, surely.'

'Dysgraphia is the term for poor writing skills. One of my students has dyslexic dysgraphia.'

'You mean has difficulty reading and writing, or can't read or write well?'

'I mean he has dyslexic dysgraphia.'

'But the label fails to tell us the degree or character of the deficit. I agree with John.' He glanced at Odlum who sat stony-faced. 'Like schizophrenia, we need to describe the problem, place people on a spectrum, a literacy spectrum, not divide the population into dyslexics and non-dyslexics, making dyslexia an exclusive club.'

'Exclusive club,' she said slowly, repeating the words to herself.

By now, other members of the team were adding examples:

'Can't ride a bicycle, you have dyscyclia.'

Dunk stood up, moved his arm as if wielding a baton and said, 'Can't compose music –'

'Dysmusica,' they chorused.

'If we abolish labels, how does anyone discuss dyslexia?'

'We don't. That's the point,' Dunk breezed. 'We discuss the problem. If someone has a reading problem you don't need some overpaid, overqualified educational psychologist to say, 'I've assessed your symptoms and pronounce you dyslexic.' Dyslexia's not a thing, it's a word, a sound we attach to behaviour.'

'A mouthful of air,' Neil added.

Standing up, voice trembling, she glared at Neil and said, 'Yes, but a mouthful of air that sucks in the funding, and the funding agency insists on labels.'

'Are we researchers or fundraisers?'

'Oh, I give up. You're all, all… You're all suffering from labelphobia.'

'The phobias,' they chorused, bouncing examples off each other like so many rubber balls.

Reaching the door, she turned and said, 'Fuck the lot of you,' glared at Odlum and said, 'And fuck your research.'

Odlum stared fixedly at Neil. 'Thanks, Neil. Most helpful.'

*

As they walked along the corridor, Wendy was saying to Neil, 'Interesting how Odlum blamed you, yet you said very little. The meeting was a bit aggressive towards the disability coordinator. I know she's a pain, but...'

'Problem is, they really wanted to attack Odlum.'

'Why was Dunk so scathing? You would think his own condition – prosopagnosia – would make him sympathetic.'

'Could be the opposite: he hates labels. You know he developed face blindness following a car accident? Found he could no longer recognise members of his own family.'

'How terrible.'

'His doctor diagnosed prosopagnosia. "What's prosopagnosia?" he asked. "Inability to recognise faces", replied the doctor.'

'We shouldn't laugh. How does he teach small groups?'

'They know his condition and stay in the same seats, print their names on cards which he laminates and folds so they can be displayed on their desks each lesson. After a time, he links voice and name. Unusual appearance helps, of course.'

'So there's something to be said for labels.'

Neil looked at her bemused.

'Would they be as sympathetic if he simply told them he couldn't remember faces?'

*

Neil felt growing unease.

He had listened to several presentations from team members and was about to present his findings on Rosenhan, aware his approach didn't chime with the rest, particularly Odlum's. Momentarily he empathised with Asch's lone subject hearing a string of wrong answers, knowing it would soon be their turn and the last to respond, conflicted over whether to conform or be a minority of one. Even if he wished to, it was too late to change the content of his talk, as this was no simple issue of judging line length. This issue was complex, beyond simple laboratory tests and single variables.

Odlum, he increasingly realised, was steeped in anti-psychiatry, a movement flourishing in the sixties and seventies, declining in the eighties only to return in the nineties under new labels minus extreme and provocative theories such as Szasz's depiction of psychiatry as modern-day witch-hunting. Very strange ideas can grow in a cloister. Earlier, Kel had shown Laing's weaknesses, carefully focusing on his later, more absurd revisions: schizophrenia a voyage of discovery beyond human experience transcending mundane reality; the schizophrenic an unrecognised mystic on a spiritual journey; or schizophrenia the collapse of the false self, attached to a false reality, sane in an insane world, psychiatry and society on the couch, not the patient.

Odlum chuckled. 'I think we can leave out Laing's late sixties, romantic hippie-cum-Marxist views, the bathwater, that is, but keep the baby.'

The 'baby' was Laing's belief that the medical model was wrong, psychiatry pseudo medicine, drugs ineffectual and dangerous. Odlum still adhered to Laing's earlier view, that voices were the controlling voices of uptight controlling parents, denying their children individuality, the interiorised family smothering the individual, the damaged teenager erroneously labelled schizophrenic by colluding psychiatrists. This resonated with Odlum. One unguarded moment, the worse for Matlock's dry sherry, that antidote for boredom, Odlum had talked about his patriarchal family: 'Don't sit there, that's Dad's chair. Don't touch the paper, Dad hasn't read it yet. Dad, Dad, Dad, the word haunts me still.' His parents were ambitious for him, their only child, burdened with compensating for their failures, life a grind towards the eleven-plus, then grammar school, followed by an academic career. Curiously, now away from his parents, he still clung to his imposed career, telling himself that no one totally escaped their family. Did he hear voices? Staff often wondered. Staff also wondered about Odlum's troublesome, or troubled, children, the picture on the lavatory wall and other stories of control and rebellion. Were they in turn escaping an oppressive family, escaping Odlum?

Neil had carefully researched Rosenhan, first reading and re-reading his original 1973 article *On being sane in insane places*. To test the idea that psychiatric diagnosis was unsound, Rosenhan and others faked symptoms and gained entry to various mental hospitals, showing psychiatrists can't tell the sane from the insane, and seeming to support Laing. Once admitted, they behaved normally thereafter. Would the psychiatrists continue seeing their behaviour as signs and symptoms of madness, once diagnosed mad, forever mad? Rosenhan claimed this to be his key finding. A much-quoted example was the pseudo-patient who openly took notes. 'Patient engaged in writing behaviour', one nurse's comment, presumably his 'compulsive' writing dismissed as an aspect of his disturbed condition. Whatever the pseudo-patients did or said was evidence of their condition, the initial diagnosis rubber stamped by the situation. Also, much quoted in the media were genuine patients voicing suspicions aroused by the continual note-taking. 'You're not crazy... you're a journalist... checking up on the hospital.' It seemed the patients were better at diagnosing than the staff.

In an era when psychiatry and psychiatric hospitals were under attack, the study was a media sensation. *Fake patients fool psychiatrists* and *Psychiatrists can't tell the sane from the insane* were typical headlines. But research that dismissed the entire psychiatric establishment as charlatans was unlikely to go unchallenged, and a torrent of criticism followed, confined mainly to scholarly journals rarely read or referred to by the media or included in psychology textbooks. Neil followed the debate with interest. There was much to criticise. Matlock had merely touched upon a few weaknesses of Rosenhan's design.

After outlining Rosenhan's study to the group, Neil set about methodically demolishing the study, citing various critics. A key problem was that Rosenhan's research findings did not match the conclusions, and the design and evidence were poor. There was even a suggestion the results were partly fixed by Rosenhan. One pseudo-patient, Harry Lando, gave a positive account of his experience and was dropped from the study.

'But was he dropped because he disagreed or was there some other reason?' asked Odlum.

Neil shrugged. 'Lando doesn't say.'

'Corroboration?'

'Couldn't find any.'

A long pause followed, and Neil finally said, 'Another problem is that the method itself limits you to underdogs not overdogs. You can sit in the gallery of a court, but you can't sit on the bench. You can pretend to be a worker on some production line, but you can't secretly infiltrate the board of directors. You can pretend to be a patient, but you can't pretend to be a psychiatrist or hospital manager.'

'Underdogs, overdogs? Where does this come from?' Kel asked.

'The sociologist, Becker. Rosenhan couldn't go behind the scenes and spy on the doctors and other staff in secret. Rosenhan could only observe what he saw. He could say what was happening in an open ward but couldn't say why, only observe and speculate.'

'Didn't he get the co-operation of the hospitals and look at records when the fake patients had left? What about, "Patient engaged in writing behaviour"?' asked Odlum.

'Straight observation. The patient, or pseudo-patient, was writing. It's Rosenhan who puts a situational construction on the comment to fit his theory that psychiatrists misdiagnose, affected by context.'

'But all of his pseudo-patients were discharged as schizophrenic, despite showing no symptoms, proving psychiatrists couldn't tell the sane from the insane.'

'The exact phrase is, "schizophrenia in remission". The psychiatrists recognised the absence of symptoms.'

'They still left the hospital labelled schizophrenics; a label shaped by context. Once labelled –'

'They could hardly diagnose cured,' Neil interrupted. 'Remember, they believed the pseudo-patients had taken antipsychotic drugs, and schizophrenia does go into remission. The pseudo-patients had told the psychiatrists the voices had gone. The psychiatrists presumably believed the medication was working, or they were in remission, or both. Anyway, the psychiatrists accurately observed they were no longer showing psychotic symptoms, showing they could accurately diagnose. This contradicts Rosenhan's conclusion that the hospital situation alone confirmed the diagnosis of schizophrenia.'

'But not on entry,' said Dunk. 'On entry, all were diagnosed schizophrenic when they were normal.'

'If someone sees a doctor and claims to have backache and want time off work, the doctor may suspect malingering but is unlikely to *diagnose* malingering, less still a "researcher" pretending to be a patient. Rosenhan went beyond the evidence. At most he shows the unreliability of diagnostics, but that doesn't prove psychiatry can't tell the difference between the sane and insane, only that they can't detect the sane *pretending* to be insane. Surely, when you voluntarily approach a mental hospital, you have labelled yourself mentally ill and in need of help. Normal people don't present themselves for treatment. Why should a psychiatrist suspect otherwise? Kety gives the example of someone swallowing a pint of blood and appearing at a general hospital vomiting blood. Doctors would suspect a peptic ulcer, not a researcher or malingerer pretending to be ill. And it wouldn't be proof doctors can't diagnose the condition or that the condition doesn't exist. When you approach a hospital as a volunteer patient you have labelled yourself ill, otherwise you wouldn't be there. The doctor or psychiatrist merely decides the precise label.'

'What about the warning to a hospital?' Kel smiled as he addressed the group. 'Didn't Rosenhan do a follow-up study where he warned a hospital that fakes would be presenting themselves. Two psychiatrists suspected fakes. One psychiatrist suspected 23 out of 193. The joke was, no fake patients were sent. Doesn't that raise doubts about diagnostics?'

'Same with physical illness. Munchausens spend years getting unnecessary treatments faking physical illness. Diagnostics, mental and physical, can be difficult. Doctors often have difficulty diagnosing conditions.'

'Point understood,' said Odlum, finally interrupting. 'But do we want to discuss this?'

There was an awkward silence as Neil surveyed the group. Deciding they did, he said, 'Imagine if doctors were warned that fakes would be presenting themselves with low back pain. Wouldn't that make them cautious? They might believe a percentage were malingerers but still give them certificates. Doctors rely on patients to tell the truth. It's difficult to disprove back pain, as it is voices. Were any genuine patients ejected or refused help in Rosenhan's follow-up study? Rosenhan doesn't say. Millon, a critic of Rosenhan, suggests a better design. Sane subjects act normally and present themselves to various hospitals, accurately describe everyday behaviour and life histories, feign nothing, and ask if they are mentally ill. If diagnosed mentally ill and admitted, that might support Rosenhan's belief that psychiatrists cannot distinguish the sane from the insane. Rosenhan –'

Neil was cut short by Odlum who loudly addressed the group. 'Do you really want to discuss this? It's drifting off the point, and time's running out.'

'I thought it *was* the point,' said Dunk, looking confused.

Odlum shook his head. 'We are not testing diagnostics alone, that's secondary. We're mainly testing staff reaction to patients refusing to take drugs. Today's therapist is supposed to be non-directive and value neutral. That's mainly what we're testing.'

Kel and Dunk exchanged confused glances.

'But –' started Kel.

'User choice,' Odlum said emphatically. 'Patient-centred psychiatry, that's the modern claim. Can users negotiate treatment, such as choosing therapy over drugs? We want to know how far things have moved on since Rosenhan. We want to test if psychiatrists now negotiate with patients over treatment, and if they do negotiate, is the patient under pressure to accept a psychiatrist's recommendation? We're not replicating as such. It's treatment that's moved on. I thought I made that clear?' He brightened. 'We'll expose the psychiatrists, don't worry. Everything's under control. The volunteers are sorted, hospitals identified, the research design finalised. Just need to decide the date. What can go wrong?'

As they left the room, he warned, 'Remember, no contact with the media, especially Andy Seedbank and that radio station.'

*

'I'm confused,' Wendy was saying as they walked along the corridor. 'We started out testing diagnostics in context, now it's what happens if we refuse to take drugs. I am right in thinking that?'

Neil nodded agreement as they entered the staffroom.

'Otherwise, why the seminar on how to deal with medication? I practised for hours with those placebos, and the bastard changes the research. Now all I have to do is refuse medication and see how they react. The truth is the bastard took your arguments on board but didn't own up. That was a superb criticism of Rosenhan. Up to then I accepted the research.'

'Same here until I read the criticisms. I bet Odlum regrets not doing the archive himself.'

Wendy laughed.

'Odlum obviously hadn't read the counter-arguments, explaining his long silences, intervening only to nit-pick. Isn't he supposed to be the expert? In fairness, I suppose, most of his time is spent organising, planning, negotiating grants and other mundanities.'

'At least it's a better research design,' Wendy said cheerfully.

Neil grinned. 'You haven't got out of not washing for a week, though.'

Wendy poked Neil in the ribs. 'You bastard. Just because you're not a volunteer.' She came close to him. 'You never know, I might call on you when I'm my most fetid. You won't laugh then.' She took his arm. 'Let's go for a drink.'

They found a secluded corner and Neil bought two pints of lager.

'Have you ever thought,' Wendy was saying, 'schizophrenics who present themselves for treatment might be unrepresentative schizophrenics? I put it to Odlum recently: what if someone hears positive voices? Voices encouraging and supportive? "Statistics show most voices are negative", he said. Based, presumably, on those who seek treatment, I countered. Odlum didn't reply, his usual defence, so I said, maybe those who present themselves do so because the voices trouble them. A skewed sample.'

'What did he say?'

'He just stared at me. Then I said, a medium who hears voices from the dead isn't troubled, believes it's a gift, and doesn't seek help.'

'Superb point.'

'I told Odlum that a better design would be to compare those who hear voices and seek help, and those who hear voices and don't. Maybe it's all about attitudes. Might learn something new. Of course, he dismissed it. "Sounds a bit CBT", he said. I didn't stop there. Even if one hears voices, I said, that doesn't explain strange interpretations. Some schizophrenics know the voices are not real, are in touch with reality to that extent, others interpret them as some external control: aliens, the devil, MI5, and so on. Why the difference?'

'What did he say?'

'He stared at me for a long moment and left. His stare is sooo threatening.'

10

They were in their usual pub drinking their usual beer. Everything was usual except Andy's edginess.

Neil broke the silence. 'You said on the phone you wanted some help. With an article?'

Andy paused. 'Confirmation. Just confirmation. I'm not asking you for inside information, exactly.'

Neil and Andy had retained contact since university, helped in part by taking the same degree and geographical proximity, but mostly an affinity despite taking different paths. He felt comfortable with Andy. People felt comfortable with Andy. Always agreeable, non-threatening, sympathetic, he would fall in with your tone or mood; a persona, Neil came to realise he cultivated. 'We all know you are a wonderful person, Andy,' was a common joke at university. Rachel disparaged him, of course, using the more formal Seedbank then 'Seedy', finally settling for 'Weed'.

'You're not still seeing Weed, are you? He's a shit.'

'You mean, he's a reporter.'

'Same difference.'

Neil supposed the same ingratiating skills gained information, put people at ease and off guard, but behind the façade (perhaps not façade exactly, he was undecided on this point) was ambition. Andy yearned to get on a national paper and hoped for a big story, his breakthrough, his Watergate, and escape his provincial backwater. He worked for a regional paper called the *Midland Post*, covering the Midlands from Nottingham to Luton, the latter a tantalising thirty miles from the capital. 'A national paper in all but name,' said

Andy. 'Remember the *Manchester Guardian*? Now the *Guardian*, and national.'

From time-to-time Neil helped Andy with articles, suggesting ideas but mostly obtaining data, such as a recent satirical column on academic psychology, a series of articles on the silliest, cruelest and most pointless experiments of all time. Odlum's media experiment headed the pointless category, Harlow's the cruelest, and silliest went to a forgotten study uncovered by Neil arguing that Joan of Arc, who periodically dressed in male clothes, was a man trapped in a woman's body, relating this to hormonal imbalance. The silly part was the experimental support, manipulating hormone levels in rats, or as Andy put it, the study didn't say if the female rats began wearing male clothes. Neil easily fell in with Andy's ridicule despite the inclusion of his own psychology department, such as Odlum's media study. After all, Odlum's study was pointless. Neil also supplied ideas and criticisms of studies, telling himself it was honest discussion and open criticism, not disloyalty to the department.

'Not asking for inside information,' repeated Neil. 'Information about what?'

Staring into his beer, Andy said, 'The hospital study. Rosenhan.'

Neil laughed ironically. 'How did you –'

Andy pulled a sheet of paper from his jacket pocket and handed it to Neil.

Once crumpled and now smoothed out, it contained names of hospitals and psychiatric units, and against these, names Neil didn't recognise. Some had been crossed out. It meant nothing to him. He handed it back to Andy. 'What is it?'

'The hospitals the researchers intend investigating and the researchers' pseudonyms. Can you confirm?'

'I don't know the names of the hospitals or the pseudonyms.'

'Obviously you can't check the file for me.'

Neil looked askance and Andy raised a hand. 'Obviously.'
They paused to sip their beers.

'Even if I was agreeable, no one can penetrate Odlum's
security system, not even to steal a photocopying card.'

'Handwriting?' There was slight urgency in his voice.
He pointed to a handwritten comment below the list.

Neil showed surprise. It was unmistakably Odlum's
handwriting, those exaggerated curls on his lower-case Ys
and Gs, like inverted coat hanger hooks.

'How did you get this?'

'So it's genuine?' He was trying to affect a nonchalant
tone, but Neil noticed his voice had risen slightly.

Turning to face Andy, Neil said, 'How do you know
all this?'

'Contacts. Deep background. For example, I know you
are part of the Rosenhan team. I know Odlum and the team
met secretly in the old asylum block. I know about your
presentation. Got hold of the handwritten minutes. Some
excellent criticisms of Rosenhan by the way, more detailed
than the edited typed minutes.'

'If you know so much, why do you need me to
confirm?'

'I have an informer. My Deep Throat. Very deep. So deep
I don't know who he is or what he looks like. Woodward,
at least, knew who his informer was. That's why I need
confirmation. Double confirmation. I need to know if he's
genuine. If the information is genuine. Interesting that he
doesn't want to be seen by me. He's obviously in your
department. Can't be an outsider. Seems to have access to
everything. We met and he gave me the list and minutes of
meetings, even explained the research in detail.'

'Why didn't he post it to you?'

'He said writing was risky, so we met in a multistorey
car park last night. The agreement was we would meet

providing I couldn't see him. An underground car park seemed the obvious place.'

'Your Watergate fantasy, you mean.'

Andy's laugh was more a nervous giggle, and he began searching for his cigarette lighter. 'My informer wanted somewhere dark, and I suggested a car park. Straight off the top of my head.'

'Straight out of *All the President's Men*.'

'Can you think of a more perfect place?'

Neil pursed his lips.

'The problem is, I need corroboration. He could be a hoaxer. He might have made the list up. As I said, I'm not asking you to inform, just confirm.'

Stalling, Neil wanted to know more about the underground car park meetings. 'Surely not the early hours? Does he access your paper?'

'Don't have one delivered. Often wondered how Deep Throat managed that. Before you ask, I don't have a flowerpot and a red flag to signal I want a meeting.'

Neil paused a moment to recall this. It was some years since he'd seen *All the President's Men*. Woodward and Bernstein investigated a break-in at the Watergate Office Building, headquarters of the Democratic Party. Their investigation, helped by an informer nicknamed Deep Throat, implicated the White House, and finally President Nixon, causing him to resign. Woodward, a reporter, kept a red flag in a flowerpot on his balcony which he moved to signal when he wanted a meeting with Deep Throat. If Deep Throat wanted a meeting he would indicate the time in Woodward's newspaper, delivered each morning, by circling the page number and drawing a clock with the hands indicating the time on the same page. The meetings took place in a car park at night.

Andy was saying it wasn't the same as the film. 'Bloody cold. You won't believe how cold it is at two in the morning.'

The car park was disappointing: cramped, no cars suddenly taking off at speed, tyres squealing, as in the film, just a struggle to extricate a small car from a small space making innumerable manoeuvres. Graffiti on walls, smell of urine, the route out a tight spiral marked from tyres and bodywork scraping the walls.

'Typical sixties car park, ferroconcrete, and cheap.'

Andy bought two pints and placed one in front of Neil. 'The problem is my editor insists on corroboration. "Who is this nobody who lurks in the shadows? Could be fantasising, hoaxing the paper".'

'How will you use the list?'

'Don't ask. Better you don't know. So you'll confirm? You have as much, anyway. After all, it's not as if you're supplying information.'

Neil adopted a moral tone. 'You do know I'm not supposed to talk to the press. Edict from Odlum. I should report –'

'Bollocks. You don't like Odlum.' He laughed softly. 'Or the research. Anyway, I'm more than the press. We go back a long way, Neil. Remember the last article you helped me with: cruelest experiments? All the textbooks, even our degree course, gave sanitised versions of Harlow. Remember? Omitted apes in isolation chambers he called the Pit of Despair to create mentally ill monkeys, claiming the induced psychosis gave valuable insight into depression. Wouldn't anyone be depressed isolated for up to three years? Some baby monkeys developed symptoms of extreme schizophrenia, terrified at the sight of their own arms.

'The textbooks say nothing about Harlow's Evil Mother or Iron Maiden, or infant monkeys catapulted onto the bars of the cage, spikes digging into them, the tiny infant monkey waiting for the spikes to retract to return for a cuddle, only to be catapulted away or spiked again. That was a much-needed article. Why did Harlow use such emotive language? A gift to his critics. You remember? Referred to female monkeys as "the bitches" in his lectures. Emotionally damaged female monkeys strapped to a device he called a Rape Rack so that male monkeys could impregnate them. Harlow was curious to know how these brain-damaged females would react to their offspring. Would they mother them? Surprise, surprise. They became real-life evil mothers, slamming infants to the floor when all they wanted was a cuddle, one blinded and partially paralysed by a brain-damaged mother. One chewed off her child's fingers, another crushed her offspring's skull with her teeth.'

Neil listened in silence, nodding at appropriate moments.

'And all the time Harlow coolly took notes. And what did he prove? That complete isolation leads to irreversible depression and babies need to be cuddled. Of course, his apologists put a gloss on it. Supposedly changed attitudes to child rearing, when all it did was spawn ethics committees galore. The usual arrogance, psychologists believing they have changed society. Psychologists need to be criticised, Rosenhan needs to be criticised. We need to get to the truth, give the reader a truer representation of Rosenhan. Didn't you just say that Odlum didn't like you criticising Rosenhan? Matlock complains that research is simplified or distorted by the media? Well, our presentation of Harlow was no distortion.'

Neil smiled. Andy Seedbank, upholder of truth.

'Your paper distorts, sensationalises, and misrepresents data. Take opposition to political correctness. *School bans racist blackboards*. Remember that? Some school went over to whiteboards and one oddball teacher was quoted saying blackboards are racist. I met up with some of the teachers and they said the boards were old, patched up and needed changing and the head decided to buy the latest white boards. None were quoted, only the oddball. Take the recent case of the school that dropped cricket because it's too expensive.

A reporter interviewed various teachers but only quoted an extreme feminist who said we need non-competitive games both sexes can play. The headline: *School bans sexist cricket – political correctness gone mad*, followed by a hate campaign and calls for the head to resign. She was hounded by reporters and bombarded with angry letters.'

Andy looked slightly sheepish. 'I agree with you. Anyway, I don't work on that side.'

'That's your excuse. Didn't Milgram's subjects who read out the word *pairs* go on to the very end because someone else administered the shocks? You work for the paper.'

'And you work for a university department that churns out research you know is flawed or pointless. Let's not argue. Rosenhan wasn't a sadist like Harlow, of course, his intentions were laudable, but you said yourself it's a poor study and needs to be exposed in the interest of truth, and we are the people to do it.'

Neil was amused at the sincerity in Andy's voice.

'Look, I'll make it easy. Remember Woodward and Bernstein's method? I'll ask you if the list is a fake. If the list is genuine, stay silent, if it's a fake, say fake. Just a game, really.'

'Stay silent or disconfirm?'

'Exactly.'

11

'This is our fantasy. No one must know. No commitment either side. Maybe in the future. Sex but no commitment. Be normal during the day.'

Neil had given scant thought to Selena's repeated stipulation that first night together, despite her reiterating on parting that their relationship at college should be professional only. 'After all, we are there to work.'

Monday showed clearly what 'normal' meant. All morning she had been distant, her gaze averted or directed past him or through him, and should they meet in some corridor moving in the same direction, she would move ahead or find some excuse to turn back. Later that day, the staffroom empty, she was standing by the window. Neil stood beside her and squeezed her hand. She had stiffened, the same way that night in the staffroom, quickly withdrew, and standing some distance away said, 'I should have realised it would be dangerous standing here. Please don't touch me at work.' Her tone was firm, as if bringing a troublesome patient into line.

'But there's no one else here, Selina. We could go to your office.'

She didn't reply and began talking about work to be done. When pressed some days later, she offered several explanations for her distance at work, some familiar such as her need to maintain a professional distance, which was unconvincing because she was less distant from Kel or Dunk, and friendlier towards Neil before their affair. Away from college she was friendlier and the further away the friendlier and more relaxed she became, and he wondered, with slight bitterness, how far they would need to go for her to be completely relaxed.

'OK,' she sighed, 'I suppose I like to keep things separate.' This was part of the stronger explanation, her privacy, something people commented on. She was a very private person, cherished privacy and feared prying eyes. 'I feel watched,' she once explained. 'Don't forget I am married, Neil. Alphonse, remember?'

Perhaps she found two relationships difficult to manage? Whatever the reason, he felt the charade was extreme. He had bought a new jacket, chosen with her help, and on the Monday she said, 'I like your jacket. Where did you get it?' Admittedly there were people in the staffroom. Neil later pointed out an irony. Might her extreme aloofness be seen as proof of an affair, protesting too much, totally ignoring each other only to be seen leaving together in Neil's car or even seen together around Nottingham.

Neil explained, 'We might have been seen without knowing.'

'Neil, don't make me more paranoid than I already am.'

Neil reflected on Alphonse, rumoured to exist but unseen, except for the possible sighting one Christmas. Maybe he wasn't her husband. He hadn't introduced himself as such. My name is Alphonse... Maybe there was no husband. Convenient myth. But to what end? Perhaps Rachel was right, perhaps Selena was gay or bisexual, Alphonse a cover? She said little about Alphonse, became evasive whenever asked about him, even withholding the date of Alphonse's next visit. She told Neil they phoned each other regularly, but admitted the relationship seemed to be going nowhere, he unwilling to move to England, she unwilling to live in France.

Pressed for answers, she would sigh and shrug dismissively. 'That's the way it is, I'm afraid. That's the way *I* am. Don't blame yourself, it's just the way I am.'

Was that it? No prospect of change? Strange defence for a therapist.

'You wouldn't accept that answer from one of your patients.'

She brightened. 'Don't you like the contrast?' Seeing his puzzlement, she expanded her point. 'There's something surreal about being colleagues by day, lovers by night or at weekends. That more than anything is why I don't want others to know. It adds excitement, mystery, piquancy. Don't you see?'

'Sort of.'

'You're not entirely convinced?'

'Not entirely.'

'Oh dear.'

'Recently you said you don't want me near you at work because I crowd you.'

'Oh, that. No, you misunderstood, I never said you crowd me, I said I felt crowded by you.'

Was that better? He supposed it was. But Selena's answers never satisfied. On another occasion she accused him of lacking romance. Where are my red roses? Perhaps this was the answer. He responded with a poem inspired by Mary Shelley's *Frankenstein* and *Mathilda*.

He showed it to Rachel. 'I must be in love to write poetry. Derivative, of course, not very good, but –'

She held up her hand and began reading it:

The world was to me a
Magic lantern and I
A poor onlooker but no actor.
In moratorium.
And then came my
Prometheus who gave
Me fire and kindled my
Metamorphosis: that

Self-transporting era of
My existence.
My rebirth.

And for a brief and
Wondrous moment I could
Pour my affection
On a warm and
Beautiful heart.
Such joy, such intensity.
Such grief.

To his surprise, Rachel was moved by the poem. 'Derivative, but only slightly, and very moving. She doesn't deserve it, but yes, give it to her. And don't forget the roses.'

12

The Rosenhan replication was a failure. On arrival, all but one of the pseudo-patients were given the same explanation, using the same words derived from Rosenhan's study: 'You're not a patient, you're a researcher pretending the be a patient.' There was no opportunity to refuse medication, and the experiment aborted.

Odlum was jubilant the day he presented to the hospital, wrapped in a bubble of confidence and control. He had scrupulously kept to procedure, not washing, adopting a pseudonym and false occupation, substituting head teacher for assistant professor, creating a fictitious school and faking non-threatening symptoms such as voices to avoid being sectioned and forced to take drugs. What could go wrong? Despite giving an accurate account of his life history and relationships, including those with colleagues, and acting normally throughout, the diagnoses was paranoid schizophrenia. He was ecstatic, a perfect example of diagnostic inaccuracy, only to be expected.

Additional to his 'voices', the psychiatrist drew support from Odlum's behaviour and life history: excessive control, preoccupation with chalk (disguised control), distrust of staff, secretly observing staff, organising furniture (not in keeping with his headship) and controlling his family. The clinching points were snatching 'alien' chalk from a teacher and recalling his relationship with his father: 'Don't sit there, that's Dad's chair. Don't touch the paper, Dad hasn't read it yet. Dad, Dad, Dad, the word haunts me still.'

This and his refusal to take medication led to his sectioning, empowering the psychiatrist to force treatment. Threatened with a depot injection he became emotional, sweated profusely, refused to lie down and laughed hysterically. 'Look. I lied. I'm a researcher and assistant professor. I'm not a patient. I'm researching you. Don't you see? I'm researching *you*.'

The psychiatrist smiled and shook his head. 'First a school head, now a researcher and assistant professor.'

Odlum made a bid to escape but was held down by two nurses while a third gave him the injection. The problem was, Odlum's pseudonym had not appeared on the list Andy showed Neil, probably because he controlled the list and felt no need to include himself, so the hospital where he presented himself had not been warned by Andy.

That week a headline appeared in the *Midland Post*: *Psychiatrists fool fake patients*. Neil misread it at first, expecting the reverse headline. And where was the expose of Rosenhan? Where were the criticisms of Rosenhan? He skimmed the article:

The aim of the research was to test Rosenhan's seminal study showing psychiatrists cannot tell the sane from the insane... showed that diagnostics have moved on since Rosenhan... almost 100 per cent diagnostic accuracy... 'wrongly' diagnosed just one pseudo-patient as paranoid schizophrenic... an assistant professor... sectioned and only released when Professor Matlock, head of the psychology department at City Centre University, intervened... 'understandable error', explained a psychiatrist... 'obsessed with chalk... snatched chalk from...'

*

Matlock met with Odlum and pointed to a follow-up article by Andy Seedbank. Odlum winced at the headline: *Assistant professor diagnosed as paranoid schizophrenic ... led the team investigating schizophrenia...* Below were details of Odlum's life history, including his relationship with his father, immediate family members and colleagues. Though not named in the article, he was easily recognisable.

Matlock shook his head. 'Pity you gained access. At least Seedbank doesn't name you.'

Matlock stood up and moved towards the window, his back to Odlum. 'There is a solution to all this. One aim was to test diagnostics, remember? Well, that's what you've done. We can say the study supports the conclusion that diagnostics have changed. They spotted you were all fakes.'

'But they didn't. They bloody well didn't. Someone alerted the hospitals. They knew we were coming. You know that. The hospitals set us up. A conspiracy.'

'I know, I know, someone set you up. How on earth did this Seedbank fellow get all this information? And you of all people, your name a byword for security. Look, what if we send a letter of complaint saying the headline is misleading? We weren't made fools of after all. Our intention from the start was to test diagnostic accuracy. Credit to the hospitals.'

'And end up supporting psychiatric diagnostics. Impossible.'

'Better than owning up to being hoaxed. That way we limit the damage. The VC's agreeable. Surely you see that? Other papers have taken up the story. Even a national paper. Have you seen the headlines? *Sham patients shrunk by shrinks.* We need to counter the headline before television takes it up.'

As Odlum reached the door, Matlock said cheerfully, 'The PTSD research is going well, I hear. Should be no problems there.'

*

Recovering from the humiliation of being hospitalised and having his research sabotaged, Odlum rose like the proverbial Phoenix and raged through the department, vainly trying to identify the informer-cum-hoaxer. His first thought was the 'enemy' of psychology: the sociologists.

'I'm certain the sociologists are in there somewhere. They don't like us.'

Matlock was doubtful.

'The Disability Coordinator, then. She has motive.' Odlum explained her recent mauling by Neil.

'Knowledge too limited,' said Matlock. 'The depth of information narrows the suspect to an insider. Keep to the team, otherwise the whole university is suspect.'

'You mean, eliminate the variables one by one until the one remaining must be the cause?'

One by one they scrutinised team members, but none had all the knowledge, though Odlum returned more than once to Neil who scored high on motive and attitude but failed on inside knowledge. Elimination and logic pointed to only one person, the one person who knew the names of all the hospitals, units and pseudonyms, the same person who locked the information in a combination safe: Odlum himself.

Matlock thought this very amusing.

*

Neil was pleased about the sabotage. After all, none of the replication team members seemed excessively concerned, other than the time wasted, replication deviating from their main research interests, and hadn't Wendy felt intense relief being rejected by the hospital, going straight to her flat to shower. But he also felt guilty, felt guilty about not feeling guilty. He had helped Andy a lot with articles, send-ups, exposés, but this was different, an ongoing research project sabotaged. And Andy had deceived him. Was he bothered? He didn't feel bothered. Anyway, he wasn't directly responsible, never knowing Andy's intention, accepting his 'better not to know', and never confirming directly, merely confirming by staying silent. And wasn't there something satisfying about Odlum's impotent raging, an exquisite sense of power knowing more than Odlum knew? But not much more. Who was this shadowy informer able to penetrate Odlum's security system?

In addition to controlling chalk, furniture and blackboards, Odlum had recently added repro paper. 'The leaner budget,' he would explain, 'the end of profligacy.' Conspicuous thrift was Neil's term for Odlum's economies, re-working the sociologist Veblen's conspicuous consumption. Chairs re-covered using old curtains replaced with blinds some years earlier, used folders cannibalised and useable sections glued together to form whole folders, a task assigned to a smouldering secretariat whom he considered underemployed and improvident, freely distributing paper and other resources to staff. What did staff do with all that paper? He suspected personal use and took control.

Shortly after, Neil wanted some paper and was directed by a secretary to Odlum.

'For personal use?'

'No. Not personal use. I want it for teaching.'

'For teaching?'

'I need paper for notes and for sticking down to make repro masters.'

'Scrap paper? There's plenty of used –'

'No. Not scrap. Clean paper for typing notes on.'

'What about lined paper? We've got loads of unused –'

'No. Not lined. Lined paper is no use. When photocopied the lines would show.'

'Are you sure you don't want it for personal use?'

'Absolutely.'

Odlum sighed. 'The only paper I have is repro paper. It costs £1.70 a ream. You realise that?'

'£1.70, is that all? Give me a ream.'

'Are you serious?'

Odlum next took control of photocopying cards. Neil wondered where he kept them. Probably some cupboard. If he could locate the key... He saw Odlum and asked for a card.

Odlum unclipped a keyring from his belt and selected a shiny brass key with numerous grooves. 'Follow me.'

'Neil followed him to a storeroom secured by a sturdy padlock, no doubt resistant to bolt cutters and similar devices.

'Five-lever lock, steel framed door,' Odlum said admiringly. He unlocked the padlock to a series of clicks.

Neil began following him to a huge bolted-down combination safe.

'If you could stand outside a moment, Neil.'

Odlum reappeared bearing a single card. '50 copies. That should last you a month. Students don't read handouts, anyway.'

'They may not read your handouts, but they read mine.'

'Really? You can't beat written notes, written by the students themselves. Muscular memory, motor learning, procedural learning, doesn't matter what you call it. Co-ordination of hand and mind. Grinds the words in. They stay put and flow out from habit on the appointed day.'

Neil tried to recall what he knew about muscular memory, but Odlum was saying, 'Serendipitous discovery years back. One of my students told me she copied out my handouts in her own writing to help memorise them, so I went back to giving notes.'

Despite a sneaking feeling Odlum might be on to something, and still trying to recall what muscular memory was, Neil said, 'My students highlight, underline and annotate my handouts. That's why I use one and a half spacing and generous margins, and why I use a lot of paper. In addition, I ask them questions and devise quizzes. Laboriously taking notes from a blackboard or OHP is time-consuming and very dull.'

'But it goes in. Take writing your name. Try misspelling it. Habit makes it difficult.'

As Neil moved along the corridor towards a set of fire doors clutching his 50-copy card, he repeated to himself 'muscular memory, muscular memory,' so as not to forget as he wanted to look up the term. Whatever the definition, he doubted if a Niagara of handwritten notes poured onto the page unstoppably on exam day. He reached the double doors and automatically pushed against the usual unlocked side, but it failed to open, groaned audibly and leaned precariously.

A member of maintenance, working behind the door, stood up and said angrily, 'What's the matter with you lot, can't you read?' He pointed to a notice on the leaning door. In large letters it read: *Use other door*. 'Is everyone blind? Call yourselves educated.'

Neil grinned, pushed the other door and said with a shrug, 'Muscular memory.'

*

Neil was telling Andy about reactions to his articles and Odlum's hunt for the extraneous variable who informed Andy and sabotaged the research.

'When he finds out who the Shadow is, he can tell me. Sorry about the deception but it keeps you out of the frame. Does he suspect you?'

'He suspects everyone with a motive, and Odlum's flexible with motives. Why do you call your informer the Shadow?'

'All I ever see is a silhouette. Hides in the shadows. If a car passes, headlights on, he steps behind a pillar. He's very specific about where we meet in the car park.'

'Voice?'

'Voice and vocabulary suggest educated. His English is strange. Slightly archaic. Few abbreviations. Has a certain gravitas, you know, weight, seriousness, dignity, substance. There's a certain substance there. Or was.'

'Was?'

'Somehow uncertain. I can't explain it. Wistful at times, even sepulchral, funereal, but mostly a quiet, soothing voice, wise and authoritative, from the back of the throat, breathy, slightly booming at times, but not so much cathedral as pastoral, small-church-in-some-sleepy-village voice. Expect a sermon any moment. "Brethren, we are gathered to discuss the sinner, Rosenhan".' He laughed. 'I exaggerate, but religion's in there somewhere. Or it could be the car park. Has a strange echo in the early hours, like talking in a church. No matter how low your voice, it's amplified and echoing. Maybe the architecture suggests a clerical connection. Where we meet is a vaulted arch, and beyond that a spiraling exit, sort of Brutalist-Gothic.'

'Could be disguising his voice. Doesn't he object to meeting in the car park? Strange location.'

Andy shrugged. 'Told you. He doesn't want to be seen. Where else could he remain anonymous? Perhaps I've met him? Don't recognise the voice. Could be another reason, I suppose. What was that psychological study showing people feel more anonymous wearing hoods and dark glasses? Easier to be dishonest or cruel. Maybe he has a conscience. Fits the religious aspect.'

'Zimbardo's deindividuation research. Flawed, I remember. Didn't Zimbardo dress half the subjects in Ku Klux Klan outfits? It's coming back to me. The other half wore their own clothes and large name tags. Sure enough, the anonymous subjects administered lengthier shocks than the identified ones.'

'And the flaw?'

'Confounding variable. The Klan outfits may have suggested aggressive behaviour. Johnson and Downing called it role expectation, clothes cueing behaviour. They set up a counter-experiment using female subjects. Half wore Ku Klux Klan outfits, half nurses' uniforms. Half of each group were identifiable with large name tags, half were not. Those dressed as nurses inflicted lower shocks on average than those in Klan outfits, regardless of whether they could be identified or not. Klan outfits are associated with aggressive antisocial behaviour, nurses' uniforms with prosocial behaviour. Clothes were a confounding variable in Zimbardo's study. Not anonymity after all, but role expectations cued by the uniforms.'

'And the flaw in Johnson and Downing's?'

Neil shrugged. 'Couldn't find one.'

'I'm disappointed in you, Neil. A study you can't flaw.'

'Doesn't mean it isn't flawed. Some overlooked confounding variable, observer bias, and a small sample. No blinds as I recall. The sample was drawn from different courses, including child development and psychology. Students were randomly assigned to groups, of course, but the lower shock groups may have contained more child development students sensitised to caring than the more scientifically committed psychology students. Randomness, as you know, is notoriously imperfect with small samples. The flaw, if there is one, could be anywhere. Who knows? How do you control all the variables if you don't know how many variables there are?'

The bar grew busy about 8.30pm, and Andy suggested they go to his flat and finish off his duty-free whisky.

Relaxing in an armchair, Andy was saying, 'The Shadow knows a lot about the routines of the department. A researcher, perhaps? Plagiarised by a superior? Been reading Broad and Wade's *Betrayers of the Truth* about fudging and faking in science. How senior staff take the credit for research and steal ideas from subordinates. Breeds cynicism, revenge, fudging, even faking results. I'm thinking about an article on the subject. We must get together sometime. Must be tons of research somewhere. Anyone in your department overlooked and thirsting for revenge?'

'Odlum's the nearest. He often implies he could run the department better than Matlock. "What's needed here are two Odlums", he told a member of staff one Christmas after a few glasses of Matlock's sherry.

'When interviewed for the job, Matlock told him, "You realise you'll do most of the work if I recommend you?"'

'Can see why he's aggrieved.'

Isn't the least obvious always the culprit in fiction, the reader led away from the real culprit?'

'Then Matlock should be the Shadow.'

'Matlock? Can't imagine a motive, other than madness. Can madness be a motive? Odlum's mad, of course. The psychiatrist's diagnosis wasn't far out.'

'The VC?'

Neil laughed, but Andy remained serious.

'After all, you said he wants to merge departments. If he could undermine psychology…'

'He doesn't fit your description of the Shadow.'

'He could be feeding information to the Shadow.'

Neil was shaking his head. 'If he wanted to merge psychology with sociology, he'd do it. Undermining psychology would only damage the university, and there's no way he could have obtained the hospital list. Only Odlum knew the details. Not all the university's men, I'm afraid.'

'So you think it's Odlum?'

Neil swirled the ice in his glass and told Andy about Odlum's delight deputising when Matlock was on a lecture tour, rearranging the room and bringing in a large angle poise lamp, casting his distorted shadow on the back wall.

'He would love to take over from Matlock. But sabotage his own research?' Neil shrugged.

'Would put people off the trail, of course, and didn't you say the Replication Team is Matlock's pet idea? What do they call Odlum in other departments? Resurrection John. Corpse resuscitator. He must hate doing it.'

'Odlum's religious, of course. Pentecostal. Boasts every summer how he divides his long vacation: third family, third research, and third charity, such as helping the disabled. Explains his asceticism, as far as anything explains Odlum. The Shadow's voice doesn't match, though. Odlum's is sharp, loud and certain.'

'As I said, could be disguising it some way. Or the car park echo. I asked him once why he was giving me the information as he didn't want money. His voice slightly haunted, he said, "One day I will tell you my story, you will be the first to know. I will tell you of the strange and harrowing events that made me what I am". He startles easily. Any strange noise and he vanishes. One odd thing, a snapping sound, a band or something, snaps it from time to time. Reverberates round the car park. Bit creepy.'

Andy persuaded Neil to stay the night. He had drunk quite a lot and agreed. Lying in bed, he reflected on the Shadow, picturing the clergy he knew or had known, mostly from film and TV. Was there any match between voice and personality or appearance? Must be loads of studies. People are often surprised meeting someone they have only spoken to over the phone, maybe on and off for years as part of their work. Radio personalities often disappoint: too old, or bald, a woman with a sexy voice peroxide and frumpish, or just the wrong age or shape. It was not that we had an image of them, more a general feeling shaped by the voice. Good research topic, probably done to death in America, shelves weighed down with rarely read journal articles on the very topic.

Drifting into sleep, the Shadow's motives floated and undulated in his mind: power, control, boredom, excitement, thrill of sailing close to the wind. *Spycatcher* came to mind: revenge for a bad pension. Or perhaps Andy had got it right, someone overlooked for promotion or having his research idea appropriated. But who?

*

Research into post-traumatic stress disorder was growing rapidly and funding no problem. Much of the research worldwide concerned returning military personnel, victims of various wars such as the Gulf and Bosnia. This aroused interest and sympathy. Kel and Dunk's variation was civilian populations. They advertised widely for volunteers who had developed symptoms following a trauma, such as numbness, insomnia, being easily startled, flashbacks, inability to work, depression, recurring nightmares, guilt, anger, detachment, alcohol and drug dependency, severe anxiety, panic attacks, poor concentration, irritability, withdrawing socially, relationship problems and avoidance of anything associated with the trauma. The range of professions from which they drew their sample was also wide.

DSM-1V was the starting point, but the list of symptoms was too wide and overlapped with other conditions and other causes, and to narrow the sample subjects were required to have experienced severe trauma: near death or serious injury experienced or witnessed, intense fear or horror, extreme helplessness. Duration of symptoms had to be more than one month but could occur sometime after the event, even years.

Neil was under pressure from Matlock to participate now the Rosenhan study had collapsed. He raised objections to the research design, drawing on his conference paper a year earlier where he had demolished a major study into family background and crime. The study found that convicted criminals were more likely to come from unstable families than a control of non-criminals, concluding family instability caused crime. Drawing on sociology, Neil pointed out that a high percentage of those caught are mentally ill or drug dependent. They are failures, out of control, often impulsive and more easily caught. What about successful criminals, those who never get caught, and therefore escape the researcher's net? Perhaps successful criminals come from stable family backgrounds? The successful criminal is disciplined, organised, in control, the unsuccessful criminal impulsive and risk-taking. A bad home life may be linked to failure generally, not crime specifically. Here was the eternal problem of muddling cause and effect and correlation. This would be a research breakthrough. Neil imagined the preamble: for more than a hundred years crime has been linked to family disorganisation, but a comparison of successful and unsuccessful criminals shows... On impulse he had rushed off to see Matlock.

Matlock wasn't impressed. 'Where the hell are you going to get a sample of successful criminals?' he sneered. 'Advertise in the newspapers? Brilliant criticism, but...'

Neil told Matlock the PTSD research somewhat paralleled the faulty crime study.

'Yes, I remember your paper,' said Matlock. 'Biased sample. Only those caught. Very clever criticism of the research. But how is it relevant to PTSD?'

Neil explained that the PTSD sample may be similarly biased, self-selected subjects with PTSD symptoms who have experienced traumatic events. 'Perhaps some people who experience trauma don't develop PTSD. Perhaps most don't. Like the crime study where you need to include those who don't get caught, you need to include those who experience trauma but don't develop PTSD. Called false positives by a philosophy lecturer I spoke to. We should select for trauma, not PTSD. Perhaps the crucial variable here is not the trauma per se but attitude towards the trauma. The person who develops PTSD may be deficient in coping strategies.'

Matlock was silent, and Neil added a quote from Adler: "No experience is a cause of success or failure. We do not suffer from the shock of our experiences – the so-called trauma – but we make out of them just what suits our purposes".'

'Adler, Adler. Sounds dangerously CBT. Enlighten me.'

'Adler broke away from Freud –'

'Stop. Stop.' He began laughing. 'Neil, it doesn't matter. Odlum is aware of the flaws, I'm certain. We all are. But even faulty research is worthwhile sometimes.'

Neil looked aghast.

'It's funding. Fodder for the department. Better than no research. Get my meaning?' He paused. 'I suspect Kel and Dunk aim to show the limitations of their study and get a further grant for a better research design. If they rushed straight in...'

*

Odlum motioned Neil to be silent. 'They're – we're – testing the DSM-1V theory that the more severe the trauma, the more severe PTSD. Now, before you say we were very critical of DSM-1V regarding schizophrenia, there's a difference. Schizophrenia in DSM-1V is a medical model and assumed a physical cause treatable using drugs, thus fuelling the drug industry. With PTSD the cause is assumed to be situational, an event in the environment. This is a new departure for DSM and to be encouraged. The stronger the trauma, the stronger PTSD. That's what we're testing. The power of a traumatic situation. Matlock is very supportive.' Odlum looked directly at Neil and said slowly, 'Which brings us to your idea that it's all down to attitude, that some might experience trauma but show no symptoms, completely denying the situation.' Odlum was shaking his head. 'One or two perhaps. Anyway, it confuses the issue.'

Neil was disinclined to argue further, except to say, 'But I thought you saw value in CBT?'

Odlum smiled thinly. 'Not to the point of total denial of the situation. CBT has a place. We need balance, Neil. If we listened to you, no research would get done.'

'Maybe some research shouldn't be done? Save the taxpayer money. Spend it on prosthetic limbs.'

'I bet you don't say that to Matlock. Whose side are you on, anyway?' He leaned back, rolled his head from side to side and said, 'Findings to date show a clear correlation between severity of trauma and severity of symptoms. Forget attitudes.'

Odlum didn't tell Neil that despite advertising widely, initial uptake was very poor, and the team worried about the sample size. Then, inexplicably, there was an upsurge of subjects. Kel and Dunk were pleased but puzzled. Seasonable perhaps? But the holiday season was in full sway and should have reduced volunteers. They settled on the snowball effect, volunteers encouraging colleagues to volunteer. Another oddity: most of the new intake were hospital staff, mainly nurses. Shrugging off these oddities, Dunk and Kel relaxed, even played devil's advocate. Could they, in the spirit of Popper, refute their own research? They tossed the theory about, stamped on the design, sample size and composition, confident it would restore its shape, as if made from memory foam. Anyway, Matlock was impressed, remarking at a school meeting, 'Beautifully situational. Great design, great funding. Great.' Odlum's name would head the eventual research report, of course, which was vexing for the rest of the team as Odlum took no part in the daily grind of interviewing subjects and recording their responses.

Expecting the clear correlation between severity of trauma and severity of symptoms to continue, many of the new intake suffering severe trauma showed only mild symptoms, while others experiencing mild trauma showed the reverse, a randomness pointing to another variable not being tested: subjects' attitudes. Perhaps they were pretending the painful events had never happened, avoiding reminders, in denial, dissociating; repressed memory even, an idea suggested by Selena. But repression was Freudian, and Freud unscientific, as everything supported the theory, even opposites, famously dubbed unsinkable theory by Karl Popper. Dora's emphatic 'No' meant 'Yes' to Freud, even more because it was emphatic. And if avoiding, denying or repressing, why would they volunteer as research subjects? No, the curse of PTSD was re-living the trauma, vivid memories and flashbacks invading consciousness and sleep.

There was no way of explaining the sudden influx of subjects showing a random pattern.

*

The answer came as a headline in the *Midland Post*: *Experimenters experimented on*. Underneath was an article: *Fake subjects fool experimenters*. Andy Seedbank, psychology correspondent:

> *In a bizarre twist, experimenters investigating PTSD were unaware they were also subjects of an experiment. Fake volunteers wanted to know if experimenters could tell real volunteers from those pretending to be volunteers.*
>
> *The fake subjects, psychiatrists, nurses and ambulance drivers assumed false names, faked various symptoms*

but gave true accounts of 'traumas', such as witnessing death or injury (typical of their professions). They came from hospitals and units recently targeted by the same researchers conducting an experiment where they faked schizophrenia to test the diagnostic accuracy of psychiatry. In that experiment all but one was spotted as fakes, whereas none of the pseudo-PTSD subjects were detected.

One researcher failed to recognise a psychiatrist who had diagnosed him as a pseudo-patient only a month ago. 'I'm amazed he didn't recognise me', commented the psychiatrist. 'But then he made little eye contact and showed unusual interest in my shoes'.

How many people are faking conditions to satisfy a craving for attention or some other strange need, the well-documented Munchausen syndrome where people pretend to have medical conditions and gain treatment, even operations? We do not know the extent of Munchausen syndrome, few admit to the condition and fewer still seek help, and they may not be limited to physical illness and hospitals. Perhaps psychologists unwittingly attract numerous Munchausens and obtain false data as a result?

On reading the article, the VC headed straight for Odlum, collecting Matlock on the way, and together they tracked him to the gym entangled and sweating on some tortuous rack. Not waiting for him to shower, or even stand up, the VC told Odlum that as team leader he was responsible for the "fiasco", the second in the space of a month, and the third if he included his media study.

Odlum distanced himself. Not team leader exactly, supervising. Dunk, Kel and Neil were in control of the detail such as interviewing, recording and collating data. Matlock and the VC maintained a stony silence as Odlum added hurriedly, 'You have to allow a degree of trust.' Silence. 'Otherwise, I might as well do the research myself.'

'But your name heads the submission,' said the VC.

'They needed my name to get funding. You know that.'

Holding up Andy's article, the VC demanded to know who the researcher was who failed to recognise a psychiatrist who diagnosed him as a pseudo-patient only a month earlier.

'Sounds like Dunk.'

'Dunk. Dunk. Is he blind, or something?'

Matlock intervened. 'Dunk has Prosopagnosia. Face blindness. You remember? Unfortunately, the psychiatrist was out of uniform, had no unusual features such as red hair, a mole, tattoo, anything that would identify him, other than brogue shoes, but possibly not wearing them when interviewed.'

'Yes. Yes, of course.'

Neil was pleased he wasn't involved in the fake. The research wasn't secret but openly advertised at hospitals to gain subjects. There was no need for an informer and Andy hadn't asked him to confirm anything. Then he remembered saying to Andy, 'Have you thought how interesting it would be if a number of people got together and pretended to be research subjects, say bipolar or PTSD?' Andy, he recalled, made notes in his small notebook. He blamed Andy's duty-free whisky. What exactly had he said to Andy? What had he revealed about the PTSD research? He vaguely recalled discussing the research. Andy's method of eliciting information could be confusing. Woodward had confused an informant when investigating Watergate, the informant reversing the instructions. Maybe Andy had confused him? 'Just make believe. Play my game.' But the VC, Matlock and Odlum wouldn't see it as a game. He felt insecure, out of control, controlled.

*

Could anything be salvaged? Not all the subjects were fakes, of course, and Odlum set about separating the fakes from the real to eliminate them from the research.

'If only Dunk had recognised the psychiatrist,' he said bitterly to Kel. 'Didn't the sudden influx of nurses, showing an opposite pattern, arouse suspicion?'

'We thought it a bit strange but relieved to get more subjects.'

The story spread to local radio and local TV, and Matlock was pressured to give an interview.

'Doesn't this undermine all research in your department?'

'An irritation only. We have dozens of ongoing studies, all running smoothly.'

'How do you know? Fakes may be turning up pretending to be subjects this very moment.'

'We would know.'

'But you didn't know about the recent fakes until the press revelation.'

'Something of a one-off. A childish prank, that's all. We now have a full list of the fakes and have eliminated them from the study. Everything is back to normal and we're getting on with what we're best at: research. As to your question about detecting fakes, we have a new vetting system in place designed to do just that.'

The editor of the *Midland Post* contacted Odlum protesting his paper wasn't involved in the fakes. Adopting a conciliatory tone, he warned Odlum there was a rumour circulating more fakes were on the way to test the vetting system.

Odlum panicked, called an emergency meeting, and told the team the new vetting system must also include greater vigilance. Reject anyone remotely suspicious.'

A week later a short article appeared in the *Midland post*: *Phantom subjects fool researchers* by Andy Seedbank, psychology correspondent.

Recently Professor Matlock stated on television that the Department of Psychology had installed a system for detecting fakes. To test this, the Midland Post told the Psychology Department more fake subjects were on the way. One researcher was convinced four subjects were fakes, another suspected three. No fake subjects had been sent. Not only can they not tell fakes from real subjects but are unable to tell if real subjects are real.

13

'Who is he?' Neil asked.

Rachel swung her chair to face him. 'Guess.'

She almost screamed when he said Dunk.

'Well, you were flirting at the –'

'I was pissed then. Anyway, I wasn't flirting. I never flirt.'

'How would you know, if you –'

She glowered at him.

Neil looked her in the eye. 'If not Dunk, who then?'

'Member of the Senate. She paused for effect, and said slowly, 'The vice-chancellor.'

Neil noted she didn't use the contraction VC, relishing his full title. Then she added, 'Harold.'

Neil smiled inwardly. Full title to first name, both conferring status, distant to intimate.

'Isn't he married?'

'Of course he's not fucking married. You really think? You do. Huh.' Rachel fell back into her chair and looked out the window, repeating 'huh.'

'Well, you once had an affair with a married man.'

She didn't respond.

'I'm sure he's married.'

'Was. *Was*. Recently divorced.'

She explained how Harold began showing interest in her, going out of his way to talk to her, at one point playfully throwing a ball of screwed up paper at her before his frowning secretaries.

'Ball of paper?' Neil's tone was incredulous.

She chuckled. 'Bit juvenile, I know. But since his divorce…'

His office staff, all female, had arranged a party for his birthday and Rachel was invited by the VC. She arrived before the party started and the secretaries, who shared an inner office, edged away, barely acknowledging her presence. Eventually one of the secretaries, pointedly looking back at her colleagues, approached her and voiced their concerns.

'Their concerns?'

'Came straight out with it. "Are you giving him a lift home?" Apparently, his car was in for repair. "We wouldn't want to see him hurt. He's very vulnerable after his divorce". What do they think I am? A black widow spider? Do they think I'm going to eat him?'

'Vulnerable?'

'They're very protective. I suppose it's those hunched shoulders and that grimace. They took me by surprise. Later I thought, what the fuck has it got to do with them? They weren't worried about me, my need for protection. He was lonely. Would he be too dependent? Too demanding? Clinging even. Would he want sex? I can't stay celibate forever, I thought. Three years... Anyway, we got to my place about two in the morning. I couldn't find my key.'

'Not again. Why don't you keep a spare?'

'Oh, you're so fucking organised! Anyway, I suggested we go to his place. A big enough hint, don't you agree?'

Neil nodded.

'We got to his place. It was well past two. And do you know what we did?'

Neil shrugged.

'We drank coffee, that's all. Well, he's older. And balding.' She laughed. 'Couldn't help but comment on his bald patch. Told me he needed a haircut, and I said, haircut! I would have thought you'd be going for a polish.' She laughed loudly and banged the table unable to speak, and recovering said, 'He automatically reached up and touched the small bald patch. "Is it really noticeable?" he said. I told him I was only teasing.

Don't think he believed me. He's sweet, really. Probably why we didn't have sex. Demoralised him.'

'There was a time when a kiss was all you had the first date.'

'We didn't even do that!'

'Are you dating him?'

'Yes. And having sex. But I'm worried. He's lonely, on the rebound, and might become too clinging. You know I don't like all the affection stuff. Just sex.'

The VCs lovemaking was scrutinised, making Neil uneasy, how he had taken to calling her to lunch in his office, complete with chaise lounge.

'The truth is, Neil, I can't stand seeing him every day.'

Rachel once had a relationship with a married man, believing it would be part-time and not too demanding. 'How can you spare so much time?' she protested. 'I never imagined... Doesn't your wife suspect?'

Smiling at her he said, 'You don't seem to understand the relationship, Rachel. You are supposed to complain to me that you don't see me often enough because I'm married. You've got the roles the wrong way round.'

Rachel vied between extremes, often quoting *Wuthering Heights*, Catherine's two kinds of love. 'My love for Linton is like the foliage in the woods; time will change it, I'm well aware, as winter changes the trees. My love for Heathcliff resembles the eternal rocks beneath – a source of little visible delight, but necessary. Nelly, I am Heathcliff!' Rachel would sigh and say, 'Why can't I find love like that?'

'Is there nothing positive you can say about him?'

'Positive?' She thought a moment. 'His penis.'

Neil smiled. 'You mean its length?'

'Why do men keep on about length?' No, the symmetry. The top is so rounded. I suppose it is quite long. When he has an erection and enters the room from the side his penis is the first thing I see. Anyway, I got revenge on his secretaries.

They bought him a tie for his birthday, a hideous patterned thing. I was in his office, and knowing they could overhear me I said, 'Where on earth did you get that tie? It looks as if someone has vomited over it. I came out, and there was stony silence.'

She changed the subject and was telling Neil about a recent equal opportunities meeting, irritated by one of the less liberal professors who said it was surely enough to employ homosexuals, encouraging them to apply a step too far. '"We are a very liberal university", said the VC. "Absolutely agree", the professor said, "but we don't want to ram homosexuality down people's throats". That was my cue. They don't do it that way, I said, they practice anal sex. Harold looked terribly embarrassed.'

Neil laughed.

'Everyone thought it amusing. Except Selena, her usual silent, self-effacing self. Said virtually nothing the whole meeting. Never have I known someone so self-effacing, and when she does speak always the soft-voiced therapist reciting platitudinous advice. At one point I said, oh, you're so fucking sensible, Selena. How can you be so sensible?

'Later, she sent me a note saying, *you're obviously not aware I have a PhD in psychology.*

'I was tempted to write back, so what? Not the same as a PhD in chemistry, a real science.' Aware Neil was silent, she added, 'But I didn't. You're not bothered, are you? Are you?'

Neil shrugged.

'Anyway, therapy is not a science, is it?'

Neil shrugged again and said flatly, 'No, not a science.'

A long silence followed, and Rachel said, 'You look a bit down. Are you a bit down?'

'No. Not down.' He brightened, and said, '"My heart is ten times lighter than my looks".'

She looked surprised, gave a short laugh and said, 'I'm impressed. Don't recall –'

'Lord Surrey, *Richard III*. The King asks him why he looks so sad.'

'Never did *Richard III*.'

'Did it for A-level.'

*

Spooner retired unexpectedly. Neil wasn't ready to replace him, his PhD problem. Kel applied but lost to a highly qualified, high-powered external candidate who had everything, from PhD to numerous journal articles, even a tan. And he was taller than Kel. Convinced the job should be his, Kel was overheard shortly before the interviews pleading with Matlock to give him the lectureship.

'The problem is, Kel, you're a bit tainted by the sabotaged research. That's how the VC sees it. Not your fault, of course, but two in a row… As the VC said, one sabotaged experiment may be regarded as a misfortune, two look like carelessness. Quite clever, really. Wait a bit and it'll blow over. You need a success or two.' He paused. 'Preferably two.'

Spooner commiserated with Neil, saying he would have supported him had the moment been right, but an unfinished PhD in abeyance… He had to leave now, he explained, because of increasing deafness and forgetfulness. He had difficulty hearing students and often misheard what was said at meetings.

'Hearing aid?' queried Neil.

Spooner told him the saga of the hearing aid, going for tests on the National Health.

'The assessor, part-time, showed me various aids for watching TV, such as headphones attached to a TV by a lead that trailed the floor. The monitor crackled when touched and had a permanent hum. "You're not the first person to notice that", she said. "Mysterious, isn't it?" If I use this, I said pointing to the headphones, can other people hear the

TV? "Oh no", she said, "only you, I'm afraid". She then advised me on managing my deafness. "If you go to a restaurant, sit with your back to the wall. If you can't understand someone, say to them, you're not making yourself clear. That way they'll blame themselves". He smiled at Neil. 'Imagine what a pain I'd be insisting on sitting with my back to a wall, and no explanation. So I said to her, wouldn't it be simpler to tell people I'm going deaf? She seemed taken aback and said, "Well, you could take that approach, I suppose".'

He decided to buy privately. The price range was large, rising to a £2500 state-of-the art self-regulating digital aid that adjusted to context. 'I chose the latter as it was the most advanced, and at that price assumed it must be the best, reassuringly expensive and all that, particularly as it was not offered on the National Health. "You'll hear sounds you haven't heard for years", promised the hearing specialist.

'There were two problems. The sound was tinny, opening a carrier bag like screwing up tinfoil, walking across a carpet a sheet of foil. The aid *was* self-regulating but completely out of control, a mind of its own. It would home in on sounds and amplify them, such as a ticking clock growing louder and louder. The background sound in a supermarket, which it was supposed to control, was more deafening, not less. Each time I went back to the shop I was told, "No problem, we can adjust that". I returned several times, but it made no difference. Finally, I boxed it up, handed it to the hearing specialist the moment I entered the cubicle, and asked for a full refund. "They are a bit tinny", he admitted. The bastard knew all along it was rubbish.

'I got one free on the National Health within a fortnight, a different hospital. Vastly cheaper model, no mind of its own, though still tinny. The problem is, an aid can't fully restore hearing loss. Deafness isn't like the volume on a radio turned down. There are imbalances, distortions, intrusive background noise; you mishear words, miss bits, which can be embarrassing. That and forgetfulness makes you appear doddery, even senile. When the students are laughing at you, you know you've had it.'

'Forgetfulness?'

'When lecturing, I say things like, what was it I said I would get back to? Or I make a long statement and forget my original point. I go to the fridge to get the milk for my tea and find I've already taken it out. At least I still know I've forgotten. I don't forget everything; where I have just come from, for instance. Immediate short-term memory is the problem. Is it that we don't remember or that we don't commit to memory? We don't forget everything. I suppose that's one difference between failing memory and dementia. I hope!'

*

'What I'm going to tell you is in strict secrecy. Not a word to Selena, anyone.' She paused, a careful pacing. 'The fake subjects are nothing by comparison. This is big. Only a few people know.' Wearing her most serious face, Rachel paused again and fixed Neil's gaze. 'Are we agreed? Tell no one? You're something of a leaky beanbag with information, gossip spilling out of you in all directions.'

Rachel liked control over inside information, dangling tantalising morsels laced with insults before delivering the main dish. Since her affair with the VC, now permanently referred to as Harold, she had been privy to what she called inside-inside, most of which she imparted to Neil, always prefaced with, 'You won't repeat this.' Neil usually found out later she had told all her friends and close colleagues. The problem was there was so much information, some secret, some not, some in-between, and Neil often forgot which was which, recently causing her embarrassment, vowing she would not tell him anything again. Hence beanbag. He felt the metaphor unjust but let it pass. Neil nodded lazily and Rachel wasn't satisfied. 'You're not taking this seriously enough. I don't want you broadcasting the information around the department with a megaphone. Harold will know it came from me. Now, are you ready?'

Neil affirmed with vigorous head-nodding and a string of OKs.

'The new lecturer, the one who replaced Spooner.' She paused and fixed Neil's gaze for several seconds. 'The one who beat you and Kel to the job. The one complete with PhD, countless publications in prestigious journals, taller than you and Kel, and tanned. Don't studies show that taller men are more likely to be promoted?'

'On average.'

She paused as Neil walked over to the window.

'Are you listening?'

Neil glanced over his shoulder, nodded.

'He's a fake. Fake references, fake PhD, fake everything. They're keeping it under wraps.'

Neil turned and smiled smugly. 'I know. And there's more.'

'You know? How do you know?'

'Andy told me last week.'

'Weed? How the fuck does he know? It's inside information. Only three people know. Harold told me, and even then I had to wrench the details out of him piece by piece.'

'Three people including you, or –'

'I'll hit you in a minute.'

Neil turned towards her and said offhandedly, 'Apparently the new lecturer walked into Matlock's office and owned up. Didn't give a reason. Matlock thought he was joking. Just walked in and said, "I'm a fake. I'm not a researcher. I don't even have a PhD".'

'Neil, look at me. I didn't realise you were still in contact with Weed? He's dangerous. How does he know so much? Someone's informing. Some insider. That's what Harold thinks.'

'It'll appear in the press soon. Andy hopes it'll go national.'

Rachel looked annoyed. 'You discussed it with him? With Weed?'

'He discussed it with me, that's all. I didn't know until he told me.'

'He discussed it with you?' She raised her eyebrows. 'A one-sided discussion?'

'Discussion essays.'

Rachel wanted elaboration, and Neil added, 'Occasionally I confirm things.'

'Hold on, what do you mean more? You said more earlier.'

Neil hesitated. 'He isn't a real fake.'

'Isn't a real fake? What the fuck do you mean? A fake is a fake.'

'He's a journalist, faking faking, part of the ongoing Rosenhan counter-research. It'll all come out in Andy's next article on fakes.'

'You're avoiding my question. What's your role in all this? Confirming things?'

'I told you, I listen, that's all.'

'You still haven't told me how Weed knows.'

Neil hesitated. 'It's confidential.'

'Confidential.' She laughed mockingly. 'So confidential he told you? Beanbag you.'

'You tell me things.'

'C'mon, we're going for a drink.'

*

Certain he was about to impress Rachel with his insider knowledge, a conclusion facilitated by generous amounts of alcohol supplied by Rachel and an assurance she wouldn't criticise, Neil gave an edited account of the system, how he didn't inform or anything, just offered criticism of research, the kind of criticism found openly in journals and elsewhere.

'You make it easy for him? You still haven't explained the listening.'

'I confirm.'

'So you keep saying. Confirm what? How?'

Neil told Rachel about the informer: meetings in a garage, always in shadow, his uncanny insider knowledge, and pastoral voice.

'And your role in all this?'

'I listen, that's all.'

'What do you mean, listen? You just sit there mute while Weed does all the talking, sorry, discussing? If Weed tells you something, he wants something. Look, I won't criticise, don't worry. We fell about laughing in the English department quoting from Weed's articles, relishing Matlock and Odlum rigid with apoplexy.'

Neil explained Andy's indirect method; what he called confirming by staying silent.

'Confirming? Nice distinction. Matlock would say informing.'

'Not if I say nothing. I don't provide new or additional information.'

'Still informing. If you didn't confirm, Weed wouldn't have a story.'

'Matlock's fond of saying many professions have some system of confidentiality, exempt from everyday moral practice, law and religion, for example. He thinks psychologists should have the same privilege and allowed to deceive subjects in the interest of science. I think it should extend to friendship. Anyway, you're criticising. You –'

'All I'm saying is, be careful. Truth borders on naivety. You could lose your job. Don't you care? Are you that depressed? Andy doesn't care about the truth. Or your job. He's a paparazzi, for Christ's sake. They're all bastards. Paparazzi is Italian for bastard.'

'Paparazzo. I is plural.'

Rachel stared at him.

'As with confetti. Confetto is singular. Or spaghetti, spaghetto is singular.'

'Singular,' she snorted. 'What use is a single piece of confetti? Wouldn't be much of a wedding.'

They laughed together.

Suddenly serious, Rachel said, 'He's still a bastard, singular or plural. Look, I'm trying to help you, Neil, but you're not making it easy.'

Neil wore the expected expression, mixture of gratitude and concern.

'He's using you. One of my feminist students goes on and on about women being treated as sex objects. Finally, I said to her, aren't we all objects of one sort or another, objects to one another? The car salesperson sees a sales object. He/she doesn't care if the car is rubbish or whether you can really afford it. God, this fucking political correctness. Have you ever come across a female car salesperson?' Neil shrugged. 'Nor me. OK, *he* is only interested in selling you a car. Paparazzo Weed only sees a story. He doesn't care about the harm he does, who gets hurt. To him, you and the psychology department are story objects.'

There was a pause while Rachel reflected. 'Not a real fake,' she said to herself. Rachel shook her head and looked towards Neil. 'The problem is, what do I tell Harold?'

Neil's face registered alarm.

'Obviously I won't mention you. But someone must warn him the lecturer's a plant. He thinks he's a genuine fake and plans some sort of cover-up on condition he resigns. Good reference guaranteed. Month's salary in advance. Unless I tell him, he'll press ahead. An attempted cover-up on top of everything else...' She shook her head.

His voice now calm, Neil said, 'Won't he want to know your source?'

'I'll say there's a rumour circulating, or a contact at the *Midland Post*. Let me sort it.' She sighed wearily. 'Now I'm part of the conspiracy. We need to find a way out of this mess. We need to find out who the informer is. Tell me everything you and Weed know about him.'

*

The article appeared in the next edition of the *Midland Post*:

Hoaxgate: fake lecturer fools psychology department, by Andy Seedbank, psychology correspondent.

First fake patients, then fake research subjects, followed by genuine subjects mistaken for fakes. Now a fake lecturer, only revealed when he confessed to the hoax. Hoaxgate goes on.

Furthering our investigation into fakes, a reporter on our staff applied for the post of lecturer in the prestigious but accident-prone Department of Psychology at City Centre University. He was offered the position despite having no relevant qualifications other than an ordinary degree in psychology. The rest he made up.

Our reporter managed to obtain blank degree certificates by pretending he was a chemist researching paper quality to reduce fraud, and registrars at different universities willingly obliged with blanks. All he needed now was a research history, so he adopted the pseudonym David Jones and cited research articles by various David Joneses in the research areas named in the job description.

Jones was no random choice. It is truly amazing how many Joneses there are out there, second only to Smith as the most common name. Years ago, a Welsh choir visited East Germany at the time of the newly built Berlin Wall. Tensions were high. One by one they approached Checkpoint Charlie and most gave the name Jones. The East Germans became suspicious, thought it was a Western hoax and refused entry to the choir. You see, it's all about expectations. You don't expect a large group of people to have the same surname. It defies statistical randomness.

The fake lecturer is reminiscent of the Piltdown Hoax. Around that time there was a race to find the missing link between ape and man, and a 'perfect' specimen, part-ape, part-hominid, materialised at Piltdown gravel pit, buried there by a hoaxer who had crudely attached an ape jaw to a human skull. Long expecting a link to turn up, most eagerly accepted it.

Knowing the psychology department wanted someone who would attract funds, we created our own Piltdown: a dream lecturer complete with Olympian funding record, mountainous research and numerous articles in prestigious journals. Believing they had found the perfect specimen for the job, they fell over themselves offering him the post, adding a senior lectureship within a year when he told them he had three more interviews lined up, one for a senior post.

*

Appearing on local TV, the VC made the usual statement about complete confidence in the psychology department.

'We have tightened recruitment policy, set up a council for academic integrity, and a training programme for all staff. There were clearly weaknesses in the system, and too much trust. We are a trusting organisation, a community of scholars committed to science. You don't expect a fake to arrive at your door sent by a local newspaper.'

'Really? Despite a Niagara of fakes pouring through your door recently.'

'As I said, too much trust.'

'So much trust that you didn't apply for a reference?'

'These things take time. He would have been found out eventually.'

'But it was several weeks before you realised he was a fake, and only then because he confessed. When were you planning to send for a reference? I know it took forty years for Piltdown to be exposed as a hoax, but –'

'These things take time.'

'What about existing staff?'

'I don't follow you.'

'You can't tell real subjects from fakes, or real lecturers from fakes. Maybe most of your lecturers are fakes? Do you plan to check out existing staff?'

The VC refused to answer more questions and went in search of Matlock, fuming when he met up with him. 'Rachel Probender seems to know more than you about what's going on. But for her contacts we would stand accused of an attempted cover-up as well as incompetence. There's an informer in your department and I want him or her found.'

*

Odlum saw the latest hoax further evidence of insider help. The fake lecturer had shown uncanny understanding of the job requirement at interview, giving perfect answers. The informer again. Insecurity spread across the department, fanned by Odlum's paranoia. Odlum blamed gossip. This had always been a key concern for Odlum, mainly staff and students talking about his foibles. 'Too much information is imparted to students, especially in the bar, too much tittle-tattle,' bemoaned Odlum.

Wendy was amused. 'What he means is, people are talking about *him*.'

Stories circulated about Odlum, passed on to each new student intake. He warned each new intake about gossip. 'If you talk about staff, I'll – we'll – know.' Warning students not to talk about him caused them to talk about him, Lemert's famous circularity regarding paranoid schizophrenia.

The top story was the occasion Odlum failed to appear for a seminar. The minutes passed and the students exchanged Odlum stories, such as his strange practice of throwing chalk, and general obsession with chalk. Shrieks of laughter greeted the story, how, one hot day he said to a small group of students, 'Let's have the seminar in the country,' and drove them to a distant field. On the way he could hear them sniggering over a story currently circulating about him, and when they got out, he drove off, leaving them stranded. As their laughter resounded round the seminar room, Odlum sprung out of a cupboard and began the seminar. Noticing their bemused expressions he said, 'Just an ongoing experiment. May as well use students as subjects. You don't mind?' Perhaps an effective way of finding out if the group talked about him, but also a new piece of gossip for circulation.

Shelrack, the evolutionary psychologist, was telling Odlum at a meeting that gossip was evolutionary. 'The equivalent of social grooming and bonding. You can't stop it. Going to the barbers, dry-cleaners, beauty salon, the dentist, are all types of grooming.'

'Like baboons removing dead skin, insects and like objects from each other's fur?' suggested Odlum.

Missing the hint of sarcasm, Shelrack said, 'In a manner of speaking, yes. A sort of social defoliating. I know it's hard to believe, but gossip builds trust, lowers stress and conflict, facilitates alliances and reduces tension. Bonding is a basic evolutionary need, more so for our ancestors perhaps. Gossip and storytelling also made men more attractive to women, in turn spreading their genes. Evolution selected us for gossip.'

'Curious,' said Odlum, 'how gossip seems to have had the opposite effect here, just distrust and disharmony.'

'Someone benefits, some outgroup. People are wired to gossip.'

Odlum smiled knowingly. 'Then I'll un-wire them.'

Convinced that curtailing gossip was the solution, Odlum created a series of posters for circulation about the dangers of loose talk, inspired by some wartime poster seen at the Imperial War Museum and the '80s HIV campaign. Staff were warned about loose talk in the bar, academic meeting or any occasion when the 'enemy' might be present, hinting at the sociologists. Even friends and relatives were suspect:

When you tell a friend
You tell your friend's friend
And eventually you tell
Your enemy.

Wendy was amused. 'Sounds like Milgram's six degrees of separation, or the AIDS' ad some years back. You remember, Neil, when you sleep with someone you sleep with all their partners and their partner's partners, and you end up sleeping with the whole world. Very frightening. Put me off having sex for a time.'

*

Rachel paused, a careful pacing, and said slowly, 'I'm going to tell you something in confidence, something Harold told me. Maybe Harold wants me to tell you, a sort of talking memo.'

'A memo object.'

'Be serious.' She paused again, looked away briefly, and then with levity said, 'You're under suspicion. Odlum's gunning for you. He's convinced you're the informer.'

'I know.'

'Is there anything you don't know? Who told you? Please don't say Weed.'

Neil laughed. 'Only indirectly. His informer. And I noticed the team is a bit cool. Then Wendy said they suspected me. She seemed concerned. "Your critical stance and the Poirot Effect", she said.'

'Poirot?' There was distaste in her tone. 'You're not back to Agatha Christie? I hate Agatha Christie.'

'What about *And Then There Were None*? No Poirot. Considered her masterpiece.'

'OK. That aside, I hate Agatha Christie. Why Poirot Effect?'

'Wherever Poirot turns up you know there's going to be a murder. Whenever I get involved in an experiment, it's sabotaged. Shelrack's on my side. Puts it down to evolution. Our ancestors had little science, saw a coincidence and assumed a cause: "Everything was alright until the strangers came, knuckles scraping the ground". For once, I'm willing to believe Shelrack's Naked Ape unconscious bias psychology. Wendy sees the humour.'

Neil told Rachel how the informer had followed a trail of memos concerning suspects but did not reveal how he obtained them. 'I've always thought the system weak; memos and other documents put in large communal pigeonholes then sorted and distributed by departmental secretaries to individual trays. According to Andy, a series of messages circulated between Matlock and the VC regarding possible suspects, including paranoid messages from Odlum to the VC naming me. All were folded and stapled. Andy said the staples were the giveaway. You might as well print on the front *Top Secret*, as in the espionage films.'

'You say Wendy sees the humour. Harold doesn't see the humour.' She stood up. 'Right, something you *don't* know, even Weed doesn't know. Harold is undecided about you. He recognises Odlum is... well, unreliable his term, meaning two sandwiches short of a picnic; "an unreliable source" his exact description. You won't repeat that, will you? He hinted that I should talk to you. Sound you out.'

'Talk to me?'

Rachel looked troubled. 'Talking memo. Obviously, I was emphatic that you're not the informer; that I would know if you were. But you are 50 per cent informer.'

'More 10 per cent, if that.'

Rachel laughed. 'Let's settle for 20.'

'Fifteen?'

As he reached the door, Rachel said gravely, 'So the Shadow knows you collaborate?'

'All he knows is that management has a list of suspects, including me. I suspect that even if he knew I helped Andy he would protect me at all costs. He values my corroboration.'

'Most comforting.'

*

Neil woke with a start, stared into the void above his bed and began ruminating on his new problem.

Was he an informer?

Rachel's percentage worried him. He decided to focus on the lecturing post and went over what he had said to Andy prior to the hoax, hoping to minimise his contribution. Shortly after the lecturer job was advertised in the

Times Higher Education Supplement Andy had contacted him, curious about the job criteria. What were they looking for? The criteria were too routine and stylised: good team member, ability to engage with and recruit students, innovative teaching, tutorial duties, publications, qualifications, experience, good record attracting research grants, and so on. But what was of greater importance?

'Why do you want to know?'

'A colleague wants to apply, that's all. He'll be most grateful for your advice. I doubt if he has a chance. Of course, if you're applying...'

'Not this time round. Too early. No PhD.' Neil said they wanted someone who had a good research and publication record, someone who could attract funds for research. 'It's all about money. The two go together: he who has a good research and publication record attracts funds, he who attracts funds...' Neil chuckled. 'Tell your colleague, more than anything else, follow the money.'

Some weeks later Neil had got a call from Andy. He sounded excited. 'My colleague got the job. Bit of a surprise.' He paused. 'But you needn't worry.'

'Needn't worry?'

Andy laughed. 'What do you think of the new lecturer?'

'He's a high-flyer. Matlock never stops saying how wonderful he is, a real researcher, at last. Tells you what he thinks of the rest of us.'

'Well, he won't be saying that after today.'

14

That summer, whiteboards replaced blackboards in the psychology department. Odlum showed mixed emotions. Delighted over the disappearance of chalk, and therefore his bugbear blue coated 'alien' chalk, staff noticed a certain wistfulness. 'He's missing throwing chalk at the students under the pretext of doing research... What will he throw at the students now?'

One day Odlum crashed into the staffroom and mounted the stage. He was seething with rage. 'Who's been teaching Ebbinghaus?'

Staff shrugged and continued working.

'Someone here has been teaching Ebbinghaus. I need to know who.'

Dunk looked up and said, 'Who's Ebbinghaus?' This question would have interesting repercussions. Later a memo circulated, and staff learned that someone had 'vandalised' the newly installed whiteboard in the lecture theatre using an 'alien' pen, the single word Ebbinghaus in black permanent ink resistant to cloth or board rubber. A technician was called, bearing a chemical, but couldn't remove the word. 'Sorry, not much we can do,' explained the technician. 'Can't use anything more powerful. Health and safety.'

Odlum obtained a camera from Resources and took several pictures. Odlum was now the protector of white boards. Ebbinghaus, he decided, offered more success than the solitary letter N. Ebbinghaus, he discovered, was a 19th century psychologist who specialised in memory. Who was teaching memory? The answer was no one. Memory was not on any syllabus and most lecturers hadn't heard of Ebbinghaus. He approached Neil, his prime suspect.

Neil shrugged. 'Sounds like a composer.'

'Not a composer, Neil. A nineteenth-century psychologist noted for his work on memory. I would have thought you would know that. Didn't you do any psychology history?'

Bet you've only just looked him up, thought Neil.

*

Some days later, Neil was called to Odlum's office. The heavy angle poise lamp he remembered from the time Odlum deputised for Matlock firmly on his desk, casting his distorted shadow on the back wall. To one side was a white screen. Odlum deftly turned on an overhead projector. A soft hum filled his office. Neil recalled a TV crime investigation, the detectives discussing the evidence, gory pictures and maps. No windows. The screen displayed no gory pictures, just an unfamiliar black and white diagram.

Odlum turned to face Neil.

'Ebbinghaus originated the learning curve and the forgetting curve and measured the speed of forgetting and remembering, but his best work is perception, especially optical illusions.' He grinned excitedly. 'You're wondering about the diagram? The Ebbinghaus illusion of relative size perception. The circles in the centre of the two diagrams are the same size, but we perceive them as different because of the different size outer rings. Rather like the Muller-Lyer Illusion but done long before. Early example of cognitive psychology.'

He switched off the OHP. 'I was looking in the wrong direction, you see. Ebbinghaus also contributed to perceptual illusions. The culprit may have been teaching perception.'

'Is anyone teaching perception?'

'No. That's the problem.'

'Could be a student. The lecture theatre isn't locked.'

'Why should anyone write Ebbinghaus on the board? That word, and nothing else. Bit like the mysterious letter N.' He gave Neil a long look. 'Which brings me to the handwriting.' He showed Neil the photos. 'Of course, you don't teach optical illusions, do you?'

'No. I recently taught Freud in the lecture theatre.'

Neil laughed inwardly at his daring, felt again that exquisite sense of power. Mentioning Freud was an oblique clue, but very oblique. Odlum was still looking in the wrong direction. There was a third possibility, not memory or perception but Freud, a quote from Sulloway's *Freud, Biologist of the Mind*, about how little in Freud was original, almost everything borrowed other than penis envy and castration fear, embarrassing theories discarded by most Freudians. Not memory, not illusions, but a quote from Ebbinghaus on originality: 'What is new in these theories is not true, what is true is not new'. A student had asked Neil how to spell Ebbinghaus. No pens available, he had borrowed one from a student, unaware whiteboards required special pens. Extraordinary coincidence, he thought, damaging two boards, neither act intentional. Then, coincidences happen.

'I'm putting a copy of the handwriting and the Ebbinghaus illusion on the staff and students' noticeboards. Should get a response.'

Neil grinned. 'Like a wanted notice, only no picture.'

*

Perhaps it was the time of year, somewhere in the middle of the long haul from Christmas to the June exams. Spring had arrived early, the students restless. Hoaxing was in the air. They needed a diversion. Ebbinghaus combined with Odlum provided one.

Neil's students were curious about Odlum's 'wanted' notice but said nothing, other than, 'Ebbinghaus, Ebbinghaus, sounds familiar,' followed by loud laughter.

Neil decided to tell his group about Odlum's investigation. He showed them the Ebbinghaus illusion, discussed attempts to explain it and surrounding research. In passing, he mentioned Odlum's fruitless search for the person who taught memory or perception, his mock surprise learning most staff had not heard of Ebbinghaus and faux disgust when one lecturer asked, 'Who is Ebbinghaus?'

This was an unusual group, fun to be with, revelled in jokes. Odlum had covered for him when he was off sick for two weeks with a fractured ankle. After a week, a deputation had called at his flat asking after his health and pleading with him to return, even offering to wheelchair him around the campus. Just before his accident, Neil had been dealing with the tricky question of prediction in everyday life, arguing we are free to choose while much of our behaviour is predictable. Someone asked, 'Isn't that a contradiction?'

Another said, 'Either we are free or not free. You're having it both ways.'

Neil pointed to predictable everyday behaviour. People say the same things, follow the same routines and responses. 'If you say good morning, the predictable response is the same greeting.' He gave the example of personalised seating; how, after the first meeting or two, each student would sit in the same place, as if claiming the seat their own. 'We all do it,' he added, 'an understood, unstated rule. But we don't have to follow these rules, we just do. That allows prediction. But it's not to be confused with cause-and-effect determinism. We don't have to obey rules, so why do we?'

A long discussion followed, and they finally concluded one reason was that we don't want to offend people or be thought rude or difficult.

'In other words, we want to belong, we conform to gain group approval.'

'Why do we want approval?' asked a student. 'Do we choose to want approval?'

The following week he arrived to find the seminar room empty. For a moment he suffered self-doubt, Asch's lines again. The wrong time perhaps? The wrong day? Perhaps they were away on a trip, had told him but he forgot? Strolling over to the window he saw the group outside sitting on the grass. The student who challenged him, saying he was contradictory, grinned as he approached the window. Still grinning and shaking his head, he said, 'You were right, we don't have to obey rules, just thought we'd prove it. QED.'

Soon after discussing Ebbinghaus, posters and signs appeared, covering staff and student noticeboards: *Who is Ebbinghaus? This way to Ebbinghaus*, and a trail of arrows. The most creative was an Art Deco-inspired poster of a twenties band, and the caption: *Coming soon, The Old Ebbinghaus Band, tickets available from John Odlum.* Ebbinghaus lent itself to other products: *For sale. Vintage Ebbinghaus, chrome fenders and chrome window surround. Low mileage. £200 or nearest offer. See John Odlum. Genuine Ebbinghaus Scrumpy Cider. See John Odlum. Hurry while stocks last.* More followed: *Ebbinghaus for chancellor*; *Ebbinghaus is innocent*; *Hands off Ebbinghaus*. Students from other departments wondered who Ebbinghaus was. This inspired *Ebbing who?* badges and t-shirts. Odlum was powerless to stop the campaign, his protests to the Students' Union and the VC met with indifference or amusement. The posters covered the noticeboards, obscuring genuine staff notices, giving Odlum an excuse to act. Adding departmental noticeboards to his area of control, he rushed out a memo to staff stating that department noticeboards were to be replaced with plastic-fronted lockable boards.

The new boards installed, a memo to staff followed from John Odlum, Space Management Committee:

The new cork noticeboards have been installed at considerable cost and this is a golden opportunity to standardise notices. In future, notices must be A6 and white, attached using four drawing pins of uniform shape, size and colour and approved by the Space Management Committee.

Under no circumstance should a member of staff, having forgotten drawing pins, remove pins from other notices or engage in the odious and unsightly practice of using a single drawing pin, resulting in a skewed notice. Notices should be in line, 2cm apart, never touching or overlapping, and 5cm from the noticeboard edge.

Once a notice has been approved by the Space Management Committee, the key to the noticeboards and a ruler can be obtained from the secretariat, signed for and returned forthwith.

A torrent of objections followed, mainly memos and phone calls. Odlum, challenged in corridors, would brush past muttering, 'It didn't come from me.' Odlum called a meeting and denied authorship. 'Are you sure?' someone said half-jokingly (half because Odlum oozed from every word). Odlum speculated and interrogated but got no further than finding that the memos originated from the communal pigeonhole, collected and distributed by the secretaries.

Wendy and Neil were discussing the memo over a drink. She was laughing merrily. 'What's that stuff about implicit personality theory?' She touched his arm. 'Don't tell me,

I remember. People believe traits go together. The warm/cold variable. It's coming back to me. You give a list of traits to two groups that describe someone. The lists are the same, but one list includes "cold", the other "warm". The groups are asked to underline those traits they think describe the person. The "cold" group underlines more negative traits than the "warm" group. Explains why so many believed the memo came from Odlum. It fits, fits everything: the chalk, the cupboard, his controlling. Traits go together.'

'His plastic arm?'

In there somewhere, I'm sure.'

15

'I heard there's a sabotage problem over in biology,' Matlock was saying. 'Experiments going wrong. So it's not just us.'

'Resolved,' said Odlum. 'They identified the culprit.'

'Really? Not the same –'

'No connection. Traced the problem to the biology storeroom.'

The head storekeeper in biology was off sick and an assistant had taken over who was lazy, often disappeared, and failed to supervise a work experience student on work placement. The student, fifteen and a mere child, was assigned to stacking shelves and giving out supposedly pure chemicals to researchers; 'supposedly pure' because he too liked to 'experiment', the chemicals a glorified chemistry set. He would pour mercury onto the table, fascinated by the strange liquid, shaping it this way and that, watch as it mingled with dirt and other impurities, finally returning it to its container. He mixed other chemicals, sometimes with alarming results. Some powders and liquids would get mixed up, unsure which bottles they came from, and handed out to the researchers resulting in inexplicably failed and ruined experiments. It was one of those situations where a set of coincidences combine to create a whole, a gestalt. Take out one piece…

'All because of a spotty, uncontrolled variable lurking in the storeroom, unaware what damage he was doing. Thinking of uncontrolled variables…' Odlum switched to making the case against Neil. 'Take research. He's more interested in what's wrong with a study than what's right.'

'Perfectionist?' offered Matlock.

Odlum shook his head. 'Self-handicapping. Excuse for inertia. He talks eloquently about blinds, knowing the cost prohibitive. Self-handicapping. Recently, I said to him, if we listened to you, Neil, no research would get done. He laughed at me and said, "Maybe it shouldn't be done. Save the taxpayer money. Spend it on prosthetic limbs". That line, incidentally, is in Seedbank's article.'

Matlock was skeptical. 'Save taxpayer money and spend it on something useful is a widespread phrase. Tabloid clichés.'

'OK, but the ideas expressed in the articles are Neil's. I asked someone in Linguistics to compare a paper by Neil and one of Andy's articles. They identified many stylistic similarities.'

Matlock shrugged. 'We all borrow from each other, draw on the same sources. They did the same degree.'

'He hasn't completed his thesis.'

'Kel only recently completed his.'

'Kel is progressing. Neil is research inactive, finds fault in every ongoing research project. You've said so yourself. And Neil's research is focused on attitudes, less on situations. No coincidence he's researching dogmatism.'

'Combined with situation, mainly at the group level.'

'He has a thing about authority. He's an untidy corner of the department. The question is, is he a contributor or an isolationist? He chose to work alone when taken on. He has the wrong attitude.'

'But that was a choice freely given by me. I created the situation.'

Odlum had approached Neil after Neil's interview with Matlock. 'Most staff prefer to join a team. Mucking in. Are you sure you've made the right decision? Are you sure you want to be an individualist, isolated, alone, following your own path, your own drumbeat?' Neil said he was sure. Odlum was insistent. 'It's your choice, Neil, and if you want to be an isolate, I can't stop you.'

'You know he expected his own office? I explained why we got rid of individual offices, the advantages of open plan, no barriers or partitions, open teams mucking in. An office is claustrophobic, isolating, incubates paranoia. "Then why have the sociologists still got offices?" he asked.'

Matlock was amused. 'Valid point. Don't we both have offices, John? Doesn't make us paranoid. Senior staff are keeping their offices, don't forget that. There's nothing wrong with individual offices, but we needed the space, you forget that. Anyway, the sociology tower block isn't designed for open plan. It's mostly small offices.'

Ignoring these points, Odlum ploughed through his list, a huge mud pie ages in the making to throw at Neil, hoping some would stick. He told how Neil joked about the damaged chalkboards; how the Ebbinghaus posters probably came from a group he taught, no doubt shaped by him; his attachment to Goffman, more sociologist than psychologist, and how he spent more time with Rachel Probender and the sociologists than with his psychology colleagues.

'He's currently researching the sociologists.'

'But it all adds up. Too many coincidences make a fact. None of it proof in itself, in isolation, but combined... Take Rachel Probender. Isn't she researching *Frankenstein*? An anti-science novel. Another coincidence?'

'Getting back to the informer, none of this explains the hospital list. Neil couldn't have access to that, you said so yourself. Only you know the combination to your safe.' He laughed. 'You would need an Enigma codebreaker to get past your security.'

'Yes. But he showed unusual interest in the safe when I gave him a photo-card recently.'

Matlock swung round to face him. 'No. I'm not convinced. Possible but not probable. At most it would explain some of the content of Seedbank's articles.'

'I'm certain he is in contact with Seedbank. It fits.'

'Motive?' said Matlock.

'Who knows how a warped mind works. What motivated the Piltdown hoaxer? Whatever, Neil is uncooperative and out of control.'

'The question is, who controls Neil?'

'Neil controls Neil,' said Odlum tersely. 'And that's the problem. We need to call him in.'

There was a pause as Matlock deliberated.

'The sabotage is creating insecurity,' Odlum added with gravity. 'We need to be seen doing something. The VC...'

'Better call everyone in, then,' advised Matlock. 'Don't want Neil to think he's being victimised. Union, and all that.'

*

Alone in his office, Matlock reflected on what Odlum had said about Neil. Uncooperative to Odlum meant not doing what Odlum wanted. Odlum criticised everyone, criticised him to other staff, saying he did all the work. Odlum was a threat to everyone. He recalled a discussion with Shelrack. 'We all have an innate sense of hierarchy, an inborn disposition to obey, enhancing the stability of the pack and reducing conflict.' Yes, but it was more complex than that. Obedience and conformity were also honed and shaped by social factors, the family, school and work. We are shaped by rules and expectations, by each other. Above all, by situations.

Anyway, wasn't cooperation relative? He recalled a study of American soldiers captured during the Korean War who refused to cooperate with the enemy. Treated as heroes on release, a researcher found they were uncooperative before capture. They were just uncooperative people. Other soldiers, models of cooperation, became model prisoners on capture, cooperating with the enemy, even converting to communism. On release they were castigated as traitors or excused as brainwashed. Why did most of Asch's subjects not conform? Why did some of Festinger's subjects change their behaviour rather than rationalise? Why did some obedience subjects disobey in situations where obedience was strongest? Cooperation, conformity and obedience were complex issues.

Matlock thought about his own obedience: years of submission and compliance, his ideas stolen by superiors, his silent rage, his slow rise through the system, his appropriation of others' ideas, particularly students and research assistants. But Odlum had a point. Neil didn't fit at all well; didn't defer, was too much of an agent only to himself. So why did he favour Neil for promotion?

*

Neil wondered where he would be sitting: confrontation, negotiation, equals. All week staff had been interviewed by Matlock and Odlum about the sabotage.

'He'll see you now,' the secretary said, smiling.

Neil faced Matlock and Odlum. Matlock leaned forward and smiled at Neil while Odlum stared impassively, one elbow on the table. There was an awkward pause and Neil glanced at Matlock who leaned back and said, 'We're very worried.' Pause. 'Do you know why we are very worried?'

Neil went through the usual routine, ending with cuts.

'Yes. We are worried about cuts. We should all be worried about cuts. Next year Blair will introduce tuition fees. The graduate population is growing and becoming expensive. The government emphasises practical courses and the so-called hard sciences. He leaned forward. 'Being more specific, more specifically, we are worried about you, worried *for* you.'

A long pause and Neil tensed himself for something disagreeable.

'There's a rumour about that you are informing,' said Odlum bluntly, cutting the silence.

'Of course, John and I know it to be untrue,' added Matlock hurriedly, 'but your connection to Seedbank...'

Neil surveyed the office. No window; no fire escape as in Holly's flat in *Breakfast at Tiffany's*, a symbol, according to Rachel, of her impermanence and escape. Door closed. No calls Matlock told his secretary as Neil entered the office. Asch might have approved: no opportunity to confer with colleagues, two against one increasing conformity. The flaw, of course, was that he knew the purpose, aware and therefore contaminated, had conferred with colleagues interviewed earlier, and only a third of Asch's subjects conformed anyway, and some later replications, one British, found no conformity. He could have brought a union rep or a friend, but felt it unwise making the meeting too formal, he piggy-in-the-middle of some battle over correct procedure, interpreting the 'rule book'.

They talked about the informer, referred to as 'some Luddite'. 'We have a Luddite in our midst who smashes experiments,' said Odlum.

Eventually Neil said, 'What has this got to do with me, exactly?' He wondered a moment why he added the word exactly.

'As we said, your connection to Seedbank. That makes you special.'

'Special?'

'Have you met Seedbank recently?' asked Odlum.

Neil shook his head a touch uncertainly, worried they might have been seen together. The pub they went to was the other side of town, close to Andy's flat. He suspected bluffing. But if they had been seen...

'Just piecing together information,' soothed Matlock. 'Contact with Seedbank could be useful. Have you thought of making contact, sounding him out?'

'Some of what Seedbank says in his articles echoes your own ideas,' said Odlum. Neil detected slight menace in his voice but balanced by Matlock's sideways glance and grimace.

'We were friends at university and did the same course. Bound to have similar ideas.'

'Exactly,' said Matlock. 'You know his way of thinking. You see your value?'

'He's a reporter. He does what reporters do.' Then slowly, for emphasis, 'His *situation*. I don't like reporters, paparazzi, but don't we all operate within constraints, the situation we find ourselves in?' Neil's voice had risen slightly.

Matlock's voice was velvety. 'We're not accusing you of anything, Neil.' He looked at Odlum whose nod was minimal. 'Things are just a bit circumstantial: Seedbank, your attitude towards psychology. See this as an opportunity to clear up any doubts.'

Neil laughed. 'Eliminating me from your enquiries? As I said, I haven't seen Andy Seedbank in a long while.'

He was gambling. If seen together his lie would support conspiracy, but saying they were in contact would fare no better. He would be asked who Andy's informant was and have to say he didn't know, didn't discuss such things. It wouldn't ring true. From the periphery of his eye Neil noticed Odlum's long gaze, iris of each eye firmly centred, pointedly infringing the eye contact rule, Goffman's delicate balance of showing attention and inattention, delivering the message: you are a liar and an informer unworthy of Goffman's civil inattention.

*

Shortly after the meeting with Matlock and Odlum, on route to meeting Andy, Neil became aware he was being observed. There are studies on whether we know when we are being observed, all inconclusive, and no strong evidence of a sixth sense, though Shelrack speculated about an evolutionary warning system deep inside our reptilian brain, the cerebellum. Neil suspected it was more about broken patterns, such as Goffman's example of looking at someone too long and making them an object of special curiosity, broken patterns that fuel the belief in intuition. He recalled a documentary about MI5. To successfully follow someone requires several people, rather like passing the baton in a relay, unlike fictional accounts which necessarily simplify. One Odlum, known to Neil, was bound to fail, especially as he ducked into doorways or pretended to look in shop windows whenever Neil paused to cross a road. Taking full advantage of the evolved human ability to rotate the eyeball round the socket without moving the head, Neil caught these strange movements unseen. Too distant to see Odlum's face, he had drawn on other clues. Everyone has his own shape or walk, Odlum very tall, neck elongated, arms and legs long, trousers too short, perhaps too mean to have them made-to-measure, shirt cuffs struggling to reach his wrists, the sort of evidence cherished by Dunk. Bizarrely, Odlum had recently participated in an identity parade comprising nine lookalikes, and Neil had tried to imagine a long row of Odlums.

Neil was uneasy. Had Odlum somehow learned he was meeting Andy, if not the venue, overheard him talking to Andy on the phone? They had discussed the day and time, the venue understood. In future he would take circuitous routes or vary venues. Neil entered a bookshop and watched as Odlum stood in front of a shop opposite observing the bookshop reflected in the shop's window, waiting for him to re-emerge, unaware the shop had a back entrance. Neil chuckled inwardly. Odlum would have a long wait. He was exhilarated, shades of Watergate, and looked forward to telling Andy.

Neil became careful on the phone, calling Andy only when the staffroom was empty, until one day, while on the phone he saw a stationary figure in the dimly lit corridor outlined through the frosted glass panel of the staffroom door. Opening the door, he found Odlum on tiptoe, and seeing Neil he began moving forward pretending he was passing by, rather like a badly timed actor's cue on some low budget soap. Perhaps Odlum had a tape recorder hidden in a cupboard or some other hiding place. Increasingly insecure, he resolved to confine calls to Andy from home.

Andy was pleased by Neil's problem. 'Definitely Watergate,' he said, making notes on the difficulty of following someone and attendant research.

'Your next article?'

'Maybe. You remember how Woodward panicked one night approaching the car park, and began running?' Neil noticed the excitement in his voice. 'Odlum wouldn't be able to follow me. I would take three taxis.'

'Expensive?'

'Expenses.'

16

Koestler's *The Act of Creation* was Neil's inspiration to study psychology. Passionate, eloquent and persuasive, the book puts forward a theory of creativity, arguing it combines hitherto unrelated ideas by sudden insight, such as Archimedes' eureka experience, creating a new whole, and introduced Neil to holistic psychology and Kohler's insight learning using apes. He could still recall the excitement, the revelatory experience, as Koestler demolished Watson's and Skinner's extreme behaviourism which denied goals, intention and mind.

A banana is placed outside a cage out of reach of the ape. Inside the cage is a stick of insufficient length to reach the fruit, but sufficient to reach a longer stick outside the cage and out of reach. After a time, the ape makes the connection, uses the shorter stick to draw the longer stick into the cage which it uses to reach the banana. Moving to people, Koestler gives various examples, such as Gutenberg's inspirational printing press, an amalgam of moveable metal type and the screw press used to crush grapes or olives, separate until one day making the connection watching a wine press. But the creative act, Koestler was keen to emphasise, does not grow in a vacuum, out of nothing; it reshuffles, recombines, synthesises. Gutenberg also had the 'prepared mind', a lifetime grappling with the problem of speeding up printing, called by Koestler the incubation period. "The whole is greater than its parts", said Koestler, "two and two make five".

Rachel was unimpressed. 'All said long before Koestler.' She lifted down *Frankenstein* and turned to Mary Shelley's introduction. "Invention, it must be humbly admitted, does not consist in creating out of the void, but out of chaos; the materials must, in the first place, be afforded: it can give form to dark, shapeless substances..." See, all said long before your Koestler.'

'She doesn't say synthesis.'

'Doesn't need to. Implicit. So much of your psychology insists on making the implicit explicit.'

'So implicit it's invisible to all but the literary critic.'

Neil and Rachel had laboured long hours trying to work out the informer's identity. Rachel, treating departmental staff as characters in a novel, got nowhere until Neil had his eureka experience. Neil likened it to trying to remember a word. You try everything, go through the alphabet letter by letter, add vowels to each letter, but it still eludes you. Then in some unguarded, relaxed moment, the word appears from nowhere fully shaped, highlighted, uppercased and underlined. OK, Neil's intuition was less than Gutenberg's contribution, less than the printing press, a point made by Rachel, peeved by Neil's insight:

'More Kohler's ape than Gutenberg.'

'Better than Odlum's efforts,' retorted Neil.

She laughed. 'Odlum's not even at the ape stage.'

Neil's relaxed moment came the day he had drunk more than usual one lunchtime and taught the students through a pleasant haze, the lecture theatre in soft focus. The subject of his lecture was Goffman's non-person which Neil illustrated through examples collected over the years: the fake window dressers who stripped out an expensive window display at an Oxford Street store in front of customers and staff, put the items into a standard container (also property of the store), and wheeled it to a van parked nearby. The only description: male and wore brown warehouse coats. His favourite was the Irish nationalists who 'liberated' paintings by an Irish artist from a London gallery. They arrived in a van and said they were collecting the paintings for an exhibition, even employing a camera operator to film the theft, telling him they were making a film about a theft of paintings. The description was similarly limited: males, dressed in uniforms, the one in charge had an Irish accent.

'Using the front door aided the deception, behaviour more likely to pass unnoticed. "No mask like open truth to cover lies, as to go naked is the best disguise". We take little notice of workers and others in uniform, seeing through them and over them.' He drew on Rachel's literary example from the Brontës: '"A private governess has no existence... It seemed as if they gazed on vacancy". Each day we encounter non-persons: caretakers, maintenance staff, and cleaners. Sufficient to note uniforms or tools and a brief explanation, such as, "Come to check the..." They are present but not as stage performers, not part of the team and easily ignored, left to get on with their background duties, themselves background, fixing or erecting staging for the main performance. They sneak about, use back entrances and goods lifts, have their own back rooms we fear to enter. They may be deliberately invisible, self-effacing, such as waiters. People often talk freely in front of them, forget they are there, treat them as non-persons.'

Neil asked the students for examples, and one said she was addressed one day by a man in the street but failed to recognise him. It was the local postman out of uniform. 'I apologised but he laughed and told me it happened all the time.' Someone had a similar experience with a decorator who wore white overalls and a white hat all the time he decorated her house. One day he arrived at the door in a suit, and she wondered who he was. 'Could non-persons gain entry and take over a nuclear power station? How secure are they? If you saw a group in white boiler suits spattered with paint carrying tool bags, you wouldn't suspect IRA terrorists about to plant a bomb.'

Neil organised the class into discussion groups, and he thought again about the informer. There was little to go on. Odlum doggedly pursued his *idée fixe* that Neil was the culprit, Andy, similarly tram-lined, was convinced it must be a disgruntled highly placed faculty member, a professor or the vice-chancellor, raising the status of his investigations to scoop level. That moment Neil had his eureka experience. Why not a non-person informer? Someone lowly? Maintenance perhaps? Lower still, a cleaner? All had keys to offices.

Engrossed in the problem, he detached from the class, only dimly aware of someone asking at one point, 'You all right, Neil?'

'Keys,' he replied absently.

Having grudgingly accepted that the informer could be a non-person, Rachel asked teasingly, 'What would Holmes do? Better scientist than all you psychologists put together. He wouldn't be deterred by a paucity of clues; one or two clues sufficient. A handwritten list, once crumpled, educated accent, cathedral voice more than enough for his inductive-deductive method.'

'Holmes is fictional, and his creator had the advantage of knowing the culprit and working backwards, planting the clues as he went. Explain the handwritten list.'

Rachel's sigh was patronising. 'Elementary, my dear Neil. Reasoning backwards from result to cause, a draft crumpled and carelessly tossed in a waste bin. Didn't you say some names had been crossed out? People are careless about what they put in waste bins.'

'You're right. A waste bin is a negative, full of rubbish. Fits Whorf's theory of linguistic determinism.' Neil began explaining Whorf's linguistic theory, but Rachel cut him short.

'For your non-person, read cleaner.'

'Right again. The only outsider with access to Odlum and Matlock's bins inside locked offices, inaccessible to all but cleaners. A cleaner, and the careless disposal of drafts.'

'And cleaners do their work before other staff arrive. You rarely see them. The most invisible non-persons. Definitely a cleaner.'

Neil leaned back and shook his head. 'There's a problem. The informer is knowledgeable, understands psychology, with an educated voice and a command of English. Andy put it well: "One of Bernstein's elaborated code users, able to explicate finer meanings to a stranger in an underground garage in the twilight hours".'

'Is that in-group Bernstein code crap necessary?' Rachel said irritably. 'And horribly stereotyping. Haven't I taught you anything? Forget psychology –'

'Sociology, to be precise. Bernstein is a sociologist.'

'Forget all your fucking ologies. Think Charlotte Brontë: "A private governess has no existence… is less than nothing". Remember the quote? But inside Charlotte was a seething creativity bursting to come forth, an original mind of great intelligence. Your cleaner-informer might be self-educated, a budding author or a weekend non-conformist lay preacher reciting the Holy Scriptures, or a shop steward by night buried in Marxist tomes by guttering candle. My advice, start with the library. If he is a self-educating cleaner, he surely borrows books.'

'Some atypical cleaner borrowing books on psychology. That's brilliant. We must see Miss Blenkinsop. Get a list of unlikely borrowers.'

'You, not me.'

Rachel related her latest conflict with Miss Blenkinsop, the librarian. She had ordered a biography of Mary Wollstonecraft. Passing the issue desk a week later, an assistant called her over and said, 'That book you ordered. Oh, I can't remember the author's name, Stone something or other –'

'Woll-stone-craft.'

'Miss Blenkinsop phoned the publisher and was told it cost £200. Well…'

'I told her the book couldn't possibly cost £200. She got out the card, and written against the book were the words, *collected works*. Apparently, I'd given her the wrong ISBN. I was being helpful, sorting out the ISBN for fuck's sake. I explained I wanted the biography – cost a mere £8.50. A few days later I ran into Miss Blenkinsop. Did you clear up the confusion over the book? I asked. She glared at me, you know, that laser glare. "*Your* confusion, Ms Probender, not mine". She stalked away, catching up with me minutes later. "Frankly, Ms Probender, I think you should borrow on interlibrary. This is a period of cuts". Her voice was cold and seething hostility. No one can say the word "cuts" like her. I'm sure she hates me. It occurred to me we can't all borrow on interlibrary. Someone had to buy books or there would be no books to borrow, but I decided not to say it.'

'Not like you, Rachel. You know she's had her capitation cut.'

'What's that got to do with it? Why are you sympathising? Are you saying she has no capitation?'

'No.'

'Well then.'

As he was leaving, Rachel said, 'How will you persuade Miss Blenkinsop?'

'I shall approach her in one of my many disguises. A researcher, perhaps.'

Rachel laughed. 'For you, that would be a disguise.'

*

Neil arrived early to observe the cleaners. Above the staffroom was a balcony facing the staffroom and stage area. Most of the seats long removed, it was now used for storage. Secure in the shadows, he had a panoramic view of the staffroom and 'stage'. The latter was long converted into two side-by-side offices, Matlock's and Odlum's, explaining their puzzling elevation and access either side by short flights of steps once leading to the stage. To the front of the stage, originally the stalls, was the psychology staffroom comprising partitioned desks.

The cleaners were permanent staff, having access to all the offices, including Matlock's and Odlum's, and he watched as they emptied the waste bins, placing the contents in black plastic bags. Immediately there was a problem: the Shadow was male and they were all female. Clutching to his theory, he recalled Popper: no matter how many instances of white swans we observe, that does not prove all swans are white. There could be a male cleaner, on holiday or off sick, his theory that the saboteur was a cleaner not yet disproved. At least he solved the mystery of the artificial perfume that pervaded the staffroom each day. Staff often moaned about the nauseating smell. The cleaners departed, and he was sitting at his desk in the general staffroom when the main door opened a few inches and a hand appeared clasping an aerosol emitting a long blast of spray that wafted across the room. Later Neil approached her and asked if she would desist from spraying in future as some staff were allergic.

The black plastic bags were stacked against a wall, each tagged with a room number. 'Follow the money', Deep Throat's advice to Woodward. Neil understood he must follow the bags if he hoped to locate the informer. Where did they go? Valhalla for bags. A female cleaner appeared with a trolley and began wheeling them away. Neil followed. The university was large, 15,000 students, sprawling buildings added over the years, mezzanine floors, walkways, stairwells and bridges connecting buildings. He followed her scenic, roller-coaster route culminating in a long corridor, one side science labs, the other continuous plate-glass windows looking out on various ad hoc buildings, mismatch of architectural forms. She stopped before a security lift operated by a coded keypad and tapped in the password. The lifts were strange here, a mystery to visitors. The ground floor started at level seven, a number continuation from an earlier building nearby, which numbered one to six. The lift descended and he scurried down a green spiral staircase in pursuit, slightly giddy on reaching the bottom. She was nowhere in sight. The lift must have continued to the basement, inaccessible by stairs at this point. Next time he would get into the lift with the cleaner.

She seemed surprised as Neil jumped into the lift as the doors were closing. 'Short cut to the basement library,' he explained. 'You don't mind?' Looking at the bags he said, 'I've often wondered where all the rubbish goes.'

'Not rubbish anymore. Not officially. Recycling. I'm taking it to the Waste Disposal Room in the library basement, officially the In-house Shredding and Baling Recycling Station. They do think up some names. I'm told some of it's baled and sent away to be made into toilet paper.'

'From scrap paper to crap paper. Strange to think that our toilet paper could be someone's memos or a telephone book.'

She laughed.

'Who does the shredding?'

'Milbro Smith, the head shredder. Why 'head' I don't know. There's no one else. Officially he's called the shredding and baling coordinator. Shred for short. He controls the shredder, baling machines and pallet trucks. Only he is allowed to operate the machines. Security or safety, or something. It's been stepped up of late. If you're interested, I'll show you around.'

Neil walked with her to the In-house Shredding and Baling Recycling Station. It was locked. Above the handle was the latest keypad lock. On the door was a prominent notice: *No admittance. Authorised personnel only*, which seemed superfluous if it was locked to the non-authorised. She produced a piece of paper containing the code, tapped in the number and opened the door. 'Shred's doing the rounds collecting the confidential waste from the VC. Collects it personally. Load of fuss if you ask me. Have a look round while I'm unloading.' She moved towards a large plastic bin and began throwing in the black bags.

Neil noticed other piles of waste, dwarfing the black bags, some on pallets, more in square plastic bins. One of the bins stood alongside a conveyor belt, which was part loaded with various documents: minutes of past management meetings, computer printouts, memos, lever arch files. One pile of lever arch files, heavily warped, showed the familiar East Light motif, recognisable as Matlock's obedience files. So he's finally put them on disk, thought Neil. He was tempted to open one, recalling the data could only be released after 50 years, but thought the cleaner might object.

He turned to the cleaner. 'Do the lever arch files go in whole?'

She nodded. 'It's a powerful machine, not called a Hercules for nothing. Cost a fortune. You should see it working.'

Neil's gaze roamed the machine. The conveyor belt fed material to a funnel or chute set upon a central structure about 10 feet above the ground. Below was a large boxed-in assembly containing the pre-shredder blades and powerful magnets to remove metals. Neil recalled a documentary about the occupation of the American embassy during the Iranian Revolution. Before leaving the embassy, thousands of documents were shredded, but the Iranian Government employed carpet weavers to reassemble them by hand. But not this shredder. A horizontal conveyor belt at ground level led from the box to the shredder, adjustable to different security levels, including an anti-espionage micro cut level four. These were minute particles, 3,000 bits per sheet compared to the standard 34 vertical strip office shredder, and no possibility of un-shredding. Once shredded to the desired security level, a chain conveyor fed the paper into a pressing container.

There was a time when almost all waste was simply baled and recycled, and the few sensitive documents, such as confidential files, burned in the furnaces which heated the water system. A change of fuel coincided with data protection legislation. At first, shredding was done on small machines by secretaries, but growing paperwork, both actual and anticipated, and security lapses, real or imagined, called for a single industrial shredder, a Hercules Integrated Shredder, the answer to all security leaks. Neil was unconvinced. No matter how minutely shredded, 3,000 bits, 5,000 bits, one million bits, the space between placing a document in a waste bin and shredding was surely a weak link. How long did the black bags lie around before shredding? The crumpled list had escaped the Hercules shredder, one tiny but important piece of paper amongst the tonnes disposed of weekly. And how secure was the code the cleaner had written on a slip of paper?

The cleaner was ready to leave. Passing some shelves, Neil vaguely noticed from the corner of his eye a Wedgwood blue spiral folder, similar in size to a lecturer's A5 diary.

'Before you go, why do you tag the bags with room numbers?'

'Milbro insists. Seems pointless to me.'

As Neil was leaving, he turned and said, 'One last question: are there any male cleaners on the staff?'

Her laugh was quizzical. 'Not to my knowledge. Why, do you want the job?'

*

Neil delayed meeting Miss Blenkinsop for over a week, explaining to Rachel he was deliberating on how to approach her.

Rachel mocked him. 'Thought you were going to pretend to be a researcher? You're scared of her. Shit scared. You are, aren't you?'

He knew he couldn't ask Miss Blenkinsop outright for information about staff, her response all too predictable. 'Confidential, Mr Denton, you of all people should know about confidentiality, a researcher no less. We are all bound by the same rules, even humble librarians.'

Her precise manner of speech, shushing, sensible shoes, defensiveness, rigidity, devotion to her waterlily pond, spinster existence, fastidiousness, and directness bordering on rudeness, was no surprise to new staff and students – only to be expected of a stereotypical librarian. No, the surprise was her off-centre attire, and stories surrounding her vitriolic swearing.

When the whiteboards began arriving to replace blackboards, she scowled out of her window disapprovingly, adding whiteboards to her long list of objections, such as renaming the library the Resources Centre and introducing computers. Only that week, a delivery man, unsure where to go, had strayed into the library carrying a whiteboard, approached Miss Blenkinsop and said, 'Where do I put the whiteboard?'

Her rage uncontrollable, she spat, 'You can take your fucking whiteboard and put it up your arse.'

When humps were installed in the car park, stoking her to a fury, she fired off a memo about the effect on her boobs which 'jumped up and down.' Neil often found himself signing one of her many petitions. One glorious summer day, the library windows open, students mingling outside on the grass and on benches, she called some across and handed out a petition. One student, eating an ice cream, spat some onto the petition, screwed it up and handed it to her, grinning broadly, no doubt believing her a safe and easy target, bound by her librarian role. Opening it out very deliberately as he grinned across, she called him to the window. Still grinning, he went up to her. 'Come closer,' she said. Still covered in ice cream, she rubbed the petition in his face. The other students thought this hilarious, and no complaint was made.

She constantly called for quiet, staff and students obliged to speak in whispers even when talking to her. On one occasion, Neil was discussing a book with her, and she hissed, 'Please keep your voice down.' Neil knew he had a better relationship with Miss Blenkinsop than Rachel did; she liked him, and sometimes treated him as a confidant, such as explaining her choice of a new assistant librarian, telling Neil she had excluded an applicant who lived in Devon.

Neil was baffled. 'Devon?'

'Because someone who lives in a place as beautiful as Devon would not want to work here,' she explained.

Around the library were 'special collections', as she called them, for her favourite staff, including a shelf devoted to clock-making. The Art Deco fashion collection was impressive, rows of weighty illustrated tomes collected by someone in computing. Lily pond maintenance was her own exclusive ensemble.

Neil did not have a specific collection, had no need for one, as she never refused a request for individual works. Despite showing favouritism, she was ruthlessly 'democratic' in public, staff and students treated equally, such as sending reminders to everyone regarding overdue books and demanding payment for those lost, regardless of status. On a third request, they were countersigned by the VC, who occasionally countersigned requests to himself, which greatly amused him. She relentlessly pursued staff for payment of lost books. Dunk had a book stolen and objected to paying. Requests followed, which he ignored. Requests were dittoed to Matlock. She badgered Dunk whenever they met, library assistants were instructed to call her whenever he entered the library, and she would confront him. Reaching the long summer vacation, he believed he had won, a new academic year and a new start, but returning found a memo in his tray demanding the book or payment. He paid.

No tweed skirt or droopy jumper attired Miss Blenkinsop. She favoured flowing, loose-fitting clothes reminiscent of a distant era, together with long strands of beads or pearls. Rachel was scathing. 'Looks like a flapper. All that's missing is the rouge lipstick and sexy pucker.' Neil thought her more late sixties than twenties, the sixties Miss Blenkinsop's era, an idea supported by a huge tome in the private collection of the computer professor called *The Sixties Art Deco Revival: Louise Brooks to Vidal Sassoon*, which argued that the early sixties drew heavily on the Art Deco era, the late sixties Art Nouveau. Watching her from a distance, Neil marvelled at her idiosyncratic flowing style, a three-quarter length dress with added material that flapped as she moved around the library; vibrant cacophony of flowers and colours, red tights, shoes admittedly comfortable (deference to past fashion than function), hair short ('Bobbed,' said Rachel with equal venom), held in place by a floral band tied at the back and pulled forward partially covering the band and completely covering her ears. Dunk had little difficulty recognising her.

His voice a whisper, Neil was explaining his latest research interest to Miss Blenkinsop, specifically social class and reading. This was his ruse to gain access to confidential information on non-academic staff. Only at a tentative stage, he explained, a pilot. Yes, confidentiality guaranteed. His voice more a murmur, he said, 'Could I see the borrowing records of staff?'

Miss Blenkinsop stepped back. 'Shouldn't you ask them first, Mr Denton? The ethical code –'

'If I want to include anyone, of course I'll contact them then. The research may come to nothing.'

'Class, you say.' She tut-tutted. 'A singularly dangerous topic, if you don't mind my saying, a topic bursting with stereotypes.'

Neil hurriedly ad-libbed. His research wasn't class as such but exceptions. 'The main thrust of my research is the class exception, challenging the stereotypes created by,' he paused for effect, 'the sociologists,' aware of her disdain for the Marxist Henry Hollow.

Miss Blenkinsop nodded appreciatively. 'Take Milbro Smith, responsible for shredding and baling, hardly says a word, goes about his business unnoticed, but a passion for theology. Perfect for your research I would have thought.'

They had halted before a huge collection of works on moral theology, noticeably Milton's *Paradise Lost*. 'That's Milbro Smith's private collection. By rights he should not be ordering books, but as he was once a man of the cloth...' They moved on as she added offhandedly, 'He's also interested in psychology.'

Making a Herculean effort to contain his excitement, and falling in with Miss Blenkinsop's pattern of speech, a mark of deference identified by psychological research and certain she would pick it up, albeit unconsciously, Neil said, 'Mr Smith sounds singularly interesting.'

Neil obtained the list of Milbro Smith's reading, along with other staff of varying status to maintain the deception. Who would have thought of shredders and balers? Blessed are the shredders and balers, as much unknown as invisible, there but not there, most staff unaware the shredding and baling coordinator existed: the perfect non-person. Later that day he looked up job descriptions of shredders and balers, found in past copies of *The Times Higher Education Supplement*. The range of duties gave access to all kinds of sensitive information along with keys and codes.

'Before you go, Mr Denton, perhaps you would be so kind as to sign my petition.'

*

Neil had just recounted the evidence to Rachel.

'Is that all? A shredder operator who reads theology, was once a vicar (fits the religious voice), has access to confidential waste and keys. Opportunity, I grant you, but no motive. Something for a *how*dunit, not enough for a whodunit, nothing for a *why*dunit.' She laughed at Neil's dejected expression. 'I'm impressed, really. Really. On a spectrum of one to 10, I'd give it five.'

'Seven, surely? You're forgetting his interest in psychology.'

She nodded slowly.

'You agree seven?'

She laughed. 'Six. Circumstantial evidence only.'

'Anyway, how important is motive? What is motive? Maybe the saboteur does it for fun or is just bored. Does he know his motive? Do any of us know our motives? We just do things because we want to, like what we like. We don't know why.'

Later that afternoon Neil remembered the Wedgwood blue folder in the recycling station and recalled seeing a pile of Wedgwood blue A5 folders in Selena's consulting room weeks earlier. At the time he was struck by the unusual colour and classical Greek motif, as much pottery as folders. It was the first time Selena had allowed him into her consulting room, maintaining distance by standing behind a barricading desk, and he'd joked about the layout and decor: no couch covered with Oriental rug, no figurines. Noticing his interest in the folders, she explained they were therapy diaries, specially made for her clients. Then he remembered the elastic bands, stored in a nearby jar, also Wedgwood blue. It was several moments before he realised Milbro Smith must be one of Selena's clients. Selena often discussed her patients with Neil. No names, of course. One puzzled her. He worked at the university but dropped therapy. Seemingly a trauma case, he was having difficulty recalling the trauma and she suspected it originated in sexual abuse. Could this be Milbro?

He mentioned the diary in passing to Rachel, combining it with a comment on the weather.

'Why haven't you mentioned this before? This could be crucial. It's imperative we look at the diary. It could contain confirming evidence, direct evidence. You'll need to observe Milbro, his routines. His breaks.'

Neil explained the problem. The recycling station was an impregnable fortress, securely locked when Milbro was absent and accessed by a long corridor with nowhere to hide and no activity he could engage in to justify his presence. Milbro would soon know he was an object of his attention. Later he recalled the cleaner, who had let him into the recycling station, looking at a piece of paper before operating the lock. This was surely the weak link. He tracked the cleaners to their base: a room which housed cleaning equipment. Once unlocked, it remained open until work was completed, and as predicted there was a list of codes against room numbers, including the recycling station and lift. The lift ceased operating when the library closed, and once closed the only access was stairs in the library leading to the basement.

'We could access the recycling station when Milbro goes home. The library doesn't close until 10pm.'

Periodically they checked the recycling station after Milbro's departure, but there was no opportunity to enter because library staff soon sensed their un-library behaviour. Rachel surprised Neil with an imaginative solution. They would stay behind on Friday, hide somewhere, wait until the caretaker had completed his rounds, and then obtain and photocopy the diary. 'Let's hope he doesn't take it with him at weekends.'

That Friday they went to a Sainsbury's to buy food and other provisions. As usual Rachel complained about the supermarket. Why was syrup not kept with jam and honey? Why were eggs always so difficult to find? The shape of detergent packets annoyed her, so tall they easily fell over. 'Why the fuck do they make them that shape?'

'Tall means more,' observed Neil.

'Meaning?'

'According to Piaget, we are supposed to conserve quantity by the age of 11 to 12, meaning we know any quantity remains the same despite changes in the arrangement of an object, such as shape. Below that age a child is dominated by appearances and believes, for instance, that tall means more. Detergent manufacturers obviously don't agree with Piaget's age limit. One brand tried putting detergent in squat containers, but customers thought they contained less and sales plummeted.'

'Always on duty. Don't psychologists have some free time? You'll be analysing the toilets next.' Laughing, she said, 'No, don't tell me.'

'Middlemist and Knowles wanted to find out if male pissing was affected by the presence of others, measured by the time it took to start urinating and the duration of each piss.'

'How did they study them? They didn't stand and watch, did they?'

'No. The observer's presence would have affected the outcome. Middlemist hid in a cubicle and observed urination through a periscope. Things were arranged so that a confederate stood at varying distances from the unwitting subjects. Closer distances increased delay and decreased duration.'

Rachel laughed uncontrollably. 'Isn't that a bit obvious? Are you psychologists still paid to study the obvious?'

'Paid to *prove* the obvious,' Neil said, feeling challenged. 'Someone I know is currently measuring the presence of others on hand washing after using the toilet. What's your impression? Do most women –'

'Yes. Definitely. Again, why study the obvious?'

'That's the problem, it isn't obvious. How do you know your presence isn't influencing them? In an alone situation...'

'Not more hiding in cubicles with a periscope? Is there nothing psychologists won't stoop to study?'

'Now you mention stooping –'

'Stop. I don't want to hear. As I said, always on duty.'

They passed through Home Baking and Neil glimpsed foil-wrapped cake boards, causing his teeth to tingle. His teeth always tingled whenever he saw cake boards. When small, he would chew the remaining icing off the cake base and inadvertently bite into the metal foil, stimulating the nerves in his teeth. Thereafter, the mere sight of foil-wrapped boards caused tingling. Conditioning, of course, Pavlov's dog salivating at the sound of a bell when no food was present. Did that mean he was conditioned forever, even though he no longer took regular bites at metal foil cake boards? What about extinction? He must revise conditioning. He was about to relate the problem to Rachel but hesitated, recalling her jibe 'always on duty'. He supposed he was. She once told him, 'You don't just study psychology, you don't even have psychology, you *are* psychology.' But was Rachel any different? Wasn't she literature?

He told her about the foil affecting his teeth.

'Maybe you have sensitive teeth. What type of toothbrush do you use?'

'Manual.'

She advised electric. 'Two minutes brushing twice a day.'

'I only brush once a day. Should I brush for four minutes? What if teeth are missing? Should I deduct so many seconds for each missing tooth?'

'Why are you always so fucking difficult?'

'Not difficult, just convergent thinking.'

'Convergent you. Another excuse.'

'Anyway, dentistry's not such a hard a science. When I told my dentist I brushed my teeth only once a day she said she was surprised my teeth are as good as they are and that I should brush twice daily.'

'What's wrong with that?'

'Fits Kuhn. She could have said, maybe the theory is wrong, I need to revise the theory, but the anomaly was ignored, anything but change the theory. It's common in science. Called shelving.'

'All this talk of teeth has made me hungry. Let's eat. This time I'll choose the restaurant.'

They had recently gone to a restaurant recommended by Neil. Usually good, the meal had been very poor. Rachel was angry. 'Won't come here again.'

'I think we should come back,' Neil said, applying probability theory. 'Probably a bad night, chef ill or on holiday, or the cooker developed a fault. Must happen sometime. Like rain in Egypt in August. Chances of it happening again…'

Unconvinced, Rachel agreed to return. The meal was just as bad.

'So much for your fucking probability theory.'

After the meal, Rachel said, 'Bit early for the library. We need to get there about nine. Let's go to your place.'

'Only on condition you don't criticise my pictures or colour scheme.'

Rachel laughed. 'Agreed.'

'Before we go, you must try a Sainsbury donut.'

'I'm not fond of donuts. Hard balls of dough.'

'Not Sainsbury's prize-winning donuts. Forget all the other donuts you've ever eaten. Forget the name even. Start from ground zero. For millions of years our hominid ancestors never had the opportunity to try a Sainsbury prize-winning jam donut. Probably the whole of noodle-eating China is oblivious to this gastronomic delight, yet here you are before a tray of soft, golden, crispy, sugar-coated donuts, an opportunity denied most of the people who ever lived, and hesitating.'

'Better than your restaurant prediction.'

'Unfailing. 100 per cent positive reviews.'

*

True to her word, Rachel avoided mention of Neil's pictures and décor, focusing instead on his books which lined one wall. One shelf, at eye level, contained a row of hardback intellectual works, except one volume, a hardback of *Peyton Place*.

'Bit lowbrow for you. Is that your way of saying you're not just an intellectual, also a bit of a pleb? Henry Hollow thinks he's a pleb. Told me he went to university to avoid going down the mine like his father. Learned later that his father was a Coal Board clerk and Henry privately educated. Lowbrow?' she prompted.

Neil sighed. 'I'll give you a clue.' Nearby was a chalkboard for reminders. He went over and drew the following:

$$\frac{A \qquad EF}{BCD}$$

'I test all my students with this puzzle.' he explained, adopting a mild lecturing tone. 'Only one ever got it right.'

Rachel was intrigued. 'Can't think what it's got to do with *Peyton Place…*'

'All will be revealed. You have to say where the letter G comes, below or above the line, and why.'

Rachel struggled, muttering, 'One, three, two. Maths is not my subject. I'm sure I would fail an intelligence test.' She looked at Neil who stared back impassively.

'You used your left hand. Is that a clue? Thought you were right-handed.'

He turned and smiled. 'Not completely. Sometimes.'

Rachel laughed. 'How can you be left-handed sometimes? You mean you're ambidextrous.'

'Not completely. Most times. On a scale of one to 10, one being the lowest, I'm six or seven on the spectrum to ambidexterity. I'm not exactly right or left-handed, or ambidextrous.'

'I really can sympathise with your Professor Matlock.'

'Give up?'

'No. Give me a bit longer. Give me a clue.'

'You're looking at it the wrong way, from one dimension only, one angle. Frankenstein's error. There, a clue.'

'A word sequence? Each letter the first letter of a word? Or an incomplete word? No. That won't work.'

Neil shrugged.

'OK. I give up.'

'The student I mentioned saw it right away: all the bottom letters contain curves; therefore, G comes below.'

'That's unfair. A trick question. So what was so special about your genius student, the only one to get it right?'

'An art student as it happens. She didn't treat it as a numerical reasoning test, more a work of art. She was alerted by my switch to capitals, my handwriting up to then mostly lower case.'

'She was into shapes. *Her* one dimension.' She looked again at the shelf and speaking slowly said, 'What has shape got to do with –' She broke off. 'Fuck. They're all hardback.'

'Go on.'

'The shelf is taller. Oversize!'

'Exactly. The only shelf they fit. Once alerted to size and shape you solve the problem.'

'I still think there's something in my pleb theory.'

'If you look at the bottom shelf, you'll see several books about village and small-town life, some plebby, some not. All fit the shelf, except *Peyton Place*. I once did a Goffmanesque paper on the importance of gossip, using various sources. The highbrow/lowbrow distinction didn't interest me. That's literature, not psychology. Do you know the origin of low and highbrow? Comes from phrenology, a 19th century science which claimed you could discern intelligence from the shape of the skull. A high forehead indicates intelligence, a low forehead stupidity. Hence birdbrain. Head size comes from craniology, such as brainy, egghead, big head and swollen head, denigrations derived from the belief that the bigger the head the greater one's intelligence. The Mekon was all head, a huge egg perched on a small body. Europeans were thought to have larger heads than Negroes. All discredited, of course. Psychology has contributed loads of neologisms. Take Cybernetics: cybernauts, Cybermen, cyborg, feedback –'

'Getting back to gossip, did you use *Much Ado About Nothing*? The plot revolves around gossip, eavesdropping, deceit, misunderstandings. If only you'd come to me for advice. Shakespeare –'

'I hadn't met you then, of course.'

*

That Friday, the caretaker followed his routine, first sounding the clearance bell to indicate the library would close in 15 minutes, switching off the copying machines and finally checking the basement. On emerging, he walked towards the issuing desk. Neil and Rachel quickly entered the stairwell. That moment, the stairwell flooded with light. They had overlooked the occupancy censor-operated lights. Leaving the stairwell, they triggered more lights. The stairwell light remained on. Seconds seemed like minutes in the glare, then relief when the light finally switched off, enveloping the stairwell in comforting darkness. Then the lights switched on again, brilliant against the white painted walls.

The caretaker descended and scowled at them. 'Closing in five minutes.'

'No problem,' said Rachel sweetly. 'We're just looking up a journal. Only take a minute.'

Moving deeper into the basement they triggered more lights, each extinguishing as they moved away. They waited anxiously as the caretaker called out a warning before slamming and locking the heavy access doors above. The stairwell light remained a problem as it would be triggered on route to the toilets and the recycling station, and visible from the ground floor, glowing beacon-like when the library was in total darkness. They solved the problem by covering the sensor with a sheet of black plastic found in the storeroom, having no choice but to activate the light one last time. Returning to the storeroom, other lights were triggered, but were not visible from the ground floor. The plan was to wait two hours, obtain the diary, copy it and leave some time after the library opened at eight.

They drank more than intended, perhaps affected by the oppressively low ceilings, enclosing and claustrophobic, and were a little intoxicated as they progressed to the recycling station.

'Your bloody shoes,' Rachel hissed. 'They'll wake the whole campus. What possessed you to wear squeaky shoes?'

Everyday noises now seemed amplified or distorted, the flushing toilet earlier like Niagara Falls. Rachel was unusually anxious, and Neil suspected her complaint about his shoes some kind of displacement.

'It's the floor that's squeaking,' he said defensively. 'My shoes don't squeak on other floors, the library, the staffroom. It must be the floor.'

'My shoes aren't squeaking. Explain that.'

'I bet they squeak on some floors. Anyway, does it matter? The caretaker's unlikely to hear them. If noise worries you, think about the photocopier.' The photocopiers were particularly noisy at CCU, groaning and clunking when first switched on.

'Fuck. I forgot. They turn them off at night. Fuck.'

*

The diary was still on the shelf where Neil first saw it, covered in a thin layer of dust which Neil attributed to the shredder.

Expectations of its content high, they would be disappointed that it contained no reference to sabotage, merely Milbro's shifting symptoms and a loosely followed CBT structure. Symptoms were wide-ranging: increased arousal such as anger (controlled by snapping an elastic band on his wrist), smell of leather, startled by buzzers, palpitations, sweating, depression and numbness, recurring dream. Another recurrent symptom was an eruption on both wrists, red and purple weals appearing and disappearing, and no apparent physical cause.

'Milbro fits the patient Selena discussed with me who couldn't recall his trauma.'

He remembered Selena saying the patient had probably suffered a trauma and encouraged him to re-experience and work through the emotions to help remember the trauma. The missing trauma was inferred from the symptoms. It was only a matter of time before it surfaced, she explained, so the immediate task was to recover the memory. His diary suggested she was focusing on sexual abuse.

Rachel was suspicious. 'I thought you said trauma is constantly remembered. Intrusive thoughts, involuntary flashbacks. Nightmares; the problem not forgetting but remembering.'

Neil, now well versed in Selena's approach, explained Selena's theory. Though it was usual in cases of PTSD for the trauma to be all too vivid, in some cases dissociation occurs, called peritraumatic dissociation. The victim dissociates at the time, distorts the memory or loses it completely. Disconnected fragments remain, pushing to the surface. The victim avoids, shuts out but suffers a host of symptoms indirectly.

'The weals or strap marks?'

'Recalling what Selena said, straps or ropes suggest sexual abuse. There are well-documented cases of torture victims who were tied up developing rope marks from time to time, even under controlled conditions in a lab. Selena is keen on sexual abuse.'

'You know, I think I'll scream if another female student tells me she was abused. It's so fucking fashionable.'

'Isn't that a bit harsh?'

Ignoring his comment, Rachel focused on Milbro's recurring dream:

I am in a white room but overwhelmed with the idea that it is green and keep switching from green to white when trying to describe it. I feel trapped. A strong smell of leather prevails. I feel numb, powerless…

'What do you make of that, a green room that is white, and further along, a blackboard that is green? And green writing on a black screen. And the recurring phrase, "continue, continue, continue" that seems to be coming from outside of him. Don't schizophrenics hear external voices? I'm starting to feel sorry for him, and a tiny bit guilty reading his diary. Some wonderful symbolism, though. A green room that is white, a blackboard that is green. Must be a metaphor for something. Good grammar and sentence structure. And look at that perfect semicolon. The semicolon is going out of fashion –'

Noticing Neil's inattention, she had stopped. 'OK, I'm off on a tangent again. Sorry. Keep to the evidence. Let's have a coffee.'

Handing Neil a steaming mug, she began summarising the evidence. 'A shredder operator who reads psychology and borrows library books on the subject. Dates borrowed and content of studies roughly correspond to the sabotage. Once a vicar, has access to confidential waste and office keys. From the diary, we know he uses an elastic band to control anger, and Weed thought he heard a band snapping. The elastic band is a gain. Pity Weed couldn't see if it was Wedgwood blue. At least we got something from the diary.

The problem is there's nothing in the diary about sabotage or meeting Weed. There again, would he write about sabotaging research by informing Weed knowing Bobbysox reads the diary and works at the university?'

'Selena is neutral.'

'Even so, would he believe her neutrality? Changing the subject, I was talking to someone in the Law Department about evidence. Apparently direct evidence in trials is unusual. Most people are convicted on circumstantial evidence. Often better than direct evidence, contrary to popular belief. Eyewitnesses can be unreliable or lying. CCTV is good. But how many crimes are filmed? We're unlikely to see Milbro rifling the bins or passing information to Weed on videotape. He probably knows where all the car park cameras are anyway, another reason for staying in the shadows. Confessions are unreliable. People confess to crimes they don't commit. If they show knowledge only the perpetrator could know, that's better. Even then the police may have fixed it by suggesting things. Nothing is certain.'

'All evidence is flawed.'

'I don't think he was saying that exactly.'

'Close.'

'What about beyond reasonable doubt?'

Neil shrugged. 'Too loose for a questionnaire. No researcher would use it.'

'Let's hope you never do jury service. Little chance of a majority verdict.'

Neil backed up Rachel's point with research by Loftus; how people reconstruct memories according to what they think should have happened. 'Memories can be distorted by implanting ideas. Called confabulation. Subjects of her experiment were shown a film of a car accident and questioned about it. There were two groups, each asked slightly different questions about the speed of the cars that collided. For one group she used the word "hit". For the other group she used "smashed". Remember both groups saw the same film. The "smashed" group on average estimated a higher speed. A week later they were asked whether there was any broken glass on the road in the film. A much higher percentage of the "smashed" group recalled glass on the road, even though there wasn't any. Makes you wonder about identity parades. You know they are supposed to choose similar-looking people, age, height, and so on?'

'What's wrong with that?'

'Odlum appeared on an identity parade last year.'

Rachel shrieked with laughter. 'A row of Odlum lookalikes with plastic arms. Impossible.' Rachel made more coffee. 'Where do we go from here?'

Neil shrugged.

'Then I'll tell you. We need another line of enquiry. You say Milbro was once a vicar? We need his personal file. That'll tell us where he originally came from, and maybe more. From vicar to shredder. Something odd there.'

*

There was no logical reason why Milbro's inscrutable diary, Selena's puzzling patient and Matlock's obligatory tour of his old laboratory should cohere into a complete idea, a combination more than its parts, a gestalt. Koestler's prepared mind, his two and two make five. Neil had been drifting off to sleep, his thoughts intermittently turning to repainting his bedroom, unable to decide on the colour. Selena suggested white. Her flat was white, every room was white, including the kitchen. She liked white. 'Pure and does not date,' she explained. 'Sophisticated.' He fleetingly wondered how a chameleon reacted to white. A green room that is white. 'Wonderful symbolism,' said Rachel, 'must be a metaphor for something.' Or gibberish. Freud saw meaning in everything. Nothing accidental. But somewhere in one corner of Neil's mind, rather like peripheral vision, he glimpsed a connection, fleeting, elusive, undulating, and impossible to pin down.

At the point of falling asleep, it cohered. He pulled the sheet from his face. A green room that is white. A white green room. He sat up abruptly. That was it: the Green Room. Matlock's obedience experiment. He jumped out of bed and rushed to his study. Should he phone Rachel? No, it was past midnight. She would be asleep. He grabbed a pad and made furious notes, realised some of the words were unreadable and re-wrote them.

New staff and students were shown Matlock's original laboratory where the famous obedience replications took place. The laboratory was originally the Green Room behind the stage and Matlock would delight at the inevitable question: 'Why is it called the Green Room when it is painted white?'

'Before becoming a laboratory,' he would explain in erudite tone, 'the room served as a waiting room or lounge for performers about to appear on stage. Universally known as a green room, the origin of the name is lost to history. The mistake is to focus on colour, not function. You see, this whole area...'

But what was the connection between Milbro Smith and the experiment? Neil went over Milbro's diary and looked up a summary of obedience experiments. Now he saw the connection, understood the voice, the voice outside himself. *Continue, continue,* and *go on.* Of course, the commands. The last command from the experimenter to a faltering subject: 'You have no other choice. You must go on.'

Was Milbro Smith one of Matlock's subjects? Only Matlock had that information, somewhere in one of his East Light lever arch files, sagging and warped. Then he remembered Matlock had disposed of the files after copying them onto disk. He must visit the Green Room again. He must inform Matlock. It all fitted: the white green room, the repeated command, the subject strapped to the chair by his wrists. What else? The weals. He kept forgetting the weals. Darwin's golden rule. The weals on his wrists were a problem, an anomaly, a voracious anomaly devouring his theory, purring with sated satisfaction. Huxley's ugly fact. Milbro would not have been strapped to the chair as that was the confederate's role. There had to be an explanation, some overlooked variable. Had to be.

*

'Matlock's right about the origins lost in history. The narrator in Charlotte Brontë's *Villette* mentions a green room while preparing to perform in an amateur play. There are even earlier references,' added Rachel, taking control of, and extending Matlock's knowledge.

Rachel summarised the position: 'A shredder who reads psychology, has access to confidential waste and keys to offices, probably wears a rubber band to control anger, once a cleric (fits the religious voice), reads psychology, was probably a subject of Matlock's experiment, which fits the recurring dream symbolism, though not the green blackboard or the green writing on a black screen, or the weals, of course. We have enough evidence for a *how*dunit, better evidence for a whodunit but nothing for a *why*dunit. The evidence advances, but –'

'But?'

'Aren't you forgetting Darwin's golden rule? You quote it enough.'

Neil looked puzzled.

She sighed. 'The problem remains, the case study Selena related to you we now believe to be Milbro doesn't refer to the sabotage in his diary. OK, he could be editing the diary because of Bobbysox but he says nothing of Matlock's experiment. Or –' She stopped and fixed Neil's gaze. 'Or has he genuinely forgotten the experiment? What is that condition Bobbysox is keen on?'

'Peritraumatic dissociation. Inhibits memory.'

'But if he has forgotten, what a strange coincidence turning up for a job here. Vicar to shredder. Can you see any connection?' She laughed. 'Do vicars shred? Why weals or strap marks? As you say, he wouldn't have been strapped to the chair. We've explained the white green room, but why a recurring memory of a blackboard that is green and a black screen with green writing? Why green? None of this proves Milbro is the informer, of course. On a spectrum of one to ten I would give it seven at the most. Key to this is Matlock's experiment. Milbro is either withholding information from Bobbysox or has genuinely forgotten. Would he forget the experiment? We need more information about this Milbro Smith. We need his personal file, the presbytery he worked at, above all the experimental records held by Matlock, and his therapy file. I'm still working on his personal file. Can't ask Harold outright. Do you think Selena...?'

Neil smiled knowingly and shook his head.

Rachel nodded. 'Completely trustworthy. Would never betray a confidence. Never gossips, never mingles. Die rather than part with a patient's file. A paragon of all therapy virtue or... Incidentally, what are you going to tell Bobbysox?'

'Nothing.'

'Nothing comes from nothing, I suppose.'

*

That night, well past midnight, Neil was woken by an excited call from Rachel.

'I've explained it. Why there's no reference to Weed or sabotage in Milbro's diary.' She paused. 'Something we both overlooked. So fucking obvious. Didn't you say the client she suspected of sexual abuse dropped therapy?' She paused, longer this time. 'The dates. The fucking dates. The diary entries end before the sabotage and meetings with Weed, which explains the layer of dust on the diary.'

'The weals?'

'Still a problem. But progressing.'

*

Matlock's old laboratory was situated at the rear of the stage and consisted of two adjoining rooms – prop room and dressing room – now graveyards for disused equipment or monuments to past experiments, depending on your viewpoint. When functioning as Matlock's laboratory, the Green Room housed Matlock's shock machine and the adjoining prop room was an observation room, the large two-way mirror still intact. Hand-painted on the door in script were the faded words *Green Room*, vestige of the sign-writer's art. Neil depressed the antique brass handle. The door grated and opened heavily, solid wood on brass hinges. To the left were cobwebs: strands of sticky threads once entrapping, now dusty and long abandoned. Centre stage was the shock machine, dust-free and gleaming, and he wondered if Matlock secretly polished it, then remembered he wheeled it out each year to impress the new student intake. To the rear was a fire escape, accessed by fire doors. He pressed a bar which grated and squeaked, and stepped onto a metal open-steel grating and felt a welcome upward breeze. He needed some air. The room was suffocating.

Back inside, he wondered if the doors were open when Matlock conducted his experiments, but doubted this, escape the last thought allowed his subjects. They were captives, enclosed in a surreal laboratory at the behest of an all-powerful experimenter in a white coat. *You have no other choice. You must go on.* The room was white. 'Sophisticated, pure and does not date,' Selena's view of white. But white was also cold and clinical, the colour of Matlock's laboratory uniform, sterile, and befitting a cold and calculating experiment. No empathy. To one side was a chalkboard. It was green. He laughed out loud. Whether green or black, most people called them blackboards out of habit. Was this Milbro's green blackboard? It fitted. Not meaningless ramblings after all. And on a shelf, a small computer dating from the time of Matlock's experiment. He recalled using one years earlier, squinting at a tiny black screen with green writing. That moment he wanted to tell Selena, Milbro's enigmatic flashbacks decoded at last, but how could he tell her without revealing he had read Milbro's diary?

Looking again at the shock generator he felt an impulse to switch it on. Nothing happened. He found the cable and traced it to a wall plug and pressed the socket switch. The machine was disappointingly quiet. He expected a more dramatic response, an expectation shaped perhaps by the sensational nature of the experiments and Matlock's amplified account. Down the centre of the machine was a long row of levers and above each lever a voltage label, rising from 15 volts to 450 volts, arranged in groups of four and labelled *slight shock* at one end and *severe shock* at the other. Neil still found it hard to believe 65 per cent of Milgram's subjects inflicted the final shock, more so as his machine read: *Danger, high voltage*. Perhaps the subjects didn't read the labels. After all, he rarely read instructions, often a cause of regret. Then he remembered they were instructed to read out the shock level to the learner before pressing the lever, giving no excuse for not knowing. The machine buzzed and a circular light above turned an impressive bright red as a blue light flashed and the dial on a large voltage meter swung to the right. There was much clicking. Rather than awed, he was amused, reminded of a machine in an episode of *The Avengers*, which fitted the period of Milgram's original experiments.

*

'It's understandable – cuts, targets, careers. More pressing today than when Broad and Wade published in the eighties. Targets corrupt, absolute targets corrupt absolutely.'

'Bit cynical.'

'Comes with the job, I suppose, or I don't have your optimism. People are often shocked and surprised when they hear others take bribes, lie, fix data. Or pretend to be. I start from the opposite end, start with the assumption people are dishonest. Take targets in Vietnam. The infamous body count. The Americans were losing the war, but rather than admit this, they chose a measure that made it seem they were winning. The military went for the body count to convince the public they were winning. Corrupting, of course, because units were encouraged to compete and grossly exaggerated the numbers; other units killed randomly to push up the count, civilians as well as enemy soldiers. As I said, targets corrupt. Extreme example, of course.'

Neil nodded. 'And they still lost the war.'

'But delayed the truth until after the next election.'

Andy was planning a series of articles on faking and fudging in psychology, drawing on Broad and Wade's *Betrayers of the Truth*, a book title he worried was somewhat tabloid and sensational. He wanted Neil's opinion.

'After all, you always were committed to the truth, Neil, getting to the bottom of everything, finding the flaws. I'm not criticising. Commitment to truth is laudable. Long hours labouring over monumental tomes, review articles.'

Neil laughed. 'Yet we both got a 2:1.'

Neil recalled how Andy would find shortcuts. Given an essay, Neil would agonise over it, feel he had to read everything, whereas Andy would go from book to book searching for a chapter that approximated to the essay title and skilfully paraphrase and edit the content, adding odd quotes to disguise its origin and give the impression of wide reading. Most galling was his paraphrase of an encyclopaedia entry on Piaget. While

Neil pored over numerous books and articles hopelessly mired in jargon, Andy gained a better grade.

'Tabloid title,' Neil agreed, returning to Broad and Wade, 'but you say the writers are sound?'

'One is a former deputy editor of *Nature*. And don't forget, the subtitle's different: *Fraud and Deceit in Science.*'

'Maybe they had no control over the title. Anyway, it's not just about fraud. It looks at what science is rather than what it is pretends to be, or some think it should be, and gives reasons for corruption.'

'Coming back to my article, the Burt scandal about intelligence testing is well covered, but most of the book is about the natural sciences.'

'Perhaps psychologist don't fudge and fake, Burt a one-off.'

'If pigs had wings.'

Neil laughed.

'Didn't Wolins write an article on replication?'

'Wolins, Wolins. It's coming back to me. He or someone contacted a large number of psychologists asking for the raw data on which their research was based. Most claimed their data was lost, destroyed or misplaced. An extraordinary set of coincidences. Of the raw data made available, a third contained serious statistical errors. Of course, this assumes Wolins' research into research wasn't biased in some way. You need to say that in your article.'

'Didn't you do a dissertation on Burt? Remind me what you concluded.'

'Burt was a fake.'

Andy laughed loudly. 'I'll need to say a bit more than that. Background?'

'Isn't it all in Broad and Wade?'

Andy was silent.

'You bastard, you haven't read it. I'm sure you know the stuff. Twin research supposedly the perfect scientific test untangling nurture from nature. Various abilities run in families, but are abilities acquired because families share the same genes or because families share the same environment? Is little Wursel bright because he inherits his parents' genes or because they are affluent, pushy and send him to the best school? The beauty of identical twins is that they more or less share the same genes. All you need are sets of identical twins separated at birth and reared in different environments. If the environment has little effect on intelligence, as Burt claimed, the twins should be similar in intelligence. If the environment is more important, they should differ in intelligence. Burt claimed there was little difference in intelligence between twins reared in different environments, thus proving intelligence is largely innate.

'He claimed to have amassed 53 pairs of identical twins separated at birth. That may not sound a lot but only four studies, including Burt's, were recognised to be of scientific value at the time, a worldwide total of 121 pairs of twins separated into different environments. All pointed to the same conclusion: intelligence is largely inherited. Burt's sample comprised almost half the world total. Hence his esteem and importance.'

'Where does Kamin come in?'

'Kamin was the first to raise doubts about Burt's research, observing that Burt's IQ correlations remained constant despite periodic increases in sample size, which was statistically impossible. And there was no raw data supporting Burt's conclusions, purportedly destroyed in the Blitz. But Kamin didn't cry fake. Burt was still alive. In 1976, after Burt had died, Oliver Gillie, medical correspondent of the *Sunday Times*, levelled the first accusation of fraud with the dramatic headline: *Crucial data faked by eminent psychologist.*

'What a scoop.'

'More so as Burt was Professor of Educational Psychology at London University for 27 years and the first English psychologist to be knighted.'

'The evidence against Burt?'

'All circumstantial. Suspicious stats, no raw data, untraceable collaborators, presumably fictitious, no reference to collaborators or twin study research in his diaries. Some still claim Burt was not a fraud. OK, the argument runs, he may have used pseudonyms for his collaborators, quirky, but not evidence of fraud. His statistics contained errors, but not proof of fraud, just human error, just coincidence that the errors were all in the direction of his preferred finding. No raw data? No problem. He lost his data during the Blitz and probably reconstructed it from memory. Unprofessional but understandable, but not proof of fraud. However, none of the twins Burt allegedly studied stepped forward when the scandal broke, nor friends or relations of the twins. Burt claimed that many came through personal contacts, colleagues and friends, yet none recollected such research. The clinching argument is provided by Mackintosh in *Cyril Burt: Fraud or Framed*. Mackintosh investigated the pre-war twin study research comprising almost half the 53 pairs, supposedly lost in the Blitz. The alleged data for these twins arose from Burt's work at the London County Council, between 1914 and 1932. This would have been a significant finding as there were no systematic twin studies at that time. So why did he take so long reporting the data – ten years before a brief mention, twelve more years before a moderately systematic report? Meanwhile, Newman in America had published a systematic study of separated identical twins in 1937. And here's the clincher. That Burt was aware of the significance of this is shown by the minutes of a London County Council committee meeting held in 1931 to consider an application from a researcher called Hogben to test the intelligence of London school twins. Burt was enthusiastic about the application, stating that no one had investigated "The great mass of valuable information accumulated over the years". Yet Burt later claimed that, before Newman, he had himself undertaken research into an even larger number of twins in London schools.

'There are other twin studies, of course, but none stand up to scrutiny, faked or not. Even Burt's most ardent fraud deniers came to admit Burt's data is hopelessly flawed and worthless.' Neil stopped and looked at Andy, strangely silent during his exposition. Andy was not taking notes. He always took notes.

Andy looked across, eyebrows raised, and Neil continued. 'Some people mistakenly think Kamin's book is only about Cyril Burt, but he assessed the raw data of all the recognised studies of separated identical twins. Remember, there aren't many. Now this is important. Take a note. Everything hinges on the key word *separated*.'

Andy looked interested and Neil continued. 'Unlike Burt's research, Kamin was able to access the raw data of the other three studies: Shields, Newman and Juel-Nielson. 68 pairs in total. All turned out to be ridden with flaws. Take Shields's UK study. When we think of identical twins separated into different environments, we don't assume they went to the same school, had regular contact, lived with relatives nearby, some reunited early on and only tested in middle age after years of daily contact. Shields's definition of separated is very flexible. The problem is, identical twins are rarely separated, and those who are usually placed in similar environments or with relatives. Yet Burt claimed to have found 53 pairs completely separated and placed in totally different environments. Not proof of fraud exactly, but bloody suspicious. Anyway, how do you measure different environments? How different is different? Burt offers no criteria.' Neil looked intently at Andy. 'Remember, Kamin is not denying the possibility of innate intelligence, only that it remains unproven. That's all. And even if intelligence is largely innate, and tests measure innate intelligence, they don't measure creativity or motivation. Not designed to do so.'

There was a long pause as they drank their beers. Finally, Andy said, 'Another key question, was Burt a rotten apple, the remainder of the barrel sound, or was the whole barrel rotten?' He briefly looked at Neil. 'What's the barrel like today? Since Broad and Wade, I mean?'

'That's a big question.'

Looking into his beer Andy said, 'Tell me about faking and fudging in the psychology department at CCU.'

'Faking and fudging?'

'Perfectly understandable, Neil. If you want to corrupt people, introduce targets, threaten jobs. As I said, all targets corrupt and absolute targets corrupt absolutely. That's the irony. Efficiency begets a new inefficiency.' He paused, offered Neil a cigarette. As they lit up, he said, 'Shadow thinks it's rife.' He paused. 'Rife at CCU.'

Neil shrugged, remained silent.

'No hard evidence, of course, just a veiled message.'

'Veiled?'

'Shadow uncovered a memo from Matlock telling a researcher who was unable to get a positive result: "Look at your sample again. I'm sure there's a result in there somewhere. Know what I mean?"'

'Is that all?'

'I know, a jury wouldn't convict. I'm meeting up with Shadow. Let's see what he comes up with.'

Later that evening, Neil thought again about the Burt scandal. Andy hadn't taken notes. He always took notes. An answer suddenly took shape. All along Andy was preparing him to reveal faking at CCU and wanted confirmation.

*

'But you helped him. You encouraged him. Did you tell Weed faking is taking place?'

Neil was silent.

'You did, didn't you?'

'I didn't confirm or deny.'

'That's encouragement. Weed will be encouraged. Maybe the informer is wrong. Is he wrong? He is, isn't he?'

'Researchers are under pressure to cut corners. The informer isn't wrong exactly. I've overheard things. People manipulate research in different ways, to different degrees. Trebling sample size, for instance.'

'Trebling sample size?'

'Overheard a conversation between two researchers. One was worried because his sample was small, and he was running out of time. "Treble the sample", advised the other researcher. "No one will know. We all do it".'

'Does sample size matter that much?'

'A sample needs to be a certain size to avoid bias, get a grant and get published. Error decreases as sample size increases. You can't research everyone so you sample the population, but the sample must be representative. Think of a sample of one, or even two. Say you wanted to research lecturers and your sample was Odlum and Hollow.'

Rachel laughed.

'Exactly.'

'Hold on. How do you know a sample is representative? How can a sample of hundreds represent millions of people?'

'Take soup.'

'Soup?'

'George Gallop invented the opinion poll and compared it to tasting soup. You don't have to eat the whole bowl to know if it has enough salt. Providing you've mixed it well, one spoonful is enough.'

'So how do you mix people? They vary, individuals, different groups. You can't stir the population. I'm not convinced.'

'Yes, you can. You take a sample from each group – age, gender, social class, and so on – and mix them. Take predicting an election –'

'Hold on. You're deviating. Back to Weed. Have you told Weed about trebling?' Her voice had risen.

'No. And I don't tell. I confirm only.'

'The conversation you overheard isn't necessarily proof of fudging. Where did you hear this conversation?'

'In the toilet.'

'Don't tell me – periscope or recorder?' She leaned back, her gaze steady and said, 'You don't know if the researcher took the advice. You don't know if the adviser was exaggerating when he said, "We all do it". He could have been joking. Maybe later he said, "I hope you didn't take me seriously". People say all sorts of things they don't mean. How often have I said I'd like to strangle my supervisor? How often have you said you would like to do the same to Odlum? But Weed won't report it that way, will he. He'll take it literally.'

Neil filled Rachel's glass, hoping she would mellow. Alcohol made most people more honest, sometimes rude or aggressive in Neil's experience, but had the reverse effect on Rachel.

Rachel waved her glass at Neil. 'Maybe your silence was good after all. Andy will think you're on his side. You're not, are you? Are you?' The alarm had returned to her voice. 'What if the informer had overheard the researcher you mention say treble the sample? Would you confirm? Your famous mute response? Think of the university, your colleagues. OK most of them are shits, but you'll bring the department, bring the university into disrepute. Every bit of research, every PhD would be suspect. Sabotaging research is one thing, but fraud… Think of yourself. Your career would be over if found out. Come on, agree with me. Say you agree a bit. I'll stop if you say a bit.'

'OK, a bit. A lot really. No, you're right. It's been troubling me, and it's got to end. It's spiralling out of control. Andy's using me, I see that. The articles were harmless fun. The sabotaged research…' He shrugged.

Rachel softened. 'OK. But don't stop seeing him. Use him. Let him think you're on his side.' She relaxed, reflected a moment and said, 'I know I keep saying it, I must get Milbro's personal file. Personal files are kept in Harold's office.'

'The chaise longue casting couch?'

She laughed. 'Leave it to me.'

17

Matlock and Odlum were discussing an article by Andy, *Is Science Science?* The article started with Cyril Burt, pointing out that more than two decades had passed since his exposure as a fraud, and more than a decade had passed since publication of Broad and Wade's *Betrayers of the Truth*, yet fraud and fudging were still rife, evidenced by recent cases. 'But is this surprising?' asked Andy. 'Refereeing and other forms of peer review are clearly not working. True replication is rare, blinds almost non-existent. The referee system is supposed to ensure only quality research is published yet no end of pointless or error-ridden research appears in the journals, peer-reviewed or not.'

Matlock leaned back. 'Research into research shows some research is flawed, we both know, but how reliable is their research? How reliable are Broad and Wade?'

Odlum nodded. 'And how reliable is Seedbank's interpretation of Broad and Wade? We can all play the postmodern game.'

Still drawing on Broad and Wade, the article pointed out that the real process of conducting research little resembled the way it is presented. 'Yet anyone hoping to get published is obliged to go through the same charade.'

Andy had used a dramaturgical metaphor derived from Goffman: science as performance, front and backstage, impression management, the impression given off more important than substance; the audience, in this case the journal editors demanding a front stage idealised performance complete with props. 'Welcome to the show,' Andy concluded.

Matlock was particularly irked by the assertion that researchers appropriate research ideas from students. 'And look at this.' He passed the article across to Odlum. 'He says we present old ideas as new by dressing them up in obscure and inflated jargon.'

Odlum adopted an ironic tone. 'Thought we were all plagiarists in this postmodern world? Nothing totally original, everything derivative. Wasn't that Seedbank's point in an article last year? Now we appropriate original ideas from defenceless students. Can't have it both ways.'

'Exactly.'

'You know, there is something familiar about these arguments. Blinds, the sociologist Goffman, negative view of psychology. Neil goes on about Goffman.'

'Sociologist in name only, remember,' Matlock said, casting a sideways glance at his row of Goffman.

'Obsessed with blinds, friend of Seedbank, joined at the hip with the sociologists. Coincidence?' Odlum shook his head.

18

They entered the castle grounds and followed a pathway through some trees. Enveloped by foliage, Neil took Selena's hand, which she withdrew.

'Friends, remember.'

'Women friends hold hands.'

She laughed. 'Not the same.'

Neil had offended Selena a week earlier, accused of being presumptuous assuming they were going to have sex one evening.

'Apparently I must never take sex for granted,' he explained to Rachel.

'Not an unfair assumption as you always have sex when at her flat. What on earth did you do to offend her?'

'I undressed and donned a dressing gown when we were at the listening-to-music stage.'

'Stage?'

Neil explained how their lovemaking followed a strict procedure: listen to some modern jazz as they drink white wine, undress, don dressing gowns, and drink more white wine.

'Always white?'

'The carpet's off-white. She doesn't allow red. Finally, she would look at her watch and say, "Let's go to bed". That night I deviated. It was hot and I undressed early.'

Rachel laughed. 'Talk about sex by numbers. Didn't she once accuse you of sex by numbers? She sounds positively Asperger's. Would explain a lot. Cold, ritualistic, distant, compartmentalising. So what happened?'

'We had sex. Two days later we met for a drink. She was unusually silent. She lit a cigarette and inhaled deeply. I knew she had something unpleasant to say. Looking into the distance she said, "I don't want us to be lovers anymore".'

'Lovers. How quaint. Go on.'

'I asked her why and she said she was mixed up.'

'You'd think a therapist with a PhD could come up with something more original than that.' Rachel leaned back. 'You think she's punishing you by going celibate?'

'Possibly. Shelrack thinks so.'

'You told Shelrack? I thought men didn't discuss –'

'No, of course not. Sexual withholding came up during my research. Shelrack has an evolutionary answer for everything. Among other things he argues women withhold sex to increase its value, making it a scarce resource. That way they get more from a man, more than just sex. Gave the example of baboons grooming. The male must groom the female before being allowed sex.'

'Didn't Selena say she doesn't want commitment?'

Neil shrugged. 'Sort of. I was really pissed off and said we should finish, and she told me I would still be a dear friend, our friendship special. Next day she was warmer, even friendly, even in the staffroom.'

'I doubt if Birkin in *Women in Love* would have put up with her celibacy for long. Her favourite Lawrence novel, you said. Who does she like most, Birkin or Nigel?'

'Birkin because he opposes conventional monogamy and wants another kind of love.'

'Birkin doesn't know what the fuck he wants. Some critics see that as a quality in *Women in Love*, uncertainty equals modern, postmodern even. I think he's just hopelessly confused because Lawrence is confused. *Women in Love* is ridden with contradiction and ambiguity. Fits Selena, though.'

Neil looked puzzled.

'Challenges marriage and commitment but offers no real alternative. 'Little mention of children in *Women in Love*. They don't feature. What does Bobbysox say about children?'

'Selena hasn't mentioned them. I'll ask her some time.'

Neil was feeling disloyal discussing Selena with Rachel, particularly so negative an account. He never discussed Rachel with Selena. Once in bed, Selena could be affectionate, as if the closed door, drawn curtains and bed covers gave anonymity. Selena often told him she felt watched, felt people knew her innermost thoughts. When making love she wore a long silk garment with sleeves and leggings. She was turned on the moment he slipped his fingers inside her sleeve, along her arm. 'Why your sleeves?' he once asked.

'Not only my sleeves. Any part of me that's covered,' she said turning and facing him. 'It's private, secret, not available to others, out of bounds, hidden, forbidden.'

And on occasion there was tenderness of sorts, such as when she commented on his paunch. 'I'll slim,' he told her.

She pressed against him, belly to belly, hers a pancake. 'It's soft and cuddly, like a Buddha.' Later, putting on weight, she sported her own developing tummy, rubbed it against his. 'There, I've got one too.'

She never appeared naked until the closing moments, clad in her silk garment up to the point of coitus. What did she call it? 'My little brown thing'. Close fitting, revealing but hiding, offering but denying, and her final nakedness in daylight mitigated by closed curtains, a muted, soft, sophisticated nakedness. He didn't mind, preferred it even. Sometimes sexual desire waned when confronted with arrant nakedness, full frontal daylight nudity, a mass of luminescent flesh. He even liked the teasing, prolonging, deferring.

Now free from the foliage, Selina was asking Neil why he disliked Leicester, his birthplace, why he preferred Nottingham. Coming from central London, Nottingham and

Leicester were just Midland towns to Selina, dull, provincial, hide-bound.

'Goes back a long way. Nottingham was always more open, more exciting,' he explained.

She stopped and turned to face him, incredulous. 'If Nottingham is open, I dread to think what Leicester is like.'

He laughed. '*Was* like. When I was a child, they chained the children's swings together on Sundays. It had a strong puritan tradition. Weekends saw an exodus from Leicester to Nottingham. It's all changed now. Nottingham's not as bad as you make out.' He paused at her askance expression. 'There's a lot here. Victorian pubs, the Trent, Goose Fair, Robin Hood.'

'Robin Hood.' She laughed uproariously. 'Sometimes I think you're very funny, Neil.'

'Nottingham's produced some great writers. Alan Sillitoe.'

She grimaced.

'DH Lawrence, then.'

She nodded approvingly.

Now clear of the trees, they followed the path to the wide steps leading to the castle.

'Doesn't resemble a castle.'

'Big house, really, but built on the site of a medieval castle. There's a bit of it somewhere at the back.'

'I need a drink,' she said. 'Something strong. You said there's a bar or restaurant?'

A waitress arrived with the menu. Selina was amused by the heading: *Baguettes by the inch – make your lunch as long as you like!*

'So these are the famous baguettes you told me about.'

She was relaxed now, the sweet, angelic, poised and demure Selina he had watched at a distance for so long, never imagining they would become lovers.

The waitress returned, order book ready, and Neil ordered some drinks. Selina deliberated choosing her filling, and the waitress said, 'Do you want a four inch or a six inch, or longer perhaps?' She drew out the word longer as she looked sideways at Neil, and with a hint of a leer said to Selena, 'You look like you can easily manage a six inch.'

When the waitress departed, Neil commented, 'Baguette doubling as a phallus.'

Selena grunted, absorbed in her baguette, undecided which end to start, and settling for the crusty end, tentatively removed a small piece. After a moment she looked at Neil and said, 'Mm, these baguettes are beautiful.'

'Best this side of Nottingham?'

'You mean they are better the other side?'

'An expression, pedant.'

She laughed. 'I like teasing you. You're so easy to tease. Why did you take so long asking me out if, as you say, you found me attractive?'

'Did I ask you out?' She didn't answer, and he said, 'I didn't think you would be interested. Anyway, I thought you were having an affair with Kel.' He reflected a moment on why he had thought this. She was in his company a lot, of course, often in deep conversation, intense sessions in the cafeteria which would last an hour or more. She talked a lot about Kelvin, talked admiringly, almost deferentially.

She did not reply immediately having bitten off a full inch of beef baguette. 'With Kel? I did consider it once, but...'

'He's a bit young? Younger than you, I mean.'

'I suppose that was the reason.'

He instantly regretted supplying a reason, feeling she was about to give a different explanation.

She became very serious, offered Neil a cigarette and said, 'Why should you think we were having an affair?'

'You were together a lot. Some time ago you said the two of you would like to move to London.'

'We both come from London. I remember now. I didn't say we were moving to London together, I said we would ideally like to move to London.' Neil looked confused, and with patience she said, 'I once discussed with Kel where we would like to live – ideally – and we both said we would like to live in London, Hampstead or Greenwich.' She looked highly amused. 'And you thought we were moving to London together. You see, quite innocent. Let's forget Kel. You often criticise Kel, but I won't have you criticising poor Kel, not when he's a bit down. Kel is having a hard time of late, his research is going wrong, some sort of sabotage. And he didn't get the lecturing job. Anyway, Kel's a good front. Do not forget I am a married woman.'

So she hadn't told Kel about their relationship. He wanted Kel to know they were having sex, or more exactly had had sex. That was the line separating him from Kel. He wanted everyone to know and didn't want them thinking there was anything between Selena and Kel.

'Don't you have a friendship with Rachel? I don't go on about that. I'm sure some people think it's more than friendship. Do you discuss our relationship with Rachel?'

This was a surprise question, and he was unprepared. 'Only generally. Not in the detail.'

'Does she know we've stopped having sex?'

'Yes.'

Her voice rising, she said, 'That's a detail. Is sex really that important to you?'

'It's obviously important to you because you've given it up.'

She looked away and said, 'I now feel watched by Rachel, an observer, judging.' She sighed. 'What a situation.'

The bar was filling, and their privacy threatened, she suggested they go outside onto the balcony to get some air and take in the view of the city. A soft breeze greeted them as they stood near a telescope. Selina was having difficulty identifying the sights and wondered about the huge Victorian clock tower.

'All that remains of the station, demolished in 1967. Much of Victorian Nottingham went the same way. It seems every city centre had to have a shopping mall.' He asked her if she had seen the film *Saturday Night and Sunday Morning*, which she had, and he reminded her of the scene shot from the very spot where they were standing, the city almost invisible because of the enveloping smoke in the early sixties. 'The film gives a distorted picture of Nottingham,' he explained, 'industrial, working class, monochrome.'

'Lawrence hated industry. Have you read much Lawrence?'

'Only *Women in Love*, and only because of you.'

'It's a sequel to *The Rainbow*. Did you read *The Rainbow* first? Obviously not.'

'Didn't Lawrence believe in free love?'

'Absolutely not. He's not just about sex. *Lady Chatterley*, the surrounding publicity, the trial, gives the wrong message.' A rare passion in her voice, she had gripped his arm tightly. 'Can we see Lawrence's birthplace from here?'

'Too far from here. Eastwood is about ten miles.'

'We should go there someday.'

How could she go without sex for so long, he wondered? He knew she masturbated. Soon after starting their affair, she produced a vibrator and asked him to use it on her.

'You could do this yourself.'

'Yes, but not the same.'

He thought about her flatmate. Did she? Did they? No, surely not. That would be a complication.

She was looking again at the clock tower. 'It's very tall and red.'

'Red, erect – and thrusting.'

'We could have a weekend of sex, I suppose,' she said, offhandedly.

Surprise in his tone he said, 'You mean this weekend?'

'Don't rush me. Maybe. When I finish my paper on –'

He had taken her hand. She was unresisting.

'You always were a bit of a hand fetish,' she murmured.

'And nipple fetish, don't forget,' he said, sliding his hand under her silky top and under her soft bra. He felt her tense then relax, then sigh. 'That's not fair.'

'Why the sigh?'

'I'm weakening, giving in. Succumbing.'

'Don't blame yourself, blame the baguette, or the tower. What did Freud say about towers and the like?'

Her laugh was ironic. 'Seduction by baguette and clock tower. Candy is dandy, but liquor is quicker, the baguette quicker still. Can we see my flat from here?'

'Not from this side,' he explained. They began walking slowly round the castle parapet, stopping at a spot facing east. He pointed out the block containing the flat she shared. He no longer believed she was gay, the sex too real, too needy on her part, though he supposed she could be bisexual. At the very least there was something odd about her relationship with her flatmate who seemed more permanent than temporary. Why had he never met her?

'Paula doesn't know about you,' she once explained.

'Would it matter if she did?'

She became tense and said, 'Not to me. I'll explain some other time. It's complicated.'

There was a long silence as they concentrated on her flat. She seemed to be deciding something. Slowly she turned to look at him and said evenly, 'OK, let's go to my flat. Paula's away.'

They never went to Neil's flat. Too many lecturers lived nearby, two in his road. 'We might be seen,' she explained. They used her flat when Paula was away, which was frequent, though not enough for Neil, and served as a convenient excuse for not seeing him more, or so Neil assumed, as usual guessing Selena's motives. Rachel said Selena preferred her own flat because it maximised control, her own space, everything hers, arranged by her, Neil on tiptoe.

*

'She asked you to read *Women in Love*?' Rachel said petulantly. 'Was that before or after you read *Frankenstein*?' Before he could answer, she was saying, 'Bet you found it difficult to understand, and probably blame yourself.'

'Was a problem at first, until Selena –'

'No one really understands Lawrence, that impenetrable, mystical language, though his followers pretend to. The difficulty inheres in Lawrence. Obscurantist, and that's putting it mildly. You read the same passage over and over. Meaningless.'

'She told me Lawrence worked out he had an Oedipus complex before reading Freud. She knows a lot about Freud.'

'Well, let's beat the drums, have a fanfare, cry eureka, Lawrence discovered the Oedipus complex before Freud. And a passionate Selena, you say? Isn't that a contradiction in terms?' She leaned back, arms folded, and Neil prepared for a diatribe against Freud, Selena and Fussel, the three now fused into a single hate.

'Literature's not her subject,' she purred, 'so we must make allowances. Lawrence, she has to understand, is a bit passé.'

This was a contentious issue in the English Department under Professor Fussel. 'Nottingham is Lawrence country, after all,' Fussel would counter whenever Rachel and others suggested relegating Lawrence on the syllabus.

'You make him sound like a bloody football team. Support your local club,' Rachel would protest.

'Yes, yes, Rachel, we are all aware of your stance on Lawrence.'

Fixing Neil's gaze, Rachel explained why Lawrence was *démodé*. 'His heyday the sixties, the Lady Chatterley trial, sexual repression and all that finally gaining him a place on the canon after years an outsider, only to see him knocked off by the feminists. Ironic really given his fame for writing about women as sexual beings. Until then followers either blinded themselves to his faults or minimised them. Trifle sexist, at times opaque, but still a great writer, they argue. I bet Selena did Lawrence for A-level. Where would that place her, early eighties? Her teacher, probably twenty years older, would know nothing of Kate Millet or other feminist criticism, or want to know. Same with modern Russian writers, such as Pasternak. Popular and lauded when repressed, Nobel Prize, the lot. Completely undeserved. Or Galsworthy. Someone recently described *The Forsyte Saga* as the thinking man's soap, yet in his day lauded as great novels because of his enlightened views, even got the Nobel Prize. Can you believe it? But is today's political correctness any better? Critics weighed down by colonial guilt, desperate not to appear racist or sexist. There's a lecturer I know who discriminates in favour of black students and teaches black literature – MA in anti-colonial literature. Dire. Nothing more than political tracts, but he says it's the content that matters, poorly written by the standards of white bourgeois criticism admittedly, but...'

Neil began making coffee, first cleaning Rachel's cafetiere left uncleaned over the weekend and growing a mould.

Rachel turned and faced him. 'I'm surprised Selena, a therapist, fails to see *Women in Love* and his other novels are all about Lawrence. What was it Freud said about mothers? A man who has been his mother's darling keeps for life the feeling of a conqueror. He could have added, and expects the same from all relationships with women. Lawrence never grew up, was ever a mummy's boy, tied to his mother's apron strings. Wasn't much of an Oedipus complex either, no mention of incestuous wishes or castration fear. Lawrence missed that. If anyone was castrated it was his father – symbolically.' She paused as Neil handed her a coffee. 'His mother saw to that. Undermined his father and taught Lawrence to despise him. Not so much Lawrence desiring his mother, father a rival, as mother desiring her son, father sidelined. Even Lawrence's most ardent supporters criticise his insistent narrative voice, his endless preaching, such as how a woman should behave sexually. Not Freud's, what does a woman want? but Lawrence's I'll tell her what she wants or should want. Lawrence wanted it both ways, to be in a relationship and to be free.

'He descried a conventional relationship as a "Horrible merging, mingling, self-abnegation of love". Of course, it was supposed to be an exchange, ideally, growth through conflict and opposition, each a door to the other's development. He hated the theoretical, what he called sex in the head, "blood and flesh greater than the intellect", depicting love to Rosalind, a friend, as "a force outside and getting us. It is a force; a God". Yet he was the arch theorist. He asked Rosalind if she would have sex with him, or as he put it, "Have a sex time together". She agreed. Nothing happened. A day passed and they finally bedded. Not exactly passionate or spontaneous, a force, beyond them, a god. Not a bad seduction line in certain circles at a certain point in history, but hardly passionate. Beats your line. What was it you said to Selena about touching?'

Neil ignored her question and began staring out the window.

'Sorry, sore point, but she asked you out again. Maybe, maybe there's a link to Kel? Was he his mother's favourite? Is that why Selena is attracted to him? Sorry. Sensitive issue, I know. You're not ready yet. But *Women in love* is surely a clue to Sox's personality. Unfettered relationships, no children, actual or proposed.' She paused to gauge Neil's response. 'Some say *Women in Love* could have been called *Men in Love*. Definitely a homosexual undertone in there, but only on the male side. Can't imagine Birkin, Lawrence's mouthpiece, putting up with Ursula having a lesbian lover.'

Neil hesitated, uneasy discussing Selena with Rachel after her strong reaction learning he had told Rachel they had stopped having sex.

Perhaps detecting the reason for Neil's hesitation, Rachel said, 'Let me treat Selena as a character in a novel. What do we know about her, what has the author revealed, and why? Of course, I only have your perspective, a narrator as unreliable as Nelly in *Wuthering Heights*. Don't take it personally, but you are emotionally involved. Rose-coloured, and all that.'

Neil was about to protest.

'But there's sufficient evidence for a writerly approach on my part.'

'Writerly?'

'Oh, the usual Barthes stuff,' she said impatiently. 'Barthes distinguishes between a readerly text, readers as passive consumers, and a writerly text, one which invites its readers to actively participate in the production of meanings which are infinite. The first puts the author centre stage, the second abolishes the author. In a readerly text the signs and signifiers are synonymous, the text a closed system, whereas the writerly text is a myriad of signifiers. We can access it by several entrances, all of equal status... reversible... no beginning...' She was pausing, aware of Neil's bemused and slightly contemptuous expression, and sighing said, 'I'll simplify. For you. Let's drop all this crap and just say, the data you present, though biased, is sufficient for me to draw my own conclusions. Tell me more about Selena. Anything. Anything that comes to mind, no matter how irrelevant it seems.'

'She keeps chameleons.'

Rachel laughed uncontrollably and banged the table. Slowly recovering, she said, 'I've heard of women substituting a dog or a cat for a child, but chameleons! Do you like them? Don't tell me you like them. You don't like them, surely.'

'Pretend to, I suppose. Have to pretend lots of things with Selena. I even pretend to like modern jazz. We listen to that a lot before going to bed, the steely, barren tones of some trumpeter. Depressing stuff. She loves it. Can't remember his name. Very famous.'

'That proves it. Tolerating chameleons and modern jazz. You must be in love. Falling in love and falling out of love are opposites, of course. In the first you focus on the love object's qualities, blind yourself to everything else and accommodate their tastes and foibles. In the second you focus on their flaws, loathsome interests and bad habits, and friends say, why did you stay with that monster for so long? You're obviously in the interim stage, poised between love and uncoupling. Don't deny it. Chameleons, chameleons. I knew someone who kept chameleons. Incredibly fussy and difficult. Easily stressed. Don't like to be handled, hate the presence of other chameleons, even their own reflection.'

'She keeps them apart,' said Neil. 'Keeps two, male and female, but plenty of space and foliage to hide in.'

'Exactly. How on earth do they mate? Controlled environment: lighting, humidity, isolation, quiet surroundings, watering. Do you know, they don't recognise still water. This friend placed a saucer of water in the chameleon's cage and the stupid thing died of dehydration. All that effort and nothing in return. Wonder if chameleons like modern jazz?'

19

'We have enough evidence for a *how*dunit, sufficient evidence for a whodunit, no evidence for a *why*dunit, but does that matter? What we are left with is a howcatchem.' She paused for Neil to digest this, and said, 'We need a trap.'

'Trap?'

'Something like *The Mousetrap*.' Rachel rose from her seat. 'You know *The Mousetrap*?'

'Agatha –'

'No. Not fucking Agatha Christie. Shakespeare. *Hamlet*. *The Mousetrap* is a play within a play.' She launched into a long exposition about the insight it gave into Shakespeare's playwriting innovations, how Hamlet instructed the actors to avoid over-acting, such as large gestures. 'Shakespeare was ahead of his time. Not of an age, but for all time, said Ben Jonson.'

By now Neil was auto involved with the catch on his briefcase which opened if the briefcase was overloaded with files. Each year saw the advance of paper: handouts, edicts from management about health and safety, student rights, evidence sheets to complete.

Rachel paused and said, 'When you decide to listen... Good. You'd like *Hamlet*, it's about the impossibility of certainty or proof. *The Mousetrap* is as close as Hamlet gets to certainty. Hamlet's problem is uncertainty about the ghost. Is it his father or the devil? After all, the ghost says he was murdered by Claudius who poured poison in his ear while he was asleep and wants Hamlet to revenge his death. No trivial request. But is King Claudius guilty? Hamlet can't act until he knows for certain. He must have proof. *The Mousetrap* is his proof.'

Neil was showing interest, and Rachel explained *The Mousetrap*.

'A group of actors arrive, and Hamlet asks them to perform *The Murder of Gonzago*, which Hamlet modifies and renames to fit his father's death, namely poison poured in the King's ear. At the point where the King is poisoned, Claudius rushes from the room. Hamlet now has his proof.'

Neil pouted his lips and looked thoughtful.

'Hamlet infers from Claudius's response that he is guilty and that the ghost really is his father demanding revenge, not the devil disguised as his father. Why else would he rush from the room?'

'Coincidence. Maybe he felt ill, a sudden pain. Food poisoning perhaps. Or just painfully bored. Or he needed to go to the toilet – fast. All correlate equally well. Did Hamlet consider those possibilities?'

'But Shakespeare didn't intend that. You're treating Hamlet as a real person. You've got to put it in the context of the play as a whole. Those interpretations don't fit the themes. Claudius shows guilt and fear.'

'You mean, Hamlet interpreted guilt and fear.'

Rachel sighed deeply. 'OK. What kind of conclusive evidence had you in mind for Milbro?'

'The best circumstantial evidence we can get, I suppose.'

'Degrees of evidence. Not like you. That's progress. Soon you'll be researching again.'

'*The Mousetrap* wouldn't work for Milbro. Impossible to set it up.'

Rachel laughed. 'Not a troupe of players suddenly appearing outside the shredding room. We could set up a drama for Milbro. After all, you're always saying life is drama, a performance. What's the name of the psychologist?'

'Goffman.'

'We'll set up a Goffmanesque drama for Milbro and Andy, something in line with their expectations. Let me work on it.' Adopting a matter-of-fact tone, she added, 'Of course, we'll need a double blind to avoid observer bias, or you won't believe the evidence, some third party to do the observing and analyse the data, someone who has no idea what the research is about. A one-way mirror would be useful. After all, we both believe Milbro is the informer, and you know how you go on about observer bias. Then there's the ethics committee.'

'Ethics committee – You're not serious? You're joking?'

Rachel leaned forward, hand on chin, and beamed.

*

Neil made a final scrutiny of copies of memos and other documents, all indicating fudging and faking of results at CCU, and set off to meet Andy.

Andy sloshed his beer as they headed for a table, saying breathlessly, 'Concrete evidence at last. My Cyril Burt. My scoop. The whole psychology department engaged in fraud. Endemic.'

They sat down and he showed Neil a collection of memos, drafts and other documents.

'From hoaxgate to fakegate. The Shadow's been busy.' He looked expectantly at Neil. 'Confirmation, Neil. Don't let me down. You know all the researchers and their research.'

Neil nonchalantly lifted his beer, took a draught and said, 'Does he include the one where the researcher forgot to state age when advertising for subjects but pressed on anyway, creatively adding their ages later?'

'Yes. *Yes*. So it's true?'

'And the researcher who got a negative result and eliminated various subjects until she got a positive one?'

'Absolutely. You're confirming?'

'The opposite, I'm afraid.'

Andy looked puzzled.

Neil placed his copies of the documents on the table. 'Take a look.'

'Andy looked at the documents. 'I don't – '

'All copies of the Shadow's documents. A simple but effective way to trap and identify the informer. You see, all along we assumed the informer was highly placed, such was his knowledge and the impact of his hoaxing. Important hoax equals important person. We overlooked Goffman's humble non-person. At first, I thought the weakness was the communal pigeonholes, but that didn't explain the handwritten crumpled note, presumably thrown in a bin. From there I suspected a cleaner – access to keys and bins. That didn't fit because all the cleaners are female. So I followed the waste bags and ended up in the recycling station run by Milbro Smith. He operates this monster shredding machine called Hercules. Aptly named. Cuts through any amount of data. Security and confidentiality, you see. The recycling station is locked and inaccessible to outsiders, making it a near-perfect laboratory experiment.'

'Except the cleaners.'

'As I said, all the cleaners are female. But would a humble shredder understand the research? And what possible motive? Then I thought, just because he's a shredder doesn't mean he's not educated. Could be self-educated, or educated but downwardly mobile, perhaps embittered by his sunken status. My next port of call was the library. I persuaded the head librarian to let me see the lending records of staff. She alerted me to Milbro. Borrows books on psychology, coincidentally in the areas sabotaged. And' – Neil paused for effect – 'he was once a vicar.'

'The religious voice, the religious voice,' Andy said faintly.

'Still very circumstantial, of course. Then I remembered seeing a therapy diary in the recycling station. It didn't register at first. Selena de Vaux's patients keep therapy diaries.

They're very distinctive, Wedgwood blue, classical laurel motif. He was undergoing therapy. One of her patients.'

'I don't follow.'

Neil smiled triumphantly. 'He controls anger by snapping an elastic band. All in the diary.'

Andy laughed. 'You're making this up. Tell me, if the recycling station is so secure, how did you gain entry?'

'I stayed behind one night and made a copy of his diary. First, I had to get the code for the keypad lock. Wasn't difficult. People are careless, or lazy. The diary was disappointing. Day-by-day emotional states and ways of dealing with them, but no mention of sabotage or meeting with you. Then I realised he stopped therapy before the sabotage. His symptoms provided the final clue. Strange flashbacks and fragmented memories, such as a white green room and a green blackboard, and a voice saying, "You must go on". Then it all made sense, all fitted. There's a white painted Green Room behind the stage, used for a time by Matlock to conduct his obedience research, now a storeroom. Milbro must have been a subject.'

'Green Room?'

Neil explained how a green room could be white and a green board black.

'You're sure he was a subject?'

'Not absolutely. Haven't asked Matlock yet.'

'How can you be certain this Milbro is the Shadow? Couldn't anyone have picked up the fake material on route to the recycling station? A caretaker or maintenance.'

'I planted bits of evidence in the bags over a period of time just before they were collected and taken to the recycling station.'

'Maybe someone else searched them. In a pile, you said?'

'I watched the bags from the balcony and followed the cleaner. Remember, once in the recycling station only Milbro has access.'

'You gained access? Maybe someone else…'

Neil shrugged. 'Possible. Can't control every last variable.'

'The researchers involved? The names on the drafts?'

'All fakes. Made up. I couldn't name real researchers and gambled on Milbro's not knowing and not checking.'

Andy pushed the pile towards Neil. 'Go through them. Something might be genuine.'

Neil went through the pile. 'All fakes, I'm afraid.' He pushed his file of copies towards Andy. 'Correspond to my copies exactly.'

'OK. It sounds watertight. Are you absolutely sure no one else can access the recycling station? Maintenance staff?'

Neil shrugged. 'It's possible. That's why we need final proof; direct evidence. We need Milbro to confess.'

'You want me to confront him?'

'It's a good story. A scoop. Fake faked research entraps saboteur, or something. Milbro won't be passing on any more information. He's no use to you now.'

'Not what I was hoping for.' Andy stared into his beer glass, now half empty. Turning to Neil he said, 'That exposes the informer, but doesn't prove there's no faking. Absence of evidence not evidence of absence.'

'You could say that about all sorts of things: existence of aliens, life on Mars, Bigfoot, the Abominable Snowman. All may exist. Just haven't found the evidence.'

Andy looked disconsolate. 'Not the VC, not all the VC's men, not even Matlock's men, not a researcher even, just a shredder. A fucking shredder. A non-person, a nonentity, a nothing. Just my luck.' He glanced sharply at Neil. 'And you've heard nothing about faking and fudging?'

Neil shook his head. 'Not to my knowledge. Getting back to Milbro, don't you think it strange going from vicar to shredder? Surely a story there?'

*

Scrolling through a file, Matlock turned and grinned at Neil.

'Glad to be rid of the lever arch files. Ungainly monsters sag under their own weight. Incapable of standing up. Academic dinosaurs. Once stored them in a damp basement, pages musty, some mildewed. But not now. All on disk. Clean, odour-free.' He chuckled. 'Two research assistants transferred the data. Could hear them coughing and wheezing. But the data's secure now. Only I know the password, and I lock away the copies.' He returned to the screen and muttered, 'A shredder. Who would have thought?'

'A non-person.'

'Milbro Smith, Milbro Smith. The name doesn't... I didn't keep names, of course, except for a few follow-ups. Gave each subject a number and initials. But I did note info on background. A vicar, you say? Let me put in the word vicar. No, nothing. Are you sure he was a vicar? Let's try priest. Bingo! One subject was a priest. Only one. Subject MS641.' He beamed across at Neil. 'Spot on. I won't ask you how you obtained Milbro's therapy diary. Easily explained, I'm sure. More impressive is how you managed to persuade Miss Blenkinsop to part with a library record. That is truly amazing. Well done, well done.'

Neil started to explain but Matlock said very seriously, 'Don't tell me. The less I know about the sordid details, the better.'

'Any more information on him?' Neil said, nodding towards the computer.

He looked again at the file. 'Need to search another disk for the exact variant he participated in, and another for debriefing. About it, for the moment. Leave it with me.' He chuckled. 'A shredder, and all along Odlum thought it was you. Of course, I didn't –'

'Yes, I know. But Odlum's paranoid.'

'Hush. Be careful what you say. I wouldn't go as far as that.'

'How far would you go? 70 per cent paranoid? 50 per cent? That's why I lied about meeting Andy.'

Neil had given Matlock a carefully edited account of his meetings with Andy, described as an ongoing friendship. Had Andy known the informer's identity and revealed it to him he would, of course, have told Matlock.

'Look, I understand your anger, Neil, but think positive. At least you're researching, even if it's not psychology.' He chuckled, leaned back, picked up a pen and began tapping. 'The next step is to inform the VC. Wonderful array of evidence. All circumstantial, but as you say, most people are convicted on circumstantial evidence, rarely on direct evidence. Still, there's always the possibility of coincidence.'

'Odlum didn't give me the benefit of coincidence.'

'Right. Right. Let's move on. Be positive. The diary, his reading, the trap – brilliantly executed I might say – all pointing to Milbro. Be interesting to see how he explains it all. God, has he got some explaining to do. Not least why he did it.'

Matlock sank back into his swivel chair and visibly relaxed. 'The sabotage is over, that's a relief. And it's not a team member.' He laughed and banged his fist on the table. 'A shredder. Who would have thought? I didn't realise we had a shredder on the premises. What else is lurking around our basements? Bin loads of rubbish removed daily, and you don't give a thought to who's taking it or where it's going.'

A long pause followed, and Neil knew Matlock wanted to say something, something disagreeable.

'Selena. Selena de Vaux.' Neil noticed his long stress on the S, the hiss of a particularly venomous snake. 'She's deep. Very private. A very private person. What's her role in all this? You seem to know her. After all, you obtained Milbro Smith's diary.'

'Not from Selena. She doesn't know –'

'Quite. Quite. Don't tell me. The less I know... Do you think she will discuss Milbro with me?'

Neil laughed. 'Absolutely not.'

'You seem very certain.'

'She has a Hippocratic Oath mentality.'

'Quite. Quite.'

'If you meet Selena, don't mention I obtained the diary. Is it possible to delay interrogating Milbro? Andy's confronting him tomorrow and hopes for a confession. The clinching piece of evidence. If he confesses...'

'Quite. Quite.'

*

Alone in his office, the door closed, Matlock thought about the ethics of obedience research and the student who said his obedience to science resembled Nazi obedience to the Fuhrer. Yes, he had caused his subjects to suffer, had deceived them as to the purpose, but recalled Milgram's justification in the original experiments: napalm, agent orange and the pineapple bomb in Vietnam, carpet bombing of Germany, levelling of Japanese cities, all done in the name of democracy and freedom by obedient citizens obeying the call of their country and its way of life. If the experiments illuminated these acts of obedience... And wasn't deception, or Milgram's preferred term technical *illusion*, an everyday occurrence, from the salesperson extolling the virtues of a product, to the politician selling his manifesto? Wasn't life a presentation, everyone from individuals to groups engaged in deception? Wasn't most advertising deception?

*

Expecting negotiation, Neil sat facing Matlock seated at the far end of the rectangular table creating maximum distance.

He was eager to tell Matlock that Milbro Smith had confessed, but before he could speak Matlock said, 'We've decided to wind up the current research into PTSD and start again. The research design is flawed.' His tone was cool and slightly formal.

Neil took a moment to recall the research undertaken by Dunk and Kel, his reluctance to participate because it was a faulty research design, mainly a biased sample comprising self-selected subjects experiencing PTSD symptoms from occupations that generated traumatic events, and how they should have included all those who experience traumas as some may not develop PTSD, the crucial variable not the trauma but attitude towards the trauma – the problem of false positives. The person who develops PTSD may be deficient in coping strategies. Matlock, he recalled, was dismissive.

'The research design is flawed,' Matlock repeated. 'Those who develop PTSD may be deficient in coping strategies, not the situation, as we thought. Why do some cope and others not? That's the new question.'

His tone questioning, Neil said, 'Not the situation? DSM-1V –'

'Not in this instance. DSM-1V assumes the situation causes symptoms. We are looking at attitudes. DSM has got it wrong. Remind me, didn't you find studies that support this?'

Neil nodded. 'A few. There aren't that –'

'Excellent. But we need more. Everything. Total demolition. I want you to team up with Wendy and look into it. I've already spoken to her.'

'What about the current research?'

'As I said, ended. Faulty from the start. PTSD is mostly myth. We need to counter the myth. Get my meaning?'

Neil didn't. It was only a few weeks ago Matlock had tried to entice him onto the PTSD team. 'Think of the litigation alone. You'll be sought after by lawyers across the land.' Now he was denying its very existence.

'Brought in funds, of course,' Matlock was saying. 'Served its purpose. Time to move on. Phase two.'

'Odlum? Dunk? Kel? How –'

'I've squared it with them. Told them we should have started with trauma to see how many develop PTSD. John protested, of course, but I reminded him that he planned a follow-up study to maximise the grant. Well, we're just speeding things up.'

As Neil was leaving, he looked back and said, 'Milbro Smith, I –'

'The VC and I met him and he confessed. Didn't have much choice, thanks to you and Rachel.'

'I was about to tell you he had confessed to Andy. Remember our agreement?'

'Yes. Yes. But the VC...'

'What did Milbro say? What's happening?'

'Another time. When things clarify. It's... it's complicated. I don't need to say all this is under wraps. Above all, don't tell Seedbank anything more. We're still negotiating with Milbro.'

'Negotiating?'

'As I said, complicated.'

*

'It was strange as he stepped out of the shadows. Would appearance match voice?'

'And did it?'

'Mostly, yes. A gloomy, saturnine face, dark watchful eyes, desolate and bleak. A touch gaunt, as much professional cyclist as vicar. You know the type, as aerodynamic as their machines. And you were right, not a vicar, a priest. A Catholic. But his personality is more in his voice, plaintiff and sepulchral. Suffering. You remember I said his vocabulary was slightly archaic? He stepped out of the shadow and said, "You wonder why I sabotaged the experiments? Let me tell you of the strange and harrowing events that made me what I am".

'We went to my flat. Even let me tape him. I knew I was in for a long evening, and it was dawn before he left. Interestingly, he had extracts from Matlock's raw data. Told me he'd read the research in its entirety, including notes on himself, or as he put it, "on his own creation".'

'Own creation?'

'Curious expression. Take it he had access to Matlock's office?'

Neil smiled ironically. 'No need. Matlock had the data transferred to his computer and obligingly sent his lever arch files to be shredded.'

They laughed together at the irony.

'Milbro blames everything on the experiment. Up to then a successful priest, but unable to live with the knowledge that he could obey a command to inflict electric shocks on an innocent person. After that he deteriorated, finally leaving the priesthood. Sad, really.'

'Are you investigating Milbro's background?'

'Is there any point? It's obvious why he left the priesthood. That experiment ruined his life. I feel sorry for him.'

Andy told Neil he was considering an article on the effects of research on subjects linked to PTSD, Milbro a case study. 'Milbro's agreeable. It's a good story.'

*

Neil was troubled by Matlock's refusal to discuss Milbro at their meeting.

'You're in the clear,' Rachel insisted. 'The black spot has firmly settled on Milbro. So don't worry.' She placed her coffee mug on the desk, the surface decorated with coffee rings. 'The job I had explaining your relationship with Andy to Harold. I hope you're grateful. Harold wanted to know how it was possible for you to hoax Andy and Milbro. "Surely, he must have been in regular contact with Andy, complicit even, supplying information. That's what Odlum is saying". Tricky question. Luckily, he doesn't know Andy needed confirmation. I reminded him you didn't have access to most of the information, such as the hospital list. Only Odlum and Milbro had access. I switched to over-reliance on the Hercules shredder. Whatever Hercules' success with the 12 labours, I told him, his namesake failed the 13th: stopping the hand that fed it. Think about it, Harold, a hugely expensive shredding machine producing shreds that can't be un-shredded, and all along operated by the informer. OK, I said, maybe Neil should have been open about his friendship with Andy, but if Neil supplied information, why would he help set up Milbro and Andy using fabricated information? Harold still wasn't convinced. "So, Neil knows nothing about Andy's meetings with Milbro, then contacts Andy and tells him the documents are fakes?" At that point I had to compromise. Ad-libbing like mad, I said you were in regular contact with Andy, of course you were, friends going back a long way. *Friends*, I emphasised. Naturally you discussed Andy's articles with him, and in the process learned about Andy's informant, but couldn't know his identity because Andy didn't know his identity. "Maybe Neil should have told Matlock about these meetings", I said, but what difference would it have made? Neil set Andy and Milbro up. He didn't want the university damaged. I told him you manipulated Andy, not the other way round, played along but never imparted anything of importance. You hoped to find out who the informer was and pretended to be on Andy's side, even helped with some of his articles, then set them both up.'

Rachel walked towards the window and stared into the distance. Turning, she looked directly at Neil. 'Look, there's something else. Let's go for a drink.'

'What I'm going to tell you is in strict secrecy. Not a word to anyone, particularly Weed.' Rachel paused, gulped a large mouthful of wine, and said, 'Milbro Smith is determined to sue. Post-traumatic stress peritraumatic something or other.' She paused again, gulped another mouthful of wine emptying the glass. 'We should have bought a bottle.'

Neil moved to buy more wine, but she held his arm. 'Sit down a moment. There's more.' Another pause. 'Selena's supporting him. Harold's furious. By the way, he knows about your affair with Selena. God knows how. That was also tricky. "Is everyone in this case linked to Neil?" he said. "You, Andy, Milbro, now Selena?" I just laughed. What else could I do? Pure coincidence, I told him. He wondered if Selena would reveal details of Milbro's therapy before it went to court. No, I said. She has a Hippocratic Oath mentality. "More peritraumatic oath", he replied. Witty, don't you think?'

Neil nodded.

'Anyway, I convinced him that despite shagging Selena, she never discusses her patients with you. He knows you helped me steal Milbro's diary. I had no choice but to tell him. Helped your case.'

'Does Selena know about the diary?'

'I don't know.'

Neil reflected a few moments. 'It's becoming clear now. His threat to sue explains Matlock's U-turns on obedience and PTSD. But why didn't he discuss Milbro with me?'

'Matlock supports you, I'm sure.'

'But the chairs. Confrontational. You know the importance of chairs to Matlock.'

'Are all you psychologists mad, or just pretending to be so? Matlock's got a lot on his mind. Maybe he forgot to rearrange the fucking chairs. An off day, felt unwell. A stomach upset. Who knows? If he suspected you, would he ask you to research PTSD with Wendy? You're not thinking. Why have you stopped thinking? Trust me, I did well for you upstairs. Has Harold asked to see you?'

'No.'

'Exactly. My advice is, get on with what you are good at: demolishing research. Have you got together with Wendy yet?'

*

'A friendly, sympathetic meeting,' advised the VC. 'Steer him away from litigation. We can sort this out internally. Invite Shelrack. He has a theory obedience is evolutionary and normal, and the authority of his discipline.'

Matlock smiled at Milbro. 'There's no need to feel guilty,' he explained, looking at the VC who nodded rapidly. 'Those who gave shocks were not evil, merely obeying an all-powerful situation. You were not alone, not untypical but *typical*. Most obeyed.'

He piled on examples, other research, a long catalogue of studies stretching from Asch to Milgram, including King's replication using puppies, but whatever excuse he provided Milbro returned to the same point.

'If there was no threat from outside, no punishment such as awaited the extermination camp guard, why did I obey? Are you saying there is no good or evil, only situations? I would like to believe that, but I cannot. You revealed to me the person that I am, and in doing so destroyed me. Did I solicit thee, maker of my clay to promote me?'

'Destroyed. Isn't that a bit –' started the VC.

'My research was not about personalities, but situations,' interrupted Matlock. 'Perfectly good and kind people like yourself responding to the situation. You were in an agentic state, not acting alone, not responsible, but obeying an authority figure. You went through an agentic shift. Once free of the situation you became your usual self.'

'Would you have said the same of Eichmann? After all, he killed no one after the war.'

Lost for an answer, Matlock hurriedly added, '90 per cent said they benefited from the experiment.'

'89 per cent to be exact, which makes me one of the 11 per cent who failed to benefit.'

'How did you –' Milbro was right, 89 per cent. In his write-up he had rounded up to 90 per cent. How could Milbro possibly know the correct figure? That moment he remembered the lever arch files, sent to Milbro to be shredded.

'According to my record, when debriefed you said you benefited.'

Milbro looked at the VC. 'Of course, I said it was worthwhile, I wanted to believe it, so traumatic was the experience. I rationalised then blocked the memory. But memories remain, gnawing away. I could not sleep. I became anxious and lost my job as a priest. I was at a loss to understand. And all along, it was that odious experiment. Slowly the memories came back.'

'Before or after therapy with Selena de Vaux?'

'After.'

'You're saying the sabotage began after you stopped therapy?' Matlock gave the VC a significant look. 'I need to clarify a point, Milbro. You are saying you had no intention of sabotage when you took employment as a shredder?'

'Absolutely not. At that point I had no memory of the experiment.'

There was a long silence.

'My specialism is evolution,' Shelrack said, finally finding a niche in the discussion. 'Think of obedience as a virtue. We are adapted to survive, and obedience has survival value.

As Professor Matlock says, most obeyed. Without obedience there would be anarchy. You were just obeying your evolutionary nature.'

'Didn't Hitler preach evolution, the survival of the fittest, and murdered those deemed unfit, so-called life unworthy of life?' Milbro glared at Matlock. 'I was not a person to you. Not a name. You created me, you and your evil experiment. Did I ask you to fill me with revenge?'

*

Matlock was franticly scrolling through the files of his obedience experiment. He and the VC were meeting Milbro again and the VC wanted a printout of Milbro's responses to the experiment.

Matlock sighed bitterly. All this extra work. We behave differently in different contexts, observed Milgram, have no hesitation exposing our throat to a man with a razor in a barber's shop. Matlock emitted a dry laugh and thought he would have no hesitation cutting Milbro's throat, situational constraints notwithstanding.

After the last meeting with Milbro the VC had criticised Matlock's research. Milbro had a point, subjects were not treated as people, were objects, research objects (a term borrowed from Rachel). Easy to criticise with hindsight, thought Matlock. The obedience research had been a Herculean task, long hours working alone on the variations late into the night and weekends, 18 variations in all and 700-plus subjects to get through, for he aimed to match Milgram's prodigious sample. The grant didn't cover everything, leaving little time to debrief subjects, just a perfunctory explanation, assurance the shocks were not real, meeting with the grinning recipient of the shocks revealed to be an actor (just a hoax really), asked how they felt about the experience (most were positive), shown the door.

At least Milbro recorded positive, whatever his rationalisation. A small, random selection was sent follow-up questionnaires a year later. Milbro was not included. All subjects had signed a disclaimer stating they had freely participated, of course, hopefully releasing the university from any legal claims. He still had the originals and the questionnaires completed by each subject. Would that stand up in a court today? Attitudes had changed. Would a court judge the past or the present? Litigation was everywhere. PTSD fashionable and everywhere. Finally, he came to the responses during the experiment and hesitated. A lot rested on this. Was Milbro one of the few who stuttered, trembled, laughed hysterically? He scrolled to Milbro and almost cried with joy at what he read. Variant 28. Milbro had gone all the way with the shocks despite being given orders by phone, a situation where a large percentage cheated by giving lower shocks. But not Milbro. OK, at two points he demurred and needed prompting, but showed no signs of distress. A model psychopath.

He made a note to humanise the records, add names and create more background, treat them as people not objects. He should have done that years ago, but there was so little time. Here was another advantage to storing information on a computer. So easy to modify. Then with sinking feeling he remembered Milbro had accessed the original lever arch files, probably poring over them that very moment. But the fact remained, a significant number of Variant 28 subjects refused or cheated by giving lower shocks. But not Milbro.

*

Matlock and the VC peered down the table at Milbro.

'We've decided you are right. Not the situation after all in your case. We wouldn't go as far as you, not an evil nature, but definitely something you brought to the experiment – something in your personality.'

Matlock produced a sheet of paper and passed it to Milbro. 'According to my record, you participated in Variant 28 where I left the room and gave orders by phone. You obeyed to the end. You could have disobeyed. Most did. Obedience dropped by two-thirds and a surprising number cheated by giving lower shocks. But not you. In that experimental condition you were a minority.'

Milbro was silent.

Matlock pointed to Milbro's comments. 'Didn't you tick the box indicating you found the experience positive? So why the trauma?'

'Cognitive dissonance,' said Milbro. A brief incongruous smile crossed his saturnine face.

The VC raised his eyebrows.

'As I explained at our last meeting, I deceived myself at the time. I wanted to feel I was in control. It was hard to admit I had been fooled and humiliated. More than that, it was hard to admit I was capable of evil. I was suffering from cognitive dissonance.'

'Could you explain what you understand by cognitive dissonance,' asked the VC.

'Festinger said in the face of contradiction we either change our behaviour or our beliefs. I could do nothing about my behaviour so I rationalised my belief by saying I found it beneficial.'

'The majority said they benefited from the experiment,' said Matlock.

'But were they truthful or rationalising? Anyway, I am not a statistical average. I am an individual.'

'Who obeyed to the very end.'

Milbro rose from his chair, placed his hands on the table and leaned forward. 'As I said at our last meeting, you created me, you and your evil experiment. Did I ask you to fill me with revenge? You gave me no choice.'

'Isn't that a bit melodramatic?' said the VC.

'I repeat,' said Matlock, 'you did have choice. Not everyone went to the end.'

'Let's get this clear,' said the VC, a tinge of hopelessness in his voice. 'You say you are suffering from post-traumatic stress caused by participating in the obedience experiment?'

Milbro nodded.

'Yet, according to your therapy diary, Selena believes you were most probably sexually abused.'

Milbro was visibly taken aback. 'How did you... it's confidential.'

The VC didn't answer, and Milbro added, 'As I said, I have not seen Selena for some time. She did not have all the facts then and I could only recall fragments of memory that made little sense. They seemed to fit her theory at the time.'

'But now your memory has recovered?'

'Mostly.'

'Mostly? So there could be more facts to come, perhaps requiring a new theory?' said the VC.

Milbro stared impassively.

'And you applied for the shredder job before you remembered participating in the experiment?' said Matlock.

Milbro remained silent.

'Extraordinary coincidence getting a job at the very university where the experiments took place.'

Milbro shrugged and smiled thinly. 'Coincidences happen.' He started to rise from his chair.

'You know, we can offer you therapy, sort out your attitude, your lack of coping strategies.'

'I have a therapist – Selena. She – she'll support me.'

'Selena. Se-lee-na. Yes, of course,' said Matlock.

'What I think you are saying is, it wasn't the trauma but my response to the trauma. Isn't that blaming the victim?

Would you say that to a victim of burglary? It is not the burglary that's causing your anger and insecurity but your response to the burglary. Doesn't your department's research support PTSD?'

'I think you'll find we've progressed from that particular approach.'

'How convenient. Seems coincidence is not peculiar to me.'

The VC adopted a conciliatory cards-on-the-table tone. 'If you drop litigation we can settle quietly. I'm sure you don't want the police involved. Malicious damage to research.'

'Then there's your reference,' said Matlock.

Milbro rose, headed for the door and said, 'I am suing. As a Christian, I forgive you, of course.'

'Yet you still intend to sue?'

'Of course.'

'Before you go,' said the VC with gravity, 'I must inform you that from this moment you are banned from the campus premises.' As he spoke a security guard entered the office. 'Security will escort you to the In-house Shredding and Baling Recycling Station to collect any personal belongings and escort you from the premises.'

The door closed.

Matlock shook his head and turned to the VC. 'Funny thing, Christian forgiveness. Most still want their pound of flesh.'

Matlock rose from his seat. 'I need to see Selena before Milbro does.'

*

Matlock had just told Selena that Milbro was the informer. She denied this initially, surely some mistake. He deftly presented the evidence, above all, Milbro's confession to him and the VC.

She stood up to leave. 'You must realise I can't discuss Milbro Smith. What happens between Milbro and me, his therapist, is confidential.'

Matlock pointed out that Milbro had openly discussed his therapy, the sexual abuse theory, all contained in his therapy diary. It was in the open.

'His diary?'

'All I want is to clarify a few points. In strictest confidence. Trust me. The police aren't involved yet. But criminal damage...' He shook his head. 'For the time being, that's the way the VC wants it. Look, I want to help Milbro. We all want to help him. Whatever we discuss is confidential.'

Selena sat down. 'He let you read his diary?'

'Copy sent to me anonymously,' Matlock said smoothly. 'Milbro isn't the only informer. Informers informing on informers. But understandable. Milbro was a threat to the department. We used every means necessary to catch him.' He looked at Selena. 'What do you make of his recollections?'

'I really shouldn't –'

'Then let's discuss the condition generally. What do you make of weals appearing spontaneously? Speaking generally.'

'Sometimes victims of abuse or torture who were bound spontaneously develop the marks of abuse. I'm linking repressed memory and PTSD. That's my research. Victims often blame themselves for the abuse, feel they encouraged it in some way; feel guilt and repress the memory. Fits his Catholicism.'

Matlock noticed she was becoming more specific.

'I suspect some sort of bondage. I'm not a strong believer in repressed memory but the evidence fits.'

'Buzzers and clicks? He says in his diary that he is startled by buzzers and clicks.'

Selena explained her belief that buzzers and clicks indicate electricity, the weals caused by electric cables, electric shocks perhaps. More than abuse, torture. Same with the commands "You must go on", and "Continue". 'Who knows what happened to him in the control of those celibate priests. As you know, child abuse was rife in the Catholic Church and covered up, a conspiracy of clergy and devoted laity. His parents were ambitious for him and pushed him into the priesthood, altar boy, then seminary. How could he tell them? And if he told them, would they believe him? Want to believe him.'

Matlock allowed her to continue unchallenged.

'While under therapy his memory slowly recovered, something about a white room, white coats, a machine. A man standing over him saying, "You must go on". The word continue repeated over and over. At that point I could get no further. He would shudder and break off. I think it is an abuse memory.'

'The fragmented flashbacks. White green room, green blackboard?'

'I can't explain them yet.'

Matlock rubbed his chin. 'But he doesn't remember being abused?'

'Repressed memory. Dissociation.'

'Of course, of course.'

Matlock stood up. 'Selena, I'm afraid you are totally wrong, and I am going to prove it.' He relished her startled expression. 'Come, follow me.'

He led her to the Green Room and pointed to the sign: *Green Room*. 'Green. OK?' The door grated open, and Selena covered her ears. Matlock pointed to the walls. 'White. Green. White? White green room.'

Selena looked bewildered.

He laughed softly. 'You still haven't got it, have you?' He walked over to the generator. 'The shock machine for my obedience experiments. The mirror facing the generator is one-way – once used to observe subjects, hundreds of subjects. 703 in total.'

Selena glanced at her watch and said irritably, 'The point?'

'The point. Yes, the point. The point is, one of them, one of the subjects, one of the 703 was Milbro Smith.'

He gave her a moment to digest this.

'You said you couldn't decipher the fragmentary memories. I can help you there. A green room that is white, a blackboard that is green.' He pointed to the green blackboard in the far corner. 'Not some paedophile torturer.'

Matlock explained the original purpose of the Green Room.

Selena was rattled. This is what he had hoped for. Free of her therapy room, her comfort zone, her abuse explanation of Milbro disintegrating, he confident, on home ground, in control, surrounded by the trappings of experimental psychology.

'What about the voices, the repeated commands?'

'Yes, the commands: *you must continue; you have no choice; you must go on.* All part of my experiment, my commands to the participant. As I said, not some priest paedophile-torturer after all.'

Selena was looking a bit shaken, and Matlock suggested that she sit down.

'I was led by the evidence,' she said falteringly. 'I am always led by the evidence.'

Standing over her, body weight evenly distributed, voice deep and low, Matlock's words were clear, measured, and projected authority. 'The problem is, the problem here, is that your kind of theory is so flexible it is supported by any evidence. Anything can mean anything. Anything can lead to anything. Everything and anything fits. That's the difference between therapy and science – real science.'

*

Selena remained looking out of the window as Matlock entered.

Without turning she said, 'You deceived me. You lied to me. You asked about abuse when all along you knew Milbro was a subject of your odious experiment. You deliberately tried to make me look foolish.'

'A technical illusion. I was only interested in getting to the truth, for Christ's sake. The department is under threat, the university is under threat.'

She turned and faced Matlock. 'You think my method lacks rigour, don't you?'

'Of course. More to the point, therapy isn't a science.'

'Not according to your narrow experimental approach, no. Despite your meticulous work on obedience, isolating this and that variable, your only finding is that most obeyed, and that the behaviour you term obedience was linked to authority. The explanation you attach to your research, the agentic state, is mere guesswork borrowed from Milgram, your luminary. You walk in Milgram's shadow, a mere replicator.'

She sat down as Matlock peered round her office, clean white walls, ornament-free desk. Focusing on a pile of blue diaries, he said, 'What do you call your analysands – patients or clients?'

'Analysands!' She laughed merrily. 'What a wonderfully quaint term, couch and Oriental rug, whiff of cigar smoke. I'm not a Freudian, if that's what you think.' She leaned back and adopted a dismissive tone. 'Patient is too medical, of course. Client is non-medical, but... I don't call them anything, really. Just their first name. Unlike your wretched experiment. What was it? Numbers? Prisoners have numbers. What number did Milbro merit? I don't suppose you can remember.'

'But I did use names, Selena, I did see subjects as people. Debriefed each one in depth.'

Selena smiled mockingly. 'Oh, how easily you lie. Not according to your written account.' She handed Matlock a copy of his account taken from his lever arch file.

'This is confidential.'

'So is Milbro's therapy diary.'

They sat in silence a few moments. Selena spoke first. 'OK. I was misled by limited evidence and thought it pointed to sexual abuse. The real reason would have emerged under therapy, of course, had Milbro completed. But it doesn't alter anything. Repressed memory and PTSD remain as strong as ever, only the cause was not sexual abuse but your experiment. Not sexual abuse, science abuse. Not a sex object but an experiment object. Milbro feels intense guilt. Blames himself. Hence self-punishment, resulting in sleeplessness, anxiety and weals.'

'Weals? At our last meeting you said they were marks of sexual abuse, such as being bound in some way. You suggested electric cable. How do you explain them now?'

'Wasn't the recipient of electric shocks strapped by his wrists to the chair?'

'Yes, but Milbro was never strapped to the chair. He was the teacher in the experiment, not the learner.'

'Perhaps guilt caused him to invert roles; guilt and empathy for the supposed victim. How could he cope with total sense of failure and complete loss of integrity? He avoided all memories that evoked anxiety. Such memories don't really disappear but reappear as something else, sleeplessness, anxiety, free-floating anger. He couldn't resolve the contradiction, couldn't continue as a priest because of his mental condition brought on by the humiliating experiment.'

'You explain his cognitions, but how do you account for his behaviour?'

'He is torn in two directions: finding out and avoiding.'

'He sabotages research he initially couldn't remember participating in, and coincidentally works as a shredder at the university where the alleged trauma occurred, giving him access to sensitive data.'

'You forget, he recovered memories of the experiment after getting a job here, and the sabotage occurred after he stopped therapy. Stopping therapy and sabotage were his way of taking control, his way of working through the trauma. When you experimented on him, he lost all control. As you yourself say, he was controlled by the situation. Sabotage put him in control, made him an experimenter manipulating variables, a creative act. Sign of progress, really. Moving towards a solution. I encourage control; facing the cause head on. The idea of therapy is to release the repressed memory and express anger to manage it. When he damaged those experiments, he was damaging his abuser. A perfectly understandable response, showing the success of the therapy. A positive response.'

'Positive. Are you fucking serious?'

'Positive in the therapeutic sense.'

'Well, bully for therapy.'

There was a long pause which Selena found less disconcerting than Matlock, as these were common in therapy. Sounds usually unnoticed overwhelmed the consulting room, the ticking clock growing louder and louder. Selena was very still, statuesque, her gaze fixed on Matlock.

Matlock broke the silence. 'I still think it's an extraordinary coincidence that he should choose the very university where the experiments took place. Don't people with PTSD avoid locations that caused their stress?'

'As I explained, my research is a synthesis of three theories: PTSD, represses memory and peritraumatic dissociation. The memory was so completely repressed he wouldn't know.'

'And took a job here by coincidence?' He shook his head.

'Coincidences do happen. Didn't Milbro say that to you? I know you experimental psychologists abhor coincidences, as nature abhors a vacuum. He lives in Nottingham, the university is well known, a big employer. The shredding room is distant from your long-disused, cobwebbed laboratory, now storeroom. He would have no reason to go there.'

'Let me tell you what I think, Selena. But before that I want to emphasise no fault attaches to your therapy, except indirectly. Milbro duped you, that's all. He's a fake. He used you, is still using you. He wants you to defend him in court. I think Milbro carefully planned the sabotage. He duped you, fooled you, that's what I think.'

'You mean I'm supposed to tell fakes from the real thing? Strange, recalling the false subjects queuing up for your experiments.'

Matlock paused. 'Yes, yes. OK, like the false subjects.'

'No, I don't believe Milbro is a fake. You don't understand my research, do you? My research is a synthesis. PTSD results from failure to process the trauma. Though it is usual in cases of PTSD for the trauma to be all too vivid, in some cases dissociation occurs, called peritraumatic dissociation. A trauma occurs, say abuse in childhood, and the victim dissociates at the time, distorts the memory or loses it completely. But disconnected fragments remain, pushing to the surface. The victim avoids, shuts out, but suffers a host of symptoms indirectly. My task, as therapist, is to make conscious the trauma and facilitate resolution. But, as always, I must be led by the evidence. Milbro is no fake. As to the sabotage, I didn't consciously encourage his aggression. He told me about his anger, how it would well up for no apparent reason and no tangible object to vent it on, which is why I encouraged him to put an elastic band round his wrist and snap it whenever he felt angry.'

Matlock roared with laughter. 'Fat lot of good that did him.'

'Milbro is depressed, clinically depressed. Confirmed by his doctor.'

'Well, I'm clinically pissed off, but I don't go round sabotaging research.'

The meeting ended.

*

'Selena's distant. She's avoiding me.'

Rachel smiled. 'You mean more distant? Distantly distant. Distant beyond distant.' Noting Neil's despondent expression, she said, 'Sorry that was mean. You're out of touch with developments, of course, your lowly status. According to Harold, you and Wendy did a brilliant job trashing PTSD research. Must have taken hours digging out all those American counter studies. Matlock didn't tell Selena how he obtained Milbro's therapy diary, but he did mention your work on PTSD. That must have soured her. Disloyal, and all that. I'd keep away for a bit if I were you, give her time to calm down.'

'How did Selena react to the counter-research?'

'I was coming to that. She wasn't exactly bowed by the evidence.'

Matlock had presented the findings on PTSD to Selena, expecting her to bow to the weight of evidence, bombarding her with numerous studies and a battery of tests used by different researchers: the *Mississippi Scale for Combat-Related PTSD*, the *Beck Depression Inventory (BDI)*, the *revised Social Support Questionnaire, revised (SSQR)*, the *Shipley Institute of Living Scale revised manual (SILS)*, the *Ways of Coping Checklist (WOC)*, and the *45-item Dispositional Resilience Scale (DRS)*.

He explained that these researchers showed disposition more important than all other influences, and most people who experience trauma do not develop PTSD. Response to trauma is what matters. The few who develop symptoms have poor coping strategies. In other words, the problem inheres in them, the individual, a personality flaw, not the situation as we once thought.

During Matlock's exposition Selena had remained silent, appeared distant and uninterested, auto involved with one of her nails which had broken.

'Put simply. Put simply,' he repeated to gain her attention, 'why did some develop PTSD, others not? Surely that shows response to the situation and disposition are more important than the situation?'

Tone even and measured, Selena said, 'Milbro stopped being a priest because of severe depression, and the underlying reason was the trauma of the experiment. I agree, someone else might not have been so traumatised, but Milbro's faith was shattered and his whole identity undermined. Yes, he did bring something to the situation, not a personality flaw as you say but beliefs, his deeply held Christian beliefs and his calling which you shattered. Milbro is a very special individual, not a statistical average.'

'I'm loath to say it, Selena argued well. Harold's less than happy. So where does it leave us? If Milbro were a character in a novel I would want a surprise at this stage, some twist in the plot. Some unexpected development. Any ideas?'Neil shrugged.

'God, you're useless. So much for the psychological imagination.'

Reaching back, Rachel picked up a folder and shook it in front of Neil. '*Voilà*. Copy of Milbro's personal file. Job application, references and, most importantly, the name and address of the parish where he was priest. Good reference from the parish, of course, but that means nothing, not even from men of God, even less in view of the paedophile cover-ups. Priest to shredder must have been tricky for him at the interview. Says he lost his calling and couldn't continue as a priest. OK, it happens, but why choose shredding? And why here? Coincidence, he claims. Of course, cost-cutting management took him on, would take on Attila the Hun at the right price. "We know you've been a bit of a bad boy in the past, Attila..."'

Neil laughed.

'The most worrying aspect for Matlock and Harold is the weals on Milbro's wrists, now interpreted as physical evidence of guilt-engendered suffering, no doubt photographed and described by some lawyer. Exhibit A. Selena says stigmata is part of his religion, guilt and empathy for Christ, or in Milbro's case for the supposed victim strapped to the chair. Clever argument. Do you think Weed will help? Special relationship, and all that.'

'Andy won't help. He's peeved about being hoaxed; disappointed the saboteur is lowly and acted alone.'

'Then if Weed won't help, we must access local papers at the British library and interview people locally. The newspaper library's at Colindale. I've checked it out. Crap area, but it's the right side of London, and doable in a day.'

Neil shook his head. 'I don't know. Long journey.'

'Two hours, max.'

'Parking? You know what London's like.'

'Oodles of parking at the library.'

'Referee? Membership?'

'No referee needed. Membership on the door. Just the usual identification. No charge. You're not getting out of this. Even Hamlet couldn't hesitate on this one.'

'Internet?' asked Neil, close to desperation.

'Checked. Yahoo showed no local papers. Name Milbro Smith drew a blank.'

20

The journey to Colindale took three hours, some inexplicable hold-up on the way, and they arrived midday. 'Oodles of parking' amounted to some ten spaces at the front of the library, all taken, no doubt for the day. Wasting an hour driving around, they headed for the nearby RAF Museum.

The attendant eyed them suspiciously, their free car park a magnet for workers in the area.

'What are you here for?'

'We're visiting the museum,' Rachel said breezily.

He seemed unconvinced.

'Battle of Britain hall,' said Neil, thinking he was at least 70 and old enough to have fought in the war.

'Churchill's speeches,' added Rachel. 'Pure poetry.'

Once parked, they slipped through a small side entrance and headed for the newspaper library. By the time they had registered and received their reader passes it was time for lunch, and they headed for a nearby pub. It had gone two before they started the search. National papers were on CD-ROM and searchable, but local papers were limited to hard copies. This was a blow. What might have taken minutes to find would now stretch into hours, or days.

They sweated through the papers (it was a hot day), month by month, starting around Milbro's departure from the parish some years earlier and working backwards, laboriously turning page after page, beginning to believe there was nothing about Milbro. On the fifth month, a result. But it was only the beginning. Milbro's story stretched back years, a bizarre tale that filled the gaps and offered a startling explanation for the weals on his wrists.

The library closed at 5pm and they needed to copy numerous articles and pictures. There were few machines, some out of order, and queues. They were exhausted, the heat, eye strain, long waits for newspapers. There was no cafeteria, just machines issuing drinks and snacks in a cramped and humid space. The weather was exceptionally hot and humid, London hotter still, a huge storage heater of concrete and bricks, emanating heat day and night. Rachel suggested they might stay the night at a friend's in Chalk Farm, a few stops down the Northern Line. 'I'll need to phone.'

Neil sighed wearily. 'Can't see a phone box.'

Rachel smiled triumphantly, and with a flourish produced a mobile phone. 'No need. Bought it second-hand. £50 new.'

Neil was intrigued. A cordless phone with built-in aerial. Rachel was up on technology, her landline cutting-edge allowing her to switch between callers or have three-way conversations.

*

Neil was poised to present the findings on Milbro to Matlock, a huge dossier crammed with articles and photos. Rachel had insisted Neil take all the credit to boost his career. 'He hates me, remember.' Neil compromised; he would say it was his idea, his planning, but include Rachel.

Before he could present the dossier, Matlock began fuming over Andy's latest article on the effect of research on subjects. 'Out of date,' he raged. 'Doesn't deal with the growth of ethics committees and all the other safeguards now in place. Typical media distortion. We couldn't do that kind of research today. Political correctness, human rights, litigation, all aided by therapists and councillors. We even run our own courses on counselling. Everyone wants to be a councillor. Flying councillors, trauma councillors ready-to-rush-to-any-disaster councillors, riding on the backs of traumatic stress disorder. What happened to toughness, self-reliance, getting on with things, pushing ahead, overcoming? When the going gets tough, the tough get going, and all that? We're creating a generation of wimps, victims, dependents, excuses and excusers, passive recipients of events. Why is everyone so fucking fragile? I blame Freud. His entire sample trapped in the first five years, fixated, unable to move on. I've always thought the most remarkable thing about most people is not that they are anchored to the past and backward looking, but sail free, so to speak. The whole of therapy is based on a biased sample.' He leaned back. 'At least Seedbank hasn't revealed anything about Milbro yet. Why is he holding off?'

Neil paused, then said quietly, 'I can answer that, but I have something more important, I have the answer to the weals. I don't think Milbro will sue.' He pushed the dossier towards Matlock.

'Bring your chair round,' Matlock said. 'We'll go over this together.'

Neil guided him through the data. Finally, Matlock looked at Neil and said, 'This is war, not research, but it's in the interest of research.' He grinned broadly. 'And you're researching again, even if it goes unrecognised, doesn't attract funds, will never appear in a journal. Research of the highest calibre, all the same. Well done, Neil. Evidence. Solid evidence. We've trapped Milbro with a clinching piece of evidence that contradicts his story. What's that modern term?'

'His narrative.'

'His narrative, yes. Not experimental, of course, not complete control of variables, but close. You set up a hypothesis and tested it. Scientific to that degree. You started with a hypothesis – a non-person – and tested it. From there you looked at non-persons. Cleaners didn't fit – all female. Popper would approve. The library books fitted, but circumstantial. Milbro's diary didn't support the hypothesis at first, but didn't contradict it, and so on. Well done, Neil, well done.'

'And Rachel. Don't forget –'

'And... Rachel.'

*

Matlock's voice was almost singing as he invited Selena to sit down.

'Sit anywhere.' He pointed to a choice of seats. 'Sit anywhere,' he repeated. 'It doesn't matter. It doesn't matter.'

'Before we start,' said Selena, 'I can't discuss Milbro with you. His request.'

'No problem, Selena, no problem. But we can go over what we discussed at our last meeting?'

She nodded.

'You are staying with Milbro's symptoms and sabotage caused by my experiment?'

'Yes. Milbro feels intense guilt. Blames himself. Hence self-punishment appearing as weals, sleeplessness, anxiety. We've been over this –'

'Yes. The weals. I'm glad you mention the weals. You're saying that stigmata – an established part of the Catholic religion – partly explains Milbro's weals? Identification with the victim, in this case recipient of the shocks?'

'Didn't I make that clear?'

'You are right, Selena. Milbro's Catholicism explains the weals.'

'You agree?'

Behind Matlock was a white screen. He rose and switched on the OHP. 'Would you mind switching off the main light, Selena?'

An image appeared on the screen of Milbro Smith impressively dressed in a cassock, ankle-length with 33 front buttons symbolising Christ's life on earth, black symbolising poverty, sash symbolising chastity, and clerical collar symbolising obedience. But more striking were his hands, held out showing what appeared to be wounds, one on each hand.

'Milbro has a history of self-mutilation.' Matlock displayed more photos and some headlines relating to Milbro, adding a matter-of-fact commentary.

'You do have roundabout ways of saying things, Professor Matlock. Does everything have to come with a performance? Please get to the point.'

'The point, the point. Of course. That's where the dates come in. All this occurred before participating in the experiment.'

Selena countered. 'If a stigmatic can induce stigmata because of identification with Christ's suffering, Milbro can do the same with the supposed shock victim. Sympathetic weals. His Catholic background, guilt. I really don't see the problem.'

'The problem, yes, the problem.' He paused, looked at Selena. 'As I said, long before participating in my experiment Milbro was a stigmatic on a grand scale, nail holes in his hands, thorn marks on his head, all five sacred wounds of Christ at different times: feet, hands, back, side, head. For a time, many of his parishioners worshipped him – reflected status, and all that. Their own home-grown stigmatic. Why should the Italians have the lion's share? But there was a problem.' He paused again, switched off the OHP and motioned Selena to switch on the light. 'The problem was, the problem *is*, the nail holes were round, whereas nails in ancient Rome were square, tapering to a point. That was his error. Secondly, the holes appeared in his hands. Hands can't hold the weight of a man so the Romans nailed their victims through the wrists, carefully avoiding arteries. They knew their stuff. He's not much of a historian, your Milbro Smith, probably misled by religious paintings and crucifixes. After those revelations, everything was suspect, such as masses of encrusted blood but superficial wounds. He described them as gifts from God, others began saying self-inflicted. The church, wary from the start, distanced itself. Strange how some stigmatists are believed and made saints… Anyway –'

'How could you possibly know all this?'

'Good question. A difference of research methods. You listen to clients' verbal statements and believe what they tell you, their stories confined to four walls –'

'You're oversimplifying.'

'Others delve into their backgrounds, their pasts. Different methods, different results. Neil, for instance, looked at Milbro's library borrowing, which tallies with the sabotage. He and Rachel went to the British Library and researched local newspapers. At their own expense. I consulted a medieval historian about stigmata –'

'Neil?' Her tone was surprise and shock. 'You said Neil?'

'My staff are very loyal. Commitment, that's the key word. Commitment to the university.'

'Commitment,' Selena said distantly, tone ironic.

There was a long silence, finally broken by Selena. 'None of this proves that the experiment wasn't traumatising, and even if the strap marks are self-inflicted, which I doubt, they could still be self-punishment for guilt.'

'Is his PTSD caused by the experiment, or is the experiment a rationalisation of his failure as a cleric? Milbro was a failed cleric on the way out before the experiment. He left the church following a breakdown. His breakdown occurred when the church doubted his stigmata. The point is, the symptoms you identify, depression, anxiety, sleeplessness, and so on, precede the experiment. He must have been angry. Such a fall in status. I think he displaced his anger onto my experiment.'

'Displaced. Who's being psychoanalytic now?'

She fell silent considering her response, turned to Matlock and said, 'You still haven't proved he is insincere about his weals, or that your horrible experiment was not an additional and separate cause. As you say, his fragmented memories – green room, and so on – relate to the experiment; surely evidence he was traumatised by the experiment.'

Ignoring the anomaly, Matlock peered at a crack in the wall. 'I must remember to report that to maintenance.' He looked across to Selena. 'Sorry, you were saying?'

'Additionally traumatised by the experiment –'

'But as I keep saying, most of his symptoms occurred before participating in the experiment. His breakdown, depression, leaving the priesthood, relate to his exposure as a fake stigmatist.'

Her voice rising, she said, 'But the experiment was additional, exacerbated his condition, re-activated it, probably. Caused him to seek revenge.'

Matlock shrugged wearily, turned to face her and said, 'Isn't that straw clutching? Don't you feel some loyalty to the university?'

'Yes. And to my clients.'

'Whatever Milbro's motives, whatever the truth, we can settle with Milbro. Put it all behind us. After all, we don't do that kind of research today. Ghosts – we're fighting ghosts.'

'You deny he was traumatised?'

'Hysterical dissociation, autosuggestibility, symptoms self-induced, displaced aggression, call it what you like, explain it whatever way you like. Your area of expertise, after all.'

'Thank you.'

'It wasn't a compliment. As I said, you're not to blame. You had a few facts derived from an unreliable witness in 30-minute therapy sessions enclosed by four walls.'

*

Neil woke from a disturbing dream, momentarily stranded between the dream and reality. Slowly realising it had been a dream, the emotion dissolved and he lay there trying to remember the content before it too dissolved. Later that day he related the dream, or dreams, to Rachel.

'I was in the staffroom with Selena. I tried to kiss her, but she was much taller and I couldn't reach. She was stiff, unbending. She threw my keys out the window. There was a child in the room. As I reached up to kiss her, the child pushed between us. We were outside. She walked ahead, alone. I followed and kept looking back. I said I should retrieve my keys. She walked on in silence. We were on a bus. Top deck. I was carrying a coffin made of cardboard, painted dark grey. I indicated we should sit at the back, the seats more secluded. She sat on the outside, blocking my way. I was worried about my keys. I stood there a few seconds, then threw down the coffin. It made a hollow sound as it hit the floor. I now knew in the dream it symbolised the end of our relationship. I knew I had to go back for my keys. The bus was old, whining, a petrol engine, open at the rear, no doors. As the bus slowly turned a corner I jumped off.'

'Worthy of the French surrealist cinema,' said Rachel.

'Next, I was at a station. Selena was arm-in-arm with Kel. I felt jealous, but not intensely so. She was alone. I began telling her about my decision, but I don't remember what it was, only that it was important. As I spoke, she no longer looked right – face too round. Then I realised it was Kel in a wig pretending to be Selena. "Kel", I said. "That fooled you", he replied. "You won't tell Selena I made that mistake", I said. He laughed mockingly. Then I woke up.'

Rachel wanted to know about events surrounding the dream. 'The child?'

'I asked her about children recently. I asked her how she saw herself years from now. She said she saw herself living in a cottage, two little ones around her feet.'

'No mention of a man.'

'Exactly what I said. Selena laughed and said, "Probably not. Too stifling". "Then where do the kids come from?" I asked. This amused her and she told me she had considered using a man to have a child but couldn't decide whether the father should know or not. I said he would have to know if she wanted support. "Oh, I wouldn't want support", she said, "I would want to be completely independent".'

'So it's over?'

Neil nodded. 'I think so.'

'What brought things to a head?'

'Researching Milbro. Matlock telling her of our involvement. She told me I was obsessed with the truth. Couldn't I have lied for once, or just kept silent? She said I was disloyal.'

'So Matlock ended your relationship with Selena and got you together with Wendy. He's better at matchmaking than he is at psychology.'

'I'm not dating Wendy.'

'Not yet. I've seen you together. You're relaxed. You relate. The evidence is staring at you. She's interested. She worries about you. She even laughs at your jokes. What do you want, experimental proof using double blinds?'

*

Selena left unexpectedly, a counselling job at a prestigious American university. Her flat mate joined her some weeks later. Three months after she gave birth.

Neil was telling Rachel of his mixed feelings, anger at wasting so much time and effort – and relief. Selena had always been hard work, never committed to the relationship, and he now agreed with Rachel's suspicion that Selena wanted him for male sex, the only thing lacking in her gay relationship with her flat mate (Rachel had moved from lesbian to bisexual to explain Selena's sexuality, Alphonse no more than a cover).

Sometime earlier, before Neil helped expose Milbro, Selena had expressed a wish to see Hadrian's Wall. It was summer and every hotel booked, but after numerous phone calls he found a hotel and booked a double room with a view. It turned out to be the hotel of last resort, bottom of a long list, the room in keeping. The window looked out on a yard full of bins, some overflowing. Against the manager's resistance, they changed rooms. The view was satisfactory, but the new room had twin beds. 'We can't ask for another room. We can put them together after dinner. I'm ravenous,' Selena said.

The dinner was the second disappointment, soup out of a tin, the steak tough, the house wine some East European heavyweight of mouth-coating density. The decor was faded Victorian, part masked by fading sixties veneer.

Put together, the beds had a hard ridge down the centre. Neil had drunk a lot and kept falling asleep.

The next day they headed for the wall. Perhaps expecting something akin to the Great Wall of China, before them were small piles of stones no more than a metre high stretching monotonously into the distance, more farmer's wall than defence (much of the wall had been reclaimed from local fields). Most of the wall had long gone, sacrificed to the road building frenzy of the late 18th century. The surrounding country was no respite, planted conifers in regiments, aircraft noise.

Selena blamed Neil for a disappointing weekend: poor choice of hotel, poor location and lacklustre sexual performance. He countered by saying he had to be motivated to perform. They endured a mostly silent journey back, and he dropped her outside her flat despite her request to be dropped a street or two away, worried her flat mate might see them.

Rachel listened with sympathetic amusement. 'I like the ridge down the centre of the beds. Symbolic.'

Neil enumerated the negatives and finally told Rachel about the day Selena gave up her celibacy. He hadn't told her because Selena had asked him not to. Definitely a detail.

Inside her flat, the door firmly closed and locked, he had reached for her hand, which she withdrew. Her voice icy and distant, she said, 'Do you want me to fuck you?'

He looked at her, a joke surely, but her eyes were cold and serious.

'Right.' She took his hand and pulled him sharply towards the bedroom, stood some distance away and undressed. 'Right,' she said again, pushing him down on the bed, 'I'll fuck you.'

After, they lay side by side in silence. At length, she turned to him and said, 'I don't know why I did that.'

Neil laughed ironically. 'And you a therapist.'

'The unconscious is a mind of its own.'

'Nothing unconscious about it,' retorted Rachel who had listened in silence. 'She wanted to be in control. She was angry because you told me about her celibacy, but at the same time felt embarrassed knowing I knew. She succumbed, but on her terms. Bet she took the top position.'

Neil laughed.

'I suspect what really upset her is that you took the initiative. Same with the dressing gown and sex by numbers jibe. She wants to be dominant in sex.' Rachel leaned back. 'You know, I was so wrong about you when we first met, never realised you were so sensitive. Criticism seemed to bounce off you, and all the while...'

Rachel eventually told Neil she thought he never knew the real Selena. She was a creation, a fantasy, an idealisation, her good points illusory. She reminded Neil that falling in and out of love were opposites. First you focus on the love object's qualities, blind yourself to everything else and accommodate their tastes and foibles. Then you focus on their flaws, loathsome interests and bad habits. Neil was seriously uncoupling. 'Maybe Selena in turn created you, the pair of you created each other. So important was she to you for a time, you saw rivals everywhere. We all need to control to a degree. That's probably why you helped Weed destroy Kel's research. You denied jealousy but subconsciously took revenge by taking control of his experiment through Milbro – surrogate revenge. Surely you have a theory for it. You must have a theory. What's that window theory you psychologists go on about? Something about... Remind me.'

'Johari's Four Windows. Self-known to self and to others; self not known to others but known to self; self not known to self but known to others; blind spots –'

'Blind spots, that's the one. Your not known self that others see through.'

Neil doubted the sabotage theory, but could only deny it by challenging Johari's theory, so he let it stand.

Rachel relaxed in her chair and smiled knowingly. 'So the demure, reserved Selena, sweet little Bobbysox, is a rampaging sex fiend. At least you had some sex,' she added, laughing. 'Getting back to the baby, do you think it's yours?'

'It's possible. The timing. Maybe she wanted me for sex, and to provide a child.'

'Keep looking on the bright side, see the positives. Isn't that the new therapy? She's not demanding maintenance, and you could be living with all those chameleons.'

She paused and moved towards the window. 'What was it Matlock said, something in your situation is stopping you researching? He may be right. What you need is a relationship, a good relationship. It'll change your perspective.'

21

'You're researching again,' Rachel was saying.

'I've included evolution for comparison with the social sciences. Shelrack's next.'

'Shelrack? I hate Shelrack. He once told me he never reads fiction. Made up, he said. Not factual. Pointless.'

'I've also changed my research design. I've dropped the structured questionnaire and the belief scale. Matlock wasn't pleased. You know how he loves numbers. I've gone over to unstructured interviews. More subjective, but more accurate.'

'Isn't that a contradiction? Subjective and accurate almost an antonym. How exactly are you researching dogma?'

'I'm not. Well, not officially, not in so many words; indirectly. Dogma's an emotive term. Researchers object to being thought dogmatic, get defensive. I avoid the word dogma at the personal level. I ask about science in general. Along the way, I casually ask about their own research or subject area to reveal their attitude towards science. You know how we all love to talk about our own research. Getting their response to contrary ideas tells me a lot.'

'Isn't that deception?'

'Absolutely.'

Rachel laughed.

'Anyway, there are degrees of deception. More a spectrum.'

'Neil, it's deception.'

'Remember, I won't name them in my write-up. Most are drawn from other universities. No one will know who's who. Especially as I don't interview, not officially.'

'Either you interview or you don't. I'm confused again.'

Neil explained further his unstructured/unstructured interview approach, how he wanted his subjects to behave naturally and speak honestly, so he included chance meetings, parties attended, conversations in corridors, overheard conversations, unguarded moments, and the pub. 'Especially the pub. You know how alcohol –'

'You ply them with alcohol? Quite a research device. Can I participate?' She descended into uncontrollable laughter, fell back into her chair, but managed to say, 'Am I part of your research?'

'Of course not.'

'How do I know? You deceive everyone. Tell me, I don't mind'

'I'm not including literature.'

Suddenly serious, she sat up and said, 'Why not?'

Mindful of her comment on Shelrack, he resisted saying literature wasn't about real people or truth as an end in itself.

'I can't include every subject. Anyway, I'm studying the social sciences. Is literature a social science? Didn't you once say literature isn't reality – "dung heap reality picked over by psychologists" your exact words.'

'You sound like Matlock. Literature's just as relevant to understanding people and life, if not more so. And no worry about ethics committees.'

'Don't writers and publishers censor for political correctness? *Ten Little Niggers*?'

'Anyway, it's not all fiction. Writers draw on life. John Millington Synge listened to conversations through the floorboards of a house he stayed in in the Aran Islands; Conan Doyle based Holmes on a professor he studied under; Joyce based Buck Mulligan on his friend Oliver Gogarty. One way to end a friendship. Isherwood's novel *Goodbye to Berlin* is autobiographical. Sally Bowles based on Jean Ross, remember? All writers draw from life in some way. Anyway, I'm more than fiction. Isn't biography a science?'

'Sociology is. History should be but doesn't seem bothered. Biography...' He pursed his lips. 'Depends on what you mean –'

'By science. Exactly. While we're on the subject of science, why do psychologists use rats?'

'Cost,' Neil said breezily. 'Elephants would cost the earth to feed. Skinner chose rats and pigeons not because they were closer to humans but conditioned more easily, bred more readily and were cheaper to keep. Cats are more difficult to control, elephants cumbersome. All the equipment would have to be much larger. Imagine a maze for elephants.'

'Isn't that biasing the research?'

'Absolutely.'

'Is there such a thing as an unbiased sample?'

'Most participants in research are volunteers, and may be different from non-volunteers, but how do you find a sample of non-volunteers for comparison? Wanted: non-volunteers.'

Rachel laughed.

'My method overcomes the problem because most don't know they are subjects.'

Rachel made some coffee and Neil elaborated on his new approach to research, such as his neutral pose and roundabout method.

'Researchers can be very emotional about their scientific status, impassioned and protective about their research. I started with an up-front approach. Most subscribed to the ideal of the open-minded, detached observer ready to absorb new ideas. It didn't ring true. I needed a better method and hit upon a roundabout method derived partly from teaching.'

'Roundabout method?' prompted Rachel, handing Neil a coffee.

'I present an alternative theory as if quoting someone else and observe reactions. Sort of side-stepping, a protective mechanism. Got the idea from teaching. When teaching something contentious, I distance myself from the subject. That way they are criticising the theory, not me. If possible, I avoid the personal pronoun *I*. *We* is better. What do *we* think of this theory? I'm mediator or intermediary. It helps when cornered by a syllabus and forced to teach a something disagreeable. Sometimes the opponents are imaginary, such as the creationist I've fabricated to test Shelrack and other biologists. A creationist I spoke to said, etc.'

'Who said literature isn't science because it's fiction? Go on.'

'The aim is to see how they respond to ideas contrary to their own, and how they manage anomalies.' Rachel looked blank. 'Kuhn's term for problems their theories can't explain, apparent contradictions, such as insects in amber that haven't changed in 200 or so million years – just haven't evolved – yet the earth has undergone enormous changes.'

'I did biology at school. I always thought evolution was a fact, a hard science; facts, proven beyond doubt. What about the speckled moth? Weren't they protected against birds because their colourings matched the lichen covering tree trunks until the trees were sooted by factories, giving advantage to black moths, and black moths became dominant?'

'And when the clean air act came in, the black moths were easy prey again and replaced by speckled moths.'

'Exactly. Surely proof of evolution by natural selection.'

Neil was distracted by a noise in the corridor.

'Ignore it. You're not getting away. What's wrong with the moth study?'

'It's very elegant, I agree, but not as black and white as it seems.' Rachel smiled at his intended pun. 'But is it evolution or adaptation? The moths are identical, just different colours;

still moths. Not quite the same as dinosaurs turning into birds or apes turning into humans. Even creationists have no problem with small-scale adaptations.'

Rachel could only manage a guarded affirmation, a very thoughtful and drawn out, 'Yes,' and sipping her coffee said, 'So you're a kind of go-between, posing as an innocent, relaying opposing theories and exceptions.'

'Works well when interviewing.'

Rachel smiled archly. 'Especially when they don't know they are being interviewed. When James Joyce was with friends, he would note down their conversations to use in his novels. Real conversation stopper. How do you record their comments?'

'A hidden recorder.'

'Christ! Don't tell the ethics committee. Matlock agrees to this deception?'

'Matlock doesn't know, doesn't need to know, and doesn't want to know.'

'But how will you write it up? Surely you won't mention the pub, corridors and recorders?'

'Broad and Wade say the research write-up is a fiction demanded by journals and examiners.'

Rachel laughed uproariously.

'The point is,' Neil said a little tersely, 'if truth's the aim, my method is more scientific.'

'So you're reading up on evolution now?'

'Currently the giraffe's long neck.'

*

Neil recalled a passing discussion with a Freudian. Quoting Popper's view that psychoanalysis isn't a science because it's unsinkable, all evidence supporting, he was met with a wall of resistance, particularly when learning Matlock was his head.

'He hates psychoanalysis.'

Neil started to dissociate from Matlock but was cut short.

'I'm not interested in what your ego has to say. I never listen to the ego, talks mostly rubbish; all rationalisations and defences. It's your unconscious that worries me, Neil. What is it saying? What is this really about? What motivates you to ask questions about science? Ask yourself.'

Before Neil could so ask, the Freudian had gone, rapidly disappearing into the distance. 'Interesting defence,' he murmured, making a note.

Another negative meeting occasioned a professor of planetary science. Neil thought it might be useful to discuss Kuhn's description of natural science with some physicists, particularly as Kuhn was a physicist and largely based his theory on physics. Most were relaxed, agreeable and secure in their scientific status, though he detected patronage in their tone and suspected they cast the social sciences a poor relation. The planetary scientist was not defensive like the psychoanalyst; was more pompous and arrogant, portraying physics as 'real' science. 'You must understand, physics is more than observation, we also use inference based on mathematics. Take Neptune.' He explained the planet's discovery by Alexis Bouvard, a momentous turning point in astronomy, how the erratic behaviour of Uranus inferred another planet the cause, later verified by telescope, and named Neptune. 'If there was a Nobel Prize then, he would have got it. A stupendous mathematical prediction, don't you agree?'

Forgetting his neutral stance and unable to resist a put-down, Neil said, 'Inference, you say? Isn't that a bit like observing your tap's water pressure is low, inferring a leak and searching for it, or inferring that the unseen creature at the end of the fishing line in *Jaws* must be big because it drags away the jetty?'

The planetary scientist scowled, and voice singing, said, 'Wrong, but too difficult to explain. After all, physics isn't *your* subject.'

They turned to the issue of usefulness. Neil was surprised to realise this was a growing concern in planetary science, the purest of the pure, unsullied by use and practicality. Cuts and funding were in there somewhere.

'What about trips to the moon or Mars? Bit extravagant according to some. Boys' toys, according to one feminist. A waste of money.'

'Rubbish. I was discussing that very issue at my local recently. All agreed it was worthwhile.'

'All. How many, exactly?'

'I don't know. Does it matter?' His tone was perfunctory and dismissive.

'Do they know you're a professor?'

'Yes, of course.'

Neil expounded on method, social science method, the importance of sample size and composition of samples, the dangers of leading questions, and the researcher's status affecting responses; how people are conscious, knowing and questioning, unlike mindless atoms. 'In your laboratory,' Neil concluded, walking away, 'it would have no effect on atoms if you stripped naked, but an unwise action in a social psychology experiment, or in your local.'

*

Was Shelrack an exception to the rule that no one wanted to be labelled dogmatic?

Head of evolutionary psychology, a new and growing area, he was blatantly dogmatic, a particularly militant evolutionist straddling evolution and psychology. A buckle which joins, intoned Shelrack when challenged; more Trojan horse, said others.

Shelrack was high on Neil's original belief scale, almost off the scale. 'Just honest,' he would say with a shrug. 'If you know something to be true, say it.'

Was he more honest or... Neil suspected Shelrack liked to shock and relished being outrageous. This troubled Neil. Perhaps he wasn't dogmatic; perhaps he was reacting to Neil? Or the imaginary opponents Neil created? Who was the real Shelrack?

Shelrack was enthusiastic about Kuhn, a theory of science that sanctioned dogma and admitted evolution to the paradigm club and, presumably, its recent offspring – evolutionary psychology. He would boast how this new branch of evolution (he never saw it as a branch of psychology) would eventually integrate the whole of psychology, sociology, economics and history, and absorb all the conflicting schools. "A paradigm in waiting", he often said. Other disciplines were resisting, in denial, but someday... Evolution was the bedrock of all theory, unrecognised but waiting, the towering figure of Darwin, like some Soviet icon. Neil has difficulty maintaining objectivity when talking to Shelrack and often forgot he was researching.

In line with his method, Neil would sometimes spy on Shelrack, observe his interactions with others at lunch, in the bar or lecturing. One day, the door of the lecture theatre open, he listened to Shelrack lecturing:

'Evolution by natural selection unites all things – plants, animals, birds – from the smallest to the largest, a single cell to the largest mammal, taking in psychology and sociology, every perspective, and beyond. Natural selection is itself an example of natural selection. It survives and grows because it answers more problems than all other theories combined.'

Some disciplines lend themselves naturally to reductionism, some all-explanatory cause – atoms, molecules, genes, the unconscious – but Neil agreed with the biologist Steven Gould that people, complicated by culture, are less reducible, despite those grandiose attempts (Freud's unconscious, Marx's economy, Skinner's conditioned reflex, Adler's inferiority complex); anvils upon which people of varying complexity are arranged and hammered into place, resulting in Popper's unsinkable theories, all evidence supporting. Was that the appeal, that God-like ability to explain everything?

To test Shelrack's dogmatism, Neil had initially quoted Kuhn, aiming to put Shelrack in a state of cognitive dissonance. Would he accept that he was dogmatic, or challenge Kuhn?

Shelrack smiled slyly and said, 'So what's wrong with a bit of dogmatism? Lots of dogmatism? Darwinism works. Until a better theory comes along... Better than wishy-washy on-the-fence mental constipation or open-door-anything-goes. Dogma gives structure and direction and allows you to move forward. Some of the greatest minds in history were dogmatic and single track but won in the end. Einstein didn't vacillate. What was it Dawkins said? "Don't be so open-minded that your brain falls out".'

'Max Radin, actually.'

'Whoever – I'm sure it was Dawkins – whoever...'

'Max Radin the legal scholar. Said long before Dawkins. Also wrongly credited to Russell and Sagan.'

'Typical, Neil. You home in on detail, scrutinise the marginalia, study every forgotten footnote, and search the appendix, anything but the body of the text. Dogmatism has survival value, whereas skepticism can only lead to inertia, stagnation and extinction.' Shelrack shook his head. 'Excessive skepticism has no survival value.'

'I like the way you turn dogmatism into a virtue.'

'What would you have us teach? Lamarck?'

'It's an alternative theory.'

'So is creationism. The problem is, it's not whether you teach creationism or any other theory, but how much status you give it. Equal status? 50/50? If so, what about Lamarck, or teleology or other theories that preceded Darwin? As I said before, science is dogma; has to be dogma. You have to choose. Kuhn said it. He was right. You can't teach and research every crackpot theory, no more than you could represent every art form in a gallery, or teach astrology alongside astronomy, or abolish the literary canon and include *Thomas the Tank Engine*. Otherwise, there would be anarchy, chaos.'

Neil realised he had a point. This was the kind of answer that his structured questionnaire on belief had failed to detect. The questionnaire merely indicated degrees of dogma. Shelrack's answer gave a plausible reason.

'But why Darwin?'

'Because it's the best we've got. The only theory that fits the evidence.'

'Or the evidence fits the theory.'

'Same difference.' He shook his head vigorously, his fleshy cheeks quivering, and said, 'Riding on the back of the plea for openness is the Trojan horse creationism intent on destroying the Troy of science.'

How long did it take him to phrase that? Neil wondered.

*

'Some insects in amber haven't changed in 200 or so million years; just haven't evolved. Is that true?'

'Living fossils, you mean? No need to evolve. Environment hasn't changed.'

They continued walking.

'Earth was one continent then. No birds or flowering plants.'

'Didn't change for that insect. Anyway, rates of evolution vary. Still time to evolve. Remember, we're talking geologic time, not your flash-in-the-pan psychology time. Earth is more than four billion years old. What's a hundred million years here or there?'

'You mean, the explanation is waiting to be found when the tools become available?'

Shelrack nodded.

'As I remember, Darwin's theory faltered because there were no intermediate fossils, just complete species, a giant anomaly, but he and his followers still clung to the theory of gradualism, believing the solution would turn up.'

'Neil, you're forgetting Eldridge and Gould's solution: evolution by mutation, punctuated equilibrium so rapid you wouldn't expect intermediate fossils.'

'Yes, Gould offered a neat solution to the anomaly, but that wasn't until the 1970s, surely the longest shelving of a problem in science history. And diehard Darwinists, like Dawkins, clinging limpet-like to gradualism, still disagree –'

'Neil, Neil…'

*

Standing in the bar one day, Neil caught Shelrack's eye. He grinned, sauntered over and said, 'Any more evolutionary conundrums? Exercises the mind, if nothing else.'

'The creationist I was telling you about, he says evolution can't explain the giraffe's long neck.'

Shelrack laughed. 'You're expecting me to say, it has a long neck to reach the leaves at the top of the tree, giving it an advantage over other animals, to which you'll reply, but female giraffes average a metre shorter, and should therefore starve.' He laughed again. 'It could be that the male giraffe has to eat leaves from the tops of trees because its neck is so long, rather than evolving a long neck to eat from the tops of trees.'

'Still doesn't explain the long neck.'

'Forget leaves. The giraffe needs a long neck to reach water because it has such long legs. Applies to both male and female giraffes.'

Here was the answer Neil wanted. 'In that case, why has it got such long legs?'

Whenever Neil confounded Shelrack, he would shake his head very rapidly, mouth slightly open, causing his fleshy cheeks and jaw to quiver, laugh lightly and say, 'Neil, Neil...' which Neil interpreted to mean his patronising, 'What are we going to do with you?'

Neil maintained a fixed stare, eyebrows slightly raised, waiting.

'OK, I'm sure there's an answer. We just haven't found it yet. Evolution is an ongoing science. Given time...'

A few days later Shelrack was standing by Neil's desk, smiling smugly. 'Your question about the giraffe's neck – I've phoned around – necks are used as clubs by males to fight for access to females. Known as clubbing. The longer the neck, the greater the chance of winning. Long necks have adaptive advantage. Nothing to do with leaves or water after all. Just sexual selection.'

'That might explain why males have longer necks than females, but still doesn't explain long necks for both. Or long legs.'

'Neil, Neil...'

Later, Neil made some notes: *Wonderful fit with Kuhnian model... able to absorb almost every awkward fact... inconsistencies shelved or explained away... explanation somewhere waiting to be found when the tools become available.*

*

They were side by side in the toilet, urinating.

'Crickets have wonderful camouflage, which protects them against predators, but make a deafening noise. Predators hear it, surely?'

'A mating call, maximises offspring,' Shelrack said breezily. 'You see, it all balances out. If it didn't balance out crickets wouldn't survive. Simple logic.'

Neil made a note: *Survives because it is well-adapted. We know it is well-adapted because it survives. Whatever it does, evidence of survival. Popper's unsinkable theory.*

*

'Morgan? You mean Elaine Morgan? Not Elaine Morgan?' He laughed uproariously. 'Her subject's literature, not biology. What does she know about evolution? She supports the aquatic theory, for Christ's sake. Need I say more?'

'Have you read her book on the aquatic theory?'

'No. Nor has she been reviewed in any quality journal.'

'She took the theory of the aquatic ape from Alister Hardy, a marine biologist – professor of natural history, and later professor of zoology at Oxford. She's only stating what Hardy says.'

'Which is?'

'Take hairlessness and bipedalism. We descend from a hairy quadrupedal ape, walk upright and are relatively hairless. How do you explain that?'

'Simple. Raymond Dart explained it well. Descending from the trees and running about the Savannah in pursuit of game required hair loss to avert heat exhaustion and bipedalism to see distant prey.'

Neil suppressed a smile of triumph. 'Morgan points out that women have less hair than men, yet women, according to Dart's theory, didn't hunt. Shouldn't women be hairier than men and still on all fours? Isn't there some flaw in the theory, namely androcentrism, the evolution of man meaning *man*?

'Of course,' he began slowly, as if uncertain where he was going, 'it's not strictly true we lost our hair. Humans, on average, have the same amount of hair follicles as apes, only the hairs are shorter.'

'Still fails to explain why we have shorter body hair; women's hair shorter still. A woman's face presumably has the same number of hair follicles as a man's, only shorter, but women don't grow beards. Why are men able to grow beards? What's the evolutionary advantage?'

As Shelrack reflected, Neil was saying, 'The aquatic theory answers some of these problems: bipedal to stand upright in water; relatively hairless to facilitate swimming; layer of subcutaneous fat like other aquatic mammals. We have a lot in common with marine mammals, such as whales and walruses. Hair protects against sunburn, and skin cancer, explaining why we retained hair on our heads. Surely hairlessness fits the idea that our ancestors were partly water-based for a long period. Any sensible ape leaving the security of the trees would not run hairless hither and thither on the Savannah in the roasting tropical sun but head for the nearest riverbank and tree shelter. Humans like water, swimming pools, paddling. Children love water. Humans need water. Savannah animals, such antelopes and lions, are hairy, heat tolerant, don't sweat, consume less water, and perfectly adapted for the hot Savannah.'

They reached the end of the corridor and Shelrack said, 'Supporters of the aquatic theory select evidence to fit. No serious evolutionist believes the theory. The majority of biologists reject it.'

'And the majority is right? Curious proof of a theory. Before Einstein the majority supported Newton. Anyway, how do you know what the majority thinks? Have you interviewed them, sent out a questionnaire? What was the sample size and response rate?'

'Neil, Neil...'

*

The aquatic theory was a variant within the paradigm, a modification of Darwin. Neil wanted something bigger, something more than a variant; a rival theory a paradigm away, a final rebuttal. He recalled Koestler's defence of Lamarck in *The Act of Creation*, evolution by use and disuse. Lamarck preceded Darwin, a rival explanation finally eclipsed by Darwin's evolution by natural selection when combined with Mendel's genetics and Weismann's barrier. Despite this, Lamarck survived into the 20th century: Freud, Jung, Pavlov, Piaget, Koestler, HG Wells and Bernard Shaw were Lamarckians. Even Darwin retained aspects of Lamarck to paste over anomalies in his own theory.

Lamarck's theory was temptingly simple. We acquire characteristics and pass them on to offspring; the giraffe stretches its neck to reach the topmost leaves and offspring acquire longer necks; the blacksmith strengthens his arms, and sons are similarly endowed. Lamarck's theory was progressive, unconstrained, and gave control over evolution, explaining its appeal to socialists. If we raised people to be cooperative and altruistic, these traits would become part of our nature. Not blind purposeless evolution after all, but evolution by design.

'Darwin wasn't right about everything. He didn't know about genes, or Weismann's barrier,' Shelrack said breezily as they headed for the cafeteria. 'As for your blacksmith's muscles, what about his daughter? What contribution does his wife make?' He looked sideways at Neil and grinned meaningfully. 'Sounds androcentric to me. What Darwin and

Lamarck didn't know is that hereditary information moves in one direction only – genes to body cells – never in reverse. Acquired characteristics are never inherited by offspring.' He raised a finger. 'Weismann's barrier.'

He gave the example of generations of mice, deprived of their tails, giving birth to tailed offspring. 'No disuse principle operating there.'

'Not disuse, exactly. They didn't stop using their tails; still needed them. Chopping off tails is not the same, no more than chopping off feet.'

Maybe Weismann was wrong? Neil researched the topic and returned to Shelrack with a seemingly irrefutable case. 'What about blind animals in perpetually dark caves, such as eyeless fish? Surely proof of Lamarck's use and disuse? Use them or lose them. Why else would they lose their eyesight? Natural selection has no answer. Admittedly eyes are no use in the dark, but why their disappearance? Darwin agreed.' Neil had found a passage in *Origins* supporting Lamarck's idea that blind fish became that way because of disuse, "… aided by natural selection".'

Shelrack protested. 'No. No. Mutation and selection must have changed them from an eyed to an eyeless state. I admit it's a bit of an anomaly… Are you sure about eyeless fish? Sure it's not a myth? Look, I'll get back to you. Remember, my specialism is people, not fish. Selection's in there somewhere. Has to be. Give me the page reference.'

'Don't forget Darwin's golden rule.'

Later that week Shelrack sauntered up to Neil's desk accompanied by two research assistants-turned-audience. Ash's majority of three. They circled, one peering at and touching a print, another leaning against his filing cabinet, flexing their reflected status, finally taking up position, one each side of Neil's desk.

Shelrack faced Neil.

'Repeat what you said about eyeless fish.'

'We read about fish that live in caves. They can't see, and they have scars where most fish have eyes. Somehow, they've lost their eyes. Surely supports Lamarck's use and disuse? Even Darwin adds disuse to his natural selection. He uses both mechanisms. Disuse "aided perhaps by natural selection", and before that he says: "This state of the eyes is probably due to gradual reduction from disuse". His exact words.'

'OK, point taken. Look at it this way: a fish without eyes is normally disadvantaged. Sight allows fish to catch food and avoid predators. Even eyesight that permits only the bare outline of shape helps to avoid predators, something Koestler failed to understand when he asked what use half an eye.' He leaned forward, fingertips on the desk. His assistants did the same. 'Fish in caves have no use for eyes, but that's no reason to suppose eyes degenerate. Just like the mice tails I told you about, the genetic information is copied and passed on regardless. This brings us to copying mistakes. Mutations damage and corrupt genetic information, including eyes. In a light environment, an eyeless fish would not survive, would have no offspring and the faulty gene selected out. It's reasonable to assume that the same mutation will occur in caves, only a blind fish in perpetual darkness is not disadvantaged and the mutant gene will not be selected out.'

'Still doesn't explain why they are all blind.'

Shelrack looked at his assistants in turn. 'On the contrary, blindness confers adaptive advantage. Eyed fish in the dark still bump into objects, causing eye injury. This leads to eye diseases and possible early death, and less chance to pass sight on to offspring. Fish born blind, say through some genetic disorder, have none of these problems. They survive and pass on their blindness. Over time, all fish are eyeless because being so confers an advantage over eyes. Hence eyeless fish by natural selection.' He paused for emphasis. 'Unplanned and,' he laughed loudly, 'blind.'

His clones, as Neil now dubbed the assistants, no doubt carefully selected by Shelrack and survivors, fell about laughing.

'Perfect example of evolution by natural selection.'

Slightly peeved, Neil said, 'But not the same as dinosaurs turning into birds, or apes into humans. Creationists I know have no problem with small-scale adaptations.'

'Are you sure you're not a creationist?'

22

Rachel had mentioned Geneva when explaining *Frankenstein*, how the Shelly's had met up with Byron one July evening at the Villa Diodati, and how one rainy night he proposed each write a ghost story.

'I must go there, the source of the novel's creation.'

She had been putting the trip off for over a year. Would Neil be interested in coming along?

'Ideally we should have gone in the winter.'

'Why the winter?'

'To mimic the year without a summer.'

Rachel made coffee and explained that the summer of 1816 was memorable for two linked events: the conception of *Frankenstein*, and a huge volcanic eruption in Indonesia a year earlier, the most powerful recorded, vaster than Krakatoa, enveloping the earth in volcanic ash causing crop failures and freakish weather. No one knew the cause of the bad weather at the time. Some blamed sunspots. It hit Geneva mid-June 1816. "An almost perpetual rain", wrote Mary Shelley, keeping them indoors for much of their Swiss holiday.

'So, no volcano, no *Frankenstein*.'

'Surely more than the volcano?'

'You mean, was she the right person at the right time, with the right intellectual background, father a famous philosopher and novelist, mother an early feminist who wrote *A Vindication of the Rights of Woman*, belonged to a literary circle in touch with publishers, au fait with galvanism (the animation of life using electricity, a theory discussed at the Villa Diodati around the time of the ghost stories that inspired the novel), and she yearned to be a writer; the volcano merely deciding the moment, like HG wells' broken leg. Is that what you mean? Of course there's more to the fucking creation than a single volcanic eruption, however powerful.'

'Sorry.'

'No, don't be sorry.' She gulped her coffee and coughed. 'It's me. It's Fussel. I'm meeting him tomorrow about the trip. The bastard's trying to block it.'

*

The pub was dark, low-ceilinged, sparingly lit, and they relaxed into upholstered curved chairs.

'It wasn't easy justifying Geneva,' Rachel was explaining. 'Fussel tried everything to keep me here. First, he questioned my grant application. Then he steered me towards a Marxist interpretation. Since when were you a Marxist? I said, after he sauntered into my office and said, "Save you a trip to Geneva", and handed me an article by O'Flinn. "Need go no further than Nottingham". Nottingham! He's obsessed with Nottingham. First Lawrence, now Mary Shelley. I told him I was aware of O'Flinn, and he said, "Then why go to Geneva when the monster's right here". Remember me saying O'Flinn is a Marxist, albeit a sophisticated Marxist, who argues that the novel is about class, the monster symbolising the rampaging mob, textile workers smashing machinery that threatens their livelihood? In short, O'Flinn's monster is a super Luddite. True, Mary Shelley was appalled by the executions that followed machine breaking. And she feared revolution and revenge, a home-grown version of the guillotine; her own neck. I didn't admit it to Fussel, but O'Flinn has a strong case putting the monster centre stage, despite the novel's title. There's ambivalence in Mary's thinking, at once championing and fearing the working class, fearing anarchy and revenge for Tory oppression.

'I've no quarrel with O'Flinn's interpretation, you understand. It's a compellingly seductive argument, imaginative. As I said, sophisticated Marxist; writers more than passive reflections of the economic base. But think of it: dreary English scenes, boggy fields, mud, midges, industrial locations, and damp. Definitely damp. I shudder to think. "All relatively close by", persisted Fussel. "Didn't Luddism start in Nottingham?"

'By now I was desperate to make a case and explained that the novel is more about Frankenstein. The title and subtitle *The Modern Prometheus* relate to the theme of unbounded ambition, Frankenstein's unbounded ambition. I said I must go where Mary went, see what she saw, go to Switzerland. Geneva is where the idea was born, the centre of creation, and many of the novel's locations. No Geneva, no *Frankenstein*, and no monster. *Frankenstein* is about Frankenstein, not the monster.

'Fussel persisted. "Didn't I read somewhere that the Shelleys travelled around Switzerland by donkey? If you want to follow in their footsteps ..." I pointed to the cost. Would cost more than flying – hotel bills alone. And the time... What speed does a donkey travel at?'

'What happened?'

'We took it to Harold. I needed something to mollify Fussel's huge male ego, an offering, a red herring, an apparent compromise, so I told him I would also have to shoot off to Ingolstadt University where Frankenstein created the monster, just a little detour, 660 kilometres or so from Geneva, rail fair, couple of nights at a hotel.' Rachel laughed. 'He took the bait. Harold supported my application to pursue Frankenstein to Geneva, but not as far as Ingolstadt. A neat compromise that wasn't. Ingolstadt's a pure tourist trap. I heard they do scary Frankenstein tours, actors in monster outfits. Couldn't face that. Anyway, I got a grant, and funding for an assistant – the theory side. I made a case for you.'

'Doesn't Harold want to go?'

'Too busy. The fact is, it's over between us. He feels a bit guilty ending it – our relationship. Got him in an emotional arm-lock. Won't cost you anything. I'm doing an exchange of apartments.' She laughed. 'O'Flinn and Fussel would have us traipsing around England's early industrial sites dwelling on machine-breaking Luddites, keeping us firmly tied to sites of the working-class struggle, dreary mills in crumbling towns, treks across even drearier moors, trench foot trudging enormous bogs, reading tracts on the Luddite struggle: hangings, transportation, sombre plaques on walls – Luddite land. Durkheim leads us to Geneva via anomie, the Shelley circle suffused with anomie, deregulation and loneliness. Remember, they were, to some degree, free of social constraint, anomic wanderers, but at a price. They defied convention, were ostracised, and suffered psychologically. Take suicide. Mary's half-sister, Fanny Imlay, took an overdose of laudanum, and Polidori killed himself with arsenic. Percy's first wife, Harriet, drowned herself after he left her. All within a few years. All consistent with Durkheim's monumental work *Suicide*.'

'What was the rate of suicide then?'

'What are you saying?'

'Do biographers compare the circle's suicide rate to the national average?'

'You're sounding like a psychologist again.'

'More sociologist.'

'Thought you told me you can't believe the suicide rate?'

'Just wondering. If I'm to be your assistant...'

'Percy's first wife was heavily pregnant when he left her and she killed herself –'

'Bastard.'

'Pregnant by another man.' Rachel laughed. 'Well, probably. Percy might have been the father. Accounts are hearsay and biased. Thought I would get that in before you challenged the evidence.'

Rachel put down her wine and adopted a mock serious pose. 'What do you think, Neil? Marx or Durkheim?'

Neil pretended to hesitate. 'A difficult choice. The needs of research...'

'Marx means crumbling northern towns, fish and chips cooked in lard solidifying the moment the chips start to get cold, rehydrated peas turned to mush, bread and dripping; whereas Geneva, close to France and French speaking, means French cuisine and exotic locations such as the Mer de Glace glacier in Chamonix.'

'Durkheim, definitely.'

'I agree. Where was it Gauguin went?'

'Tahiti.'

'Imagine researching Lowry's matchsticks. Damp, rain-soaked Manchester. Didn't the cotton industry originate there because of the damp?' 'Rachel stood up. 'Another drink?'

'Better not. Driving.'

'How much have you had? Beer here is four per cent. I read that four units is the limit, and the average liver processes about one unit of alcohol an hour. We've been here two hours.' She started calculating.

'The average liver? How on earth do they arrive at the average? Bet it's mice. I'm not an average, or a mouse. My liver might be lazy or weak. Then there's the effect of eating, type of food eaten, body weight. The average shoe size might be 10 for men, but what use is that to me when buying shoes? What I need to know is my own liver, its position on the spectrum –'

Rachel laughed dryly. 'I really can see why Matlock despairs of you.'

*

They were on their way to Geneva, a circuitous route taking them to the site of the Polygon near Euston and the Hardy Tree in St Pancras Cemetery, way posts on a long trail of Shelleyana.

Rachel explained the connection. 'The Polygon was a 15-sided Georgian structure comprising 32 houses. Mary was born there and lived there with her father. Dickens was also a resident in the early 19th century. Engulfed by the railway, it declined, was demolished, and now a huge housing estate.'

Rachel wanted to walk the route taken by Mary and Percy from the site of the Polygon to St Pancras churchyard where Mary's mother, who died giving birth to her, was originally buried. Observing the plaque of Mary's mother, Mary Wollstonecraft, they quickly escaped the estate and headed for the churchyard and the Hardy Tree.

'Her body was interred in 1860 and moved to Bournemouth. The railways demolished huge swathes of the surrounding area and a large part of the churchyard was poised to go. Bodies were exhumed, numerous gravestones removed and unceremoniously piled against a tree, now known as the Hardy Tree. A monument to Mary Wolstonecraft and Godwin is all that remains. The family moved their bodies because the surrounding area had become dreary and rundown. Once rural, it deteriorated rapidly.'

The churchyard was a mini oasis caged in by railways and council estates. The Hardy Tree immediately captured Neil's interest.

Rachel explained. In 1865 Thomas Hardy, then a student of architecture, was given the onerous task of exhuming the bodies. He piled the gravestones round an ash tree vertically in pairs, completely encircling the tree. The tree grew over the years, enveloping and embedding some of the stones, those closer to the tree raised by the tree's roots, some lower down almost totally buried. Were there more tombstones underneath? None of the inscriptions were readable, such was the decay. Rachel was surprised they had survived so long. Were there no vandals? Perhaps they were completely overgrown by ivy for a time, invisible, before being protected by a surrounding railing. Despite the decay, Rachel felt it was better that way, shades of crumbling grey patterned by green lichen and moss, branches intertwining the stones, an organic whole.

Rachel quoted two stanzas from a poem by Hardy, *The Levelled Churchyard*:

O passenger, pray list and catch
Our sighs and piteous groans,
Half stifled in this jumbled patch
Of wrenched memorial stones!

We late-lamented, resting here,
Are mixed to human jam,
And each to each exclaims in fear,
I know not which I am!

'Most don't know Hardy wrote poetry, less still humorous poetry. Hardy's poem is comic, albeit blackly, a rare feat for him. The muddled graves result in muddled people. He imagines a teetotaller getting the inscription of a drunkard, and vice versa, or a maiden dreading Judgement Day lest she rises half-virgin, half-harlot. I expect he found the work gruesome. On one occasion a coffin split open and a skeleton and two skulls fell out. Macabre.'

Leaving the cemetery, Rachel said, 'I'm surprised you accept the story. Not like you; challenge the evidence you.'

'Why challenge it? You're not going to spoil it.'

'That's the problem. People love the story. To start with, there's no evidence Hardy placed the gravestones around the tree, and no mention is made of Hardy handling bones or gravestones, by him or anyone else at the time. His job was to drop in occasionally unannounced to ensure the bones were properly re-buried and not sold to bone mills. You see, there were hundreds of graves to remove to make way for the railway viaduct, bones galore, and money to be made on the side. Finally, the clinching evidence: a book published in 1926 by St. John Adcock, *Wonderful London*. He mentions a rockery made of tombstones. The book includes a photo showing the circle of gravestones – but no tree. A 1960s photo shows the tree surrounded by gravestones.' She sighed. 'A nice story embellished over the years. Sadly, the Hardy Tree is a myth.'

'The tree grew between 1926 and 1960?'

'Ash trees grow fast. Presumably self-seeded.'

'Conveniently in the middle of the circle of stones?'

She shrugged. 'Chance, just chance. Had to grow somewhere, the story added over the years.'

'Maybe the original died and was replaced.'

Rachel laughed. 'You're clinging to the story, but I understand.'

*

On the plane to Geneva, Rachel defined the situation: 'Forget Selena, forget the university, forget my affair with Harold, forget everything. But before we forget, I must tell you about a meeting just before we left. It was about funding and cuts. Odlum was particularly scathing about my research, a contempt that extended to Switzerland generally, to him an uncultured wilderness. Have you seen *The Third Man*?'

Neil said he had.

'That makes the joke easier. Remember the speech by Orson Welles on the Ferris wheel in Vienna about the cuckoo clock? I can't remember it exactly, the gist is: Italy, under the Borgias had warfare and terror, but produced Michelangelo, de Vinci and the Renaissance. The Swiss had 500 years of peace, brotherly love and democracy, and all they invented was the cuckoo clock. Odlum quoted it. That moment I remembered *Life of Brian*, you know the scene, *what have the Romans given us*? So I said, what about Jean-Jacques Rousseau? "OK", he said, "apart from Rousseau". Someone else called out Le Corbusier. Amazingly he persevered. "OK, apart from Rousseau and Le Corbusier". Then there was a torrent: Carl Jung, Jean Piaget, Ferdinand de Saussure, Johann Pestalozzi, Paul Klee. At that point I said, apart from Rousseau, Le Corbusier, Carl Jung, Jean Piaget, Ferdinand de Saussure, Johann Pestalozzi, Paul Klee, and George de Mestral, I suppose the Swiss really have produced nothing, not even the cuckoo clock which was a German invention. This got a round of laughter. Then Odlum said, "George de Mestral? Who's George de Mestral?" I was waiting, and said, the most useful and practical of them all, the inventor of Velcro.'

Neil shrugged. 'George de Mestral?'

'De Mestral was puzzled by the burs that kept sticking to his clothing and his dog's fur when out walking. Under a microscope, he noticed hundreds of hooks that secured to anything that had a loop – clothing, hair, animal fur. The imaginative leap was to see the possibility of binding two pieces of material together to create a new type of fastener.'

'Fits Koestler's theory of creativity: synthesis, two and two make five.' He produced a notebook. 'How do you spell his name?'

'I'll tell you when we get back. Forget university, remember.'

*

There were few tourists in Geneva in 1816, but enough to irritate the internationally celebrated poet Lord Byron who left a trail of scandal in his wake. Having earned the appellation "Mad, bad and dangerous to know", tourists observed his every move, even peering through his window and watching him in his garden, deciding him to rent the more isolated Villa Diodati in Cologny, overlooking Lake Geneva.

Rachel was commenting on the Shelley visit as they walked along a hot winding road to the villa. Neil had suggested a bus.

'No busses or taxis when the Shelleys were here.'

'Donkeys?'

'Only to carry luggage.' She laughed. 'You're not getting out of walking.'

The walk was almost six kilometres from Geneva to Cologny. 'Under four miles,' said Rachel breezily. 'The average walking speed is three to four miles per hour, three in your case; we'll be there in little more than an hour.'

But Geneva has a variable climate, the day hot and excessively humid, and the last part of the journey uphill, every step an effort, their rests growing more frequent and longer, their bottled water near depletion. The vast expanse of lake, still and glittering in the intense heat, offered no cooling breeze.

Neil wondered what had lured the Shelleys to Geneva that summer.

Rachel explained. 'Claire Claremont, Mary's younger stepsister and only 18, had thrown herself at Byron and become pregnant. She pressed the Shelleys to go to Geneva, hoping to become Byron's official mistress, a fantasy the Shelleys shared. They rented Maison Chapuis, within walking distance of the Villa Diodati. Up to then, the Shelleys hadn't met Byron.'

Two hours later, exhausted and perspiring heavily, Neil and Rachel reached number nine Chemin de Ruth, the word *Diodati* chiselled into a stone gatepost, and stood outside the gate. Rachel had explained there was no possibility of entry, the villa privately owned, so they went to a small public park where the villa was clearly visible, an impressive house with a colonnade, surrounding balcony and huge step-out windows.

She produced some pictures. 'Much as it was in 1816,' she said with satisfaction. 'That's the expansive balcony Byron would view the lake from, partly replaced with iron.' She chuckled. 'The hotelier on the opposite bank hired telescopes for his guests to view the goings-on, Villa Diodati now seen as a bordello, a veritable league of incest. Byron had allegedly shagged his half-sister, and he and Percy supposedly shagging Mary and Clare. The Byron watchers mistook tablecloths hanging out to dry for petticoats. Imagine being turned on by the sight of a wet petticoat. Bit table leg.'

'You're saying the Shelleys weren't libertarian?'

'Judge for yourself. Godwin, Mary's father, believed in free love. His wife, Mary's mother, had an affair, resulting in a daughter, Fanny Imlay, Mary's half-sister. Mary was raised by her stepmother, who came with two children, followed by a third from her marriage to Godwin. Mary was one of five children, none of whom had the same set of parents. Today we'd call them dysfunctional.

'Shelley eloped with Harriet, left her with a child and pregnant, and then eloped with Mary. The Shelleys believed in free love, shared property, everything shared, though I suspect Mary was less enthusiastic about free love, more in the abstract than the concrete. Percy wanted her to sleep with his friend Hogg, but Mary demurred. She was committed to Percy, you see. Interestingly, the relevant pages of her diary are torn out. So we don't know what happened, though her biographers have no problem filling in the details. One often overlooked fact, free love favoured men; there was no reliable contraception, and unwanted pregnancy a woman's burden. Percy and Byron seemed oblivious to the problem. Byron was particularly cruel to Claire and her child. "Is the brat mine?" he wondered in a letter to his sister, reluctantly concluding it was. He distanced himself from Claire and grudgingly took control of their daughter on condition Claire had no contact, eventually handing her over to a convent where she died.'

Their feet were burning, the road intensely hot and dry. Everything was hot, even the stone gatepost. They decided to walk down to the lake and bathe their feet, eventually finding a spot where they could sit on some rocks and eat their lunch, feet dangling in the cooling water, reminding Neil of a blisteringly hot day in London when he joined tourists dangling their feet in the Centrepoint fountain.

'So clear and blue,' Neil observed.

'"Blue as the heavens which it reflects", Mary Shelley's description in a letter. Vineyards swept down the hill from the Villa Diodati when Byron was here. Some call it the Swiss Riviera. The water's warm enough for swimming. We must buy some costumes.'

'You said it wouldn't be hot in Geneva.' Neil sounded a little reproachful.

Rachel laughed. 'I was misinformed. Someone said the heat was mitigated by the cooling Alps. In the distance you can sometimes see snowcapped peaks. What we need is a cooling breeze.'

They peered at the mountains, distant, very blue, caps covered in cloud.

Now recovered, they headed for the site of Maison Chapuis, long demolished, where the Shelleys stayed and Mary claimed to have her creative dream resulting in *Frankenstein*. Rachel showed Neil photographs taken in the late 19th century, the Shelleys' dwelling a much humbler building close to the lakeside. 'Byron was wealthier than the Shelleys and came to Geneva in a replica Napoleon coach, bevy of servants, an unstable personal physician called John Polidori, and a menagerie, including a peacock and a monkey.

'Accounts of the creation of *Frankenstein* are conflicting. Biographers obsessively argue about the exact date, how long after the evening Byron asked the assembled to write a ghost story. They pour over journals, seeing deep significance in what might be passing comments, what is unsaid more important than what is said. But does it really matter? One day, three days, a week – what the fuck. No, the real question is: do we credit the creation of *Frankenstein* to Mary or Percy Shelley? After all, he was an established writer, older, and involved in her early draft.'

There was a cafe further along the road where they bought ice-cold lagers and sat under a huge parasol watching various craft on the lake.

'Mary claimed to have had a nightmare of a monster brought to life. Creative dreams were fashionable, of course. Remember Coleridge and *Kubla Khan*? Obviously, she drew on experience, and says so herself. Electricity was new, of unknown potential. Some scientist passed an electric current through a dead frog, causing its legs to jerk. See where the idea of animating a cadaver came from? Remember the quote?'

Neil looked blank and she pulled a copy of *Frankenstein* from her bag. Numerous pages were marked by post-it notes of various colours.

'"Invention, it must be humbly admitted, does not consist in creating out of the void, but out of chaos; the materials must, in the first place, be afforded: it can give form to dark, shapeless substances, but cannot bring into being the substance itself".'

'Not the materials, but what she did with the materials. Not the volcano, but the opportunity it provided. The strength of *Frankenstein* is not in the detail, but in the meaning. Who originated the brilliant idea of an over-reaching scientist who mistakenly creates a monster? Mary or Percy? When I started this project it seemed so simple, until I found out there are several versions of *Frankenstein*. So it was several trips to the Bod.'

'Bod?'

'Bodleian Library in Oxford where the originals are stored.'

'Doesn't it bother you that you can't get at the truth?'

'I can improve on the evidence; get closer to the truth. I can interpret. That's all I can hope for. Mostly the journey's more important than arriving. I love researching. As I was saying, there are so many versions of *Frankenstein*. There's the uncorrected 1816-1817 written by Mary; the Mary-Percy corrected version 1816-1817, published in 1818; the corrected 1823 version containing 123 word changes, corrected by her father or the printer. Few copies were printed. Finally, the 1831 corrected copy by Mary. But how genuine is the 1831 text? After all, it was modified and added to under pressure from her publisher who wanted to secure a new copyright, and she needed the money.

'Did you know, all the famous women writers in the 19th century, other than Mary, were childless? Hardly surprising, you say. Most women spent their fertile years pregnant and in a state of lactation. Miscarriages were common. Someone calculated that for every successful pregnancy, a woman had two miscarriages. Many women died in childbirth. Mary's mother died giving birth to Mary. The infantile death rate was high. Mary lost three of her four children. How many stories from that time are about evil stepmothers? *Frankenstein* was written between 1816 and 1817, a particularly difficult period in her life. She had a young child, she assisted Claire through her pregnancy; her half-sister, Fanny, committed suicide; Harriet drowned herself in the Serpentine, and Mary, in opposition to her father, married Percy and became pregnant. Yet she still managed to write *Frankenstein*. If she had failed to write the novel the feminists would say hardly surprising, but she succeeded, so how do we explain that?'

Neil shrugged.

'She was steeped in literature and philosophy, of course. Famous literary parents. Yes, she was only 18, but so was Francoise Sagan when her first novel *Bonjour Tristesse* was published, and most 14-year-olds don't write like Ann Frank. Mary wasn't your average 18-year-old; she was Mary Shelley, a one-off individual. What most people can't do is not evidence of what one individual can do. Forget your psychology and sociology averages. Isn't that what you keep telling me? Mary was an individual.'

'Didn't she publish the book anonymously?'

'Fronted by Percy, yes. He described it as a novel by a very young friend who wanted to remain anonymous, apparently a common way to publish at the time. Difficult to know the reasons exactly. Feminists see prejudice against women, but Jane Austen was well-established, albeit under the pseudonym "By a Lady". She didn't masquerade as a man. Mary was young and unknown and thought she wouldn't get published.'

'Percy's help? You were saying.'

'Shush. You mustn't say things like that – not PC – the feminists might hear you. Mary must be presented as totally independent of the men around her. You're allowed to argue the other way, a famous male writer helped by his wife or sister, albeit uncredited. Remember that novel you helped me with? *Breakfast at Tiffany's*? One of my students interpreted it as a novel about stalking, claiming Fred – that's the name Holly gives the narrator – is a stalker because he looks through Holly's trash to gain information about her. Male control; male power. I said to her, surely the main initial contact between Fred and Holly is when she climbs through his window naked under a robe. Imagine that the other way round.

'I'm deviating. You must stop me when I deviate. Back to Mary. Some critics are dismissive of Mary, not the same literary stature as Byron or Percy Shelley, you see. They either dismiss *Frankenstein* as poorly written or, if meritorious, written, or partly written, by Percy. The fact is, Mary's *Frankenstein* is now better known than Percy's poetry. Who reads Percy Shelly today? Of course, if you ask people, they'll tell you he was a great poet, but it's easy to remain great if no one reads you. Mary is more famous than Percy, that's what galls the dwindling Percy followers.

Percy added 4000-5000 words to Mary's total of 72,000, some good, some bad. But it's quality that counts. Most of his revisions improve grammar and spelling, but others impair the novel by removing colloquialisms. He insisted on a more formal style. Mary's "The use I should make of it" becomes, "The manner in which I should employ it"; Victor's father's "...did not see of what use learning could be to a merchant", becomes "...in compliance with his favourite theory, that learning was superfluous in the commerce of ordinary life", and so on. Percy elevated her prose into a more Latinate idiom – stilted and ornate. Mary's style is more direct and natural. Her journals and letters attest to that. Today, these colloquialisms are standard English. That Percy made some good changes is undeniable, but no more than a good editor would do. However, he did make the monster more human, with human feelings, corrupted by society. But remember, the 1831 revision, emphasising the all-important triad, was Mary's work alone, Shelly long dead.

'What is help, anyway? Lots of writers get help: friends, spouses, partners; agents advise, editors edit, proofreaders correct grammar and punctuation. Wilfred Owen was guided by Sassoon, but Owen was the better poet. DH Lawrence's *Sons and Lovers* was reduced by a tenth by his publisher, and the reduced version is better. Pity all his books weren't reduced. Have you ever wondered why most novels are grammatical and well punctuated? You probably thought it was the skill of the writer?'

Neil nodded.

'So much for the psychological imagination. Don't psychologists get help?'

Neil reflected a moment. 'Researchers get help with their PhDs, grammar, spelling, punctuation, structuring, even help with statistics. Supervisors give advice.' He paused. 'I hadn't really thought about it, but yes, you're right.'

Neil was piecing together Rachel's method. Never trained in methodology, she was adept at evaluating evidence. Sometimes, Rachel mentioned a method picked up in passing, say a casual conversation. 'A historian I talked to recently said you must look at unwitting evidence and gave the example of a message written by a slave in Rome. The unwitting: the slave was literate. Got me thinking. Mary was shown considerable equality by the men assembled at the Villa Diodati. They included her, encouraged her, and took her idea for a novel seriously. That's unwitting, and more important than obsessing about the exact night *Frankenstein* happened.'

After the Villa Diodati, the nearby Mont Salève. The day was still hot and humid.

'Too far to walk,' said Rachel wistfully, 'you wouldn't stand the heat. We'll take the bus. 20-minute ride. It's on the French border so we'll need our passports.'

They took the cable car to the top of Mont Salève, dubbed the Balcony of Geneva. Neil thought the view stunning. The lake, 74km long and 14km wide at its maximum, stretched into the distance, a sheet of intensely blue glass. They could just see a ferry, a small dot barely moving. Further along was the Jura Mountain range.

'That's where the Shelleys crossed in 1816, travelling from Les Rousses in France to Geneva over the Jura. Their passport specified a more treacherous, impassable route, the rules very strict on this point, but as Percy put it, "easily…softened by bribery". They hired a four-horse closed carriage. 10 men were needed to dig them out of snowdrifts. Undaunted, snow pelting their carriage, they endured until they reached Geneva.'

'Even more enduring for the men,' Neil said.

Rachel frowned at the distant Jura Mountain, verdant green, not a flake of snow. She shook her head. 'Frankenstein observed an electrical storm in the Jura Mountains, prelude to creating his monster. Don't suppose we'll get any violent electrical storms or torrential rain, but you never know. Don't forget this trip is unrepresentative of Shelly's trip. I didn't tell Fussel it was the year without a summer: lashing storms, lightning flashes leaping across mountain peaks, overcast and cold, torrential rain. They were forced to stay inside much of the time.'

Two days later they headed for Chamonix-Mont-Blanc to get the early cable car for Aiguille du Midi, some 80km away.

Rachel explained: 'At 3,842 metres it dwarfs Mont Seleve's mere 1,379. Expect snow and huge glaciers. Like a huge hurricane, Byron's impression of a glacier; palaces of nature his description of the alpine mountains. Isolation, wilderness, snow, the inspiration for *Frankenstein*.'

Though hiring a car was appealing, they decided on the bus as neither had driven on the right before, and there were dire warnings about parking in Chamonix.

'Hard to believe the Shelleys did the journey by donkey in 1816.'

'More so, considering the weather,' added Rachel.

*

Reaching Chamonix, they bought tickets for the cable car and advanced into a hurricane of statistics: one of the highest restaurants in the world (2,354 metres), highest cable car in Europe (3,842 metres), and steepest incline in the world. The ascent would be in two stages, but before that, a small detour. Neil wanted to see the Ice Grotto and Cave cut into the

Mer de Glace, France's largest glacier at 7km long, 200 metres thick.

Rachel was resistant. 'Mary Shelly visited the glacier in 1816 and made it the setting where Frankenstein meets his creation and promises to create a mate for him. No ice cave here when Mary Shelly came in 1816.'

'No cable car, either' retorted Neil. 'Does that mean we should climb to the top.'

Access to the ice cave was by funicular train, climbing to an altitude of 1,913 metres, followed by cable car or a 20-minute very steep descent by foot. Rachel favoured the latter. Expecting Byron's Persil-white frozen hurricane, the glacier was covered in an ugly grey scree of rocks, masking the ice completely.

'Perhaps in the winter when layered with snow,' consoled Neil. 'The leaflet says in winter skiers descend on Montenvers station en masse for the train back to Chamonix.'

Descending to the glacier, the statistics told of declining levels, each marked by a year spanning a hundred years or more, the culprit global warming, the cause perhaps more problematic. Out of their laboratory comfort zone, faced with innumerable variables, the natural scientists cobbled a consensus and ridiculed sceptics. Each year the glacier moved 70 metres or more and a new cave cut. Once the glacier advanced relentlessly, ever thickening, devouring whole villages, now diminishing in height and in retreat. When opened, the cable car reached the cave entrance. Now there are 106 steps, 12 more added each year. They passed tourists heaving and puffing back to the cable car.

At the entrance Rachel brightened. Like entering a 200-metre-high ice cube. You must read Fitzgerald's *The Ice Palace*. Sally Carrol, the heroine, gets lost in its labyrinthine corridors of ice, ending in black voids.'

'Don't expect too much, Rachel.'

The opening was an orifice of washed-out emerald green. Inside was coloured lighting, alternating from blue to pink and green, mood music and an incongruous soggy blue carpet. The grotto contained items of ice furniture, slowly melting and difficult to recognise. Was it warmer some days? Tourists' body heat? Whatever, it was considerably cooler than the 30 Celsius outside and they put on their jackets.

'Impressive walls,' Neil said, clutching a positive. 'Transparent as glass to an amazing depth, not cloudy like an ice cube.'

'Yes, impressive,' agreed Rachel.

They explored the tunnels, but all the time Neil sensed Rachel's restlessness.

Exiting the cave to a wall of heat, she breathed heavily and said, 'Snow. That's what we came for.' She looked up at the snowcapped peak of Aiguille du Midi and said, 'Mary Shelley's network of frosted silver. That's where we are headed for next. I want snow; I want to touch it, walk on it. I want cold. All the way from England, and no fucking snow. Even the glacier looks as though it's made of rock. And shrinking. The glaciers in the valley were larger when the Shelleys came and advancing a foot a day, relentlessly, and you could hear the advance. Mary experienced delicious sounds of destruction, an avalanche, pine trees chewed up by the ice, constant rumblings, and wolf packs. Chamonix was a village when Mary visited in 1816. Imagine packs of wolves roaming the mountains, raiding the villages in winter. Even avalanches.' She sighed. 'Wonderful.'

*

'No doubt psychology has something to say about snow?'

Neil leaned back, clasped his hands behind his head and intoned, 'The Linguistic Relativity Hypothesis, originated by Whorf.'

Rachel's laugh was friendly and relaxed. 'That's right, torture me with jackhammer jargon. Remember, I have an ear for euphony and harmony.'

They were in the restaurant, partway to Aiguille du Midi, eating very large croissants and drinking a local wine, awaiting the final lift to the summit. The queues had been long, and the cable car packed, finding themselves in the middle hemmed in by a group of mountaineers with huge Alpine rucksacks, the temperature 30 Celsius. At this altitude there was a strong breeze, the air pleasantly cooler, prelude to the final ascent to the frozen summit.

Neil sipped his wine, dry and very cold. 'Whorf believed language shapes and limits the way we think about the world. Language determines thought.'

'What's that got to do with snow?'

'Whorf was originally a fire insurance inspector. One workplace he visited contained empty gasoline drums stored in a separate room. Workers would smoke in the room with empty drums, but not in the room containing full drums. The point being empty drums are more dangerous than full ones because they contain flammable vapour. The word empty unconsciously shaped their response to the drums, regarding them as harmless and believing them safe because empty is a negative.'

Rachel was silent. Neil knew that silence, shapeless thoughts awaiting their moment to spring into words and shred his theory.

'Snow?' she repeated impatiently.

'Whorf applied this to different cultures, such as Hopi Indians and the Inuit. Whereas the Inuit have 27 words for snow, we have only one. Because of this they can distinguish more types of snow.'

'Only one word. What about slush?'

'OK, that's a type of snow, I suppose. Very icy. But still not 27.'

'Sleet, hail.'

'Not 27.'

'Icicles.'

'Not snow.'

'Formed from melting snow.'

'So is water.'

'What about blizzard, snowstorm, snowdrift. How many does that make it?'

'Seven, including snow. But not icicles.'

She paused, looked at Neil slyly, and said, 'How do you know these psychologists are right? Not like you to accept evidence at face value. Maybe it wasn't 27 at all.'

Neil sipped his wine and focused on the view. 'I didn't say I believe the theory. I did it years ago, in passing. Secondary source. I'm sure it must be flawed, like everything else.'

'In passing,' she said slowly, 'usually means haven't read but won't own up.'

There was a pause.

Rachel brightened suddenly, and her voice close to a shout, said, 'We use adjectives. Wet snow, powdery snow, driven snow, pelting snow, dusting of snow, crunch-under-your-foot snow, slip-on-your-arse snow. I could go on. What's that poem by Longfellow?' She paused a moment. '"Over the harvest-fields forsaken, silent, and soft, and slow, descends the snow". Maybe Eskimos don't have adjectives. Have these psychologists heard of adjectives?'

'Anthropologists and linguists, to be precise, and I never said I agreed with them. You asked for –'

'Oh, I see, dissociating, are we, now I've kicked the shit out of them. Hopi Indians, you said earlier.'

Neil hesitated, sighed and said, 'The Hopi Indians are the other extreme, have only one word for insect and aeroplane.'

Rachel's laugh was close to a shriek, causing some climbers nearby to turn and look. 'So they think all insects are the same and can't tell a bee from a jumbo jet?'

'As I said, I don't necessarily agree –'

She was now in full flight and Neil fell silent.

'We use the single word foot for many objects – foot of a mountain, a limb, unit of length, foot of a page, foot in poetry, foot the bill. One word, very different meanings. We don't think the foot of a mountain is the same as the limb below the ankle. Just because you don't have a word for something or have the same word for many things, doesn't mean you can't recognise or distinguish them. What's the Gracie Fields my mother loved? About a girl who makes a thing for a thing-ummy-bob, but has no idea what it's all for, other than to win the war:

She's the girl that makes the thing
That drills the hole
That holds the spring
That drives the rod
That turns the knob
That works the thing-ummy-bob.

My car engine is full of parts I can't name, but I can still see them. If you never experienced snow, had no word for snow and went to a country where there was snow, you would still see it, and if a snowball slammed into their face, you would feel it. Bet Eskimos don't have a word for fake snow.'

'Eskimos or Inuit?' Neil said, hoping to move to safer ground and a winnable argument.

'Eskimos – does it matter?'

Neil laughed. 'Only to an Inuit, I suppose.'

'Has anyone bothered to ask them?'

As they were leaving, they passed the table of climbers. One said, 'Couldn't help overhearing your conversation. If it helps, skiers have a whole load of words for snow because it is important to them.' He recited a list: 'Champagne powder, corn snow, crust, granular snow.'

'There,' said Neil. 'Fits the Inuit theory. Snow is important to them, so they have specialist words.'

'Without specialist skiers' words we would still recognise the types of snow, wouldn't we. Wouldn't we?'

Approaching the lift to the summit, Rachel was saying, 'Wasn't it all said long ago by Orwell? Orwell's Newspeak?'

'Remind me,' Neil said a little wearily.

Rachel laughed at his tone. 'You remember, the party eliminates dangerous words from the language so that no one can think subversive thoughts, all remaining words given precise meaning with no possibility of unorthodox secondary meaning. That way the Party controls thought. Language controls thought.'

'So you're supporting Whorf now?'

'Of course not. Orwell, at least, knew he was writing fiction. Pity Whorf failed to realise the same.'

Neil was peering up at the huge granite pinnacle two vertical miles above Chamonix and felt his heart thumping. Never had he been so high.

*

Despite warnings, neither believed that at 3,842 metres the temperature could change from 30 Celsius to zero, perhaps fooled by the strong sun.

'Surely the top of a mountain is closer to the sun and hot air rises?' queried Rachel, her tone petulant.

Neil tried to recall something about warmth and air pressure, but the effort was too great. He was rigid with the cold, their warm clothing minimal, no hats nor gloves, and they had not counted on the chill wind. Neil was breathless and suspected Rachel was similarly affected as she was breathing heavily. He was annoyed to find he was lightheaded, though slowly acclimatising. At least his ears had stopped popping, pressure finally equalised. He needed to sit down. He looked around, but no seats were available.

Rachel was unsympathetic. 'You can't take the heat, now you can't take the thin air.'

Neil sighed. 'That's right, Rachel, blame me.'

'I'm not affected. Anomaly, I suppose?'

'No, different tolerances at different altitudes.'

'Or different attitudes.'

Neil didn't respond. It would lead into Rachel's oft stated view that women got on with things more than men and tolerate pain better. Neil looked around. He wasn't alone. People nearby, men and women, slumped in chairs, looking as if they had completed a marathon rather than a short climb to the platform. Someone had fainted leaving the cable car, the attendant looking on nonchalantly; no doubt fainting routine. The thin air was another thing they had brushed aside. Neil needed a distraction and concentrated on the view. The glacier below was a thick carpet of white and they watched as a string of climbers, roped together, slowly crossed a ridge of perfectly white snow. The view prompted the usual epithets and flashing cameras, and a nearby party of Americans wowing the scenery took endless pictures. Mont Blanc dominated – huge, snow-covered, daunting. 'As close as you can get to Mont Blanc without climbing,' one of the Americans said. In the far distance was the Matterhorn.

'A region of perpetual snow,' Rachel said with satisfaction. 'We must go to the ice tunnel.' She looked at Neil. 'OK, first let's go for a coffee. You need to rest.' She laughed and touched his shoulder. 'OK, we both need a rest.'

Once recovered, they explored using a system of wooden walkways, tunnels cut into the mountain and bridges. One bridge spanned a gap, spaces between the planks, which some crossed without hesitation while others drew back paralysed. Vertigo was never a problem for Neil, short of walking a tightrope over Niagara on a windy day. For the vertiginous there were sufficient viewing terraces, solid wood underfoot. As they wandered, Neil felt himself adjusting, his breathing returning to normal.

The snow tunnel, a hole carved in the mountain, was the exit for climbers heading for Mont Blanc. They stood at the entrance as climbers flowed in both directions, entering and checking equipment, fitting and removing crampons, the familiar rucksacks and ropes of TV programmes. Tourists watched and took more pictures. The walls were solid ice, unlit and unadorned, unlike the ice cave in the valley below. A sign warned of the perils ahead. Rachel was keen to exit and walk in the snow, but they could not go far. A metal barrier enclosed a safe area, and at the end of the barrier a small gate led to an ice ridge churned up and peppered by crampon ice boots.

Rachel leaned over the gate, poised to go through to the ridge. That moment a voice warned, 'I wouldn't if I were you, not without crampons and ice pick, and even then...'

It was the mountaineer who earlier named skiing terms for snow. He seemed dressed for Mount Everest, complete with a huge rope coiled over his shoulder, ice pick firmly held. He grinned as he explained that the ridge, or arête, was knife-edge thickness dividing two glaciers, with 40 degree drops either side. It fell away sharply and was one of the most dangerous points on route to Mont Blanc and the spectacular 20km-long ski descent down the Vallée Blanche glacier to Chamonix in winter.

'If you insist on going and slip, fall to the right; it's little more than a hundred-foot drop. The other side will take you all the way to the valley bottom.'

Their ropes secured, he and his party were ready to leave and they filed through the gate. 'Off to the wilderness,' he shouted and disappeared over the ridge, reappearing a dark speck in a line of dark specks along the perfectly white ridge below.

'Wilderness,' said Rachel wistfully. She picked up some snow. 'Not skiers' powder, for sure, it hasn't snowed for some time, and a bit dry for snowballs. I wonder if Eskimos play snowballs.'

Deciding they had exhausted the sights, they took the lift to the pinnacle and the promised 360-degree view of Mont Blanc and the Italian French and Swiss Alps. The Alps were certainly more impressive from this height, the view less restricted, but there wasn't much to do after that. The return time stated on the ticket was two hours away and they sat with a huge crowd of tourists, reminiscent of an airport departure lounge.

'I've remembered, most Inuit call themselves Inuit,' Neil said, more to kill time than out of genuine interest, though he hoped to salvage something from his mauling earlier.

'This sounds like one of those white, middle-class liberal arguments, like calling Boadicea Boudicca, all because the Romans Romanised her name, and for some reason we are supposed to be on her side. Cosy liberalism, variant on cosy catastrophe. Curl-up-in-your-armchair liberalism, all safely in the past; don't have to do anything except shed the odd tear over colonialism or slavery. And it doesn't cost anything.'

'Doesn't Eskimo mean eaters of raw meat?'

'What if it does? Or did? Today, we don't picture an Eskimo peeping out of an igloo chewing uncooked seal. Some people eat their steak rare, raw inside, blood oozing out as it's cut. As for the Japanese... Since when were you an exemplar of political correctness? Are you going soft? Why are we so precious about certain groups? Is it because they are, or were, oppressed, we the oppressors? We call the Nipponese Japanese, Deutschlanders Germans. Has anyone asked them how they feel? Take the Swiss.' She began reading from a holiday guide. 'We call them Swiss, the Germans call them Schweitz, the French, Suisse and the Italians, Swizzera.' Rachel laughed merrily. 'Should all countries call us English, then? The French call us Angleterre, the Italians, Inghilterra, the Finns, Englanti, and the Romanians, Anglia. A thing I dislike about academia is the widespread delusion that you can change the world by manipulating words. Say the right thing, get the word right... It's a game like Monopoly. Call it The PC Trap, or something. Use a wrong word and you move back five squares or go to jail.'

Moving on to more secure ground, Neil had remembered Rachel's temperature question. Some hard science for once, a winnable argument: physics. 'Your mountain question,' he said casually, 'that the top of a mountain should be hotter because it's closer to the sun and hot air rises. To start with, distance to the sun has nothing to do with it. The sun is about 93 million miles away. You're closer by only a few metres, not a meaningful difference. Lower atmospheric pressure is the cause. The air is thinner the higher you go up a mountain. Put simply, for you, air holds heat. The thinner or more expanded the air, the less heat it holds. Gaps between molecules don't hold heat.'

'So why is it thinner?'

'Air closer to the Earth's surface is more compressed or dense, the molecules closer together, pressed down by the air above. That's why we find breathing harder at the top of a mountain. That's why I felt faint.'

'I didn't feel faint.'

'I'm sure you would at the right height. Everest, for instance. The molecules are spaced out even more. Put simply, there is less air.'

She lapsed into silence which Neil interpreted as defeat.

'As I said, much physics is rarely obvious, rarely common sense.'

She turned and smiled thinly. 'Unlike psychology.'

23

'Not you as well,' she sighed.

Neil had just posed an anomaly about educational attainment to the sociologist Weena Grovecot. In the context of the school-intake debate, she and her team were researching why the poor do less well despite numerous reforms, concluding it was lack of know-how combined with the poverty penalty, and coming down on the side of intake. Knowing her views, Neil had come prepared. A London comprehensive with an intake of poor children, once dubbed the worse school in Britain, had been turned around by a new Head. Surely this was leadership surmounting poverty, not intake after all, but school structure and leadership. Would she change her beliefs about attainment, or challenge the knowledge?

Unknown to Neil, Weena had just taught a class of unusually critical students. Another lecturer from a different discipline might have shrugged and said bad luck, but the sociologist Weena looked deeper, searched for a cause, looked to group dynamics, the very subject of her PhD, how one group of students differed from another group because strong individuals shaped them. This group was led and shaped by a particularly strong personality with Thatcherite leanings, the same student who earlier that year had challenged Matlock, utilising the same body language: folded arms, looking to other students for support, his chair askew, looking from the class to Weena and back again.

'Didn't Margaret Thatcher say there is no such thing as society? There are only individual men and women.'

This had gone down well with the group, a mixture of defiance and entertainment, wanting to get home on a bleak Friday afternoon.

'And families,' Weena corrected. 'Thatcher added families. The exact quote: "There are individual men and women and there are families". A family is a group, is more than a collection of individuals. Thatcher also hated the idea of class, whatever she understood by the term, but the family is the basis of class. The family is the root of inequality. Call it what you like, background, milieu, upbringing, society.'

'Go on, give an example of class.'

'This isn't botany or entomology, a specimen mounted, a flower pressed into a book. There are no pictures, no fossils, I'm afraid.'

'Admit it, class is all in the sociologist's mind.'

She sighed but understood. A concrete individual was more sensual, more tangible, and more real than de-humanising averaging columns of statistics. Understood, but knew it was essential to beat them and show who was in control, and the importance of sociology.

'You sociologists are always generalising. You can't generalise.'

Not an original observation and one she had honed an answer to over the years. 'Of course you can generalise. You have just made a generalisation about sociologists.'

The students laughed as the questioner waved his hand dismissively.

'Even the word sociology is a generalisation. It implies the subject has common characteristics distinct from some other disciplines such as psychology. You can see sociologists as individuals, focus on difference, or see them as a group. We are not all the same, but we have things in common. You can't avoid generalising. Some women are tall, some men short, but you can still generalise; you can say that on average men are taller than women. You might say Americans are loud. Does a quiet American refute the rule? Sociology recognises exceptions, individuals. Of course it does.'

She scanned their faces, detected a grudging acceptance, and to compound the victory said, 'Take the planets.'

She paused at this point, long enough for someone to ask, 'Planets?'

'Yes, planets. All the planets are different, so why do we call them planets as if they are all the same?'

No one had an answer and she said, 'Philosophers call it the level of generality. You can look at difference or similarity in any object, what things have in common, what sets them apart. The planets are all different but have one thing in common: they all revolve around the sun. Same with moons. Some moons are bigger than some planets, but they are still moons because they revolve around a planet. That's what they have in common.'

The ringleader, not open to persuasion, persisted. 'People are not planets.'

This evoked a small ripple of laughter.

Sensing she was winning them over, she relaxed and asked them to name something, anything.

'Giraffes,' someone said, causing more laughter.

'All giraffes are different, but you know a giraffe when you see one, know it's not an elephant. It's the things giraffes have in common which makes them giraffes, gives them their giraffeness. A green giraffe would still be a giraffe.'

The group was laughing now, laughing with her.

'People. Not planets or giraffes. People. Keep to people.'

Weena sighed. 'Maybe we should leave it there. Move on. The next task might resolve the issue.'

She handed out statistics on Nottingham school pass rates, showing considerable differences between schools. Some were situated in poor areas, some the affluent suburbs. Arranging the students into two groups she asked them to explain the differences. Each group appointed a spokesperson to state their conclusions, and she was pleased that group two appointed the ringleader. The conclusions were similar for each group: poverty, wealth, family background, parental attitudes. One school with a high pass rate was fee-paying, selective, and had small classes. One group was divided over whether low-performing schools were blameworthy.

Taking control, Weena elaborated on the school-intake debate. Were pass rates the outcome of intake, or the structure and ethos of the school? The government believed the latter, better school management and tougher inspections the solution, yet pass rates, she insisted, correlated more with intake and catchment area. This was consistent across time, and predictable. 'Predictable,' she repeated.

Looking at the ringleader, she said very quietly, 'That collection of reasons, other than school management, that's what sociologists call class. Call it the family or by some other name. It doesn't matter. Whatever you call it, it affects pass rates and life chances.' She explained that class was measured by occupational background and that children from unskilled backgrounds were, on average, less likely to obtain good GCSEs than children from professional backgrounds. Class was not evenly distributed across catchment areas.

Weena looked at Neil. 'Sorry,' she said, referring to her opening 'Not you as well,' but I've just taught a particularly resistant group. And it's Friday. They're always difficult on a Friday afternoon.'

She summarised the lesson and worried she had given the impression she was blaming working class children for failing. 'I should have emphasised the point.'

Neil had come to realise it was an article of faith held by many sociologists never to blame the victim, be it class, race, gender or some other underdog. He reminded her of the anomaly: a London comprehensive turned around by a new Head.

'I know the school,' Weena said, 'or know about it. But can you generalise from one school?'

This seemed a curious question to Neil as Weena's team had recently studied a single school, an observational study of a comprehensive.

'Isn't that Woodhead's point about sociological research,' said Neil patiently, 'that it's all small-scale and observational and therefore open to bias? Left-wing bias, Woodhead claims. I'm only quoting him.'

Woodhead, the Chief Inspector of Schools in England, had compiled a report on educational studies, claiming that the millions spent on numerous small-scale studies would be better spent on a few well-designed larger studies.

'Woodhead's right-wing.' She fell silent, as if this was self-explanatory.

'You've read his report?'

'Woodhead's report is small-scale and biased, namely his own reactionary right-wing opinions masquerading as research. Anyway, it depends on what Woodhead means by big. Stephen Ball's team studied 15 schools in three local authorities in 1994. Bet Woodhead didn't mention that. Remind me of this turned-around London school?'

Neil suspected she was unaware of the school, only recently reported in the *Telegraph*, a paper she probably didn't read, a suspicion strengthened by her question and not naming the school.

Neil explained again how it had been turned around. 'Even English and maths. Astonishing pass rates yet a deprived area. Large working-class intake. 80 per cent pass rate for English.'

She laughed mockingly and said, 'And do you believe it? Have you thought they might fix the results? I'm sure they must be fixing their pass rate. You can't turn a school around that easily. It contradicts everything sociology knows about class and achievement.'

Neil shrugged. 'Class and achievement?'

'Ask yourself, why are speaking and listening grades usually higher than grades for writing?'

Neil was silent, stroked his chin and smiled.

'I'll tell you why. It's assessed exclusively by teachers. Bumps up the final mark. Then there's help with coursework. I learned a lot observing teachers and classroom interactions. You see the advantage of observation? Wasn't part of my research, of course, I was a fly on the wall.'

Neil glanced at her figure, very large, bordering on obese. Big fly, he thought.

'Education is becoming cynical. Even extends to examination boards. They compete for customers – sorry – teachers. Teachers increasingly teach to targets. You need a C to pass, and they put their efforts into borderline students. Some students obtain model answers and rephrase them. One entrepreneurial student – a model Thatcherite – was running a profitable business writing assignments for a fee. Although 100 per cent coursework has gone, GCSEs are still 40-60 per cent. Easy to fix. Plagiarism is rife. Students write the same English assignments numerous times. The teacher proof-reads, the parents proof-read, siblings proof-read. Some have private tutors who correct or even re-write their assignments before final submission. I overheard one student tell a teacher her assignment was late because her tutor hadn't seen it. When I asked about this, the teacher described the tutor as a resource. "What's the difference between someone helping and using a book or the Internet?" he asked. Then there's the Shakespeare play. When I did Shakespeare at school it was under exam conditions. You did the play back to front and memorised numerous quotes. You had to know the language thoroughly and all the characters. Now it's taught as coursework. There was this weak group, so the teacher set a question about the murder of Duncan. *"Who influences MacBeth most: the witches or Lady MacBeth?"* Duncan is soon dead so all they had to study was act one of the play and ignore the remaining four acts. I asked the students if they'd read the whole play. One laughed and said, "We've read the video". The rots had even got to them. Then there's the possibility some teachers or heads have access to exam questions, either as members of examining boards or as examiners, privy to the questions before students sit the exam. Some even write exam questions. You look surprised? Quite a few heads are on the appropriate panels. Of course, it all done on trust. No checks.

'Wouldn't be risky revealing the question paper to students?'

'Done indirectly. Hints, or the teacher revises only the topics coming up. Not all teachers fix results, but I suspect many do. Who knows the exact number? Schools vary. Couldn't include it in my research, of course, but would make a good research topic.' She shook her head. 'Impossible, of course. What school would allow you past their gates to research fixing and faking?'

'The school I mentioned. Deprived area.'

'Bet he selects.'

'Oversubscribed but claims he doesn't select. Doesn't interview parents even. High percentage of free school meals.'

'Oversubscribed, you say. Doesn't need to interview parents. Knowing where they live sufficient. Postcode, and all that. And not all those on free school meals are low-attainers. He probably selects the best; selects the best of the worst, so to speak.'

Neil was feeling challenged. 'The Head claims 10 per cent of pupils are autistic.'

'Not surprised. Flexible term; fashionable label; long spectrum, from mild to severe. People want labels. Schools need them to get extra resources. Doctors distribute the label like confetti. Maybe his autistics are mild. Some argue that numerous famous people were, or are, autistic, including

Einstein and Darwin. An intake of Einsteins.' She laughed. 'Who wouldn't want autistics in the class?'

Her dismissals fitted Kuhn's theory of dogmatism, pleasing Neil, but he simultaneously felt a powerful urge to counter her arguments.

'Disproportionate number of ethnic minorities?' He was aware of growing desperation in his voice, which he checked.

'Bet they're Chinese.' She noted Neil's puzzled expression. 'Despite poverty and English often a second language, ethnic Chinese do exceptionally well. Do you know the school's ethnic composition?'

Exasperated, Neil shook his head and said, 'What about dyslexia? More than his share of dyslexics, apparently.'

'I'm pleased you said apparently. Same as autistics. There are dyslexics and there are dyslexics. As you know, we like to pull in so-called dyslexic students to claim our disability fund.' She nodded knowingly. 'Labels abound. Look how many celebrity dyslexics there are and those with bipolar. It's fashionable. Four Yorkshiremen, and all that. To achieve is one thing, to do so against the odds... Give me a class of dyslexic autistic Chinese students any day.'

Neil fell silent. Was she serious, or joking?

Weena made some tea. Without turning she said, 'Remind me about the catchment area. You say it's deprived yet the school is oversubscribed. That's suspicious.'

'According to what I read, every ambitious parent wants their child to go there. The Head is a disciplinarian; ex-army, uniform mad – designer uniform. Wear it right into the sixth form. Some argue that people need discipline, thrive on discipline. Maybe poorer children see liberalism as weakness. Their homes are probably –'

He was cut off as she exclaimed triumphantly, 'Was it a new school? Purpose built? I remember reading about it. He didn't take over the school exactly – a brand new school built on the site. Three-year gap between the two schools. All sorts of things can happen to a local population in three years. Some parents research the best schools, even move house or temporarily rent a flat to get into the catchment area. One family I know trawled estate agents for recently sold houses proximate to the best school. They didn't buy anything, just pretended to be living there knowing they wouldn't be found out because it was too early for the new occupants to appear on the electoral register. Then there's the God moment. They suddenly find Christ and attend church to get their child into a church school. A friend of mine was so desperate for her son to go to a prestigious Catholic secondary school they went to mass at the local cathedral, learned that the cathedral youth orchestra was short a double bass player, bought a double bass, found it didn't fit in the car and bought one of those very long Volvos. That's dedication. Special uniform, you say. Expensive. Probably puts off poorer parents – poverty penalty, that thief of high performance.'

'You blame parents whose children fail?'

'Absolutely not. Parents from all classes have the same level of ambition and motivation but vary in know-how. That's our main finding.'

'Isn't that contradicted by studies that show middle-class parents are more interested in their children's education, play educational games with their children and, as you say, move house etcetera to get into a better catchment area?'

'Still know-how. They show more interest because they are in the know. Same thing.'

'Isn't that stretching the definition of know-how?'

'Links to the poverty penalty. You can't deny differences in income. The expensive school uniforms? Then there are expensive school trips and equipment. Expense of travelling to a distant better school. Can't afford to move or rent a house or spare the time driving the greater distance. That's if they have a car. Can't afford private tutors. Forced to take holidays in term time. Know-how is not much use if can't do.'

Neil finally saw a small opening: the Chinese. 'Didn't you say poor Chinese children do exceptionally well? Against all the odds? Against sociological expectations? What makes them different? Where does that leave the poverty penalty?'

Motioning Neil to the door, she said tersely, 'The poverty penalty explains most poor children. Sociology is about averages, the norm, the majority, not the odd exception.'

Standing in the passageway, Neil turned as the door was closing and began saying, 'The majority of Chinese children –'

The door closed.

*

Neil was outlining his encounter with Weena and other sociologists to Rachel.

'So the Chinese are a chink in the sociological armour.'

'I wouldn't phrase it that way, exactly.'

'I'm being positive about the Chinese. What's wrong with that?'

Neil shrugged.

'What about inability to defer gratification?'

'Blames the poor. Definitely out.'

'Sound like fashion.' Rachel swivelled her chair to face Neil. 'So one hand in a packet of crisps, sucking on a bottle of Coke in front of a cinema-size TV screen is a stereotype. Labelling, then. All the rage when I did O-level sociology.'

'Labelling's out. Well, almost. Dominated the eighties, but limits research to classroom interactions. Ignores the wider society. And before you mention ambition, all classes are now equally ambitious, according to Weena.'

'Just because parents say they are ambitious for their children doesn't mean they are. They might tell Weena they want their children to do well then take them on holiday during the school term and see no contradiction.'

Neil felt a need to defend himself and sociology. 'Remember, I'm researching dogmatism, drawing out contradictions. There's a lot in what sociologists say about class inequality in education.'

'Is class still important? More working-class children are going to university, surely?'

Neil smiled. 'That's what I said at a meeting of sociologists. Adopting an innocent tone, I said I'd been reading *The Death of class* by Pakulski and Waters. You know, just to provoke them. The meeting erupted. Denying class or the importance of class to most sociologists is like denying God to a mullah.

After the meeting Paul Ewing, a social mobility specialist, invited me to his office, and told me to sit down as he closed the door. "Coffee", he said. Seated in front of me, he set me right about class. "Pakulski and Waters are postmodernists", he explained. "OK, postmodernism has a place. Society is changing, new identities, increasing fragmentation and greater individualism. Lifestyle and consumption patterns also define who we are, not just class. They have a point. But the fragmentation is nowhere as great as they say, and choices are not as free as they make out. No, we are still shaped by class. Lifestyle and consumption patterns are dependent on money power. None of us choose our parents, and Parkin long ago recognised the family as the basis of class. People may be less class conscious today, or even want to deny class exists, but it still shapes them. There are still massive inequalities".

'He pointed out two aspects to class: rewards for different positions and access to those positions. Even the postmodernists can't deny inequalities in the former, so that leaves access to positions. More working-class children than ever are attending university, but that's not proof of class decline or the declining influence of the family, let alone the death of class. Mobility is relative. More children from all social classes are going to university but the proportion from each class remains constant.' Neil paused and said, 'Did you know that?'

Rachel shook her head.

'Ewing explained that going to university is a very crude measure of attainment, anyway. People misuse or misunderstand statistics. Children from privileged backgrounds are more likely to access the prestigious Russell Group. 40 per cent of students attending Russell Group universities are from private schools. It gets worse. Students are not equal on graduation. Russell Group graduates are destined for better jobs, such as the higher professions, and are more likely to have good connections and affluent parents. They can afford to work for nothing for a year or more after graduation and can afford to self-fund further degrees and research.'

'So, it's more than the school attended.'

'Exactly. Private education correlates with success but may not be the only cause of success. Wealth and connections correlate with both.'

Her laugh was slightly ironic. 'So class is not all in the mind of the sociologist.'

'And just because class may not be someone's conscious identity, doesn't mean it's unimportant, less still non-existent. Even those who deny class are still affected by their class of origin. Ewing was very convincing. Consciously or not, class pervades everything. Even dyslexia.'

Rachel looked intrigued.

'I asked him about the disability coordinator's oft quoted examples of famous dyslexics overcoming their handicap, such as Ron Llewellyn-Buckfast. He did badly at school, now a millionaire. Self-made, he claims. Ewing found that amusing. "Ron Llewellyn-Buckfast, or Fastbuck to some, went to a top public school and his parents initially funded his business. As for his dyslexia, secretaries deal with his correspondence. He never writes anything. Doesn't matter if you can't spell once you reach a certain level".'

Rachel chuckled. 'He has an answer for everything.'

'Well, everything to do with class. Take class attitudes to university. One study showed that working class pupils – those from manual backgrounds – are disinclined to choose Oxbridge, feel they don't belong, whereas privately educated pupils feel entitled to go. Private schools boast percentages progressing to Oxbridge, or the big two as the pupils expressed it to Ewing. Working class children self-exclude, and teachers possibly expect less.'

Rachel seemed impressed. 'Ewing's so right about the Russell Group. How many privately educated students come to CCT? The privately educated student automatically assumes access to an older university, preferably Oxbridge, as a right. They don't ask, will I fit in? Will I belong? How many lecturers at CCU were privately educated?'

'Or Oxbridge educated.'

There was a pause and she leaned back. 'You seem to be progressing with your research.'

'I'm meeting Henry Hollow next week.'

'Henry Hollow?' She raised her eyebrows. 'You're interviewing Hollow? Good luck. He's got children, you know. God knows how. Hollow and sex the contradiction of contradictions. Tell me, what sort of schools do these Marxist sociologists send their own children?' She looked at her watch. 'Let's go for a drink.'

*

Relaxing in her favourite leather armchair, Rachel was saying, 'Henry hates people to know, but he was privately educated. And pampered. Those doleful eyes, anguished look, that withering smile. Some revolutionary. Some women are attracted to him, though.' She laughed at Neil's disbelief. 'Not as a man, someone to fuck, but as a child, someone to protect. His little-boy-lost pose. Some of the female staff are very protective; don't like to see him bullied.'

'I bait him from time to time. Is that bullying?'

'Don't feel guilty. He needs baiting, and more. I never miss a chance.'

'Claims to be a feminist.'

'Some feminist. Dominated by his wife. He might stand up *for* women, but he can't stand up *to* them. Take his marriage. Bit bourgeois for Henry the revolutionary to marry, I thought, until I found out it was his wife's decision. She's very religious. No, he was forced into marriage, and married late. Had children late. Rarely mentions he's married. Pretended at the time it wasn't happening. Went into denial. Called his forthcoming marriage a "festival thing".'

Henry had told staff he was going to some 'festival thing' and asked his supervisor for time off during term time.

'Got to go to this festival thing.'

'Festival thing?'

'I need at least a week.'

'A week? What festival thing, Henry? What are you talking about?'

'I'm getting married.'

'Congratulations. But why can't you marry in the holidays?'

Rachel refilled her glass. 'Henry likes to think he's outrageous, likes to shock. Marriage is prostitution, he often says, or used to say, quoting some American feminist. One day I said to him, does that mean your wife is a prostitute, Henry? If someone offered her the market rate, would she sell her body? "That's a different sort of prostitution", he said. That's just pissing about with words, I replied.'

'Most of the sociologists I've met are not like Henry. Most are not Marxists, but like Henry most are obsessed with protecting underdogs. Most seem to dislike the middle class but are all middle class, if not in origin. They have that in common with Henry. You've got to be careful what you say about the working class or ethnic minorities to a sociologist.

Maybe it reflects their backgrounds? They're all quick to boast or claim humble origins, even Henry.'

'As I said, privately educated.'

'But pretends proletarian origins. "Went to university to avoid going down pit", he told me, adopting a slight Yorkshire accent and leaving out the definite article. Most of the time his accent couldn't be more educated southern. "Parth" instead of path, "barth" for bath. Turns out his father worked for the Coal Board as a wages clerk. Most sociologists I've met are leftish-liberal, pay the usual lip service to genes, but have a blank-slate view. That's their guiding paradigm, though Kuhn wouldn't have called it as such.'

'How do you explain them?'

'I'm working on it. Maybe the subject attracts such people, or are they, in Kuhn's terms, initiated into one of the many sociological paradigms? One sociologist, after a few pints, told me he altered his views the first term of his degree, believing you couldn't progress far if you held the wrong views. His impression was most sociology students adopted a liberal pose very quickly. Perhaps it's cognitive dissonance: change your view or drop the subject. Or Bem: I am studying sociology; therefore, I must be...'

'So you're saying sociology's left-wing, and biased?'

'They wouldn't say so. If challenged, they tell you bias affects choice of subject only, but thereafter the research is objective, or tries to be. Sociology also gives the appearance of being left-wing because of its subject matter, or much of it. As I said, currently obsessed with underdogs and inequality.'

*

'I've often wondered, what exactly is the difference between psychology and sociology?'

'According to a phenomenologist I was speaking to, all subject boundaries are arbitrary and artificial – mere reifications.' Neil expanded with examples as Rachel's body stiffened and lips pursed.

Shoulders hunched, she said, 'When you look at a sociology textbook it's obvious it's not psychology, and vice versa. Now tell me the fucking difference. Tell me what *you* think.'

Neil gave an awkward laugh. 'OK. Subject matter, for a start. They often deal with different problems, or different aspects of the same problem. Nurture-nature is explored in psychology but ignored by sociologists. This closely relates to methodology. Sociologists prefer the comparative method to the experiment and shun the laboratory.'

'Comparative?'

'Studying and comparing people and groups in context, in real situations. Weaker results, but despite that sociologists can make predictions – contrary to what Matlock believes. Take education. On average, middle-class children do better in education than working class children. Every year it's the same. Therefore, prediction is possible in sociology. But they want to go beyond prediction. They want reasons. The outcome is an ever-moving conveyor belt of explanations: income, ambition, amount of TV watched, culture, teacher expectations, know-how, and so on. Know-how is in vogue, not differences in ambition as previously believed. You can't quantify the variables, of course, say put a percentage on watching TV.'

'So how do they choose one explanation over another?'

'Common sense, for a start. Take trees. Trees correlate with achievement.'

Rachel laughed and thumped the armrest on her chair. 'Trees?'

Neil remained serious. 'Yes, trees. But do trees cause success, or does success give greater access to trees? The middle classes live in leafier suburbs, but no sociologist would suggest that planting more trees in working class areas would raise pass rates.'

'Couldn't trees be linked to air purity, in turn affecting intelligence?'

'Shhh. Intelligence is a dirty word in sociology.'

'So more common prejudice than common sense.'

'Partly. They use common sense ideas about causality providing it fits their environmentalist assumptions. But is common sense a good guide? At one time common sense suggested that women achieved less because, on average, they had smaller brains than men. It correlated. It seemed obvious. Absence of a Kuhnian paradigm doesn't mean they are more open than the natural sciences, a free for all, or inherently less dogmatic and more tolerant. Not paradigms as such, but unshakable beliefs all the same. Sociologists I spoke to vaguely talked about sociological perspectives, in the plural. Functionalist, conflict, Marxist and interactionist perspectives feature strongly. And within each perspective a kaleidoscope of conflicting mini perspectives tenaciously clung to, and within these, multiple methodological disagreements. Dogma is there, but more fragmented than in the natural sciences, more splintered and transient. Same with psychology, of course. Perhaps more so. The more eclectic draw on different perspectives or hop from one theory to the next, often the opposite of what went before to establish their own reputation. A series of mini paradigms, and within these, more paradigms, an endless fragmentation, a mirror reflecting a mirror reflecting a mirror, ad infinitum. There's no agreement over methodology, of course. Each claims scientific status or greater truth.'

'So is sociology a science?'

'Some sociologists deny the possibility of a social science at all. More than one sociologist told me sociology isn't a science, meaning it's inaccurate, even denied the very existence of facts, so I said to one of them, what's the point of research if you think that? Surely sociological research is better than the racist rantings of the National Front? Are sociological studies no better than *Mein Kampf*? At that point he agreed. He just hadn't thought through the issue. The problem is there's no agreement about what science is. The social world is more complex than the natural world, of course. Sociologists go beyond prediction. Atoms aren't about meaning or motivation. Atoms don't think. As I've said before, we can predict that working class children on average will do less well in education, but that's only the starting point. We also want to know why. Explanation adds another layer of complexity. Put another way, the social sciences involve a far greater range of variables.'

Rachel looked thoughtful. 'You *are* changing. Where has Hamlet's absolute search for the truth gone, your Hamlet complex? You'll be telling me next you've finished your PhD.'

*

Some days later, Neil found a note in his tray from Rachel: *Come to my room to discuss Durkheim. Urgent.*

Neil had since 'interviewed' Roger, Rachel's Durkheimian, to include in his research.

Roger once applied Durkheim's Suicide to Nottingham boroughs modelled on Sainsbury's study of London. He began with areas of low and high integration, and confirmed Durkheim's and Sainsbury's findings that suicide was inversely proportional to integration. Suicide was higher in bedsit areas and lower in areas with strong family ties, and within these groups singles had a higher rate than married, the rate diminishing with each child added to the family – a perfect correspondence to Durkheim.

His study was cited in major textbooks and for many confirmed the view that Durkheim's theory of suicide was akin to a paradigm, an exemplar with its own methodology, and his replication fulfilled Popper's first commandment of science: thou shalt be open to replication. Unknowingly, he had replicated a flawed research design and a short time later Douglas, a phenomenologist, demolished the statistical data on which Durkheim's imposing structure stood, an erect building built on sand. How did Roger cope with Douglas's demolition of Durkheim's suicide statistics? Did he change his beliefs about suicide, or somehow explain away the criticisms?

Rachel was stressed. Before Neil sat down, she was saying, 'Durkheim says sociology and psychology are totally separate. Does that mean the theory can't be applied to the Shelleys as individuals? Durkheim says, "A social fact can be explained only by another social fact". What the fuck does that mean exactly? Does that mean it can't explain an individual act of suicide? Two levels of reality, social and individual. Render unto Caesar. I'm confused.'

'Have you asked Roger?'

'Roger's away. Visiting lecturer. The Sorbonne.' She gave a withering look.

'Very inconsiderate.'

She glared at him, and he said hurriedly, 'You know he learned French so he could read Durkheim in the original?'

'What does Durkheim mean by "Consider social facts as things"?'

Neil suggested they go for a drink.

'I've got students –'

'They can come back another time. Pin a note on your door. Let's go. I'll drive.'

Dropping into an upholstered curved chair, Rachel, now calmer, took a gulp of red wine and reminded Neil, '"Social facts as things…"'

'You obviously haven't read Durkheim's *The Rules of Sociological Method*.'

She nodded. 'So?'

'First you must understand the historical context. At the time, natural science was the exemplar of science and

Durkheim set out to create a science of society separate from psychology that paralleled the natural sciences, which he believed to be objective and exact, arguing that to be a science and a discipline in its own right, sociology needed as its subject matter objective, observable and regular facts using methods drawn from the natural sciences. There were two aims: sociology as a separate discipline from psychology and sociology as an objective predictive discipline. The sacrifice, so to speak, was that sociology had to be limited to observable phenomena.'

'So you *are* saying Durkheim can't explain individuals?'

'I'm coming to that. Bear with me.'

'What are social facts, and what are things? You still haven't explained. Why are you stalling? Are you sure you know the answer? After all, it's not your discipline.'

Her voice had risen but Neil remained calm and said, 'Neither is psychology Roger's discipline, and the background of my research is the history of science. I read up on Durkheim before interviewing Roger. As you said, rambling, meandering Victorian epics.'

'Sorry, sorry.'

'That's OK. I was saying, Durkheim wanted to emulate the natural sciences, the hallmark and model for science in the 19th century. The natural sciences study objects outside individuals, material forces or things which affect us and pattern behaviour independent of individuals, such as climate affecting mortality.'

'Like the volcanic eruption and the year without a summer that kept the Shelleys indoors, a force external to them that shaped them. No volcano, no *Frankenstein*.'

'Durkheim believed there are social facts external to the individual, greater than the individual, exercising control over the individual, akin to the facts of nature.'

'So how do you know a social fact? Give a tangible, concrete example.'

'Suicide. Durkheim applied this to the suicide rate, a social fact not reducible to the motives of individuals but detectable through statistics which are independent of individual motives and therefore a force beyond individuals, as much a fact as climate. If he could show that suicide – a very individual act – could be linked to society and not individuals, he could justify sociology as a separate discipline. He believed society is more than the sum of its individual members, exists beyond individuals and has an existence outside the individual at the level of the group. He called these social facts. Psychological factors, such as intentions, though a cause of suicide, are untidy, erratic, uncontrollable, and can't explain variations between groups, which remain constant over time. Group variations are therefore the subject matter of his sociology and can only be explained by other social facts, such as egoism, altruism and anomie.

'Now you see what Durkheim means when he says a social fact can only be explained by another social fact. It can't be reduced to individual psychology, such as an individual act of suicide because such acts are just too individual, too erratic and unstable. They don't allow prediction. Also, they don't allow for the separate discipline – sociology.'

Rachel gulped the remains of her wine. 'Let's get a bottle each and go to my flat. There's a quote in *The Sign of Four* I think fits what you're saying.'

*

Rachel reached over to her bookcase for a copy of *The Sign of Four* and read from a marked page: "...while the individual man is an insoluble puzzle, in the aggregate he becomes a mathematical certainty. You can, for example, never foretell what any one man will do, but you can say with precision what an average number will be up to. Individuals vary, but percentages remain constant. So says the statistician".'

'Holmes puts it well.'

Rachel nodded. 'But you still haven't said if I can apply Durkheim to *Frankenstein*.'

'I'm getting there. First, we need to deal with Catholics and Protestants, the main subject of Durkheim's *Suicide*.'

Neil was enjoying teasing Rachel, dangling her on the end of the rod for a change. He settled back into the armchair, and rearranging the cushion, said, 'Variations in suicide rates, such as the consistently lower rate amongst Catholics, must therefore relate to some group characteristic of Catholics, something that differentiates them from Protestants, something above the myriad of individual intentions. That something, Durkheim concluded, was higher integration and regulation. He likened social facts to a thermometer measuring heat –'

'So that's what he means by saying suicide is a measure of social health, namely declining social integration and anomie. The less integrated and anomic a society, the higher the suicide rate.'

Opening a second bottle of wine, Rachel continued. 'OK, it's clearer now, but you still haven't said if Durkheim can be applied to Frankenstein, an individual, or to the Shelleys individually.'

'That's where the criticism comes in, the flaw in Durkheim's theory.'

Rachel was alarmed. 'I don't want you demolishing Durkheim. It's because of Durkheim we went to Geneva, don't forget that. We owe a lot to Durkheim. He's integral to my research. Tread carefully. Are you sure you're not reverting, getting all nihilistic again?'

Neil laughed. 'Don't worry. The critics are also flawed. There will be enough left of Durkheim for your research, I promise. Let's start with Hell. Durkheim wanted to show that a single variable – integration – explained the difference between Catholic and Protestant suicide rates. But there was a problem.

What if Catholics condemned suicide more than Protestants? Being told you'd go straight to Hell for eternity would make you think twice about topping yourself. Durkheim solved the problem by claiming both religions condemned suicide equally, leaving the only difference integration, his a priori theory.'

'OK, it's flawed, I see that. Very convincing. Frankenstein?'

'I'm almost there. First Douglas and Atkinson, the main critics of Durkheim's *Suicide*.'

'Douglas? Atkinson?'

'Jack Douglas, *The Social Meaning of Suicide*. Atkinson followed with *Discovering Suicide*, a more extreme phenomenological account. Both demolish suicide statistics. You see, Durkheim relied on official statistics, accepting them as facts, unaware, or choosing not to believe, they are socially constructed, and therefore not facts. The decision whether a death is suicide is made by coroners drawing on evidence from family and friends. Douglas cleverly parallels Durkheim's use of integration, but instead of seeing this as constraining the individual, he sees it as an opportunity to fix the evidence. Remember, at the time of Durkheim's study suicide was a mortal sin in the Catholic Church and the suicide condemned to eternal damnation. Family members must have been under pressure to cover up, and doctors and coroners more cautious returning a verdict, especially if they knew the suicide's family, often the case at that time.'

'Hamlet hesitates to commit suicide, his dread of something worse after death because God had "fix'd His canon 'gainst self-slaughter". "...conscience does make cowards of us all". He can't act.'

Neil nodded. 'Exactly. When someone is well-integrated, such as living with their family, the family can cover up the suicide by destroying a suicide note or personal diary and lying about the suicide's state of mind before committing suicide, especially if the suicide blames them, bringing added shame on family members.'

'And even without blame, parents would still have a sense of failure as parents,' Rachel added.

'For someone less integrated, such as living alone, this is less likely to happen. The less integrated a suicide is, such as living alone in a bedsit, the more likely their death will be explained as suicide because family members don't control the evidence. Suicide may bear an inverse relationship to integration not because integrated groups constrain an individual but because they can cover up more. Another problem is that coroners use different degrees of evidence. Douglas says we need to get behind coroners' labels to ascertain the real rate of suicide. Atkinson believes we can never know the true rate of suicide. All we can ask is, how do deaths get categorised as suicide? Who decides using what criteria?

'Durkheim conveniently assumes all coroners used the same criteria deciding if a death is suicide, but Douglas found this wasn't so. One coroner insisted on a suicide note, another didn't. Take Brian Epstein. Objectively we know he died of a drug overdose, but we don't know his intention. The coroner recorded accidental death. Another coroner might have recorded suicide. Durkheim ignored intention and coroners' interpretations.'

'What does Roger say to all this?'

'He knows all the criticisms, of course. I cited Douglas and Atkinson to test his dogmatism. He made the point that if suicide statistics are no more than coroners' interpretations, then the observations of coroners by phenomenologists are no more than their interpretations of coroners' interpretations.'

'A theory that takes us nowhere ends up nowhere.'

'Interestingly, Roger says it doesn't invalidate Durkheim's theory of integration and suicide. He still believes in Durkheim's theory and believes there is a suicide rate out there. Getting at it is the problem. So he put his Nottingham study on hold and moved on to other things.'

'So where does that leave me and Frankenstein?'

'Durkheim's wrong to separate sociological factors from other factors. For a complete picture of suicide, we must integrate all levels of explanation.'

'Can I use Durkheim's theory to explain the Shelleys and Frankenstein.'

'Of course. Call it your interpretation of Durkheim if you wish.'

'Barthes's readerly and writerly, death of the author the birth of the reader.' Rachel reflected a moment. 'Hold on, isn't all this is really no more than your interpretation of Durkheim?'

'Absolutely. I was coming to that. See it as an advantage. Call it your interpretation of Barthes's readerly and writerly argument.'

'Is Durkheim writerly?'

'He wouldn't have thought so, but isn't everything a bit writerly, everything on a spectrum? Didn't Barthes say that?'

Rachel laughed. 'According to someone's interpretation based on someone's translation of Barthes, who in turn interpreted what Barthes is saying.'

'Scholars disagree about what Durkheim is saying. Same with any theory. Barthes's no different. Apply Kelly's rule: can a theory explain its own creation? If the works of Barthes are writerly and there is no single author behind his texts, no originality, everything borrowed and re-combined, then where does that leave Barthes?'

She laughed. 'I'm sure Barthes didn't see himself as irrelevant, otherwise he would have remained anonymous. I don't know. I don't think he applied his theory to himself.'

'And if a book is writerly, where does that leave copyright and royalties? If the reader is the author, who sues for libel or copyright infringement?'

'And where does the poetry of language fit? Interpretation isn't everything. The writerly approach can't write like

Shakespeare. Surely, we must credit Shakespeare for the poetic language and eloquence. Shakespeare, not the reader?'

She banged her wine down, causing it to splash. 'Durkheim! You still haven't –'

'Getting there. Durkheim is confused over individual suicide and tries to edit out the individual. He tries to separate the individual from society and make society transcendent. He's right to say sociology is concerned with averages, but so is all science, including psychology.'

'History? Biography? Deals with individuals.'

'Sort of. Biographers often infer motives based on averages, likelihoods, past behaviour, social context, or merely infer or guess motives.'

'Like why did Mary Shelley write *Frankenstein*? Was it a re-play of her own life, or fear of the mob?'

'Exactly. As I said, Durkheim's sociology is not the exact science he imagined. An individual is obviously a mixture of pressures, internal and external, psychological and sociological, the two interacting, acted on and acting.'

'Then I can apply Durkheim to the Shelleys.'

'I don't see why not.' He grinned at her. 'Did I mention, there's a footnote in his *The Rules of Sociological Method* where he discusses a sociopsychological fact, how an individual may influence the social. He qualifies it though, plays it down.'

'Then why the fuck didn't you say so at the beginning? Give me the reference. You and your forgotten footnotes.'

Neil shrugged. 'It's only a footnote.'

'Only a footnote! Thought that was all you ever read. Anything but the body of the text. Didn't Shelrack say that?'

Neil fell silent, gazed out the window.

'Sorry. That was a bit hard.'

Neil turned to face Rachel and smiled. 'You could say *Frankenstein* symbolises egoistic and anomic society, rather in the way that Marxist portrays the monster as symbolising the mob. Your choice, your interpretation. After all, you don't have to be a slave to his theory. Take from it what you want, modify it. Despite the flaws, it's still a good theory, still relevant today. Unlimited aspirations, unlimited consumption, endless growth and consumerism destroying the planet, anomie and egoism everywhere. Most of us are caught up in it, a market system turning people into consumption slaves. Got that from Henry. Well, sort of. Circuitous route via Feuerbach and Marx. Feuerbach said man made God and became a slave to his own creation. Marx applied the idea to the capitalist economy; we create an economic system and lose control. It controls us. The world economy revolves around growth. A nation's success is measured by growth. Politicians boast about growth, are criticised for lack of growth. Advertisers manipulate us. We are what we spend.'

'So many women I know delay having children and buy a dog to compensate. They work after they have children, all to maintain a lifestyle, the latest kitchen, desires distorted and out of control. Think of the stress, the conflict, the guilt. Cooking is in decline, or so a recent study showed. People eat out more or buy ready meals. They don't have time to cook.'

'Yet cookery programmes are very popular and kitchen design more and more expensive. Very strange.'

By late evening, halfway into a third bottle of a particularly smooth Côtes du Rhône the world becoming increasingly hilarious by the glassful, they flawed the home cooking study. What exactly was home cooking? Opening a can of baked beans and heating them? Rachel wondered if it was real cooking. After all, we don't grow or harvest the beans, or the tomatoes that comprise the sauce, or the bread we turn into toast.

*

Consciously walking towards the staffroom, in cognition terms guided by a cognitive map and therefore more pulled than driven, Neil reflected on similarities between Durkheim and Skinner and how he might fit them into his research.

Skinner's psychology fitted the idea of a psychology paradigm rather well, though at a terrible cost. To have a 'science' of psychology Skinner limited psychology to observable behaviour. The goal of psychology was prediction and control, and subjective states, such as mind or motives, that is, conscious experience and intentions were unobservable and could form no part. Inheritance was similarly dismissed. Anomalies – and there were many – were dealt with one by one. The mind was a problem, a staggering anomaly. Deemed unsuitable for investigation and initially pushed to one side, it was finally abolished as a myth; what we think are motives and consciousness are illusory. Now behaviour replaced the mind it was logical to research 'mindless' lifeforms such as rats – hence ratology – and generalise to people; well, not people exactly, 'organisms', people implied consciousness and motives. For decades numerous psychologists, mainly American, studied rats in mazes, and pigeons pecking for food pellets, behaviour shaped this way and that by rewards.

Skinner's level of explanation was more than another level, it was the only level, a paradigm forged at the expense of human freedom and unashamedly reductive. Freedom and choice were also myths, of course. But there was an anomaly. Skinner couldn't explain *himself*. As an experimenter he was in control, conscious, knowing, pursuing an idea, a goal, pulled not pushed, therefore contradicting his own theory.

*

Was he changing? Less concerned with the truth? Rachel implied as much. And he was researching again. Bem…

Recently a student had posed a conundrum. 'You're always criticising research, Neil, finding fault, demolishing, yet you back up your arguments with research and use it to counter our personal experience.'

The group was silent, some grinning, wondering, no doubt, how he would escape the conundrum, a Festinger cognitive dissonance trap. To gain consonance, according to Festinger, he must say that research was hopelessly flawed and accept experience or reject personal experience and accept the superiority of research. There again…

Recalling his counter to a sociologist who claimed sociology wasn't a science, he said, 'Yes, research is flawed. I stick to that, but it must be better than no research, more proximate of the truth than our own very limited personal experience or untested assumptions, better than the I-know-a-man statistic, the statistic of one against the sample of thousands. Think, think of truth as a continuum, the National Front, and similar groups, at the very bottom, their ranting about race surely less objective than social research based on data. The National Front isn't committed to the truth, it selects and distorts its so-called evidence. And our experience is very limited, a few friends, family circle, the workplace.' He shook his head.

At that moment he realised he was thinking positively about research, thinking relatively, not absolutely, but was it was genuine cognition change, he wondered, or rationalising to win the argument? After all, Festinger said we are more rationalising than rational, but where did that leave Festinger?

*

From the window of Henry's office, Neil peered down at the Department of Psychology, low-level, red brick, T-shaped and sunless, and wondered if there was some message in the architecture.

Henry's room was on the ninth floor of the tower, accessed by paternoster, stairwell or closed-in lift. The paternoster, an open continuously moving chain of boxes, seemed dangerous to Neil as passengers were expected to jump on and off, but no one had been injured to date, and any risk outweighed the long haul up the winding stairwell (the lift was being serviced).

Henry's room was its usual ordered disorder. Scattered papers and Marxist tomes occupied every space. His wife often complained about his disregard for more mundane matters, such as paying bills, and every so often a threatening final bill would arrive, the first bill and reminder unopened and used by Henry as bookmarks. Henry thought this very amusing. Perhaps shades of the absent-minded professor?

A typewriter occupied one corner, obviously in use: paper in the platen, a spare typewriter ribbon and a box of carbon paper to create copies. Neil moved closer. The smell of carbon paper now recalled blue carbon on his fingers. Next to the typewriter was a card index box, scuffed and patched up with tape. Was it fear of new technology or inverted snobbery? Henry's appearance suggested inversion: threadbare jeans and pullover full of orderly holes. Didn't Socrates say to someone who wore rags to show his lack of vanity, 'Young man, your vanity peeps through the holes in your clothes'.

'Orderly disorder, carefully careless, mindedly absent-minded,' said Rachel.

Unknown to Neil, Henry's scruffiness was residual, having long shed his earlier more radical sixties image, his ensemble, though scruffy, regularly cleaned by Mrs Hollow. Like a Catholic struggling with sin, Henry struggled to live by his Marxism, recently spotted being pulled into a store by his wife to look at washing machines, audibly muttering 'consumerism, consumerism.'

Neil had researched Henry before their meeting, focusing on some articles by Henry on education defending the

Marxists Bowles and Gintis against Lyotard's postmodernism and a sprinkling of sophisticated Marxists who dismissed Bowles and Gintis as vulgar Marxists, in turn dismissed by Henry as revisionists. To Lyotard's criticism that Marxism is a grand narrative, he rejoined: 'Better than a kaleidoscope of fragments, ever shifting and changing shape. Marxism offers permanence, stability, contextualisation – tectonic plates underpinning and shaping a myriad of surface detail. Bed rock.'

Not for Henry the sociology of detail and trivia blinkered to wider issues, or the minutiae of daily interactions such as labelling and Goffman. Nor the daily squabbling over ever-diminishing finer points, but a soaring edifice peering down at the rubble of small, transient and squabbling theories, a transcending, all-pervading superstructure of a theory.

Neil was now well versed in Bowles and Gintis, an imposing but flawed theory attracting a long line of critics, including many Marxists. While liking its totality, such as placing education in a wider context unlike psychology's boxed-in and isolated fragments, this was also its weakness: too generalising and too reductive – the all-explanatory underpinning economy. He knew Henry must know the flaws but how did he cope with them?

He mentally went over Bowles and Gintis, reciting the main points to an imaginary audience. The structure of the school corresponds to the structure of the workplace. The classroom reproduces each generation of workers, trained to accept their roles in capitalist society. Schooling operates under 'the long shadow of work'. Fragmentation of the school curriculum mirrors fragmentation of work tasks. Lack of control in school mimics lack of control at work. Unfulfilling jobs for a wage parallel studying for grades, not knowledge as its own end. A small number of private schools prepare an elite for management, inculcating leadership. Bottom line: schools reproduce inequality.

Their re-working of the hidden curriculum captured Neil's interest. Whatever the content of the syllabus, relevant to the economy or not, the hidden curriculum, unspoken, often unrecognised, is pervasive. Schools are about hierarchy, obedience to authority, rewarding cooperation, conformity, punctuality and rule-following. Not the content of the curriculum, more the way it is organised and delivered. School is the perfect preparation for the capitalist workplace. Building on Marx's idea that rulers cannot rule by brute force alone and need to legitimate their rule, Bowles and Gintis assert that education serves this need by creating an illusory meritocracy where jobs are gained through merit because education is free, fair and open to all. The myth of meritocracy stops people who fail from rebelling by convincing them it was their fault, their lack of ability or motivation, creating the illusion that everyone has an equal chance of becoming unequal. This in turn justifies income inequality. Those who gain high qualifications are deemed more valuable and deserving of higher pay, the poor in turn blamed for their poverty.

Neil applied his standard test to Bowles and Gintis: Kelly's question whether a theory can explain its own creation. The theory failed the test. If we are all duped, conditioned, made unreflective, why were Bowles and Gintis immune? Here was an anomaly. And did everyone believe the system was fair, and knuckle under? One study showed that most workers did not believe education fair or the school all-important. They emphasised family background and social connections (who you know). But Henry would surely fault the study, the methodology, sample size, ideological bias, or neutralise it with an alternative study that supported Bowles and Gintis (Neil noticed that researchers were astute at faulting studies that conflicted with their own).

A better criticism was the obvious lack of correspondence between education and the economy. We have a liberal, humanities-based education only indirectly related to the needs of industry. How often do employers criticise school leavers' limited skills, such as spelling, and why is Shakespeare built into the curriculum and made compulsory? What use is Shakespeare to the economy? Did Bowles and Gintis ever teach? Did Henry ever teach outside university? Neil drew on his own school teaching. Students, he recalled, were not passive recipients of education. Bowles and Gintis overstated the power of education and the power of teachers over people's lives.

Neil presented the list of anomalies and contradictions to Henry.

Henry laughed and said, 'I partly agree.'

'You agree?'

'Partly, but not completely.' He nodded rapidly; mouth open in the form of smile. 'More disagree than agree.'

Neil decided he needed to be specific. 'Do schools reflect the economy?'

'Largely.'

'If education largely reflects the economy, is a creature of the economic base, how do you explain Marxism at degree level and A-level sociology syllabuses, which include Bowles and Gintis, and capitalist publishers publishing the works of Marx?'

'Tokenism, part of the liberal veneer,' he said breezily. 'Potential revolutionaries are shunted into academia where they are rendered harmless. Talk shop, or eunuch Marxists, we call them.'

'So where does that leave you?'

His tone confidential, Henry said, 'My Marxism extends beyond academia. I'm actively involved in revolutionary politics and operate under a nom de guerre.' His voice close to a whisper, he added, 'My house is a cell. I can't say more. Come along some time.'

Neil nodded agreeably. 'I would like that.'

Henry made tea, some Fairtrade brand, slightly green in colour and very weak.

'If the school curriculum is shaped by the ruling class, how do you explain literature, history, even Shakespeare on the syllabus? Can't all be tokenism. Doesn't that show a degree of independence? Education not the total creature of industry, the infrastructure?'

'National pride. Our heritage. Cultural imperialism. Flag waving, and all that. Cultural superiority. Cultural arm of national economic self-interest. Anyway, the arts and humanities are part of the economy. Films, plays, novels are products that sell. Bowles and Gintis are a bit narrow economically. I'm not a Bowles and Gintis clone.'

'Explain Labour governments.'

'Wasn't it Baldwin who said, "Whatever government is in office, the Tories are always in power"? Parliamentary democracy is a facade. Parliament's a facade. Multinationals are the real power, the money.'

'Follow the money,' nodded Neil.

Henry frowned momentarily.

'The film, *All the President's Men*.'

'Haven't seen it. Tend to avoid Hollywood blockbusters.'

'Blockbuster?'

Henry made a little cough, and his voice a little higher, continued countering the criticisms. 'Since Thatcher, Major and now Blair, Bowles and Gintis are increasingly relevant. Education is increasingly linked to the needs of industry.'

'A-level sociology?' Neil reminded him.

Henry coughed again; a cough that told students he was about to say something important. 'You're forgetting the hidden curriculum. Whatever is taught in the curriculum is infinitely less important than the hidden curriculum. Your A-sociology student learns about Marxism and other radical ideas within a framework of conformity. She learns hierarchy and learns to compete. She is more interested in the qualification than the content. The qualification is the message. Not the content of the syllabus, but the way it is taught shapes the future workforce. Teachers give orders, pupils obey. Teachers in turn obey the Head, who in turn...' He made a gesture with his hands. 'You progress if you conform, fail if you don't. Pupils learn to defer to authority, learn that the world is bound by rules; learn obedience. The school stamps uniformity on the pupils and suppresses individuality. Hence uniforms, rules and punishments. Pupils are motivated by external rewards and gain little intrinsic satisfaction from didactic teaching. They regurgitate and don't create. School prepares them for unsatisfying work mitigated by the wage packet and their training to consume. We are a nation of consumption slaves manipulated by advertising. The syllabus is fragmented and allows little connection between subjects. Same at work. An alienated workforce motivated by money and consumerism – false needs.'

'Someone might ask, why aren't you a consumption slave?'

He laughed. 'I've read lots of Marxism, I suppose. Insulates and protects.'

*

Neil was amused as he told Rachel about an agitated call from Henry. 'Accused me of deception. "Was that research the other week?" He was angry. Or what passed for anger, a muted Henry anger.'

'Muted anger? Almost an oxymoron.' She adopted a knowing expression. 'Didn't I say deception was risky?'

'I told him what I was doing was near the bottom end of the spectrum from casual chat to research, an exploratory pilot. And of course, I would have asked his permission if included, but wanted him to be his natural self, not on guard – in the interest of research. He wanted to know the purpose of my research and I said subject boundaries.'

'Sounds harmless enough.'

'Matlock wouldn't agree. Anyway, dogmatism is partly about subject boundaries. Henry huffed and puffed but came round. He wants another meeting.'

*

Sipping Henry's weak tea, Neil listened attentively as Henry said, 'Marxist theory is at stake here. We've got to get the theory right. I'm worried I gave the wrong impression when we last met. You asked questions about Bowles and Gintis. I put up the best defence.' He laughed. 'You probably have me down as a deterministic, mechanistic Marxist. Absolutely not. If everything is reducible to the economy there is no objective truth, and Marxism no truer than any other theory, and my own position untenable. Got your drift. To know ideas are determined we must be partially free. If we are partially free we cannot be completely determined. I'm more towards Bourdieu these days. Moved on since my Bowles and Gintis articles. That's the trouble with the printed word, fixes you in time, ideas in amber.'

He settled into his chair. 'Bourdieu's not a true Marxist, more a Weberian.' He looked at Neil. 'The sociologist Max Weber. One of the founders of sociology. You must read up on him. Weber spent his life refining Marx. Famous for the Protestant ethic. Argues that religion has some autonomy from the economic base and shapes economic development as well as being shaped. Weber also said religion could inhibit as well as promote economic development. Weber asked, why did capitalism develop in the West? Some Eastern religions, such as Hinduism, were too rigid to permit social mobility and economic development. Caste system. Did you find time to read the articles on Bourdieu?'

Neil had scanned the articles and found them unremittingly abstract and opaque: habitus and doxa, elimination and self-elimination, class reproduction, symbolic violence, reflexivity, bourgeois parlance and common parlance, pedagogic work and pedagogic authority, each word, each sentence an obstacle course of jargon. As is often the case, researchers came away clutching a word or phrase, namely cultural capital and habitus from Bourdieu's profuse and abstruse argot, in turn prompting numerous educational studies. Neil suspected the usual need to elevate research by attaching some heavyweight theory, all the better for being esoteric or obscurantist, all the better being French. He now realised Weena's 'know-how' was derived from habitus, a pure distillation into plain English, leaving behind a thick sediment of opaque jargon. Neil was unclear about the difference between habitus, cultural capital and taste, and did Bourdieu really believe all cultures are equal? What did Henry think?

'In plain English,' insisted Neil.

Henry objected. 'Impossible. Bourdieu's ideas are so novel they require a new vocabulary.'

It was some time before Neil, by a process of interrogation and rephrasing, managed to extract a plain English version of cultural capital, a tortuous route through institutionalised state, the objectified state and family pedagogical action. The plain English version stated that the middle-class advantage their children by stressing qualifications and surrounding them with books, paintings and dictionaries. In short, the middle-class and higher-class child has a head start because home culture is like school culture.

'Bourdieu explains Shakespeare better than Bowles and Gintis,' Henry was saying. 'Remember your question about Shakespeare? Shakespeare's on the syllabus because it favours the more cultured middle-class. Shakespeare is elitist, impenetrable, part of bourgeois parlance, not common parlance, familiar to the middle-class family but not the working-class family. The school teaches through bourgeois parlance and culture.

'I mentioned cultural capital at our last meeting,' Henry continued. 'Did I mention cultural capital? Whatever. I didn't make it clear. You see, the curriculum content matters – of course it matters – because it comprises bourgeois culture. The content is as important as the hidden curriculum. Bourdieu's curriculum is less a reflection of the infrastructure and more a reflection of bourgeois parlance and culture. Education reproduces and legitimises inequality by creating the myth of meritocracy. Similar to Bowles and Gintis but emphasises bourgeois parlance and culture. The poor might dream of flying but are held back by the gravity of the social field. The terrible thing is, they think it's fair; blame themselves for failure. That's a key Bourdieuian point: self-elimination.'

Neil detected a sob in his voice.

*

Neil chuckled as Rachel handed him a coffee. 'I think he suffered a partial paradigm shift between our two meetings. All those anomalies piling up, attacked from all sides. Something had to give. I brought it to a head. I was the catalyst.'

'Why partial?'

'He still retains his Marxism, of course, even some Bowles and Gintis. The theories are very similar. Both claim schools reproduce the class system, but Bourdieu emphasises culture, social capital and milieu. Henry compromised, but still believes the economic base is paramount. Both believe education creates a myth of meritocracy.'

'Bourdieu's hardly original. It's obvious middle-class children have a more cultured environment. Now we have a word for it: cultural capital. Bourdieu coined a term, that's all. A word, a sound, a mouthful of air. Now everyone is breathing out the word. Not the same as inventing the internal combustion engine.'

'Don't forget economic and social capital. Bourdieu combines all three – economic, cultural and social.' Neil defined the three kinds of capital for Rachel. 'All confer advantage and maintain the rule of the dominant class. All these forms can be exchanged.'

'So he's saying that as well as a more cultured environment, middle class children have parents who can spend more on their education and better support them, are more socially connected and use their connections to further advantage their children. And we needed some cerebral, pompous, pretentious, bourgeois French intellectual to tell us that. Nothing but disguised platitudes.'

Now realising it was a game or sport for Rachel, and falling in with this, Neil said, 'And that's not all. Bourdieu also coined habitus, symbolic violence, field, doxa, and pedagogic authority, to name a few.'

Rachel laughed and slopped her coffee. 'Habitus? Habitus? Are you sure it's not habitat?'

'Definitely habitus.'

'A habitat, habitus revolutionary. What is habitus?'

Neil adopted a pose of open-mouthed awe, and voice full of wonder said, 'Everything, really. That's why, according to Henry, Bourdieu needed the special word *habitus*. Who we are, what we are, where we belong, the community, appropriate behaviour, expectations past and present, ways of perceiving, schemata, conscious and unconscious assumptions, spectrum from implicit to explicit, non-reflective and reflective actions, muscular memory, dispositions, ways of speaking, artistic tastes on a spectrum from low to high, life chances, deportment, social skills, notions of normality, grammar and speech, where we are going or can go, what we expect from life, knowns and unknowns, and what shapes us shaped in turn. Choice is in there somewhere but constrained and limited. Everything that makes us what we are. Life, the universe –'

'Socialisation,' offered Rachel. 'Habitus is socialisation. I did socialisation on some course, but that's far too commonplace a word for Bourdieu. You can't discover socialisation. Everyone knows it. Old wine in new bottles, Bourdieu du Plonk. Thinking of plonk...'

*

Rachel sank heavily into her favourite curved, soft leather upholstered chair and drank greedily from a large glass of red wine.

'What's Bourdieu's opinion of programmes like *Coronation Street*?'

'Bourdieu classified knowledge into highbrow, middlebrow and lowbrow. Bruegel is highbrow –'

'I hate Bruegel.'

'Gershwin's *Rhapsody in Blue* is middlebrow, or semi-cultured.'

'He's saying I'm semi-cultured? Bastard. What's lowbrow?'

'Anything popular.'

'Circularity. It's popular because it's lowbrow. We know it's lowbrow because it's popular. Does he just make up this stuff? As for Shakespeare and bourgeois parlance, everyone finds Shakespeare difficult. My parents are professionals, yet I found Shakespeare difficult at school. Chaucer more so. Hardly the typical languages of the middle-class home. Or anyone's home. Did you say that to Henry?'

'I try not to criticise too much. Might get defensive.'

'Bourdieu is right about education, a fair description, but as I said, nothing we don't already know. Habitus adds nothing, just another word to ruminate over, debate, write scholarly articles on, and disagree about. It's as if things have no existence, no acceptance, until an academic captures, labels and mounts it and has it accepted by a prestigious journal. Explain something to me; something that's been puzzling me. Working class failure suggests that manual work is inferior. Yet we need plumbers. If I had a leak, I wouldn't want Henry Hollow arriving with a copy of *Das Capital*. Why does he see manual work as inferior? Surely, as a socialist, he should argue all work is equal and advocate greater income and status equality.' She leaned back. 'Did you find out what school Henry sends his kids to?'

'I asked him, and he said they are moving house to get the eldest into a better secondary school. The new house is only a hundred yards from the school.'

'Selection by geography. How did he justify it?'

'He said it wasn't his decision. His wife and eldest child decided. It was a democratic vote and he lost.'

'His conscience is clear and his eldest is going to a better school. Very neat.'

*

'Perhaps working-class children achieve less because they are less intelligent on average?'

Henry's response was unexpected. 'I agree.'

'You agree?'

Henry laughed at Neil's surprise. 'I agree they are less intelligent.'

'Let me say it again. Working class children achieve less because they are innately less intelligent. On average.'

Henry shook his head. 'You didn't say innately. I'm saying educational successes have higher intelligence, ergo working-class children must be less intelligent because they are less successful on average. Bowles and Gintis point out that achievers do not achieve because they have higher intelligence but have higher intelligence because they achieve.' Amused at Neil's puzzled expression, he laughed and added, 'You see, they have time to develop intelligence through study. Intelligence correlates with achievement but is not the cause. Achievement is the cause of intelligence. It rather neatly dovetails with Bourdieu's cultural capital.'

'You're saying the working class have a cultural deficit?'

'Absolutely.'

'Explaining their relative failure.'

'Absolutely.'

'You blame them for failing?'

Henry coughed gently, slowly rotated his head and explained why he had no problem with the idea that working class children have a cultural deficit, but no blame attached because, along with intelligence, it isn't their own culture, but bourgeois culture.

'You see, there is no objective measure of intelligence or good taste. All tastes are equal, but the powerful can impose their taste on the rest and call it good taste. They call everything they achieve intelligent and impose their definition on the less powerful.'

Using Bourdieu's symbolic violence, Henry explained how the dominant class defines what is valuable in education. Those at the top define their own culture as superior. Education promotes and legitimises taste. If your habitus includes legitimate taste, you fit into the school regime and make better progress. Middle-and upper-class children are advantaged because their culture is closer to school culture. Teachers collude unconsciously by rewarding legitimate taste. The working class are the losers.

'Not a deficit after all but a false, imposed, alien culture. One group has the power to impose its culture over other groups and convince these less powerful groups it is higher and truer. Cultural capital reproduced economic capital which in turn reproduced culture. No need for the syllabus to parallel the factory. It's an alien, unnatural culture that eliminates the class outsider.'

'Are you're saying there is a real working-class culture, equal to bourgeois culture, but oppressed?'

Henry was vague on this point and slipped into obscurantism. Neil persisted. 'Are you saying all cultures are equal?'

His 'yes' was slow but definitely an affirmative.

*

Was Henry saying *Coronation Street* is equal to Shakespeare? Neil had avoided putting this to Henry knowing it was argumentative as it was impossible to prove one art form was superior to another, whereas you could say a fridge freezer was superior to a larder.

Neil put Bourdieu's idea to a physicist.

'Physics,' the physicist explained, 'is objective and classless. There is no proletarian physics. Put that to your Marxist sociologist.'

'Surely natural science isn't bourgeois science imposed on the rest?' Neil put to Henry. 'There isn't a working-class natural science. Bourdieu's cultural capital doesn't seem to include the natural sciences. Natural science isn't arbitrary or relative.'

Henry nodded sagely, repeating 'good point' several times. Finally, he mumbled slowly to himself, 'Not the content of the sciences so much as the way they're presented.' His voice rising, he said, 'Got it. Science is presented through bourgeois parlance not common parlance, giving middle class children an advantage.' He expounded again on habitus, how the dominant classes possess the code of the message, the key that unlocks the classroom messages.

'You mean accent, grammar, vocabulary?'

'Among other things. Also, the opaque language of science.'

'But you agree there is no separate proletarian science?

Henry made a small cough to avoid the question and said, 'Despite differences between Bowles and Gintis and Bourdieu, they concur on the idea that the ruling class rule also as thinkers, as producers of ideas, and regulate the production and distribution of the ideas of their age. Even if ideas are not there in the service of the economy directly, they still serve class interests indirectly. They act as barriers to working class children. It wasn't so long ago you needed Latin or Greek to go to Oxbridge, languages taught only in the public schools and grammar schools.'

'Then why did they drop Latin and Greek?'

'Tokenism.'

As Neil entered the corridor, Henry's voice boomed, 'All said by Marx long ago: "The ideas of the ruling class are the ruling ideas".'

*

Ed Kulcher was something of a social leper in the sociology department.

Ed promoted three heresies: intelligence is largely innate; middle-class children on average achieve more because the middle-class have higher innate intelligence on average; top jobs go to the more intelligent. Society is therefore an intelligence hierarchy. How did he justify it?

Before meeting him, Neil asked around. 'Low on the autism spectrum,' Rachel explained, 'but definitely there.' Notoriously bad team worker was a common complaint (meaning he disagreed with the team, or the team disagreed with him). Dogmatic and biased, agreed most sociologists. But who was the more dogmatic – Ed who didn't conform, or the blank-slate-following sociologists?

Ed chuckled. 'You have probably heard negative things about me. Neo-fascist, neo-eugenicist, or worse. 'You got the book I sent you.' He nodded toward a book Neil was holding.

Neil placed *The Intelligence Hierarchy* on Ed's desk. Short, succinct, accessible and clearly written, it was intended for a wider audience than academia, widely reviewed in the press but largely ignored by academic journals. Radio and TV interviews followed, angering other sociologists.

On the wall above his desk was a chart – *The Animal Intelligence Hierarchy.* At the apex were the great apes, followed by whales and dolphins, then dogs. The octopus came next. How do you measure an octopus's intelligence? Birds followed. At the base were horses. This bothered Neil slightly. He liked horses. Then he recalled *Animal Farm.* The cart horse had a low rating: likeable, hard-working, but naive and gullible. Pigs were Orwell's most intelligent. He looked again at the chart. There were no pigs.

Neil nodded towards the chart. 'How do you measure an octopus's intelligence?'

'You're a psychologist.'

'Social psychology – people. Never octopuses. That's comparative psychology.'

Ed laughed, and nodding towards the book said, 'Contrary to my critics, I never said intelligence was the only factor, only the most important one. Since the sixties we have retreated from innate intelligence, baby-bathwater, and all that. We over-socialise people, reduce them to their environments or situations; blank slates waiting to be written on by society and the sociologists. Sociology has become a repository of the nature-denying liberal left. Those who accept innate intelligence limit it to the individual, minimise its importance and claim it is randomly distributed.'

He rose from his seat. 'But biology is making a comeback.' Ed took Neil through the logical stages to prove intelligence varies across class. 'Those sociologists who agree individuals vary somewhat in innate ability fail to see where this logically leads. If people vary in innate ability, and selection for top jobs is based partly on ability, we would expect those occupying top jobs to have greater innate ability. Logical so far?'

Neil nodded.

'People choose partners from similar social backgrounds – for example, they meet at university or at work. If ability is partly innate, their children will inherit, in part at least, their abilities. It follows that more ability will be concentrated at the top, average levels of ability will vary between classes and the assumption that ability is randomly distributed across classes is false. See where this is going? Therefore, class inequalities in attainment are partly – I would say largely – the result of innate intelligence. You see the argument? Intelligent women tend to mate with intelligent men, producing intelligent children. More dull parents are concentrated at the bottom of the social ladder and more likely to produce dull children.'

Dull was not a word Neil had heard for some time, abolished along with thick, lazy and stupid, and before that, cretin, idiot and imbecile.

'What about motivation and ambition?' asked Neil.

Kulcher nodded approvingly. 'Like the question. It also seems likely that levels of motivation and ambition vary between the classes, something denied by most sociologists today.'

'Is motivation innate?'

'Quite possibly. Same argument, really. Employers want motivated workers...'

'Know-how?'

'Know-how is another word for intelligence. You must be intelligent to know how.'

'Poverty penalty? Surely a handicap?'

'They are poor because they lack intelligence and motivation. Poor mate with poor and produce dull, less motivated offspring. Not all, of course. On average.'

Ed settled into his chair preparing for a long exposition. 'Look. How do you explain the vast differences between schools? There are schools that have 90 plus GCSE and

A-level pass rates all grade A.' He laughed. 'Henry once tried to convince me that if children from a low pass-rate school had the same cultural and economic advantages they too would have 90 plus pass rates. Everything is class conspiracy to Henry, including "bourgeois" IQ tests. Someone's probably told you about the new IQism. Children segregated into sets by ability. Left-wing sociologists call it intelligence testing by the back door. But to me it demonstrates we badly need a test for intelligence. It's obvious, but sadly must be smuggled in. The left want us to believe failure is down to bad society, not bad genes.'

Most sociologists Neil had interviewed readily agreed ability was a mixture of nature and nurture, but he doubted their sincerity because intelligence was not included in their educational research and if discussed quickly dismissed, suggesting none really believed innate intelligence contributed much to individual attainment. Intelligence testing was indeed taboo and dead. Ed was right to that extent.

'Let me get this straight. You seem to be saying most sociologists are wasting their time identifying social reasons for underachievement because all along ability's largely inborn, and middle-class parents are therefore wasting their money having their children privately educated as it's all in the genes?'

Ed hesitated, and said more slowly, 'Not completely. Intelligence must be nurtured, given room to develop.'

'So you do give some credit to social factors?'

'As I said earlier, I never said intelligence was the only factor, only the most important by far. You must know the studies. Intelligence is some 70 per cent inborn. That leaves 30 per cent or so to nurture.'

'According to…?'

He hesitated. 'Twin research. OK, before you say it, Burt's research is suspect, I know.'

'Faked, I thought.'

'Never proven. Circumstantial, inferential, suspect. That's all Kamin showed.'

'Remember, Kamin wasn't limited to Burt. He looked at all the main twin studies, such as Shields', and showed they were all flawed. Observer bias. No twins properly separated. That was the real flaw of Shields and others. Plus, a flexible definition of separated.'

'All that is by the by. We now have Bouchard's Minnesota research, The MISTRA study.'

Neil looked blank.

'I can see you are unfamiliar with MISTRA. Separated identical twins. Huge sample. Should satisfy critics. Before you ask, blinds in abundance. No testers knew if the twin being tested was identical or non-identical. Therefore, no observer bias. IQ correlations average 70 per cent. Fault that.'

'As I said, the problem with earlier studies was that none of the identical twins were properly separated. Were Bouchard's sample properly separated into different environments?'

Ed paused. Neil now realised Ed's pauses signalled uncertainty.

'I am sure they were, but Bouchard never published their life histories – confidential. But he was meticulous about everything else, so it is reasonable to infer...'

'Explain something to me: the Chinese. Their high achievement rate regardless of class.'

Ed laughed ironically. 'Contentious point, and I see where it's leading. You'll ask me next why blacks underachieve.'

Neil laughed. 'OK, other sociologists I've since talked to say selection by IQ after the war was tried and failed.'

Ed waved dismissively. 'Wish you'd come to me first before getting such a distorted version. Ask yourself, why was the eleven-plus implemented by a radical Labour government, the same government that created the health service? As I said at our last meeting, teachers today select by ability. They put children in streams or bands, but are their tests any better? I would say they are worse. The eleven-plus didn't judge accent or attitude, was indifferent to appearance or teacher prejudice. The test was snob-free and prejudice-free. That's why it appealed to socialists. The problem for socialists who came later was that the eleven-plus, contrary to expectations, appeared to perpetuate the class system because a higher percentage of middle-class children passed the test. Suddenly intelligence testing was deemed unreliable. But was it? And if it was, by how much?'

Neil looked doubtful. 'Didn't it penalise late developers? What about regional bias? A failure in one region would have been a success elsewhere because the number of grammar school places varied.'

'Not the fault of the eleven-plus.'

'Didn't I read that girls were discriminated against – outperformed boys, and gender quotas imposed?'

'Girls mature earlier. It was only fair, I suppose, but I take the point. The test was a bit of a blunt instrument. But aren't all exams blunt instruments? SATs, GCSEs, A-levels? Degrees? No system is perfect. That's where the critics of intelligence go wrong. They measure the eleven-plus against a utopian standard. The test needed refining, not abolishing. Perhaps there weren't enough grammar school places in some areas. Today sociologists complain about teacher bias and discrimination against black children. At least the eleven-plus was colour blind. We agree ability varies between classes, don't we?'

Neil was silent.

'You would expect a higher percentage to be middle class, wouldn't you? You have gone silent. Argue with me. Think up some challenging questions.'

'I'll get back to you.'

*

Neil took Kulcher's argument to Weena.

'Even if ability varies between classes – and it's a big if despite the logic of Kulcher's argument – even if, it can't explain Douglas's findings on IQ and class.'

She handed Neil two volumes by James Douglas: *The Home and the School* and *All Our Future*. 'Old studies, done and dusted, really, but Kulcher's resurrecting old arguments.'

*

'Extraordinary sample.'

Neil was telling Rachel about Douglas.

'Longitudinal study, over 5,000 children, born in the first week of March 1946. Imagine the cost. Puts the usual samples to shame.'

Rachel smiled. 'Doubt if the astrologers would agree.'

'Astrologers? Oh, I see. Of course. The month. Douglas looked at a whole range of issues, health, income, parental interest, but quite overlooked zodiac signs. What a missed opportunity.'

'Douglas. Didn't he do suicide?'

'Suicide is Jack Douglas, education James Douglas. The important point is there's no mention of Douglas in Kulcher's *The Intelligence Hierarchy*. Fits Darwin's golden rule: the tendency to forget or ignore inconvenient facts. What Douglas and his team did was measure IQ using all the main tests and compare children of the same intelligence from different class backgrounds over a period of 18 years.'

'He held IQ constant.'

'Exactly. Twin research in theory observes related people of the same IQ placed in different environments. Douglas studied unrelated people of the same IQ in different environments. His results differed markedly from twin research. High ability upper middle-class children had twice the chance of achieving good results than high ability lower-class children. But we are talking high ability, the sort of child who sails through. The telling result was the struggling below average ability child. Those from the upper middle-class were 13 times more likely to gain good certificates than lower-class children of the same ability, which indicates the importance of social factors, such as help and encouragement.'

'The less able a child, the more important the environment. So how did Kulcher react?'

'Badly. He rejected Douglas.'

Rachel laughed.

'"All born in the same week, you say. I can't put my finger on it, but I suspect bias somewhere. Has to be. That's an unusual sample. I need to look more closely at this Douglas. I'll get back to you". We left it there. Haven't heard from him since.'

'Before you go, I'm having a problem with a student.'

'Problem?'

'She knits during tutorials. I've tried telling her it's distracting, but the rest of the group say they don't mind, and she says she's listening. All I hear is this *click, click, click*. It's fucking torture.'

'Tell her to read Goffman's *Behaviour in Public Places*, the sections on situationally appropriate behaviour and autoinvolvements. Better still, explain it to her. I've used it to manage inattentive students. Tell her it's not enough to be attentive, we must appear to be attentive. Not enough to be listening, we must appear to be listening.'

'Won't she say that's dishonest?'

'Shows concern for others. Goffman says we are all actors to a degree. It's a way of proving sincerity. If someone tells you a close relative has died, you wear an appropriate expression, no matter how you feel. Would your student knit if she was being interviewed for a job or at a funeral?'

'Don't suppose you could drop in on my group and give a talk on Goffman, and slip in knitting as inappropriate behaviour?'

*

Neil had a final meeting with Kulcher.

At an earlier meeting Kulcher had raged against Henry's view that anyone can be anything, given the chance. 'I said to him, anyone can learn to be an Einstein or a Mozart, can they? "Just put in enough hours or have pushy parents". That's Henry all over.'

'Your point about Einstein or a Mozart to Henry – isn't that confusing intelligence and creativity?'

'Intelligence tests are not designed to test creativity, of course, but you need a good level of intelligence to realise your creativity. Einstein and Mozart were no idiots.'

'That still doesn't explain creativity. Creative people might be intelligent, but all intelligent people are not creative. A musicologist I spoke to gave the example of Stravinsky. Stravinsky's children may have been as intelligent as their father but lacked that essential ingredient: creativity. We admire Stravinsky for his creativity, not his position on some Mensa intelligence scale. You don't get prizes for –'

'Bach? The Strauss family? Line of composers. Surely inherited?'

'Exception that proves the rule. Out of the thousands of composers, biologists select those two because they fit the theory of inheritance. This musicologist I met was researching creativity and composers. Composing families are rare. How often do all members of a composer's family compose? How often do composers' children compose? Most composers just emerge, often struggling against parental wishes. Why not be honest, Ed? We just don't know. We can't explain Mozart, and Mozart couldn't explain himself.'

Kulcher wandered over to the window and took a long, lingering look across Nottingham. Turning, he said, 'Wasn't Mozart's father a composer?'

'Nowhere near as good.'

'Some argue he sacrificed his musical career to promote his son. And didn't one of Mozart's six children compose?'

'Not a touch on his father. And only one of the six.'

'He may have lacked motivation, interested in other things; his other children the same.'

'If it's in the genes, Mozart got most of them.'

'May have been in all their genes, but they just did other things.'

Neil persisted, reciting a long list of poets and painters, all one-offs.

'Other things.'

*

Neil had just completed an interview with Horace Garvey.

Another sociological anomaly in the department, Horace was castigated (savaged, his term) for blaming black Caribbean males for their academic failure.

'Not exactly what I said,' he explained to Neil. 'My critics exaggerate. Not all fail, but enough to lower the average pass rate for blacks. They deliberately misrepresent me. But then, how else can they counter my arguments?'

His heresy was to largely reject racism as an explanation of black underachievement in education – such as critical race theory, or CRT – a position he felt secure holding because he was black, avoiding accusations of racism. The son of Jamaican professional parents, he considered most white sociologists overly protective towards blacks, mistakenly seeing them as victims, underdogs, not responsible for their plight, more sinned against than sinning.

'None of the teachers who taught me in England could be described as racist,' he recalled, 'and my own teaching experience confirms this.'

They countered Horace by saying racism was not, of course, overt but unconscious, invisible racism, posing as fairness when allocating and selecting pupils but informed by unconscious negative stereotypes. That way they can even imagine themselves liberal and free of racism while unconsciously stereotyping black pupils as less academic and relegating them to lower streams, and those pupils who protest dismissed as difficult or disruptive. Why else are so many blacks excluded from school?

'Because they are more disruptive?' suggested Horace, pointing out that the exclusion rate for black Africans (as distinct from black Afro-Caribbeans) was not only lower, but lower than the white population.

Horace considered their approach to teachers patronising, the all-knowing great white God Academia descending from Mt University onto lowly school teachers. What about the successful Chinese, African and Indian pupils? he asked. Surely that shows the relative failure of black Caribbean pupils is down to their own shortcomings, something they bring to the school, or actively create in the school, and nothing to do with prejudice?

Example of positive stereotyping said his critical race theory opponents. Teachers play favourites, have positive as well as negative stereotypes, and expect more of Chinese and Indians, who in turn give more. Horace countered: do they achieve more because teachers expect more, or teachers expect more because they achieve more? Where do expectations come from? Can't a stereotype be true?

Horace saw the explanation in class differences. Comparing white and Caribbean pupils ignored possible class imbalances, the white population comprising a larger middle class, thus raising their average success. Where do you find a black middle-class suburb? Less still a black upper-class.

A proper comparison should compare blacks and whites from similar class backgrounds. He recalled the strong anti-school culture of so many black males at the school where he taught for a time, their macho anti-school values, styling education effeminate, the pull of the peer group and the street, aspiring to be rap artists. Many (but not all) chose to fail. It was macho to fail, feminine to succeed.

Horace piled on the blame, adding absent fathers and undisciplined homes. More heretical still, he reduced their culture to their history – to slavery. Slavery explained the black Caribbean fragmented unstable family structure – the well-documented matrifocal family, the irresponsible absent father, a common family structure in the Caribbean. Slaves bought and sold; families split up becoming a way of life. His critics countered. Not culture, that's blaming the victim, but situational constraints, current poverty, the present not the past, definitely not the past, blacks no different from whites but responding to a different situation.

Horace recalled a study by Paul Willis, *Learning to Labour*, explaining how working-class kids get working class jobs, a neo-Marxist ethnographic study of 12 rebellious white working-class boys who formed a close friendship group. They rebelled, consciously and willingly opposed the academic school culture, and remained working class because they rebelled, a neat synthesis of phenomenology and structure, freedom and determinism. These were not Bowles and Gintis's docile and passive working-class pupils indoctrinated into manual work, school an appendage to industry; they came to school equipped with a macho class culture, and further developed their own counterculture, affirming their masculinity. They scorned the middle-class world of the school, dismissed book learning as irrelevant, dubbed conformers soft and effeminate. Office work was for prissy pen pushers, was not real work. Their anti-school culture emphasised style, smoking, drinking, avoiding school uniform, 'having a laff', thus gaining status within their peer group but keeping them where they were. The study resonated with Horace.

Horace knew he made white liberals uneasy. The only black lecturer in the department made him an object of special attention, patronage and expectation. They wanted to parade him, sport him, to prove their liberalism. In turn he was expected to perform. Why couldn't he just be Horace? An individual? A lecturer like the rest, colour-free? Black culture was elevated by some white liberals he knew, yet he hated bebop, more so rap, loved classical music, and each summer holidayed in London to attend the Proms. The Proms were predominantly white, of course. Some hidden prejudice? Some ethnic glass ceiling? Not if you see below skin colour to class. How many white manual workers attend the Proms? Surely people of different races with similar education have more in common than people of the same race with different backgrounds? His love of classical music and political orientation baffled more than one sociologist, as if being black he should have natural rhythm, love bebop and vote Labour, and he wondered if there was something in unconscious stereotyping after all?

24

Shortly before Neil started researching again, there had been some sort of break-in.

'Some sort' because it wasn't clear what had happened. The alarm had been triggered. The police had arrived and found the fire door closed. Automatic bill of £200 for wasting police time. Next day, the cleaners reported the door to a tutorial room had been forced open, the jamb splintered, curtains pulled down. A solid metal window catch had been torn from its mooring.

Odlum was convinced there had been a burglary.

The police were skeptical. 'Catch broken from the inside, glass intact,' said the officer.

'Explain the alarm bell.'

'It was a windy night, the fire doors rattling. This is an old building. A false alarm.'

Odlum persisted. 'Maybe he/she/they entered before the alarm was set, hid somewhere, emerging after the caretaker had set the alarm. What about the damaged door? The vandalised curtains?'

'To what end? Nothing was stolen from the staffroom despite computers and valuables carelessly left on desks, even coffee money.'

'The tutorial room, then. An act of vandalism.'

'But, according to staff, the room was never locked, the catch permanently on. No need to break into a room permanently open, left permanently on catch. What sort of vandal closes a door and then breaks in, pulls down curtains and leaves them neatly folded?'

'Explain the two champagne glasses found on the windowsill in the tutorial room, one impregnated with lipstick. No one recalled them there the day before. Doesn't that suggest at least two burglars, one female?'

'So not only did the burglars or vandals steal nothing, they came with a bottle of champagne, broke into a room that was open, vandalised then folded the curtains, and celebrated with champagne and, presumably, took away the bottle.' He shrugged wearily. 'Who knows what goes on in a university staffroom at night? Alcohol consumed...'

'You're surely not suggesting staff?'

Neil and Wendy had attended a meeting called by Odlum to discuss research ideas. It was peripheral to Neil's research, but Wendy applied gentle pressure, finally appealing to his protectiveness. 'I need you there to protect me against Odlum. That plastic arm. I'll give you a lift there. Door to door.'

He was secretly pleased. He was missing Wendy's company. They had spent considerable time together researching PTSD, mainly at her flat, their meetings ending abruptly after presenting their findings to Matlock.

The night of the meeting they were the last to leave and walked together across the car park towards Wendy's car. The evening was warm, the sky clear. Wendy was in no hurry, seemed hesitant, at one point stopping at an unlit area to gaze at the night sky. Reaching her car, she said she had left her bag containing her car keys in the staffroom.

Inside she lingered by the window. 'Turn off the lights. Mars is very red. Come closer.' Turning, she said, 'There's some wine in the fridge.' She went to the staffroom fridge and returned with a bottle of champagne and two glasses. She didn't explain what it was doing there, or where the glasses came from. The pop was extraordinarily loud and metallic in the stillness, the cork ricocheting of the ceiling, and they both giggled. She smiled and came close, touched his hand. She was tense, her hand shaking slightly, and gazing out the window said, 'Let's go into the tutorial room. Darker, better view.'

The room was small, their voices lower and softer, and Wendy said it had been fun researching PTSD together and how she missed his visits. Neil said he felt the same, a vacuum, an emptiness. She placed her hand on the nape of his neck and they embraced, kissed passionately and began undressing, the professional poses falling away garment by garment. Neil pulled down the curtains, the rail left hanging askew, and spread them on the floor. Wendy released the door catch, making a loud click. 'The caretaker,' she murmured.

They never heard the caretaker. Seeing the room in darkness, he had set the exit alarm and departed.

Sometime later they dressed, folded the curtains and cautiously opened the door. The staffroom was dark and surreally silent. Wendy closed the door, forgetting to reset the catch to open. 'My bag,' she said turning to face the door. 'Do you have a key?'

Neil didn't think there was a key, it was never locked.

'I could come back for my car in the morning, I suppose. What time do the cleaners arrive?'

Neil knew this well. 'Normally 6.30am. But it's Saturday tomorrow. They won't be back before Monday.'

Her voice rising, she said, 'I can't wait until Monday. I need the car and the keys to my flat.'

'You can borrow my car. Stay at my place.'

'That's awfully sweet of you, but there are things in my bag I need before Monday. There must be some way of opening the bloody door.'

Neil impulsively heaved against the door, the impact reverberating round the staffroom. It was surprisingly solid, and his shoulder hurt. He opened his wallet and took out various cards: debit, credit and library. In films a detective often opens a door using a card. Reluctant to risk his debit or credit cards, he decided on the library card. The film detectives had no problem, but the door jamb made inserting the card impossible.

'Obviously there are no door jambs in the films, or they have very long and flexible cards that go round corners.' He looked at the card now bucked and scratched. An image of Miss Blenkinsop flashed through his mind, scowling, disapproving, tut-tutting. 'I'll have to prise the door open.' He looked around for a suitable tool, but there was none to be found. Then he remembered the window catch, solid, long and tapered. It wrenched off the window surprisingly easily. Inserting the tapered end between the door and the jamb, the splintering wood made a terrible noise.

Wendy grabbed her bag and the remaining champagne and they headed for the fire exit. Opening the door, a bell sounded, loud and insistent. Neil turned and closed the door hoping the bell would stop, but it persisted. They fled to Wendy's car, exiting the university as a police car slowed momentarily to observe them, then accelerated towards the psychology block.

*

Neil sank into Wendy's jumbo cord settee.

He liked corduroy, so soft and warm, reminding him of *Corduroy*, his favourite story as a child, curled up in bed and being read to. Selena's settee was tight white leather, cold in winter and sticky in summer, his arm glued to the armrest on hot days. And no chameleons in Wendy's flat, just a reassuring disorder, even a wine stain on the carpet, reminded how precise Selena was, everything in place, ordered in cupboards and drawers – sterile. And no bouts of celibacy.

He didn't tell Rachel he was dating Wendy until after Geneva. He wanted to see how it went, wanted to avoid the usual interrogation, wanted to keep things separate.

Rachel was exultant. 'Didn't I predict it? Didn't I say you would get together? And you're researching again. And don't say coincidence.'

Wendy had asked about Rachel. 'You seem very close. I hate to own up to being jealous. After all, you went to Geneva together.'

Neil explained their platonic friendship, how it worked so well precisely because it was platonic, how he felt no sexual attraction for Rachel, nor she for him, and how Rachel had predicted and encouraged their budding relationship. He could have said more. When Rachel had told him about her relationship with Harold, something in his expression caused her to say, part-jokingly, part-defensively, 'It may come as a surprise to you, Neil, but some men do find me sexually attractive'.

Wendy didn't know about his relationship with Selena, of course, which was not surprising; anyone observing them in the staffroom would assume total indifference, bordering on dislike. He decided to leave it there. He felt relaxed, complete. Away from Selena, he had slowly unwound, she so critical and precise, he ever on tiptoe. 'Don't move so fast, you'll frighten the chameleons!' Destiny or Matlock? A bit of both, he supposed, plus Rachel. 'Don't you realise Wendy is interested in you? Are all you psychologists blind?'

How could he have been so blind?

*

Some distance from CCU, tucked away in a mews, exclusive yet inexpensive, the pub was a haven for staff wanting to be free of students for a time. Neil, Wendy and Rachel were seated next to a window. Opposite were Shelrack and two research assistants. The conversation had drifted, patches of silence, and during one of these Wendy had mentioned a documentary on television the night before about macaque monkeys. Shelrack, nodding enthusiastically, enthused about the similarities between humans, monkeys and apes, particularly apes, adding toolmaking chimpanzees to the creative Japanese macaque snow monkeys. One macaque, particularly inventive, was filmed improving on the separation of wheat mixed with sand by throwing a handful of the mixture into water, the seed floating and easily scooped up. Thereafter other monkeys copied.

'There you are, creativity and culture. Not so different from us after all.'

Wendy and Rachel looked at Neil, but he was busy sinking his teeth into a cheese and onion roll.

'Interesting,' Wendy said, 'but a long way from splitting the atom.'

They laughed as Neil, washing down the roll with a mouthful of beer added, 'So when is a macaque monkey going to turn the wheat into flour, bake bread and make a fridge freezer to store it?'

'What is it with you social psychologists that you keep banging on about fridge freezers?'

The group laughed loudly, compelling Neil to join in, and Shelrack, boosted by the applause, offered to buy a round.

When Shelrack finished distributing the drinks, Neil said, 'Monkeys don't have a sense of self, of course.' He said this offhandedly, lighting a cigarette. '"The self is an object to itself". Herbert Mead. Have you read Mead? An early social psychologist.'

Shelrack looked in turn to his assistants. 'Listen to him: chimps don't have a sense of self. Neil, I'm surprised at you. You a social psychologist. You of all people. Surely you know of Gallup's mirror test?' Not waiting for Neil to respond, Shelrack recited Gallup's celebrated test where monkeys were presented with full-length mirrors, eventually recognising themselves. To test this more thoroughly, odourless red spots were painted on the monkeys when anaesthetised, only visible using a mirror. When the mirrors were returned the monkeys showed awareness of the spots by touching them.

'Yes, I remember. Imaginative design. But even if it shows that chimps recognise themselves physically, so what? It doesn't demonstrate the extent or quality of awareness. How far is a chimp knowing and conscious? Is a chimp aware another chimp has a sense of self? How far has it got a sense of self as we understand it?'

'Surely, the difference is not just knowing, but knowing that we know?' said Rachel. 'Does a chimp know that it knows? It may have a sense of self, of knowing, but does a chimp reflect on itself, have an opinion of itself? Can a chimp hate or love itself? I don't suppose a chimp gets up in the morning and thinks, fuck, I'm failing, I must do something with my life before it's too late.'

Ignoring the laughter, Shelrack shrugged and looked about, smiling pleasantly, which Neil recognised as disdain disguised as benignity.

'OK, it knows a red spot shouldn't be there,' Rachel continued, 'has a sense of self to that degree, albeit crawling onto the very bottom of the knowing spectrum. Removing a spot is one thing, discovering natural selection another. Does a monkey speculate on its origins? *We* know. We're supremely, at times painfully, conscious. We know we will die. We shape the world. We don't need nature to select out the hairiest in a cold climate, innumerable deaths between. We wear clothes. We build houses and make fires. Not Morris's naked ape, more the clothed ape. What animal wears clothes?'

'Rachel's right,' added Neil. 'Herbert Mead went beyond Aristotle's observation that we are rational. He wanted to explain our rationality and linked it to our ability to symbolise the world. We store the world symbolically, allowing us to think about the world in its absence, plan far into the future, take out insurance, pensions, make wills. Does an ape know it will grow old? We symbolise the world using numbers and words. We create new worlds in our heads by rearranging the symbols: fantasy worlds, science fiction. Mathematics allows feats of engineering, advances in science. The ability to symbolise gives us our sense of knowing, our sense of self, our ability to create and control the world, accumulate, store and expand knowledge. In other words, it sets us free. Read Herbert Mead.'

'Rearranging, inventing and combining words allows great literature. What ape could write *Hamlet*?' offered Rachel.

Ignoring these points, Shelrack expounded on evolution, the genome, DNA, selfish genes – a real science making giant strides. 'We share 99 per cent of our DNA with chimps. Just one per cent difference in DNA between chimp and man,' he added triumphantly. 'We're just another species of ape, part of the ape family, a little more advanced, that's all. Just one percent.'

'Yes, but what a percentage. There must be more to it than counting genes and DNA. Didn't Schopenhauer distinguish between quality and quantity, water turning into ice and wheat becoming bread? Critical shifts. That degree of difference between humans and apes, statistically small, is a giant difference of quality.'

'I read somewhere we share 50-per cent of our DNA with a cabbage. Is that true?' said Wendy, incredulity in her voice. 'Yet we're not remotely like cabbages.'

*

Neil and Shelrack were in the student cafeteria. The smell of fried food overpowering, the sound of metal cutlery and tableware chosen by the Students' Union near deafening, drowning whatever music was being piped through the system. Neil wondered if his recorder, hidden in his bag, would cut through the cacophony.

Neil dipped a slice of sausage into a dollop of brown sauce and said, 'What about dysfunctional behaviour, the overweight population? Obesity's not adaptive, the opposite surely, life shortening and limiting, inconsistent with your oft-stated principle that everything has an adaptive purpose.'

'We were hunter-gatherers for 99 per cent of our history,' Shelrack said smoothly, 'and evolved ways of adapting to that way of life. We naturally store fat, a survival mechanism that once helped overcome food shortages. Some of those adaptations are no longer suited to modern living – a mismatch. Appetite was perfectly adapted to hunting and gathering. Fatty and sugary high energy foods were scarce and highly valued, now they are everywhere. That's why we eat too much. We are selected to eat sugar and fat. The time transition is just too short for our appetites to change. Blink of an eye in evolutionary terms.'

He put down his fork and leaned back. 'Have you ever wondered why we get bored eating the same food, even two days in a row? Also adaptive. Our ancestors were ignorant of vitamins and the need for a varied diet. Those who found the same diet boring and varied their diet survived and passed on their genes. Science has taught us the reason, we now know the reason, but still have an inbuilt craving.' He nodded significantly. 'Craving outweighs knowing. The problem is our modern skulls house a Stone Age mind.'

'OK, we evolved a liking for fat and sugar, but how do you explain other addictions, such as alcohol, gambling and tobacco? Alcohol addiction is surely dysfunctional, yet it's rife.'

'By-products. Must be by-products. Some things are by-products of useful adaptations. At a cost. Take bipedalism. Walking upright freed the hands but bending results in back problems. Half the people I know have back pain. But the gain outweighs the cost.'

Neil made a mental note, adding mismatch and by-products to the long list of anomalies and ad hoc solutions.

Shelrack stood up to leave.

'And alcohol is a by-product of...' prompted Neil as they headed for the exit.

Shelrack stopped, turned and placed a hand on Neil's shoulder. Sucking air through his teeth he shook his head rapidly and said, 'Neil, Neil, I'm sure there's an answer, we just haven't found it yet. Evolution's an ongoing science. Given time... Do you know a better theory, one that encompasses so many facts, draws together so many hitherto unrelated facts?'

*

Neil often noticed Shelrack wore glasses as he drove from the university.

'Bit short-sighted,' Shelrack explained later. 'We myopes were once a rare breed. Would not have existed in hunter-gatherer society, or not existed for long. We didn't evolve to live in rooms – fluorescent lighting, books, computer screens. We evolved to hunt. Open savannah, sunlight, space and distant horizons.'

'Sounds Lamarckian. Use it or lose it.'

Shelrack grimaced and intoned the word 'selection', picked up his glasses and waved them as he expanded on the evolutionary process. 'For millions of years we were hunters. Eyes evolved to spot game or the enemy at a distance, the gene for short-sightedness ruthlessly selected out. Now it's increasing. Called degradation. All sorts of disabilities are now tolerated in our affluent, welfare society.'

'So you credit sociology with something. The welfare state affects gene selection.'

Shelrack laughed. 'Sociology has its place, of course. An environmental shaper or two. Society shuffles genes around a bit, hangs on to the odd one or two our ancestors would have discarded as uneconomic. Society gives a certain shape or direction. Not nurture or nature per se, that old dichotomy, but interaction of the two. So yes, there's a small place for sociology.'

'Generous of you.'

There was a long pause as Shelrack donned his glasses to peer at the sociology tower from his office window, an edifice of 16 floors, huge phallus representing the fertile god Sociology, sighed wistfully and murmured, 'Someday evolutionary psychology will occupy that tower.'

'Feminists I know would say evolution is androcentric,' Neil was saying, 'your evolution more hunter than gatherer. Hunter, man, mankind.' Shelrack was silent, and Neil added, 'You do use those terms a lot. Where do women fit in to your myopia theory? They weren't hunters, you say so yourself, more gathers and mothers, so it wouldn't matter if they couldn't see into the distance, and short-sightedness wouldn't be selected out. Is myopia higher among women? Is there research?'

'These feminists – sociologists, I presume?'

'One is. The other two are psychologists.'

Shelrack placed his glasses in their case, closed the lid with a snap and selected the easier question. 'When evolutionists say man or mankind, they include women.'

'Doesn't sound that way.'

He shook his head and rose from his chair. 'Just words. You often say so yourself. Mouthfuls of air.'

As Shelrack walked away, Neil realised he had avoided the main question.

*

'Men and women differ interpreting a smile,' Shelrack was saying. 'Men are inclined to infer sexual interest when none exists. All part of our evolution. Men want sex and women also want commitment. Women fear abandonment, you see, protection for children. Bit Stone Age maybe, a mismatch with today's welfare society possibly, but inherited from our evolutionary past.'

'All women?'

'No. Not all women. Evolutionary psychology's not about individuals. You know that as a psychologist. Averages, not individuals.'

He cited various experiments by psychologists into male-female interpretations of videoed male-female interactions. Was the girl flirting or sexual in intent? Male observers were more inclined to see sexual or seductive intent than female observers. As usual, Shelrack imposed an evolutionary interpretation on the findings, but when pressed he conceded the differences were minimal. Most men didn't infer sexual intent.

'A feminist I know says, whatever the origins of this difference and however widespread, men can take control and correct the error once the error is pointed out. Unlike apes. We're not gene slaves. We can learn, learn from experience and the studies you've cited. Otherwise, what is the point of research?'

Shelrack fixed Neil's gaze. 'Works both ways, of course. Why are men expected to make all the adjustments? Say that to your feminist. Women need to understand us men.'

*

'Let me state it as a hypothesis,' Shelrack was saying as they left the library. 'Evolution predicts that women evolved to be choosier regarding a mate to maximise the survival of their children, and you would expect them to seek well-resourced and committed males.'

'A hypothesis, not a fact? Unusual for you.'

He laughed knowingly. 'Bear with me. That's where Popper comes in. The hypothesis has been tested empirically.'

'And?'

'Anthropologists *and* sociologists have observed women across cultures and found that women universally prefer men who are better resourced. Of course, most women have to say they marry for love, at least in our culture.'

'Again, culture can override evolution?'

He laughed and lifted a finger. 'Only superficially. Study after study supports the hypothesis. Men rate attractiveness more highly than females, and women rate status and wealth more highly than men; exactly what evolution predicts. Think of young attractive girls marrying older, unattractive rich men, or some ageing celebrity. Women may talk about love and romance, but underneath romance is secondary. Women are choosier than men regarding a mate, an evolved response to protect offspring. Fault that.'

'Whatever the accuracy of the studies, a sociologist would put a different take on the findings. Culture, nurture, situation. Situational constraints. Women know the constraints of their situation. No need for genes, evolutionary pressure or culture even, just the situation. Sociologists would have no problem with the data, the findings, the facts as you call them, but would argue that most men are still the breadwinners, shown by sociological research and government data. Women have and rear children, work or career interrupted. In short, most women are wholly or partially dependent on men for long periods. On average women are promoted less and earn less, are more likely to uproot to follow a partner's career, and so on. In some cultures women don't choose – an older man might be forced on them by their family, and if they refuse severely punished. Hardly responding to an evolutionary call. There is nothing in the studies you cite that proves evolution. Culture, nurture, the situation fit the evidence as well.'

Shelrack sucked air through his teeth, lifted his index finger and said, 'But no better.'

*

'A feminist sociologist I was talking to wonders how you explain rape if everything is evolved for a purpose and has a genetic component.'

'I don't follow.'

'You said men want sex, women, additionally, want love and security. Evolved responses, you said. Men are aggressive and striving, women less so. Bit me Tarzan, you Jane, her opinion. Does that mean men are naturally rapists obeying natural impulses?'

Neil leaned back; hands clasped behind his head. How would Shelrack manage the dissonance – evolution or sociology? If deterministic evolution, rape is obedience to a natural impulse; if not, men can control their urges.

'Of course we are not inherently rapists. Typical feminist. Men like non-committed sex. Man pursues, but –' Seeing the conundrum, he hesitated, gritted his teeth and said, 'Men are predisposed to behave in certain ways, that's all. We all need food, but most don't steal food. We can control our nature. Culture has a place.'

'Quite a big place, by the sound of it. Sociology has the final word you're saying. Sociology triumphs.'

Shelrack sucked an unusually deep breath through his teeth, a response to the painful word sociology, as if symbolically vacuuming it out of existence. 'No. Evolution has the final word. Misconception, that's what this is all about. Muddying the water. Misconceptions put about by our opponents.'

'So men are by nature rapists?'

'Not all men. As I keep saying, science isn't about individuals. Science deals in statistical averages. Men are predisposed to behave in certain ways.' He brightened. 'The rape gene is in there somewhere, not in all of us, mixed in with other genes. Stronger in certain individuals. Even then, a pressure only. No excuse for rape.'

'Not even for those certain individuals?'

'Absolutely not.'

'Why not?'

'Because we can control our nature.'

'You're saying sociology does have the final word?'

'Neil, Neil...'

*

'If characteristics are transmitted genetically and homosexuals have few offspring, homosexuality should disappear.'

Shelrack sighed. 'You're not the first to ask that. OK, just because it can't be explained now doesn't invalidate natural selection. I'm confident it will be explained someday. Darwin couldn't explain eyeless fish, remember. Don't forget, some are bisexual, and some homosexuals have offspring. More so in the past when gays were pressured to marry. Take Oscar Wilde.'

'Were some of Wilde's children homosexual?'

Shelrack shrugged. 'Possibly. Probably. Wouldn't be surprised. Perhaps in our more tolerant age fewer will pass on their gay gene and homosexuality will finally disappear.'

'Because society has changed.'

'Interaction of nurture and nature, yes.'

'Doesn't the inclusion of society weaken evolution for humans, make it more complex and less predictive, a myriad of social variables to contend with?'

'Interaction of nurture and nature, yes, but nature first.'

*

'I'm meeting Lombard.'

Rachel was silent. She filled the kettle, switched it on, and arranged the mugs.

'Lombard?' he prompted. 'The historian?'

He explained again that Matlock wanted him to read Goldhagen's 622-page epic *Hitler's Willing Executioners* (couldn't Matlock do some reading for a change?) and how Lombard once taught a course on Nazi Germany. He would pick Lombard's brains.

She turned and faced Neil. 'Expect a seamless flow of words. No pauses, no gaps, flitting from topic to topic, Joyce's stream of consciousness, only less coherent. Doesn't matter what you do, what body language contortions you engage in – motioning to speak, hand held up, vigorous nodding, backing to the door – he won't let you speak or escape. Some time ago I went to him for help with a course, *The Gothic Novel in Historical Context*, and asked for some reading. After a long circuitous tour of his research obsessions, he asked me to remind him what I had come to see him about. The Gothic novel, I almost shouted, in context. "Sorry", he said, laughing, "there is no context, singular or permanent. History, you must understand, is not the past but a reconstruction of the past, more flowing lava than solid rock". What's the fucking point to it then? I said, walking away. I hate Lombard.'

*

Lombard's laugh was gleeful.

'Hear you're having a spot of bother over in psychology? Hope you haven't brought it with you. Strange how it's only psychology. Bit difficult to sabotage history, of course.'

'It's under control. We –'

'Goldhagen, you said on the phone. Not surprised Matlock's switching to disobedience. Milgram was first with obedience. No one cares who is second. Who was the second astronaut into space after Gagarin? Who sailed to America after Columbus? Who ran the four-minute mile after Bannister? Matlock's a mere replicator.'

Neil listened, hoping Lombard's dogmatism, or otherwise, would emerge, as the meeting was also an opportunity to make Lombard a subject of his research.

Slowly, in snatches, Lombard's historical method emerged, such as his oft stated 'history is where the historians are researching.' He was keen on integration, incorporating other disciplines, but drew the line at psychohistory, such as Gorer reducing Japanese cruelty in the war to potty-training, or the reduction of history to personality quirks or physical features, such as Hitler's alleged single testicle or the Kaiser's withered arm. Was this dogma? Neil decided it paralleled Shelrack's argument that you can't teach every crackpot theory, and raised again the issue why one theory is chosen over another. Between these topics, Lombard was pointing to problems of evidence in psychohistory, such as unverifiable unconscious motives. 'It's simply not historiography, and therefore not really history. Bad history at the most. Anything-can-mean-what-you-want-it-to- mean method.'

What was history? Henry was dismissive: '"Sociology relates to history much as an erect building relates to the rocks and stones that surround it", quoting Herbert Spencer.'

Lombard laughed mockingly. 'Bit dated, but Henry's a Marxist, of course, head buried in the 19th century.' He paused sufficiently for Neil to approve his dismissive tone, which he confirmed by two nods.

'Anyway, history's more factual than sociology, of course. History asks different questions and is focused on personalities and dates and events a bit more than sociology. It's more chronological and less generalising than sociology and deals exclusively with the past. Don't misunderstand me, history does have structure. We've moved on since the Victorians. We're no longer so obsessed with dates, which has not gone unnoticed by the tabloids and some ignorant Tories. You know how it works: a government minister asserts that school history should return to teaching more facts, meaning dates. It's a vote catcher, of course. Isn't everything in politics about votes? Apparently, a poll showed a large percentage of children didn't know the exact date World War Two started. Shocking, said some tabloids, and echoed by the minister. A group of historians, including me, soon put him to right.'

He showed Neil a newspaper cutting of an article signed by several historians. Neil read a passage:

> *We must avoid being ethnocentric by assuming the war only began when Britain went to war. For the Czechoslovaks the war started in 1938... for others it started later than 1939... then there's the phoney war...*

'The past is untidy and unsatisfactory. Bit of a mess, really. Unlike writing fiction. You can give order to a work of fiction, select your characters and names and give it your preferred ending.' He chuckled. 'Wordsworth was born in Cockermouth. If you created a fictional poet and wanted a romantic birthplace you wouldn't come up with Cockermouth. But the historian is stuck with the truth, the facts.

'Now, what was it you came to see me about? Goldhagen, wasn't it? Nazi Germany? There are so many myths about the war. A recent study showed a high percentage of children thought Churchill declared war on Germany. It's not surprising given the hype surrounding him and the popular fixation on personalities. People tidy up the past, re-order, impose false logic and false chronology. Chamberlain was weak and unpopular, Churchill strong, so Churchill must have ousted the appeaser Chamberlain and declared war on the tyrant Hitler and saved the nation. Nothing to do with the Channel, of course, a natural defense, a super moat.

'Take literature. Literature isn't reality. The number of literature specialists who've tried to convince me that literature is another way of presenting reality. It isn't. The needs of the reader impose constraints on the fiction writer. Characters must be distinct, separate and few, otherwise the reader becomes confused. The novelist may deliberately make the hero sympathetic for fear of alienating the reader, and usually avoids loose ends for the same reason. The writer must entertain, sustain interest, create excitement, atmosphere, and so on, deviating further from reality. Finally, and often forgotten, publishers – those portal guards worried about sales – select what they think is marketable or current and reject the rest. How many writers write to please the publisher? Those who don't remain unpublished. What we call literature is mostly the unrepresentative few texts that pass the market test. How many mute, inglorious Miltons? Take teeth.' Lombard smiled broadly and Neil, now alerted to teeth, noticed Lombard's varied in colour, some yellowish brown. 'The Victorians rarely smile in photographs. Why? The popular answer is camera exposure time – difficult to hold smiles for long periods. But after 1845 exposure time took seconds not minutes so doesn't explain the grin-free, unsmiling Queen Victoria. Not even the flicker of a smile in her poses. Let it be said, dental hygiene was grim in the 19th century. Chipped teeth, crooked teeth. Notice how I'm working here? Set up a theory, test it, if wanting, move to another theory and test that. Anyway, the Victorian solution to a rotten tooth was to pull it. No crowns, bridges or caps, just gaps. You wouldn't want to grin in a photograph, a missing tooth fixed and passed down the generations. However, there was nothing to stop you from smiling, but very few even smiled for photographs. So I hit upon a test of sorts: drawings and paintings. No exposure time of rotting teeth, all filled by the artist, yet there are few grinning portraits. Take *Alice in Wonderland*. Carroll's photographs rarely show a smile, let alone a toothy grin. Exposure time? Maybe. But what about his drawings of Alice and other characters? No grins or smiles there. The published drawings were done by Tenniel, also grin and smile-free.'

'Humpty Dumpty?' interjected Neil.

'OK, Humpty Dumpty has a wide smirk of sorts. There's always some bloody exception, which proves the rule, of course'

Neil persisted, 'The Cheshire Cat?'

'Just a cat. Doesn't apply. Which brings me to the third explanation, my preferred explanation: not exposure time, not bad teeth, but social convention. Photography was expensive, exclusive to the affluent – those in authority. Grinning undermined authority. You had to be stiff, formal, severe, and maintain a haughty distance to command respect in Victorian times. Only the silly, foolish and less well-off grinned at you. Idiots grinned. It was a prim and proper age. Anybody who was anybody was serious and composed and controlled their emotions. This persisted into this century. Baldwin, HG Wells, Lloyd George, even Churchill struck serious poses, at most a thin smile. Today it's different. If you want an unsmiling pose you have to ask people, otherwise they grin insanely. We are expected to smile, say cheese, not prune, cast aside hierarchy, and pretend to be equal and friendly. Take professors and doctorates. Once, you insisted on being addressed as professor or doctor. Now, even mister is dropped at the first opportunity. Tony Blair grins at the camera, and glottal stops when talking to young voters. People play down status today, hide it under shirt sleeves, jeans, and toothy grins. But it's just as constraining. You must grin, smile or dress down, otherwise you're aloof, unfriendly, standoffish, distant or cold. Whatever the Marxists say, personalities do matter. Hitler wasn't just swept along by events, as some Marxist sociologists imagine. Without Hitler the course of European history would have been different. He mattered.'

They were closing in on Goldhagen again, but Lombard veered away, a paper he was preparing on differences between history and fictional representations, such as novels, TV dramas and films. Rachel was right, Lombard provided few cues, a seamless flow of words, flitting from topic to topic.

'Spittoons were popular in the 19th century, considered more hygienic than spitting on the floor. Today spittoons would be repugnant – fragment of a pause, and Neil began opening his mouth to speak – 'but remember, the past must be judged by its own past, never by the present. What were things like at the time, or before? Take Freud. I came across a passage where Freud justifies spitting on the stairs of a patient's house he visited.'

As he was speaking, he went to his bookcase, lifted down Freud's *Interpretation of Dreams*, and began reading from a marked page:

When I pay my morning visit at this house I am usually seized with a desire to clear my throat; the sputum falls on the stairs. There is no spittoon on either of the two floors, and I consider that the stairs should be kept clean not at my expense, but rather by the provision of a spittoon.

Lombard chuckled. 'I like the expression "sputum falls on the stairs", almost involuntary, separate from him, beyond his volition. I've seen many dramas and films about Freud but none where he spits, not even into a spittoon. Dramas clean up and sanitise the past; make it more palatable and acceptable. Lawrence of Arabia must be tall, and Francis Drake denuded of his Devonian accent. God knows what accent Elizabeth I had; nothing like her representation on TV, I suspect. I could go on. Anachronisms are rife in TV dramas, but we'd be here all day. Now what was it you came to see me about? Goldhagen, wasn't it? Your Professor Matlock might be disappointed, I'm afraid. Can't do experiments on history. If only we could remove the variable Hitler, have him assassinated and do a rerun.' He held up his hand. 'But there's a lot we can do. Browning tested Milgram's obedience research using testimony from death squads in Poland. Moral there: fear the state more than the serial killer. The state kills millions. The greatest killers this century were Hitler and Stalin. If you want to avoid mass murder, don't hand the state over to a psychopath, and try to avoid war. No war, no Holocaust. Forget all that Niemöller poetic crap about speaking out. Too individualistic; too late. He stepped out and stepped into Dachau. Not because he opposed anti-Semitism – was himself something of an anti-Semite and initially supported Hitler – but because Hitler opposed the Protestant church. Once Hitler gained power it was too late to stop him.

'You're the expert on science, of course. Read your article. Once taught a history option to some physics students. Outside their laboratory comfort zone, they were at sea, no sea legs, in a perpetual storm throwing up all over the place. Too many ifs and buts and loose ends, degrees of evidence, conflicting interpretations. Little control. You can't recreate history in a laboratory. History's far too untidy for the physicist. But even physics, gold standard of fact and prediction, separating cause from correlation, has its limits. Oh, it works well enough in the laboratory, but less well outside. Your article put it well, A boulder pushed over a cliff will fall, thus far the physicist's prediction, but could the physicist predict exactly where it will land, precisely how many pieces it will break into and the final resting place of each piece? You're right. All physical science is limited in the wild, so to speak, beyond that enclosure we call the laboratory. History has no enclosure. Meteorology operates in the wild, an open system dealing with the physical world, limiting prediction. I once taught the history of science. People have wrong ideas about science, an outdated Victorian model. They confuse it with some content or other, usually physics or biology. Science can be about anything.

An approach, not a content. People think it's law-like accurate prediction, but science is not an end state of final laws, not an absolute; science is a process, method or methods, incomplete and ongoing. Take meteorology. Imperfect, getting better at predicting the weather, but only two or three days ahead at the most, not even that before satellites, but a science because of its methods. More scientific than praying for good weather. Same with medicine. Doctors can't predict who will become ill or when. They engage in averages. Think about it, if your family has a history of heart disease they say you are at greater risk of a heart attack. Smoking's linked to lung cancer, but they can't predict that a given smoker will get cancer, let alone when. They talk of probabilities, increased odds.' He raised his hand as Neil was about to speak. 'Physics, then, you're thinking? Rotation of the planets, surely a hard science.' He shook his head. 'Accurate to a point. They pond skate their way round the earth, flea hop to peep at a planet. What if a dirty great meteor heads our way? No one can predict the next one. Once detected they can observe it, even predict when it will land, but not where exactly, less still how much damage it will do. No, science is not absolute truth, but methods bringing us closer to the truth. 'History's not all wilderness or chaos, not all rocks and stones, of course, we have some control, some structure, some edifice, looser of course: logic, comparison, chronology, inference. Did the Holocaust take place? How do we know? Why did Hitler fight the wrong war? His master plan was to expand into Russia and ally Germany to us Brits, fellow Aryan colonialists he admired, part of the master race, yet found himself at war with Britain and signing a peace treaty with Russia. What went wrong for Hitler?'

He paused a millisecond and Neil inserted the name 'Goldhagen?'

'Goldhagen, yes Goldhagen, that's what you came to see me about, wasn't it? His book *Willing Executioners*.

Goldhagen and Browning used the same data and came to rather different conclusions about the Holocaust. Who is right? Goldhagen came to the Holocaust with a fixed belief the Germans had long wished to kill the Jews and Hitler gave them their opportunity. In other words, the Germans were willing executioners, not shaped by the situation but given opportunity by Hitler. His book is a response to Browning's *Ordinary Men*, and indirectly, Milgram.

'Goldhagen is what we call an intentionalist. Did you know that? Intentionalists insist that Hitler intended killing the Jews from the start, whereas functionalists argue that the murder of Jews wasn't intended but evolved incrementally. Why else, they argue, did Eichmann initially plan to send all the Jews to Palestine, and failing that Madagascar, and failing that banish them to Siberia? And failing that, the Final Solution. Think about that when evaluating Goldhagen. So there we have it.'

Neil turned towards the door.

'Or do we? It's not quite that simple...' He paused to swallow; his mouth suddenly dry.

'Not quite that simple?' prompted Neil, turning to face Lombard.

'Because the road to Auschwitz was something of a twisted road. While Eichmann plotted some kind of resettlement of the Jews, firing squads directed by Himmler were murdering Jews in Russia. You see, there was no consistent approach. Forget the *Heil* Hitler goose-stepping columns, legendary German efficiency and order. Behind the facade of a monolithic state was disorder, feuding and competing agencies, even chaos. Hitler left day-to-day decisions to lower officials. Nazi agencies competed and moved towards increasingly extreme policies, believing this was Hitler's intention to gain rewards, what Kershaw calls "Working towards the Führer". Initially there was no genocide master plan, only improvised solutions culminating in the Final

Solution to which Hitler gave his approval. Or did he? Some even challenge that. The radicalisation was cumulative, widening from forced emigration in Germany, ghettos, to outright extermination. Huge resources were directed towards extermination, detracting from the war effort, so Hitler must have known about, and approved, the Final Solution.'

25

Ascending the steps to Matlock's office, Neil recalled what Lombard said about natural science: 'All physical science is limited in the wild, so to speak, beyond that enclosure we call the laboratory … Outside their laboratory comfort zone they were at sea, no sea legs… throwing up all over the place.' Yes, the more a science ventures beyond its controlled comfort zone the less accurate and less predictive it becomes. He made a mental note to add history to his research, but not literature. He chuckled over Lombard's comments on Matlock: 'Not surprised Matlock's switching to disobedience. Milgram was first with obedience. No one cares who is second.'

Was this the deeper reason for Matlock's conversion to disobedience, Milbro a mere catalyst, bringing to the fore a long-held ambition: to shake off the epithet "mere replicator"? Neil was initially surprised at Matlock's conversion. Matlock had called him in, and before Neil was seated said, 'I'm thinking about research into disobedience.'

'You mean obedience?'

He had chuckled at Neil's surprised tone. 'No, disobedience. What kind of person disobeys? We've done situational obedience to death. Endless repetitions. Now we need to look at attitudes, choice, and disposition. Something on the back burner all along; always a possibility. Fits current trends, CBT. What do people bring to a situation? No one enters a situation a blank slate. Even the disposition to obey comes from outside, the agentic state. You with me?'

Swivelling round to face Neil, he added, 'This is big, Neil, and I'd like you on board. You understand attitude. You have the right attitude to attitude. Have you read Goldhagen yet? He might be on to something after all. I'm going over my research, the handful who disobeyed. What made them different? The situation or…'

Was this really Matlock? Was he mishearing? Asch's lines again. Matlock's commitment to the situation seemed set in concrete, his persona, image and status enshrined in the situation. He *was* the situation. Or had Milbro and the threat of litigation set him free, Prometheus finally unbound, a paradigm shift to resolve the Milbro anomaly? Perhaps there was something in Matlock's belief that we are different people in different situations; no contradiction after all.

Before Neil could comment, Matlock was insisting disobedience research wasn't a U-turn but an extension of obedience, leading on from obedience. 'After all, some disobeyed and I explored the circumstances of disobedience, you remember. If I left the room some disobeyed by giving lower shocks. It was always there waiting to be developed. And didn't Asch obtain only one third conformity? Two-thirds didn't conform. That's the real statistic, the one the textbooks ignore: the majority didn't conform. And why not?'

Before Neil sat down, Matlock was saying, 'Goldhagen, Goldhagen. Not the situation, not obedience, but Germans freely choosing to eliminate the Jews. Freely, that's the key word.'

Neil placed five books on the table to one side of Matlock: Goldhagen's *Hitler's Willing Executioners*, Browning's *Ordinary Men*, Arendt's *Eichmann in Jerusalem: A Report on the Banality of Evil*, and Raul Hilberg's *The Destruction of European Jews*.

'Willing and ordinary, ordinary and willing. So what did you find?'

'The key word is ordinary. Arendt argues that Eichmann was, well, ordinary. She made famous the phrase "banality of evil".'

Matlock scoffed. 'Banality of labels, you mean. You can say something obvious in plain language and no one listens, but coin a phrase... And based on Eichmann, you say, a statistic of one, no doubt acting Mr Ordinary in court – obeying orders, mere cog in the machine. Am I right?'

Neil nodded agreement.

Matlock leaned back. 'Tell me about Goldhagen.'

'I went to Lombard for advice. Nazism's one of his areas of expertise.'

'One of his many areas. Hard to keep count.'

Neil suppressed a sigh and said, 'The subject's complex, more complex than I thought. Conflicting approaches. Above all, conflicting interpretations.'

Matlock was tapping the desk. 'Goldhagen?'

'Browning comes first. Goldhagen's book is a counter to Browning. Browning and Goldhagen investigated one of the many battalions that murdered Jews, the same battalion, Battalion 101, not because the battalion was necessarily typical, but because the data is very detailed. The battalion had been in Poland for less than three weeks before massacring 1,500 Jews in a single day. They hadn't killed Jews before then, though other battalions had helped SS squads kill Jews in Russia. I was surprised to find most of the killing by shooting in Poland wasn't done by special SS squads trained to kill but units called the Order Police. The Order Police weren't soldiers as such, more paramilitary; not selected because they were killers but mostly because they were too old to be soldiers. Browning gives the grim statistic that three months before Battalion 101 arrived in Poland in the summer of 1942 about a quarter of the Holocaust victims had been killed, mostly in the Soviet Union by special SS squads, but a mere six months later only a quarter remained alive. It was a huge task completed over a very short time by a large number of battalions. Initially whole communities were eliminated by firing squad, then rounded up and sent to extermination camps. Hilberg estimates that 25 per cent of Jews died by shooting, around 50 per cent by gassing in the six major camps, the rest starved in ghettos or worked to death.'

'Goldhagen?'

'Right. Just let me say, Browning and Goldhagen agree about the carnage – that's undisputed by mainstream historians. But they disagree about motivation. As you know, Goldhagen claims Germans killed Jews because they always wanted to. Killing was cultural and nothing to do with the situation. They brought their culture to the situation, came to the situation hating Jews. Hitler merely provided the opportunity. Interestingly, Goldhagen's fully aware of obedience research and the importance placed on the situation, but dismisses it as ahistorical, particularly its implication that any group of people would have killed in the same circumstances. Situation or place has no relevance, only what's brought to the situation, namely German eliminationist hatred of Jews.'

Forgetting for the moment he had asked Neil to devalue the situation or context, Matlock began defending obedience research. 'The fool misses the point of obedience research. The point was to isolate obedience to authority from strong motives, such as hatred for the victim, to make it ahistorical. There would have been no point selecting a sample of racists and asking them to inflict suffering on some hated minority. Obedience research isolates the variable obedience to authority to show that ordinary people will inflict suffering on a stranger if ordered to do so, regardless of race or anything else. The situation overrides everything else. That's why, like Milgram, I drew my sample from a wide occupational range, a cross-section of society.'

Matlock fell silent and Neil chose the moment to relate the bad news about Goldhagen. 'The problem is, Goldhagen is rejected by mainstream historians.' Aware this wasn't what

Matlock wanted to hear, Neil wore a sympathetic grimace before adding, '"Totally wrong about everything", and "worthless", Raul Hilberg's verdict.'

'"Everything" might be an exaggeration. We need to know Hilberg's bias.' He leaned back and placed his hands on the table. 'What are we saying here?'

'Goldhagen's eliminationist theory is the problem. He believes anti-Semitism was entrenched in Germany, awaiting a catalyst. Goldhagen commits Popper's error: selecting evidence to fit his theory. He ignores or explains away counter evidence.'

Matlock looked at Browning's book. 'OK. Tell me more about Browning.'

'As I said, Browning researched Battalion 101 before Goldhagen and uses the same data but puts different interpretations on the same witness evidence. In the end, it's mostly about interpretation. Take Trapp's offer.'

'Offer? Trapp?'

Neil barely suppressed a sigh. This was going to take a long time. Perhaps if Matlock bothered to do some of the reading…

'The debate between Browning and Goldhagen revolves around Major Trapp, the platoon commander, and his offer.'

'The statistic of one again.'

'Yes and no. Major Trapp's offer seems to contradict the belief that the Germans were simply obeying orders, fearful for their lives. It's this aspect the media homed in on when Goldhagen was published. Before the first massacre, Major Trapp gave his men a pep talk. Tearful, he told them the assignment was not to his liking and highly regrettable but ordered from the highest authority. If it helps, he reminded the men, women and children were being bombed back home. One witness recalls him saying the Jews had instigated the American boycott against Germany; two recall him saying the Jews in the village supported the partisans. However, if the men were so anti-Semitic, as Goldhagen claims, why would Trapp feel the need to persuade them to kill?'

Matlock leaned back and nodded. 'Seems to be justifying the action for the men.' He paused. 'Or himself.'

Neil nodded. 'Goldhagen manages a radically different interpretation. Despite conceding Trapp was disturbed by the order, shed tears and expressed his reluctance to the battalion doctor, Goldhagen emphasises Trapp's reference to bombing in Germany as proof of anti-Semitism. Why else, Goldhagen asks, would Trapp link the bombing of German civilians and Jews in Poland, a link illogical to us, but perfectly logical to Trapp because he knew the men hated and demonised Jews?'

'He has a point. Explain Trapp's offer.'

'He made what Browning describes as an extraordinary offer to the men: to step out if they didn't feel up to the assignment. Out of the 500 or so, some 12 stepped forward.'

'Not many,' said Matlock. '2.4 per cent, or put the other way, 97.6 obedience.' He laughed drily. 'Beats all the obedience studies.'

'And appears to support Goldhagen. Except there are problems with the evidence.'

Matlock's laugh was ironic. 'Go on.'

'Depends on which witnesses we believe. Browning discusses the evidence in a long footnote.'

'Not a footnote. Go on.'

'Some witnesses said the offer was limited to older men – Browning's preferred version – others that it was made to everyone, young and old, which Goldhagen prefers to believe. We don't have Trapp's testimony. He was extradited to Poland after the war, tried and executed for killing non-Jewish Poles. Witness statements differ. Only two recalled Trapp's offer was limited to older men. Some witnesses said he never made such an offer, or they never heard it. How do you decide? Few witnesses, conflicting testimony.'

'So why does Browning come down on the side of witnesses who claim the offer was made only to older men?'

'Browning says their evidence is more vivid and precise.'

'Bit subjective. Go on.'

"Goldhagen admits the testimony is conflicting but favours the testimony that the offer was made to everyone, proving that the majority were willing to kill Jews because so few stepped forward. His supporting evidence that Trapp made the offer to everyone is inferred from younger men later asking to be excused. Would they have done so if the offer had not been open to everyone? However, this was after they had started killing, perhaps sickened by the killing. Browning is not consistent. He starts by saying the offer was made to older police and later mentions there is contrary evidence which he relegates to a footnote. His problem is explaining why the majority obeyed. Later in the book he argues the men had no time for reflection, were taken by surprise, had only seconds to react and no time to confer – the same problem with your obedience experiments.'

Matlock scowled, remembered he had asked Neil to refute obedience, and beamed broadly. 'Very thorough, Neil. Trust you to read the footnotes.'

These were Lombard's observations, but Neil was happy to take the credit. His tone ironic, Neil said, 'Goldhagen also makes interesting use of footnotes. Whereas Browning in the main text cites eight witnesses who saw Trapp weeping, Goldhagen cites only one witness out of the eight and relegates him to a footnote.'

'It must be tempting to assign inconvenient facts to footnotes, a form of shelving or filing. Did anyone refuse to kill Jews?'

'Depends on what is meant by refuse. There was one definite refusal cited by Browning, and that was accepted by Trapp. More typically, those unwilling to kill requested to do other duties when the killing began, and these were granted, at least by Trapp and most officers. One officer told refusers they should lie down alongside the victims. Others didn't refuse as such but hid in the woods, or shot past their victims, or took excessive time rounding up Jews. Obedience was lower when alone and unobserved, which contradicts Goldhagen's view that Germans hated Jews.'

'Fits my variant. When I left the room and gave orders by phone most gave lower shocks and lied about the shock levels given.'

'Goldhagen counters by arguing that those who asked to do other duties were repulsed by the gore. Killing was messy: spattered with brain, blood, bone splinters. Goldhagen asks, if they hated killing, why didn't they all ask to be excused knowing some had been excused?'

'Good point. Do we know what percentage requested to do other duties or found other ways of avoiding killing?'

'Browning estimates 10-20 per cent.'

'So about 80 or even 90 per cent continued to the end.'

On the strength of Matlock's earlier positive response, Neil ventured another criticism of obedience research. 'The strange thing is' – he coughed slightly – 'you would expect it to be lower because they didn't kill by increment.'

Matlock was scowling as he intoned the word 'increment'.

'I came across this criticism of obedience research. Shocks were administered in stages, from small to large, one small step at a time. Apparently, we judge by contrast and not by an absolute standard. Or that's the theory.'

Matlock was silent.

'The point I'm making is, the Order Police didn't kill by increment, killing for them was absolute, unlike the obedience experiment where they progressed slowly to the final shock. The theory is, people are more easily persuaded if asked to do things in stages, one step at a time. So you might have expected less obedience from the Order Police, not more.'

Matlock was silent, raised a finger and said, 'We're still talking obedience. Tell me about those who refused.'

'Asked to be excused rather than refused. Most who asked to be excused felt they had to try then fail and claim weakness. "Weak" was a recurrent word, rarely "wrong".'

'Some would say it was weak to obey, strong to disobey or challenge.'

'I think too much is made of Trapp's offer. As I said, it's what the media homed in on. It wasn't only about obedience to authority. Browning emphasises the power of the peer group. Whatever his offer, to all of them or just older members, it must have been difficult for anyone to step forward in front of their comrades. Not obedience to authority so much as conformity to comrades. Stepping out risked rejection and isolation, leaving the dirty work to others. Refusals might have been higher if he had asked for volunteers, or better still, told the men to go away and discuss the request and volunteer later. Maybe we just can't put ourselves in their place, at that point in history, Germany under Hitler's brutal dictatorship, Poland a distant conquered country, different language, the Jews more different still, oppression and slaughter all around. Some recalled other reasons for asking to be excused, such as being assigned to kill Jews from their hometown of Hamburg deported to Poland. They identified with them, the same language.' Neil shrugged impotently.

Matlock looked fixedly at Neil, a question looming on his face. 'Tell me more about the sample used by Browning and Goldhagen. Didn't you say something about the Order Police being older? Surely most of these witnesses must be dead or in their dotage? Memory loss, dementia.'

Neil smiled. 'They used old data produced by others for a different purpose – trial evidence.'

'Trial evidence!'

Neil explained that the evidence was collected in the early sixties, pre-trial interrogations of battalion members, and selected by Browning and Goldhagen because the data was unusually detailed, vivid and complete, not formulaic and self-evidently dishonest, like so much testimony from other battalions. Browning was confident he could sift out the honest testimony.

'Pre-trial interrogations of battalion members. And we're expected to believe they were truthful? No wonder some said they couldn't remember Trapp's offer.'

Faltering slightly, Neil said, 'Browning believed he could tell reliable from unreliable evidence. How did he put it? He felt many of the testimonies had candour.'

'Despite faulty memory 20 years on, deliberate forgetfulness, repression or just lying to save their skins.'

'In fairness to Browning it was all he had – that evidence or nothing.'

'What did these witnesses say about anti-Semitism?'

'That's another problem. None said they hated Jews. The pre-trial problem again. Browning explains that to do so would have been self-incriminating. Anti-Semitism provided a motive, a willingness to kill, so they claimed they had no choice and were ordered to kill.'

'Telling on each other?'

'Identifying anti-Semitic comrades risked being a witness against them. On balance, Browning's selection is poor but better than Goldhagen's restricting self-fulfilling test, that the only believable evidence was self-condemnatory, admitting to being willing genocidal Jew-hating killers.'

Matlock chuckled. 'If they deny killing Jews willingly they're lying, if they admit killing willingly they're telling the truth. Variant on the witch swimming test.'

'Despite disagreeing with Goldhagen, Browning doesn't believe it was all coercion. There was no recorded case of anyone being punished for refusing, and considerable evidence for voluntarism. However, they weren't totally free. To refuse entailed some loss, if only loss of promotion, and some officers were threatening, such as one saying that those unwilling to kill should lie down alongside the victims. Above all, peer group pressure. Accusations of cowardice were common. Remember "weak" was a recurrent word, rarely "wrong". And there were other indirect forms of punishment.'

'So we've come full circle. After the war people blamed the Germans – the Germans are different – or Adorno's some were different variant, his authoritarians. Then the explanation switched to the situation; we would all do the same in the same situation. Now with Goldhagen we're back to saying the Germans are different.'

'*Were* different. He believes they've changed since.'

Matlock echoed 'changed since' and fell silent.

'Browning, at least, offers several explanations: obedience to authority, peer group allegiance, careerism, fear of punishment, real or imagined. As I said, some asked to be re-assigned to other duties. Trapp implied ethical concerns, telling the men that the task was frightfully regrettable but ordered by the highest authorities. The men who asked to be excused depicted themselves as cowardly to their peers and avoided the implication "good", implying that the obedient were tough, strong and courageous.'

'Good would imply moral superiority over officers and peers, difficult in the circumstances. No, I can see why they had to blame themselves.'

'There is conflicting evidence about unwillingness to kill. Browning points out that others were eventually brought in to do the killing, mainly prisoners of war from Lithuania and other eastern countries. The Germans now rounded up Jews and handed them over, now killing indirectly, at a distance, making the task easier. Think of allied bombing of German cities. The bomber crews didn't see the victims, children burned to death by phosphorous bombs, burned through to the bone, couldn't be put out, not even under water.

Anti-Semitism was stronger in many East European countries and volunteers plentiful, or so some historians say, though they were prisoners, and gained privileges. Himmler had come to recognise the traumatising effect of face-to-face killing on the German police and soldiers. Handing over the task to others and distant extermination camps solved the problem. Himmler even made a speech to SS personnel recognising the problem, which suggests Germans were not all that willing to kill.'

Matlock sighed witheringly. 'Is there no concrete evidence? What about Goldhagen's argument that the problem was not face-to-face killing that traumatised them but the gore. Up to now it's been differing interpretations. Give me something concrete, coming down on one side or the other.'

'As I said, Browning is aware of obedience research and his findings concur with most of the findings.'

'But not all.'

'Strangely, unlike obedience findings, proximity to the victim didn't reduce obedience, though it clearly increased stress. Again, Goldhagen puts stress down to the gore, not ethics.'

'Unlike my variant when subjects had both voice and visual contact compliance reduced to 40 per cent. Interesting.'

'But fits the situation where they were reluctant to kill Jews they identified with, such as Jews from Hamburg, and some avoiding shooting if unobserved. Then again...' Neil paused, but felt compelled to say, 'others volunteered to kill, the so-called Jew Hunt of those who escaped being rounded up for execution. Some enjoyed killing, others became increasingly disturbed and couldn't kill anymore.'

There was a long silence, broken by Matlock.

'You said Trapp made clear to the men his distaste for the killing. That's a variable not tested in obedience research. It's as if I told the subjects of the obedience experiments that I didn't want the learner shocked, shed tears, but said it had to be done for the experiment.' Matlock leaned back and swivelled from side to side. 'How was the killing done?'

'This was the battalion's first massacre and done badly. Most of the victims were women and children, the men taken to labour camps. At first, they paired off with a victim who was led to a spot in the woods, told to lie face down and shot. The killing was brutal, women and children, face-to-face, Jews begging to live. Simply paired off one to one. How could someone lead a child to the woods, tell them to lie down, and blow their brains out? Yet most complied. Maybe, maybe some things are impossible to explain. It wasn't that the Order Police were young and malleable; most were older and had families of their own. Maybe we would *all* do the same in the same situation. Ordinary people.' Neil laughed drily. 'But that doesn't say much for humanity. Lombard believes the only solution is to avoid creating such situations. No war, no Holocaust.'

'Am I right in thinking you are coming down on the side of Browning?'

'He seems to be the better historian.'

'Goldhagen could be right. Are you sure you are not selecting Browning because the historians favour him? Or you want to believe the Germans were at heart unwilling? Is there no clinching argument?'

Neil spoke slowly and deliberately. 'You mean bypassing all the clutter of different interpretations?'

'Neil, don't keep me in suspense.'

'The clinching argument is against Goldhagen's eliminationism, I'm afraid. Goldhagen ignores the fact that the Nazis murdered non-Jews: the disabled, Gypsies, Poles, Slavs, Russian prisoners of war – two million or more prisoners of war left to starve or die of disease. Hitler's Hunger Plan, racial or ethnic groups on a hierarchy, Jews at the top, French and Dutch nearer the bottom. Himmler planned to murder millions of Slavs to make way for

Germans. Germans came first. Had they won the war against Russia, millions more would have died. In short, Germans killed anyone they were ordered to kill, and killing wasn't limited to Jews. It doesn't fit Goldhagen's idea that Germans were genocidal towards the Jews, part of their culture dating back to the 19th century.'

'I agree. Sounds absurd and doesn't fit the fact that the Final Solution was just that, final, preceded by several aborted non-eliminationist solutions such as deporting all the Jews to Palestine or Madagascar. However, if most hated killing, as Browning believes, why didn't more follow the example of those who were allowed to be excused and make the same request? What does Goldhagen say?'

'That permitting some to do other duties suggests the officers were confident most would comply.'

'Inferential, but a good argument. Goldhagen is too monocausal, we agree. Tell me, how does he explain the sudden disappearance of anti-Semitism in Germany after the war?'

'Re-education. He claims the Germans are now just like us, meaning Americans.'

Matlock laughed. 'Just like that.'

Matlock rose, moved to the window and looked out across the staffroom, hands clasped behind his back. 'Browning and Goldhagen attest to a high degree of voluntarism, more so Goldhagen, but disagree about motivation, namely cultural eliminationism. Take that out and we still have a high degree of willingness to kill.'

'Don't forget, Himmler recognised face-to-face killing was difficult.'

'Was anyone punished for refusing?'

'Jager says there is no evidence of anyone being punished for refusing. But would they have known this at the time? We act according to what we believe now. Most perpetrators said they were obeying orders and had no choice. Much has been made of the fact that there is no case of anyone being punished for refusing to kill unarmed civilians, but Browning says they wouldn't have known this.'

'Putative duress.'

'Exactly.'

'Isn't this contradicted by what you said earlier, that many who asked to be excused were excused and not punished? So why not the rest? Goldhagen still has a point.'

'I still think it was a different time and place. War, killings all around.

Matlock pulled his face into a pained expression. 'Situation again.'

Feeling a need to be conciliatory, Neil added: 'Don't forget, Browning reckons about a third were predisposed to cruelty. The volunteer Jew hunt, remember.'

'You're right. Browning support predisposition for a third. Say no more.'

Neil motioned to speak.

'Done. That's obedience out the way. What we need now is a good research design to demonstrate disobedience experimentally, subjects unaffected by the situation and freely disobeying. That's your next task.'

*

Neil ruminated on Matlock's directive for a week.

He started with obedience studies that included disobedience: Rank and Jacobson's study where nurses were allowed to confer with colleagues and senior staff about the excessive dosage prescribed by a doctor, resulting in minimal obedience; Milgram's two teachers where one – an accomplice – refused the other usually refused.

What if subjects had some way of escaping the situation, other than refusing to continue? Escape was not tested under controlled conditions. What he needed was a concise label like 'cultural capital' or 'banality of evil'. People like labels; the label often more important than the message.

Neil took the problem to Rachel.

'Something to symbolise escape.'

'*Breakfast at Tiffany's*. Remember? Holly uses the fire escape to flee an obnoxious client "who bites". The fire escape also symbolises escape, along with unpacked boxes and an unnamed cat. Holly won't be tied, remember. Didn't you say Matlock's old laboratory has a fire escape? The subjects could use it to flee the experiment. Call it the Golightly Effect.'

Neil put the idea to Matlock, expecting ridicule.

'Golightly Effect. I like it. Succinct phrase. From *Breakfast at Tiffany's*, one of my favourite films. But we'll need some ruse,' he said thoughtfully.

'Subjects could be shown the fire escape, a short-cut to the car park when the experiment's complete. Door left open, ostensibly to let in some air. Could even enter the lab by the fire escape.'

Matlock looked doubtful. 'Would detract from the status of the building, hardly an awesome entry. A confounding variable. Better if subjects were left alone at some point during the experiment, the fire door open, say at the point of inflicting the more severe shocks.'

'Short-cut to the car park?' reminded Neil. 'Or tell them to go for a break and reconsider if they want to continue, or even confer with a friend invited along and waiting outside or questioned by a confederate pretending to be the next subject. That should get obedience down.' Matlock was silent, and Neil added, 'Your conformity to peers. Subject witnesses two confederates refusing to obey. In that situation most subjects also refused when it was their turn. Conformity to peers was more important than obedience to authority. Fits Browning.'

Neil sensed Matlock wanted more. Finally, Matlock told him it was a variant on obedience, and he wanted clear separation. Disobedience was to be a new departure, a clean break.

Matlock stood up and said, 'Think about fear. In extreme situations extreme measures are often needed to make people risk their lives. I read somewhere that Russian soldiers fighting the Germans faced machine gunners in their rear and few retreated. To advance was possible or probable death, to retreat certain death. Not obedience to authority, just naked fear. Sometimes you need more than the agentic state to force people to fight and risk their lives.'

He indicated the meeting had ended and Neil made for the door.

'Clear separation, remember.'

*

Neil searched the indices for articles on disobedience, but nothing went further than the Milgram variations, or included fear. Then he recalled Lombard mentioned fear, how top-ranking Nazis deserted and disobeyed Hitler when defeat seemed inevitable. Only later would he link the idea to Milgram, uncovering a forgotten footnote. Milgram had started with a pilot study of obedience. Having inflicted severe shocks, the same subjects were asked by the experimenter to shock themselves but refused. For some reason Milgram discarded the finding, relegated to a footnote as an interesting variant. Confident Matlock was unaware of the variant, a mere footnote unworthy of the main text, Neil decided to take credit for the idea. After all, he had connected it to events in Nazi Germany.

'Clear separation,' started Neil. 'I think I have the answer.' He paused, momentarily dangling his knowledge out of Matlock's reach.

'Don't keep me in suspense. This is not Shelrack's geologic time, I haven't a billion years.'

'Hitler's Nero Decree.'

Neil paused again, and Matlock tapped the desk impatiently. 'Nero Decree? You seem to be moving at glacial speed again.'

Neil outlined the Nero Decree, how at the war's end, the allies advancing on all sides, Hitler ordered the complete destruction of Germany's resources but Albert Speer, entrusted with the task, persuaded the generals to ignore the order (while before that not averse to using slave labour and other war crimes). Similarly, Paulus, ordered by Hitler to fight to the last man at Stalingrad and expected to commit suicide to avoid capture, surrendered. Hitler also ordered the destruction of Paris, explosives to be placed round the Eiffel Tower should the Allies enter the city. Military governor, Dietrich von Choltitz, admirer of Parisian architecture, refused and surrendered to the Allies. Then there was the July Plot, several top Nazis coming close to killing Hitler. Some were opposed to Hitler's genocidal policy, more had participated in slave labour and genocide, but at the end, defeat inevitable, they opposed Hitler. Even Goering and Himmler disobeyed Hitler once the war was lost. When it came to being self-harmed, they acted to save their own skins.'

Matlock sat back and reflected. 'How do we translate this to the laboratory?'

Neil hesitated. The ethical issue. How would Matlock react? 'We could ask subjects to inflict shocks on themselves. We could rig the experiment so that the subjects became learners, but instead of the teacher pressing the lever, they would be asked to punish themselves if they made a mistake.'

'I like it. Ethics committee might pose a problem, but I like it.'

As Neil was leaving, he said, 'You see what this means. Milgram didn't draw on this aspect of German history, only the Holocaust. This will free us from Milgram. A clear separation, a clear separation.'

＊

'You do realise I came up with this idea years ago?'

Neil was about to protest, but Matlock was saying, 'Bit like Wallace and Darwin. Wallace independently came up with the theory of evolution, but Darwin had been working on it for years, testified by friends and colleagues, and justifiably took the credit.'

Matlock leaned back, hands clasped, poker face.

Neil felt a surge of anger, and for a moment was tempted to say name the friends and colleagues who can support your claim.

Matlock chuckled. 'Don't look so glum. Just my little joke.' He leaned back. 'Then again, I did come up with the idea of fear, pointed you in the right direction. The problem is, Neil, you won't get funding or recognition from RAE. Such research is expensive. If I apply, attach my name, funding will be likely and more substantial. Then there's the ethics committee. Could you steer it through the ethics committee?'

His tone now conciliatory, he said, 'Unfair, you're thinking? Not really. You'll be in my position someday, doing and saying the same. Some call it the Matthew Effect. "For unto everyone that hath shall be given, and he shall have abundance: but from him that hath not shall be taken even that which he hath". Well, not totally Matthew, I can give something in return. What was it Aneurin Bevan said after bribing the hospital consultants to get the NHS off the ground? "I stuffed their mouths with gold". Well, I can't stuff your mouth with gold exactly, but your name will be on the research after mine and –' he paused, enjoying Neil hanging on his every word, 'and then there's the lecturing post.'

He paused again, relishing Neil's intense interest. 'I need help with this disobedience research and I'm tying it in with the lecturing post. You're the front runner. Nigel is keen on disobedience, of course, a sudden convert.' He laughed. 'Don't worry, I'm supporting your application. Consider it in the bag. What with finishing your PhD and exposing Milbro. Of course, there's still the viva to get through, but we can work on that.'

The viva, yes, the viva. It was suddenly real. He would face three examiners and a battery of questions about his research.

*

Popper, the main critic of Kuhn, was a philosopher of science. Rational and logical according to some, transcendent and ethereal to others, he descended periodically to lay down the law like Moses bearing stone tablets. Thou shalt... Kuhn was a physicist-turned-social historian, commenting from the inside, the "how" rather than the "should". Kuhn challenged two basic beliefs about science: that science is the steady accumulation of knowledge; that science is ever open to new ideas. Science, he maintained, progresses in jumps, such as the Copernican and Darwinian revolutions, then closes to new ideas and thereafter becomes governed by rigid paradigms which guide research and becomes necessarily dogmatic. Once in place, the dust settles and scientists thereafter collect supporting evidence and engage in problem-solving, such Darwinians finding support for the theory, until accumulating anomalies force a revolution, and a new paradigm.

Scientific progress would be impossible, maintained Kuhn, were a theory dropped the moment an anomaly occurred. For this reason, science is very protective, rather like political party loyalty, three-line whips imposed on dissidents, ridicule or expulsion if they persist. Kuhn said science is less rational than Popper imagined it to be or should be. Scientists are not open-minded but strongly attached to their theories, individually and collectively. Scientific communities are a way of life. Most of the time science is conservative and conforming, and scientists rarely attempt to falsify their theories. The old guard in particular resist change. Revolutions are championed by the young who are less committed to a paradigm. Natural science maintains boundaries, ridicules wrong knowledge, controls journals, defines problems, ostracises non-believers. This was the background to Neil's research applying Kuhn to the social sciences.

It was a long time before Neil pinpointed weaknesses in Kuhn's theory, a seemingly perfect working model of the sciences, a well-oiled mechanism, neat set of stages, exception and anomaly-free. Ironically, it was Kuhn's assertion that the social sciences, ever in flux and divided, were not true sciences but pre-paradigmatic that led him to suspect Kuhn's model was too neat, just too elegant. No loose ends, in-betweens, uncertainties. Did he select clear-cut examples of revolutions and generalise to the rest? Did he crush, compress and squeeze science into his theory?

The flaws crystallised further when Neil recalled Lombard's observation (so irritating to Rachel), history is not the past, but ever-revised interpretations, more flowing lava than solid rock, an endless reconstruction, and the professor of planetary science who said the general public supported Moon and Mars trips by quoting a handful of people at his local who agreed the trips worthwhile. 'Even my taxi driver is an enthusiast', he shouted as Neil was leaving. Though eminent in his field, once outside the laboratory enclosure and making social observations, he was at sea, bobbing along uncharted territory. So how much of a social scientist was Kuhn? How secure was Kuhn's territory?

When Kuhn did his historical research into science, he had no comforting paradigm to draw on, no controlled enclosure. He drew on subjective personal experience, biography and sociology, but mostly the history of science, disciplines described by him as weak in method and theory. His elegant structure was built on shifting methodologies and mercurial disciplines, his certainty based on uncertainty. There could be no controls, no blinds, no possibility of experimentation, no exact measuring device, and no revolution thermometer. His vague, abstract, loose and shifting terminology offered no solution. Where did normal science begin, and revolutionary science take off? There was no experimental design that could demonstrate a paradigm, hunt down or predict a revolution, isolate an exemplar of normal science or repeat the whole process in a laboratory variable by variable.

Once Neil realised the flaws, the anomalies stacked up, such as Kuhn's claim that revolutionary change was absolute, no compatibility of old and new, one paradigm replacing another. Yet Darwin, Neil discovered, did not completely replace Lamarck, needed Lamarck to solve the problems of dilution and explain anomalies, such as cave-dwelling blind animals, raising the problem of identifying the point of paradigm shift or revolution. Lamarck persisted alongside Darwin into the 20th century, especially in France, the problem unresolved until the new synthesis incorporating Mendelian genetics and Weismann's barrier. But was the new synthesis a new paradigm or a modification subsumed under Kuhn's "normal science"? When does a paradigm start?

When writing *The Structure of Scientific Revolutions* in 1962 there were two competing models of the universe: steady state and big bang. Were these two paradigms? Kuhn recognised disagreement within a given paradigm, of course, but easily subsumed these under 'normal science', but how normal is normal? No, it wasn't as tidy as Kuhn made out. Kuhn was emerging as increasingly dogmatic, his theory that science is dogmatic itself dogmatic, replete with anomalies, which he didn't set aside so much as ignore. This, Neil decided, was his interpretation of Kuhn, his writerly approach to Kuhn's abstract work open to myriad interpretations.

*

Matlock chuckled as he told Neil how he got the research design past the ethics committee.

'Told them we would start with a mild sample shock to show it's real. After that, there would be no shock, sufficient for the subject to grasp the nodule and press the button marked *Strong Shock*. No shock would be given, and no harm done to the learner. This won on ethics. No need to employ an actor, either. This won on economy. They loved the term Nero Effect, a re-working of the Nero Decree, an order given but disobeyed. I gave you full credit for the term.'

To cover themselves further, Matlock agreed subjects would be asked permission to suffer pain, the initial mild shock.

'Won't that ruin the experiment?'

Matlock chuckled. 'Depends how you ask them.'

Matlock's solution was a long questionnaire, the permission question buried deep in the questionnaire: Would you be willing to participate in an experiment which involved inflicting pain on yourself? If "no" they would be excluded. There would be a time limit for completion to minimise reflection, further reducing the number of refusers. This passed the ethics committee. Matlock flagged up debriefing, a weakness in his obedience research. Each subject would be given extensive debriefing time. It would reduce the number of subjects, but that was a price to pay.

*

Neil often had his bleakest thoughts at this time, awake but not ready to get up despite knowing once he did negative thoughts would dissolve, helped by broad daylight, a mug of strong tea, shower and breakfast.

He was worried about the viva.

He recalled telling Rachel the viva was all a matter of presentation, the arrival not the journey, order created from the chaos we call research insisted on by refereed journals. 'Yes, but yours goes slightly further, mostly presentation.'

The viva was then a distant problem, but now that it was imminent, now that it was real, he rationalised the other way. He had exaggerated when discussing it with Rachel, mostly bravado to amuse her, that was all. It wasn't all deception and presentation. Hadn't he conducted a small number of unstructured follow-up interviews and planned more had time not run out? He was under pressure to finish. The lecturing post was in the pipeline, hovering. And Nigel was applying.

Guided by the Broad and Wade framework, Neil creatively expanded his sample. After all, much time and effort had been expended on indirect and informal contacts, endless parties and socials, becoming immersed in the social life of academia, even staying over at others' houses or flats sleeping on settees and gaining a reputation for sociability, someone who could be relied on to attend. Casual corridor conversations, overheard discussions in toilets and the cafeteria, debates at conferences and, of course, pubs, easily transposed into unstructured interviews, which were, after all, no more than elevated conversations. His sample size expanded.

What if the panel saw through his deceptions? His heart jumped and he sat up. One panel member worried him, a veteran, battle hardened who homed in on weakness. 'A lie-seeking guided missile,' warned Duncan. No, he was worrying about nothing. All his subjects were anonymous, disguised by false names and fabricated locations, the true number known only to him and scattered over various universities, the raw data backing his results securely in his control. Why create problems for the ethics committee and the viva panel? Matlock agreed. Well, not in so many words, more a creative interpretation of what Matlock said. 'What matters is how it is written up, you with me?' Wasn't it obvious what he meant?

He returned to his conversation with Rachel about his method. 'I just get into conversation about their research or subject. You know how we all love to talk about our research. Puts them off guard. I don't mention dogma, or that I'm researching.'

'Isn't that deception?'

'Absolutely.'

'Anyway, there are degrees of deception. More a spectrum.'

'Neil, it's deception.'

OK, it was deception. Then wasn't everything deception? Backstage and front stage came to mind, Goffman's impression management, the impression given off, the illusion, the performance most of us see, and usually want to see; and wasn't Goffman's *The Presentation of Self in Everyday Life* itself a presentation posing as all-knowing and demystifying while omitting the deceptions of his own profession, never venturing backstage to dissect his own presentation of presentations? For a moment he recalled with amusement Rachel's initial reaction to Goffman's impression given off, mocking Goffman's jargon. 'Impression given off. Sounds like something has died.' Anyway, his viva write-up was no ordinary deception, was not some tawdry fabrication, but deception in the interest of that most noble scientific pursuit: the truth. If truth was the aim, his method was the more scientific. Truth, method and deception were one.

And he had conducted a small number of formal interviews using a structured questionnaire for comparison, the subjects asked directly about the meaning and aims of science. Some of the most blatantly dogmatic researchers ticked the boxes indicating tolerance of opposing ideas and open mindedness, even claiming to test their theories and refute their own research if necessary. Most espoused caution, described their findings as 'tentative', at most 'supporting', never 'proving', humbly recognising the need for further research. He could accept this of course, evidence that the sciences, physical and social, were less dogmatic than Kuhn supposed. So why did he conclude they were dogmatic? Where was the proof?

There was verbal leakage: the sarcastic tone, contemptuous shrug, faint praise for opposing views (has a place...) the pregnant pause, everyday signals, disregarded or overlooked by the statistically minded, number obsessed box-ticking social scientist. They start by researching what they value and end by valuing what they can research – constricted by their own methods. These verbal leaks easily translated into examples of dogma. His original 7-point scale imposed by Matlock and his structured questionnaire produced columns of statistics, looked more scientific, but failed to pick up these nuances and hidden signals.

And some not so hidden. Their response to anomalies – his litmus test – attesting to the academic ideal like Catholics mindlessly reciting the catechism. I believe in... Science, a human science he now firmly believed, should delve below the surface, not the elusive, untestable Freudian unconscious, but closer to the surface: rationalising, self-justifying, explaining away, avoiding, ignoring, actions more subconscious than unconscious. The dogmatists grew in number and open-mindedness diminished. No contradiction or anomaly after all: science – including the social sciences – was indeed dogmatic.

But would the panel accept his more nuanced interpretation, devaluing the surface, the spoken word? A touch too Freudian, a touch too unconscious? No, not even that, somewhere between Adler's conscious and unconscious, more subconscious, but only a touch. And what about his own rationalisations? Observer bias perhaps? He shut away the thought, slid under the bedclothes and drifted into a restless sleep.

He awoke with a start from a disturbing dream. An image remained, vivid, disembodied, the face of the hostile Freudian, omen of Yet-to-Come looming over the viva panel, repeating over and over, 'We're not interested in what your ego has to say, we never listen to the ego, talks mostly rubbish, all rationalisations and defences'.

Shaking slightly, he got up, switched on the light and made some tea.

*

Neil faced the four members of the viva panel, familiar from the photos yet unfamiliar, rather like meeting a TV celebrity, appearance not quite matching the cosmetic larger-than- life TV image. Two were older than their photos, more gnarled, one decidedly balder. Four members were unusual, he was told, but his PhD was multi-disciplinary and required a range of expertise. One was internal, a physics professor.

He felt in control – well, almost. Matlock had conducted a mock viva, Rachel had acted as a sounding board (payment for putting up with *Frankenstein* lectures), and Wendy had collected background information on the panel, which Matlock had gone over and added to. Neil created a dossier on each panel member, including photographs. Then there was paid help: a proof-reader and editor friend of Rachel's who restructured his thesis and reduced it by a third.

Following Popper's edict that it didn't matter where a research idea came from, he included his inspiration: Isaac Asimov's short story *Belief*, written long before Kuhn's book, about a professor of physics who develops the ability to defy gravity and levitate. No one believes him as it defies the laws of physics (Kuhn's paradigm). An offer to levitate in front of a disbelieving professor is rejected: 'If I saw you fly, I'd see an optometrist or a psychiatrist'.

Once craniometry ruled academia, shaped by the needs of colonialism. Reflecting more than testing, craniometry set out to prove, rather than disprove, convenient beliefs. It looked scientific and had the appearance of science: meticulous measurement, skulls filled with sand carefully weighed, numbers galore, the 'objective' researchers forced by the evidence to conclude that Negroes achieve less than Caucasians because they have smaller brains on average, and women achieve less than men for the same reason. Later research, informed by liberal values, discredited craniometry and similar sciences, and promoted social explanations. Better science, more objective, or... He pushed the thought aside. Challenging the current scientific enterprise was not part of his viva.

Poised to face the viva panel, clutching a copy of his dissertation, he felt unreal. Goffman again. Performance, impression management – from the jacket he last wore for a wedding to the carefully rehearsed presentation. No tie. That looked too obvious, false even. No academic his age wore a tie. He would present his ideas in an orderly fashion, a smooth and logical progression, strike a pose of strict scientific procedure couched in the language of science, show modesty by indicating weaknesses in his research, say he deliberately used structured and unstructured interviews for comparison (obtaining conflicting results) and justify placing greater weight on the unstructured results while fully aware identifying non-verbal leaks and other body language was open to observer bias. Neil suppressed a smile as he looked at the examiners. The one noted for giving PhD applicants a hard time was easily ten years older than the youthful photo on the back of a recently published book. Vanity, or needs must? Perhaps the publisher insisted. Whatever, he was notorious for challenging definitions and concepts, the subject of his recent book, but luckily critical of Kuhn. Neil had read his book, bought by Miss Blenkinsop. Matlock warned he would most likely dominate the panel.

He smiled across at Neil. 'Let me introduce the panel...'

*

'You're helping Matlock with *your* disobedience research.'

'I wouldn't call it that exactly. It's more than helping.'

'What would you call it?'

Neil stared out the window, and without turning said, 'I don't care what people call it. I'm in. I beat Nigel. I'm a lecturer, and I'm engaged in a major piece of research with Matlock.'

Rachel sighed. 'I suppose so. Yes, you're right. But it's so unfair Matlock taking over the research, stealing your ideas. God, I hate Matlock.'

'He's found me an office. His old laboratory is being restored and I'll get a room nearby. One of the perks assisting the head of psychology.'

'Better not be bigger than mine. It's not, is it?'

Neil laughed. 'At least twice as large, has a Holly Golightly fire escape, a huge window and –'

'You had better be lying.'

'– herds of migrating caribou thundering by. Drop in some time, if you can navigate your way there.'

*

After revealing Milbro was a fake to Matlock, Neil had phoned Andy asking him to delay his second article on negative effects of experiments on subjects using Milbro as a case study. 'There's something you need to know...'

Andy had resisted the idea that Milbro was a fake. A lot rode on Milbro, his star witness: victim, informer and saboteur who claimed life-altering damage resulting from Matlock's obedience research, the very fashionable post-traumatic stress disorder. The evidence that stigmata preceded his participation in the obedience study overwhelming, he finally, if reluctantly, accepted that Milbro was a discredited source. Perhaps an exposé on Milbro? His editor was uneasy. He admitted the story was appealing – exposer of fakes a fake – but the story was tangled, Milbro unreliable, first an informer, then revealed to be a fake, now bent on litigation. If he sued CCU and won...

Andy's tone was ironic. 'So many fakes. Fake patients, fake subjects, fake lecturer, now Milbro a fake. Fakegate goes on, and I can't use it.'

26

Neil peered out the window of his office overlooking the ground level part of the old asylum block, a long expanse of flat roof punctuated by skylights illuminating its depressingly long corridor, culminating in a square tower. He smiled recalling Rachel's first visit a year earlier, remembered bracing himself for her criticisms. Around this time, he and Wendy were house-buying, and estate agent euphemism came to the rescue.

'Call this an office? More a cupboard.'

'Compact, cosy.'

'Bit isolated.'

'Secluded, private, tucked away.'

'Draughty.'

'Airy, invigorating.'

'How will anyone find you?'

'You found me.'

Rachel had since been elevated to assistant professor. Fussel had retired and D.H. Lawrence retired with him, leaving an opening for the Gothic novel.

'I was blocked for years,' Rachel explained. 'I hate the bastard.'

'But he's gone.'

'Still hate him.'

One afternoon, not long after the disclosure that Milbro was the saboteur, Miss Blenkinsop halted next to Neil as he poured over a volume in the library. Staring into the distance, she said, 'Curious how your anti-class research into class and reading coincided with the search for the person informing on your department, and how it was none other than the singularly interesting Milbro Smith, a person on the list I gave you to help your research into anti-class stereotypes. A coincidence, no doubt. Though of course, as a psychologist, you do not believe in coincidences. Everything must have a cause.'

'On the contrary, Miss Blenkinsop, coincidences happen all the time. Must happen. We call them correlations. If you remember me saying once, trees correlate with educational achievement, but correlations must not be confused with causes.'

'A singularly interesting explanation, Mr Denton.'

The Milbro problem was resolved. He accepted a deal: good reference for non-disclosure and dropping litigation. 'After all,' said the VC massaging the ethics, 'he is unlikely to sabotage research elsewhere.'

Andy settled for a general article about PTSD, coming down on the side of attitude or disposition. 'PTSD is in fashion,' his article ran, 'people cast as victims of circumstances, but recent research... Are we creating a society of victims, passive recipients of events?' This pleased Matlock. 'On our side for once.' Was Andy on Matlock's side? Neil likened him to an estate agent, neither buyer's side nor seller's side, but the estate agent's side. 'Follow the money', concluded Andy's article '...symptoms exaggerated to get compensation aided and abetted by lawyers and psychiatrists...' It was an OK story, not his Watergate, he told Neil. On a scale of one to 10, 10 the highest, he gave it three.

Neil was alarmed to find that Matlock suspected he had embellished his data. 'Tell me, off the record, did you do all those interviews? The viva panel was impressed.' He chuckled. 'I heard a rumour you conducted some interviews in unorthodox venues, one in a toilet. I didn't mention that to the panel, of course.'

'All interviews took place.'

'Of course, of course. The venue is irrelevant.' He laughed loudly. 'When you were in that toilet, urinating side by side, I bet you were structuring the material, mentally completing a questionnaire. All said and done, the interview's a concept not a location, or so the postmodernists tell me. You showed great skill presenting your research. The panel was impressed. Your wide reading and criticism of Kuhn bowled them over.'

And Wendy? After moving in with Neil, they bought a house in West Bridgford, a small town turned outer suburb of Nottingham but retaining its separate identity helped by the River Trent-cum-moat. Notably middle class with good schools and good catchment areas, or vice versa, Wendy looked to the future. She was pregnant.

Scrutinising their house, Rachel resisted criticising the decor, pictures, books and furnishings, settling instead on the location.

'We just want our children to attend schools comprising the more academic child, whose parents show interest in their children's education; parents committed to education, parents who motivate their children,' Wendy explained to a silent Rachel.

'You mean middle-class parents?'

'No. Not middle-class, necessarily. Motivating.'

'Isn't that the same thing?'

Neil laughed. 'What Wendy's saying is, that they happen to be mostly middle-class is just coincidence.'

Rachel smiled wryly. 'So you accidentally stumbled into a middle-class area lured by better schools.'

'Coincidence.'

Acknowledgements

George A. Kelly, A Theory of Personality, *The Psychology of Personal Constructs* p.5, reproduced by permission of W. W. Norton & Company, 1955

Noam Chomsky, reproduced by permission of BBC – The listener', 6th April 1978

Mary Shelley, *Frankenstein,* 1834 revision

Frankenstein, the Mary-Percy corrected version 1816-1817, reproduced by permission Bodleian Library Manuscripts, 2008

The Project Gutenberg eBook, *The Life and Letters of Mary Wollstonecraft Shelley, Volume I* of 2, by Florence A. Thomas Marshall.

On the Origin of Species, Charles Darwin, 6th edition.

Thomas S. Kuhn, *The Structure of Scientific Revolutions*, The University of Chicago Press,1962

Erving Goffman, *The Presentation of Self in Everyday Life*, Anchor Books, 1959

Ervin Goffman, *Stigma: Notes on the Management of Spoiled Identity*, Prentice-Hall, Inc

Erving Goffman, *Bahavior in Public Places*, The Free Press, 1966

Sigmund Freud, *The Interpretation of Dreams*, Wordsworth Classics, p135, 1997

Stanley Milgram, *Obedience to Authority*, Pinter and Martin Classics, by arrangement with HarperCollins Publishers, Inc

Isaac Asimov, Belief, short story from *Through a Glass, Clearly,* New English Library Ltd,1969

Truman Capote, *Breakfast at Tiffany's*, Random House, 1958

Wallace Stevens *The Necessary Angel: Essays on Reality and the Imagination*, Vintage,1965

W. Beran Wolfe *How to be Happy Though Human, p.15,* George Routledge & Son, 1937

D. H. Lawrence, *Women in Love*, pp. 2-3, Penguin

Paul O'Flinn, *Production and Reproduction: The Case of Frankenstein* (*Literature and History*, Vol 9.2, pp. 194-213, Autumn 1983)

Rosalind Thornycroft & Chloë Baynes, *Time Which Spaces Us Apart,* pp. 78-79, privately printed, 1991(permission unobtainable), cited in John Worthen, *D. H. Lawrence: The Life of an Outsider*, p.232, 2005

Ebbinghaus Illusion, Alex Worth, free under Creative Commons, public domain.